Please return / renew by date shown.
You can renew it at:
norlink.norfolk.gov.uk
or by telephone: 0344 800 8006

D0278151

Ride Upon
the Storm

Ann Neve

Matador
9 De Montfort Mews
Leicester LE1 7FW, UK
Tel: (+44) 116 255 9311 / 9312
Email: books@troubador.co.uk
Web: www.troubador.co.uk/matador

ISBN 978-1905886-999

Cover image of Happisburgh (Haisbro) Lighthouse courtesy of Happisburgh Lighthouse Trust

Typeset in 11pt Bembo by Troubador Publishing Ltd, Leicester, UK
Printed in the UK by The Cromwell Press Ltd, Trowbridge, Wilts, UK

Matador is an imprint of Troubador Publishing Ltd

*For my late mother, born Annie Neve in a
Norfolk village, the daughter of a farmworker*

'God moves in a mysterious way
His wonders to perform;
He plants his footsteps in the sea
And rides upon the storm'

William Cowper 1731–1800

The poet is thought to have written his famous hymn after watching a storm gather over the sea at Happisburgh, (Haisbro) Norfolk.

Acknowledgements

I am grateful to my son, Russell O'Keefe, for reviewing the first draft of *Ride upon the Storm* and suggesting amendments.

I am also grateful to the writers of the many books and articles I consulted whilst researching for this novel. In particular, I acknowledge the work of David Butcher, David Chandler, G.M. Dixon, Frank Dunham, Jock Haswell, Joanna Hunter, Ray Kipling, Jonathan Mardle, T.H. McGuffie, R.E. Pestell, C.F. Snowden Gamble, Edward P. Stafford, The Times, William Webb, the Viking Press and of course, the Great Yarmouth Mercury.

1914

I

Tovell, a tall well-built man, left the train at Stalham. He called out to a porter, shouting above the noise of carriage doors slamming, people yelling and the steam engine hissing, to ask how far it was to the coast.

'That int more than five mile,' the man replied.

Tovell thanked the man and stood for a few moments on the steps of the station entrance considering what he should do next. It was mid-morning and already hot. He decided he needed a drink to prepare himself for the walk. The street was busy: there were so many farm carts trundling to and fro he thought it must be market day. As he crossed the road to the nearest public house, his khaki uniform attracted many curious stares. Some elderly men even touched their caps. He was mildly surprised that anyone should notice him. He had to force his way into the public bar. It was crowded and the air was thick with smoke and the stench of pigs and cattle. At last he managed to reach the counter. Whilst the landlady served him, the men leaning on the bar on either side of Tovell, regarded him with the same interest as the passers by in the street.

'Blast, if it int another one!' exclaimed the man on his left.

'How many's that make now?' asked his companion.

'They'll be falling over themselves!' laughed the man on Tovell's right.

'Now, now, boys!' interrupted the landlady. 'Remember there's a war on. There'll be a lot more to do now – that there will.'

'Reckon the war'll be over afore they learn what they have got to do.'

Tovell placed his beer carefully on the counter and glared at his tormentor. 'You're a lucky bloke,' he said menacingly. 'If I weren't in such a hurry, I'd ask you to come outside for what you've just said. I've been a soldier for twenty years and I've never had any trouble yet learning my bloody duties.'

The landlady, her voice full of concern, reached over and put a restraining hand on Tovell's arm. 'Don't you pay no regard to them, Sir. They're only a-teasing you. We're all glad to see you – that we are.' When Tovell continued to glower at his neighbour she added hurriedly, anxious to avert a possible fight, 'You don't want to walk all the way to the coast on a hot day like this. Old Ted's here somewhere; he'll give you a lift.' The landlady stood on tip-toe and beckoned frantically at someone in the far corner, shouting his name above the din.

A small wiry man in his sixties pushed his way to the bar. He wore gaiters and was dressed, as were most of the other customers, in the stained garb of a farm worker. 'What are you hallering about, Kath?' he asked.

'You won't mind giving this gentleman a lift, will you, Ted?' Somehow the landlady managed to convey the predicament she was in, to her friend.

Ted glanced sharply at Tovell and then deliberately placed himself between the two antagonists. He banged his empty tankard down in front of the soldier and said archly, 'Hold you hard, my old beauty – I hent had my fill yet!' He grinned impishly at Tovell.

The latter looked down at the wrinkled weather-beaten face and could not resist returning the smile. Tovell nodded to the landlady. 'Alright – give him another.'

'That's right charitable of you, Sir.' Ted drank his ale straight down without a pause for breath, smacked his lips loudly and rubbed a grimy sleeve across them. 'Come you on then, bor! Drink up! I hent got all day. Busy time o' year on the land – that that is.'

Tovell quickly finished his drink, paid his dues, picked up his kitbag and with a last hostile look at the labourers around the bar, followed Ted outside. The old man led the way to a farm cart, unhitched the horse and climbed onto the driving seat. Tovell threw his kit into the back of the cart and climbed up alongside Ted. Soon they had left the small town behind and from his vantage point on top of the cart Tovell surveyed the flat landscape of East Norfolk. A panorama of fertile arable land stretched before him: a patchwork quilt of fields, lush green vegetation alternating with acres of ripening corn, all neatly partitioned by rows of carefully planted hedges and trees. Tovell forgot the encounter in the pub which had left him so chagrined. He stretched himself like someone waking from a long sleep, placed his hands behind his head, leant back and gazed up at the clear blue sky. He inhaled deeply, savouring the mellow odours which wafted up to him from the rich earth all around.

'You don't have any problems with droughts here, do you?' Tovell stated rather than asked, breaking the silence for the first time since leaving Stalham. 'This couldn't be more different from the parched countryside I've been used to.'

The old man considered for a moment before he replied. 'Yes, rare good land hereabouts. Reckon it'll be a good harvest. We've got a lot of it in already.' Nothing further was said for a while and Tovell closed his eyes. He became conscious of the sounds around him: the rhythmic noise the cart wheels made as they jolted over the rough road and the varied notes of the birds singing in the hedgerows. He allowed the music to flood his brain and enjoyed the sensation to the full. Suddenly, the old man announced, 'Can't take you all the way – only as far as Whimpwell Green. You'll have to walk the rest – that's only half a mile or so.'

Tovell, annoyed at being disturbed, protested. 'But you don't know where I'm headed.'

'Course I do,' laughed Ted. 'You're headed for the Coastguard Station at Eccles – near Cart Gap. Your officer arrived yesterday morning, y'see. That must have been late afternoon afore the sergeant and the rest of the men got here. Reckon now, you must be the last.'

'I got held up,' Tovell explained casually. 'I stayed overnight in Great Yarmouth.'

'I like Yarmouth. When we've done with the harvest, the master always takes us for a day out to Yarmouth. Hire a char-a-banc, he do.' Both men returned to their own thoughts until Ted observed in confidential tones, 'That was a rum old do that was.'

'Eh?' said Tovell, startled once more out of his reverie.

'About the Coastguard,' replied Ted. 'I was drinking with two of them the Thursday night afore war broke out, and they dint know nothing about it.'

'About what?' asked Tovell.

'The mobilisation! According to what we heard later, they all got their telegrams the Friday. Yes, whole damn lot of them. 'Course they knew they'd have to go to sea if anything happened – that's what they've been trained for. They're all experienced men, y'see – Royal Navy men, most of them. Once a man's done his time at sea – at least eight year I think it be – he can ask to come ashore and transfer to the Coastguard. Well, like I was telling you, bor, they all got their telegrams the Friday, and you'll recall that was the Bank Holiday weekend, yet from what we heard, they'd all boarded their ships by the Monday afternoon. I reckon the Fleet was at sea, ready and waiting, afore we even declared war. August 4th 1914 – that'll be a date for the history books, even though that'll all be over in a matter o' weeks. Blast! You gotta admire 'em! That took some doing to get all them blokes mobilised and all them ships ready to sail. 'Course, that fellow Churchill's in charge at the Admiralty, int he? Him what escaped from the Boers. You remember the Boer War, don't you?'

'I should do! I fought in it,' laughed Tovell.

'In that case, you know more about Churchill than I do,' conceded Ted. 'He must be a master fine organiser. We hent heard nothing about the German Fleet, have we? All them ships carrying our soldiers to France and the Hun hent sunk one of them. Yes, I reckon it's all due to Churchill. I bet he had their Fleet bottled up in their home ports afore our troopships started to cross the Channel.' A sudden thought occurred to Ted. 'If you're an experienced man and fought in the Boer War like you say, what are you doing here? Why aren't you with your regiment?'

'I wish I was,' replied Tovell with feeling. 'They're in France, of course. I'd be there too if I hadn't caught pneumonia on the ship bringing us home from India. They took me to hospital as soon as we docked. I only got out yesterday morning. They've given me six months light duties. I pleaded with them to let me rejoin my regiment but they sent me here instead.'

'Six months,' mused the old man. 'Reckon you'll miss it all.'

Tovell nodded. 'I don't care so much about that – I've seen plenty of action over the years – but I don't like being parted from my pals. I've been with the same blokes for nearly seven years.'

'You've been in India for nigh on seven year?'

'Yes, and I was there in the 1890s as well, 'til we got sent to the Sudan. After that it was South Africa, then England for a while and then back to India again. But changing the subject, if the coastguards were mobilised the weekend before war broke out, who's been running the Station?'

'No-one! No-one official, that is. There hent been one ruddy coastguard along the entire Norfolk coast for more than three weeks now and that must be the same all around the coasts of the British Isles. 'Course, I can only speak for here, but the women have been keeping things going nicely – that they have.'

'Women? What women?' demanded Tovell.

'Coastguards' wives – they've been taking care of the patrols between 'em.' Ted chuckled. 'Do you know, I was up on the cliff the other day near Haisbro Light. We've got a field of sugar beet up there and the master say to me, "You'd better go take a look at that there beet, Ted." Well, I did – coming along a treat that is. Anyhow, I looked up and striding along the cliff edge was Ma Gillings. She had her old man's gun under her arm – what he used to use for rabbit shooting. I asked her what she thought she was doing and she said she was a-keeping watch for the Hun. I told her she needn't worry 'cause they wouldn't come ashore while she was on guard. They'd take one look at her and swim back home again. She say, "If I have any more of your cheek, Ted Carter, I'll fill your arse full o' buckshot." And she would an' all! Blast! I pity the poor bugger that gets billeted with her.'

'Billeted? You don't mean we're going to be billeted with the coastguards' families?' Tovell made no effort to conceal his alarm at the prospect.

'Course you are. Where else are you going to live?'

'But the Station's near Eccles. That's a village, isn't it? Surely there's a barn or something where all of us could billet together?'

'Yes, that's right. Eccles is a village and you could live there – if you were a fish! You could have your pick of the whole bloomin' place – so long as you don't mind sharing with a few skeletons. Yes, according to the history books, Eccles was a rare fine village – afore the sea took her. Well, like I was a-saying, bor, you'll have to live at the Station 'cause that's all that's there. There int nothing else – 'cept the sea and the sand dunes, o' course. There's plenty of that – oh dearie me, yes.'

Tovell groaned. 'As if being parted from my pals isn't bad enough, they have to send me to the edge of the ruddy world.'

After a few more miles Ted brought the horse to a halt. 'This is where you get off. That int far to the Coastguard Station – you just follow the track across the fields. It leads to that gap you can see in the marrams. If you look to the right of it you can just make out the cottages of the Station. Now look along the coastline to your left. That bloomin' great lighthouse on top of the cliff is Haisbro Light and further along from that you'll see houses and a church on a hill. That's Haisbro village where I live. I drink in the *Admiral Lord Nelson* every night. Come you along when you're off duty and we'll have a good yarn. I promise you, you won't have no trouble like you had in the *King's Head* today. People won't torment you if you're under Ted Carter's wing – no, that they won't – even though you are from away.'

Tovell laughed at the last remark. 'Thanks, Ted, I'll take you up on that. And thanks for the ride.' He climbed down from the cart, shouldered his kit and set off in the direction Ted had indicated. He turned and waved as Ted took up the reins and started to move off.

'Gee up there! Get a move on, gal!' Ted urged the horse. Then he remembered something and called out to the soldier. 'Hey! What's your bloomin' name?'

'It's Tovell. Just call me Tovell.'

'Fare ye well, Tovell,' and Ted was gone.

II

The men assembled in the Watch-room and lined up in front of their officer. Sergeant Harris, a seasoned soldier, stood to one side. The lieutenant, a grim faced man of about fifty, turned first towards Tovell. 'And why are you a day late reporting for duty, Tovell?' he demanded.

'It was like this, Sir. I only got discharged from hospital yesterday morning. I caught the first train I could from London but when I reached Great Yarmouth I found the train for Stalham left from another station. I had to walk right across the town, Sir. By the time I got halfway there I was feeling done in. The Medical Officer had told me that if I felt bad on the journey I'd got to rest, so I found a bed and stayed in Yarmouth overnight.'

'And are you feeling quite well now?'

'Yes, thank you, Sir.'

'I'm very glad to hear it,' said Richard Collins with a note of sarcasm in his voice. 'Perhaps I may be permitted, at long last, to address you all on the subject of why you are here and what your duties will be. Attention, please.' Everyone responded to the command instantly and came to attention. The officer was visibly confused. He coughed nervously and retreated to a new position behind his desk. He rephrased his order. 'At ease men and pay attention.' He caught sight of the smirk on Tovell's face. 'You there – what do you find so amusing?'

'Me, Sir? Nothing an officer says is amusing to me, Sir.'

Lieutenant Collins coloured. 'I'm warning you, Tovell! I'll have no insolence here.' He shuffled his papers and began again. 'The Admiralty has maintained the Coastguard Service principally as a naval reserve. Consequently, almost the entire force was despatched to ships of the Royal Navy Reserve just prior to the declaration of war. We, the Army, are to fill the gap. You will appreciate that it was necessary for coastguard stations to be manned as a matter of urgency and half-trained men are better than none. Sergeant Harris and Private

Tovell are both regular soldiers with many years service behind them. I shall, therefore, arrange for them to continue your basic training. They will give you instructions in firearm drill and so on.

I should mention at this point that the Admiralty has appointed one wife at each station – in our case, Mrs Brewster – to act on their behalf. In practice this will mean that only Mrs Brewster is permitted to take Admiralty calls – at least for the present. I would hope that in the course of time, their Lordships will come to realise that the Army can be trusted … And whilst we are on the subject of the ladies, I should mention the matter of behaviour. I want no drunkenness, no swearing, no brawling and quite definitely, no improper behaviour.

And now for your duties: His Majesty's Coastguard has always been responsible for the defence of the coasts of the Realm and now, in time of war, it must be our primary duty. Whether in the Watch-room, on patrol or manning one of the look-outs, you will be ever vigilant for any sign of the enemy. Remember the Norfolk coastline is the nearest to Germany. During the hours of daylight there are also others whose mission is reconnaissance – aviators from the Royal Naval Air Station at Great Yarmouth. Do *not* fire on them! I have already written to the Admiralty pointing out, respectfully, the folly of operating machines which carry no distinguishing marks. They could be fired at by any farmer thinking they're enemy reconnaissance 'planes….'

Richard Collins took a further twenty minutes to run through the many and varied duties expected of the replacement coastguards. They were all glad when he brought his address to a close. '…. and whenever you are not on call, you may leave the confines of the Station. Since at the present time nowhere is out of bounds, you may go where-ever you please.'

Until this point in his discourse, the officer had been heard in silence, but suddenly Tovell interrupted, demanding in exasperation, 'Go? Where the bloody hell is there to go? This is the edge of the ruddy world!'

Everyone waited for the lieutenant's reaction to the outburst. He leaned forward on his desk, glowered at Tovell and pointed a finger at him. His voice was stern but studiously quiet. 'Private Tovell, you have just illustrated my previous point perfectly. That language is the kind I do not wish to hear again. I will excuse your behaviour on this occasion because you have been ill, but I must insist that you refrain from swearing in future.' The officer straightened and directed his next remark to the sergeant. 'You may take over, Sergeant Harris. Dismiss the men who are not on watch. We will begin our training schedules in earnest tomorrow.'

The sergeant called the men to attention as the lieutenant crossed the length of the Watch-room, descended the narrow internal staircase and disappeared through the door into the Station Officer's quarters.

Richard Collins sank thankfully into an armchair beside the fire in the parlour. He was shaking slightly as he wiped his sweating palms on his handkerchief. He did not notice Mrs Brewster until she was standing beside him. She had a cup of tea in her hand. As he took it, she said kindly, 'I always found a new class quite terrifying.'

'I, too, Mrs Brewster,' replied the officer. 'And I fear this will be the most terrifying class I have ever had to handle. Would you believe, ma'am, that it even has a problem pupil? Chap by the name of Tovell. Something tells me that he's going to be a trouble maker extraordinary.'

III

'That's no way to hoe, Lily,' said David Wilson, a slightly built youth who was the youngest of the soldiers. 'Here, let me show you – or better still, let me do it for you while you sit and rest.'

'I do try, David, but I can't seem to get the hang of it,' explained Lily, handing over the hoe without protest and seating herself carefully on the edge of the wheel-barrow. 'It's such a big garden to weed and I seem to bring up as many plants as weeds.'

The boy smiled. He glanced around at the carefully tended vegetable patch – all the cottages on the Station had small back gardens – and added, 'If you think this is a lot of land to work, you'd better come home with me. How Father's going to manage on his own, I don't know, but he agreed I could go. Never guessed I'd end up here, coast-watching in my own county. I was looking forward to seeing foreign places. But I worry about Father. Annie will do her best to help him though. Have I told you about Annie?'

Lily giggled. 'You've scarcely stopped talking about her. You don't half miss her.'

David nodded. 'There's not quite a year between us. We've been more like twins than ordinary brother and sister. First time I set eyes on you, Lily, I thought you were Annie. You look just like her from the back view.' The boy laughed. 'Only from the back view, mind – she doesn't look like you from the front, and that's a fact!'

Lily blushed and tried to stretch her apron so that it concealed her bulging form more adequately.

'I don't know why you do that,' commented the young soldier. 'You look alright to me. I'm so used to seeing Mother and my aunties like that they look funny to me when they're not carrying.'

To hide her embarrassment, Lily asked, 'Do you like living at Mrs Brewster's?'

David applied himself to the hoeing more keenly. He mumbled a reply. 'Mrs Brewster's very nice but I wish I was back in your house.'

'So do I,' confided Lily.

'Mrs Brewster's kind but her children are all grown up and left home. I've got a great big room all to myself. I'm used to sharing with my four little brothers. Pity your mother-in-law didn't like me. I don't know what I did to upset her – that I don't.'

'That's a mystery, David. All the other mothers like you – I've heard them say so. You're always so willing to help with anything and they all love your blonde curls.'

The boy scowled at the mention of what to him was a very sore subject. He ran his fingers through his mop of unruly hair and vowed, 'One of these days I'm going to black-lead this lot.'

There was no opportunity for further discussion because at that moment Lily's mother-in-law returned from the village. She snatched the hoe from David's hand and said brusquely, 'I told Lily to do that.'

'I was only trying to help her, Mrs Gillings,' the boy protested.

'She don't need no help. She's gotta learn. Now be off with you.'

For a moment, David considered arguing further, but then he decided it would be useless. Mrs Gillings, a stout and muscular matron, had a daunting effect on everybody when she was angry, and quite clearly she was angry at this particular moment. Without daring to look at Lily, the young soldier shuffled away, eyes downcast, feeling like a naughty school boy caught misbehaving. He made his way onto the beach, intending to tell his troubles to the sea, but the need for human contact was too great and he soon returned to the Station.

The men who had finished their watch at midday were stretched out on the grass in front of the single storey, flint and red brick cottages, enjoying the warm sunshine. As David approached he could hear that Tovell was holding forth on one of his favourite subjects – Lieutenant Collins.

'.... and there he was, striding up and down the bloody room with a book in one hand and waving the other hand in the air. I tell you, there's no doubt about it ....' Tovell stopped in mid-sentence as David slumped to the ground beside him looking thoroughly miserable. 'What's the matter with you?' David did not reply. 'That old bitch has been at you again, hasn't she?' David nodded. 'Well, Davey boy, if you listen to old Tovell you'll stop wasting your time with young Lily. She's no good to you.'

Bill Westgate, a very large heavily built man with a battered face, sat up and joined in the conversation. 'Leave the boy alone. He doesn't know what you're talking about.'

'Oh, yes I do!' David retorted. 'But Mr. Tovell's got it all wrong – I only want to help Lily. I always help my mother.'

'Of course you do. You're a good lad. Tovell doesn't understand decent folk like you, David. He thinks everyone is as rotten as he is.'

Tovell rolled onto his side and glared at the speaker. 'Watch what you're saying, Westgate. I'll bloody have you.'

'You'll need help then,' replied Bill Westgate. 'When I was a travelling man with my own boxing booth, I used to make mincemeat of twenty like you in a night.'

'Aren't you forgetting one thing – you're not so young anymore?'

'I'm still young enough to give you a hiding you won't forget.' Bill turned once again to David. 'Pay no attention to Tovell. Try to understand, David, that Mrs Gillings is only doing what she thinks is best. You're the same age as Lily but her husband is twice her age. She's his second wife – so I've been told. The old lady feels responsible for her daughter-in-law now that her son's away.'

'I don't mean no harm, Mr Westgate.'

'We know that but the old girl doesn't. You'd be better staying away from Lily,' advised Bill. The group was silent for a while until Tovell came up with a proposal.

'Tell you what, Davey boy. You forget about Lily and as soon as we get some leave I'll take you to Yarmouth.'

'I went to Yarmouth once – when I was a littl'un.'

'Maybe you did – to play on the beach – but old Tovell won't be taking you to the beach. Yarmouth's a port, Davey. Where there are mariners there are women. You'll have a ruddy sight more fun playing with them.'

Bill Westgate interrupted again. 'Don't listen to him, David. Those sort of women will give you a disease.'

'I've had women all over the world and I've never caught anything.'

'You wouldn't! You've got the luck of the devil. Young David would catch a dose first time.'

'Father told me about that afore I left home.'

'You pay heed to your Dad,' urged Bill.

The fourth member of the group was Sergeant Harris. He had given every appearance of being asleep, but at that point he opened one eye and said, 'If its company you want, Tovell, I'll go with you; must be cheaper here than in London.'

Tovell grinned. 'You're right *and* you'll get your money's worth, believe me. The lady I met the other night was very obliging.'

'So that's what kept yer,' laughed the sergeant. 'I thought as much. Lucky for you our officer swallowed that pretty tale about your delicate state of health.'

'Well, it was true − in a way. I did feel done in − afterwards. Pneumonia takes it out of a bloke. This charming lady said it made a change to entertain a soldier and since she was enjoying my company so much, I could stay the night for no extra charge.'

'You're a damn liar, Tovell,' said Sergeant Harris. 'I bet it was raining outside and she didn't fancy going out in it again.' Only Tovell and the sergeant laughed at this remark.

Tovell returned to his original proposal. 'Well, Davey boy, coming with us? We'll show you what to do.'

'Shouldn't need to,' said Jack Harris, 'should come natural to a country boy. There must be plenty of it going on around his farm.'

'Ah − but it's not quite the same with animals, is it?' argued Tovell. 'Not unless you've got the tastes of our Lieutenant Collins!'

Bill Westgate, who had been inwardly seething for several minutes, had heard enough. He grabbed Tovell by the neck of his tunic and forced him flat on his back. Putting his face close to the other man's, he hissed menacingly. 'Tovell, we haven't been here for more than a few days but already I'm sick to death of you. I'm sick of your boozing, sick of your whoring, sick of your boasting, sick of your blaspheming. You're a foul-mouthed bastard not fit to be with decent folk. They should have billeted you in a pig-sty. By heck, if I thought someone like you was going to be billeted with my missus, I'd desert!'

Try as he would, Tovell could not throw off the heavier frame of Bill Westgate. The latter continued to pin Tovell to the ground while he spoke his mind. 'I'm warning you, Tovell. If you so much as lay a finger on that nice little Mrs Adams you're billeted with − or any of the other women for that matter – I'll break you myself and enjoy doing it.'

Tovell, desperately trying to force Bill Westgate's thick muscular forearm away from his throat, could only gasp a reply. 'Don't you worry – I shan't touch any of them here. Don't need to – there's plenty a-begging me at the village.'

Bill Westgate suddenly leapt to his feet dragging Tovell with him. 'You shouldn't be here. You need putting in your place.'

'And you're the man to do it, are you, chum?' sneered Tovell, raising his fists.

Sergeant Harris decided it was time he intervened. He hastily got to his feet but before he could remonstrate with his men, Lieutenant Collins arrived looking very flushed.

'I thought I told you there was to be no brawling,' said the officer angrily. 'I could hear you shouting at one another from the Watch-room. Whatever must the ladies think of such behaviour? Tovell – come with me! I want to see you alone.' Lieutenant Collins turned abruptly on his heel and returned the way he had come, expecting Tovell to follow.

As the soldier bent to retrieve his cap which was lying on the grass, Sergeant Harris whispered 'Watch yourself – you could be in grave danger!'

The joke roused the actor in Tovell. 'Coming, Sir!' he called in a high-pitched voice and with one hand on his hip and mincing steps, he made after the officer.

Once inside the Watch-room, the lieutenant told the only man there, Fred Mannell, to wait outside. He then sat down at his desk and indicated that Tovell should stand in front of him. He reached for a file which lay in one of the trays, glanced through it, stood up and came round to Tovell's side of the desk. To the soldier's increasing alarm, the officer proceeded to walk slowly around him, looking him up and down carefully. He ended his inspection immediately in front of Tovell. Being several inches shorter in height, his nose was directly in line with Tovell's mouth. He sniffed twice and returned to his seat. The soldier inwardly sighed with relief.

The lieutenant regarded Tovell in silence for several seconds before he spoke. 'Well, Private Tovell, I can find no fault with your uniform. You are a very smart man. I admire a man who takes pride in his appearance.' Tovell began to feel even more uncomfortable. He deliberately avoided meeting the officer's penetrating gaze as he continued. 'Such a pity you spoil everything by your excessive drinking. You've been drinking now, haven't you?'

'Just a nip or two, Sir, since I came off duty,' replied Tovell, staring straight ahead.

'From the flask in your hip-pocket, no doubt. Please do not let me see it there when you return to duty.'

'Yes, Sir! I mean, no, Sir!' stammered Tovell.

'I have your record here on my desk. Let me read a few extracts to you. *Drunk and disorderly* …. *Drunkenness accompanied by insubordination* …. *Assaulting an officer* …. Pages and pages of it, Tovell – such a pity. A good man – a brave man – wasted! You have been promoted to corporal three times and you even reached sergeant once, yet every time you were reduced in rank because of drink.' He paused for a moment, then asked quietly, 'Tovell, wouldn't you like to win back your lost promotions?'

Tovell swallowed hard and replied in a voice which croaked slightly. 'Only if I can do so in the proper manner, Sir.'

'Think about it, Tovell,' urged the lieutenant. 'Think very carefully about how you can win back those promotions.' There was another strained silence before the officer announced, 'I have decided that it would be better if you joined my watch.'

'I'm quite happy working Sergeant Harris's watch, Sir.'

'But I prefer to have you on my watch, Tovell. I shall inform the sergeant accordingly. As for our little talk – I hope that it will bear fruit. Now you may leave.'

Tovell saluted smartly and beat such a hasty retreat down the Watch-room's external steps that he almost felled Fred Mannell who was waiting at the bottom. He brushed away the beads of perspiration from his brow as he hurried towards his billet. He recalled the sergeant's words and reflected on the old adage that many a true word is spoken in jest. 'This is a right turn-up, Tovell my old pal,' he muttered to himself. 'The bugger fancies you!'

IV

It was necessary for Tovell to stoop as he entered the back door of the cottage in order to avoid hitting his head on the lintel. He wiped his feet with excessive care before stepping into the scullery – a task made difficult by the family's black Labrador dog which had been sitting at the door eagerly awaiting his arrival. The animal jumped up at Tovell, tail wagging vigorously. Two small children, the boy about eight years old, his sister about six, were busily engaged upon setting the table in the living room. They abandoned their chore immediately and ran into the scullery to greet the soldier. Taking a hand each, they pulled him into the living room and guided him towards the large armchair which stood beside the cooking range. Laughing, he allowed them to drag him along, trying his best not to tread on the dog which was running in circles around the trio, barking excitedly. Once he was seated, the little girl climbed onto Tovell's lap while her brother squeezed into the chair alongside him. The dog had to be content with sitting at his feet, chin resting on the soldier's knee. Tovell put an arm around each child and gave them both an affectionate hug.

'Mother's just gone next door to see Mrs Gillings, Uncle Tovell,' explained the boy. 'She say she won't be long and dinner's nearly ready.'

'I'm not in any hurry, Bobby,' said Tovell.

'That's stew and dumplings,' the little girl informed him, pointing at the cooking range.

'I smelt it as soon as I came in the door,' said Tovell glancing at the large saucepan simmering on the hob. 'But I'm not feeling very hungry at the moment. The fact is I've come over a bit sick.'

'I know where there's some castor oil,' offered Bobby, wriggling forward in an effort to slide off the chair.

Tovell held the child back. 'Thanks Bobby, but I think it will pass off alright.'

Lizzie reached up and patted Tovell's cheek to get his attention away from her brother. 'While you're waiting for it to pass off, couldn't you go on with the story?'

'Which story was that?' asked Tovell.

'You were hiding in the desert,' Lizzie explained.

'And all your pals were dead. Dervishes were coming at you – hundreds of them,' added Bobby helpfully.

'Oh – that story,' said Tovell with a grin. 'Yes, I think I can manage that. You'll have to give me a moment or two to remember what happened. It was a long time ago.'

Whilst Tovell pondered on the direction his fairy tale should take, the children fidgeted about until they were comfortable. They had just settled down and the episode begun when their mother burst through the back door. She caught sight of the little group as she hurried into the living room. 'I can see I haven't been missed. Story-telling again, are we?' She clucked her tongue reprovingly but there was laughter in her eyes. 'Sorry I wasn't here when you got home, Tovell. I'll dish the dinner up straight away.'

'Uncle Tovell doesn't fare well,' announced Lizzie.

'Not my cooking, I hope!' said her mother anxiously.

'Hell no, Ginny!' exclaimed Tovell, adding hastily, 'I mean, no, of course not.'

'You mean, "Hell no!"' Ginny asserted. 'Don't let's start that all over again.'

Tovell smiled and conceded the point. When he had first arrived, he had been so overcome by the strangeness of his surroundings and so concerned not to lapse into his normal barrack-room expressions that he had scarcely dared to utter a word. When he had spoken, he had peppered his conversation with, "begging your pardon, ma'am," every time he feared he might have said something to cause offence. By the second day the phrase had begun to jar on his landlady and she had shouted at him in exasperation.

'Mr. Tovell, if you say, "begging your pardon, ma'am," once more, I shall scream. I'm not used to living with saints. My husband isn't one and nor are my brothers – and I don't reckon you are, thank the Lord! Now why don't you just make yourself at home?'

Tovell had apologised again. 'I'm sorry, ma'am. I don't mean to cause you any bother. I'm not used to living with a family – in fact I haven't lived in a proper house since I was a child. Even then, it wasn't like this – seven of us crammed into one room in a city slum. I'm used to living with other blokes in army quarters. I'm afraid my ways will upset you.'

'They won't upset me, Mr. Tovell. Like I say, I'm not used to living with saints. The way I see it, my Robert's doing his duty and you're doing yours. We all have to make the best of it now – it won't be for long. And my name's not ma'am, it's Virginia. Everyone calls me Ginny and I'd like you to do the same.'

'Alright, Ginny,' Tovell had agreed, 'but only if you'll stop calling me, Mister Tovell.'

'What's your Christian name then?'

'It's Alec, but only my mother called me that. If you call me Alec I'll think it's someone else you mean. I've always been Tovell – to my officers and to my pals. Just call me Tovell.'

Ginny had consented but insisted that the children use the term, uncle. Tovell had not objected; he found he liked being addressed as uncle. The children had taken to him immediately – a fact he found quite astonishing since he had had no previous adult contact with infants. Equally astounding was the ease with which he had adapted to family life. Unbeknown to his comrades, he only joined them if he had no other choice. He much preferred to make himself useful about the house and insisted that Ginny leave all the heavy work to him. He delighted in the company of the children and would go to any lengths to amuse them. He even agreed to accompany Lizzie on a bishy-barneybee hunt – he was quite relieved to find they were only looking for ladybirds – and shared the pleasures of fishing for stannicles – the Norfolk name for sticklebacks – in the nearby dykes with Bobby. The children, for their part, loved imparting what little scraps of knowledge they had – snippets of information about the countryside and its wildlife, or about the sea and the ways of those who earned their living from the sea.

Frequently, Tovell only left the cottage at Ginny's insistence. 'I can't stand a man under my feet when I'm trying to do my work,' she would protest, but there was no malice in her voice. The top of her head only just reached Tovell's shoulder and she was so slim he knew he could have lifted her effortlessly off the ground with his hands round her tiny waist. He resented nothing she said to him and before long he realised he enjoyed being ordered around by a woman.

'What's the matter with you?' enquired Ginny, bringing Tovell's thoughts back to the present.

'I'm better now,' answered the soldier. 'I felt sick. I've always had a queasy stomach; I don't know why.'

'Don't you? I do!' laughed Ginny. 'It's all that booze you pour into it. The amount you drink would rot anybody's innards.'

'Not you as well, Ginny – Lieutenant Collins has just been having a go at me about the evils of drink.'

'Pity you don't listen.'

'Er – Ginny,' Tovell said sheepishly, 'there's something I wanted to ask you. I promised to meet old Ted tonight ….'

'In the pub, of course, and you want to borrow my bicycle again so you don't waste good drinking time walking the two miles to Haisbro. What's the good of talking to you? You're beyond help. Take it! At least you'll get home quicker – provided you don't end up in a ditch.'

Tovell was not the only soldier to quickly settle down in his new surroundings. As had been observed, Richard Collins soon felt comfortable enough when he was off duty to walk around his quarters reading aloud. '*They flash upon that inward eye, Which is the bliss of solitude; And then my heart with pleasure fills, And dances with the daffodils.*' He sighed and closed the book. 'When have you ever made pastry in the company of Wordsworth?'

'Never 'til now – I'm sorry to say,' replied Lydia Brewster, smiling as she finished cutting the excess pastry from the pie she was making. Lydia, a handsome woman in her early fifties, was one of those people who managed to look elegant whatever she was doing – even when she was performing a mundane domestic task like cooking.

The movement of a vehicle outside, near the perimeter wall of the Station, caught the officer's eye and he gestured dramatically towards the kitchen window. 'But what see I through yonder casement? Methinks tis Boadicea astride her chariot.'

Lydia wiped the flour from her hands as she joined the lieutenant at the window. She laughed when she saw Mrs Gillings standing up in her cart urging her horse on.

'So where's she off to?' asked the lieutenant.

'She's off to peddle her wares around the neighbourhood.'

'So Boadicea is really a pedlar?'

'No… It's complicated. This is the start of the Home Fishing. Vast shoals of herring are off this coast from September. They're gone by December. The local fishermen go after them and they bring some of their nets to our Mrs Ellis to mend. She was a beatster by trade. They pay her for her work in herrings. Mrs Gillings takes them, guts them, pickles them, smokes them – that was her trade. She keeps a certain amount for the families on the Station and the rest she takes to the surrounding farms. She'll return later today with eggs, chickens, fruits, cream – all kinds of things, and she'll share those with the other families as well.'

'So the art of bartering is alive and well in East Norfolk. Yes, you're quite a community, aren't you? *All for one and one for all,* and you're the Chief Musketeer. You're like a well-run army unit.'

'Or a ship's crew.'

'My apologies, ma'am – I forgot for a moment that I was standing on Navy territory. I should have said you run a good ship, Captain.'

'But you are the captain now and might I remind you of that particular captain's duty which you wriggled out of last week and the week before….'

'Oh no – not that …! Well, if I must, then let's get it over with.' Lieutenant Collins opened the back door with a flourish, bowed and waved Mrs Brewster out ahead of him. 'But, ma'am, no matter what you say, I shall not test for dust.'

The soldiers had soon realised that the cornerstone of their landladies' lives was the Admiralty. None of the women had wasted any time informing the newcomers that they must be meticulously tidy in the house since the one thing the Admiralty abhorred, as far as the wives were concerned, was dirt! Their cottages could not be anything less than spotless; their vegetable patches could not be anything less than weedless, and to ensure that this was the case, the Station Officer inspected homes and gardens once a week, the Divisional Officer once a quarter, the District Captain once a year, and the Admiral Superintendent once every three years! The women saw no reason why a war should make any difference to the established routine and Mrs Brewster had advised Lieutenant Collins that, as acting Station Officer, he must find time for a weekly inspection of living quarters. The very idea had appalled him and he had protested strongly that he would not violate the privacy of the ladies' homes. Such a concept would never occur to the ladies, Lydia had assured him and failure to perform a duty expected of him might even cause offence. She felt quite jubilant, therefore, as she accompanied him from cottage to cottage – even though he kept his hands tightly clasped behind his back throughout the tour of inspection as though to emphasise his resolution not to test for dust. He spent most of each brief visit enquiring after the welfare of the children of the household or asking whether there was any news of the absent husband. He made the same parting comment to every wife. 'You keep everywhere immaculate, ma'am – immaculate.' When all his subsequent inspections followed exactly the same pattern, the coastguards' wives quickly concluded, not unnaturally, that Lieutenant Collins was a perfect gentleman.

V

Sergeant Harris came through from the living room carrying his cup in his hand. Mrs Ellis was busy mending a fishing-net which she had suspended from a hook in her scullery. The sergeant leaned against the sink sipping his tea whilst he watched her at work. 'You're a dab hand at that,' he said admiringly.

'I should be,' she laughed. 'I was apprenticed to a net stores as a beatster straight from school. I lived at Gorleston then – the other side of the river from Yarmouth. That's how I met my Wilfred. The crews used to come to the stores to collect their gear. That was a special time afore the start of a new voyage. The master would let us stand out in the yard to watch the loading up and the christening. Yes, that's what the skippers do – christen the nets with a little whisky for luck. Then all the men have a little drink. 'Course, they wouldn't let us girls have whisky but we used to have something to wish them luck. They needed it! Many's the time my Wilfred's come home from a voyage to Devon and Cornwall, or to the Shetlands, and had no money to take up after the boat's expenses had been met. I don't know how some large families would have managed without the shop-keepers giving them credit. We were lucky though. I used to work all the hours I could get at the net stores. During the Home Fishing season that'd be eight in the morning 'til nine at night. That's a long old day when you can't sit down. You have to stand to mend nets.'

'Sounds as bad as being an infantryman,' said the sergeant with a smile.

'Yes, like guard duty, but I doubt you were sneezing 'til your nose bled from inhaling dried jelly fish dust! You couldn't make a fuss, though. You had to keep the right side of the master so he'd let you go on working for him even after you couldn't come to the stores no more 'cause you had littl'uns. Yes, it's a good trade for that. As I recall, the master had more than a hundred home workers at one time. Many a night I'd be mending nets in our scullery – just like this – 'til one in the morning. That didn't pay a lot but that kept our heads above water.'

'You must have been much better off once your Wilfred joined the Coastguard Service.'

'Oh, that didn't happen straight away. I persuaded him to join the Royal Navy. I knew he'd have a chance then, once he'd done his time, of coming ashore and joining the Coastguard – just like my brother had. But how I used to worry about him when he was at sea…. The day he left the Navy I was so happy. Now look what's happened – he's back with the Navy again. But I reckon there's nothing to worry about this time. They're only in the reserve ships so they won't be in any proper battles, will they?'

'I shouldn't think so, Mrs Ellis.' The sergeant finished his last drop of tea and put the empty cup in the sink. 'Well, I'll have to be going. I've got the first watch.'

'I've packed you something in case you get hungry mid-watch.' Mrs Ellis indicated a package lying on the draining board.

'That's very kind of you. I'm not used to being looked after. I'm going to miss it.'

'You're very welcome. See you later.'

As Sergeant Harris left his billet he caught sight of Tovell, who had been on watch all night, returning from patrol. He waited for him and they walked to the Watch-room together.

'Bet you're glad that's over. Twelve hours is a long stretch.'

'You ain't wrong!' replied Tovell. 'I'll just report in, then it's the breakfast and the pot of tea Ginny will have waiting for me.'

'Don't get too used to home comforts,' laughed the sergeant. 'I've just been saying to Mrs Ellis how much I'll miss her taking care of me when we get back to real soldiering.'

There was no time for further discussion because Mrs Gillings was bearing down upon them carrying a basket brimming with fish which she had just gutted and cleaned. Tovell made a slight movement towards her with the intention of offering to help her carry the heavy load. She found his action provocative. As she drew abreast, she ignored the sergeant but scowled at Tovell whom she had taken a dislike to from the first day he had arrived at the Station. 'Don't you darst hinder me, bor, do I'll give you a clout you'll never forget!' she announced belligerently. 'I've met your kind afore. When I was a gal, working Yarmouth fish market, they was a rough old lot, but there wasn't one o' them – no, not man nor woman – that could get the better o' me.'

'I believe yer, Missus!' replied Tovell, hastily jumping out of the way. The men looked back at the retreating figure as Mrs Gillings continued on her way to her smokehouse. They were both chuckling and Tovell observed, 'Her old man must have been a brave sod. I wouldn't dare touch the old bat with a barge pole let alone my valuables!'

Tovell was still thinking about the encounter when he was eating his breakfast and he asked Ginny about Mrs Gillings's statement. Ginny explained to Tovell that Mrs Gillings's boast had probably not been an idle one. Gutting, cleaning and pickling fish on Great Yarmouth quayside in all weathers and temperatures was, in itself, hardly the following for a weakling, and during the Home Fishing season, when the market was overrun by invaders from north of the border, she would have had more than her share of disputes with the 'foreigners'.

'Every autumn a thousand boats pack into Yarmouth Harbour. You can walk from one side of the river to the other across them. More than seven hundred of them are from Scotland – from Fraserburgh and Peterhead. They follow the herring shoals, you see. The men come down on the boats and the women on the train. Some of them even bring their children with them. They have their own coopers too – men who see to the barrels after the women have gutted the fish and packed them. Yes, I bet Mrs Gillings must have had many a t'do with the Scotties in her time.'

Mrs Gillings might resent assistance in so far as it implied incompetence on her part, but she was not averse to an audience – provided it was respectful and admiring – whilst she went about her appointed task. She held court outside her back door surrounded by buckets and tin baths. As she worked she lectured her audience. '....and they make master fine bloaters and kippers and o' course, you can turn 'em into red herring or have 'em soused. There's nothing to beat 'em. When I was a littl'un, I was brought up on fish. Red herring and swede – lovely! They do say fish make brains. That'd do you all good to eat more fish.'

The soldiers found they had little choice in the matter, but thanks to the skills of Mrs Gillings, the meals were not monotonous since the herrings were served in a variety of ways. Standing in pride of place in Mrs Gillings's back yard was her smokehouse. This was a tall wooden structure with a tiled roof and a brick floor, upon which the fire was laid. And it was no ordinary fire as the soldiers were to discover when they helpfully brought her branches to feed it. 'That int a mite o' use,' was all the thanks they got for their trouble. 'That has to be oak smoke, do you won't get the right taste. The littl'uns know what to do.'

This remark was interpreted as meaning that the men had permission to accompany the children of the Station on foraging expeditions to the woods where large numbers of sacks were filled with oak leaves and twigs. Even this was not enough to satisfy the fire's voracious appetite; oak logs had to be sawn up and bags of oak sawdust were delivered at regular intervals by a nervous gentleman who never managed to escape before Mrs Gillings had interrogated him as to the quality of his product. The fuel was stored in another specially constructed wooden shed and protected by threats, frequently repeated, that anyone who went near the place would suffer dire, but unspecified, consequences.

The preparation of the fish for smoking involved even more ritual and, it appeared, a secret formula. Polite enquiries as to the most favoured method of curing elicited the reply, 'I ent a-going to tell you all my know.' When Sergeant Harris was caught peering anxiously into the butt which collected rain water from Mrs Gillings's roof – together with assorted insects and wind-blown debris – he was assured, 'Soft water's the only thing for *smokes*. That'll be perfect once the muck's strained out.'

In time, Tovell came to share Mrs Gillings's opinion that, 'There's nothing to beat a red herring toasted on a grid iron in front of a clear fire.' His only regret was that there was no easier way of turning an ordinary herring into a delicacy than to suspend it over smoldering oak sawdust for weeks on end. 'I swear I'll never forget the stink of that damn fish-house,' he complained to Ginny. 'When you're out on patrol, miles from the Station, you can see the smoke curling out of the holes in the roof. Even on a pitch black night, I could find my way back home just by following my nose.'

VI

During the second week in September, one of the children had a birthday. That weekend the event was celebrated, as was the custom, in Mrs Brewster's parlour – the largest room on the Station. All the women contributed to the worthy spread set out on the table and all the soldiers were invited. Each one attended for part of the session – when he was not on watch – and since the time for changing shifts was six in the evening, the women were at pains to ensure that each one of their lodgers was adequately fed, either before he went on duty or when he came off duty. They were equally keen to see that the men enjoyed themselves, so the children's games alternated with singing and dancing.

'Well, I never!' exclaimed Ginny at the expert manner in which her partner whirled her around the room. 'Who'd have thought that you could dance like a gentleman.'

'Who'd have thought that once I was a gentleman – or rather, a sergeant,' responded Tovell. 'Oh, Sergeant Tovell was much sought after by high class ladies' maids – but only because he could get them invitations to the dances in the Sergeants Mess.'

Bill Westgate was no dancer but he was an unexpectedly good singer. His contribution to the festivities was a stirring rendition of that popular song of the Boer War, *Dolly Grey*. This prompted Mrs Gillings to prove that she too was in good voice with an impersonation of Marie Lloyd. So impressive was her performance that even Tovell, who considered himself to be a connoisseur of the art of Marie Lloyd, applauded her enthusiastically.

Sergeant Harris, who had returned to duty but had popped his head round the internal door to the Watch-room to see if there was any food left, remarked to Tovell, 'The old girl's not so bad looking when she's dressed up. Maybe I could fancy her myself – after I'd had a few pints!'

David enjoyed himself too because he was allowed to organise all

29

of the children's games. The highlight of the party for him, however, came when Lily announced that she felt a little sick and needed some fresh air. Mrs Gillings was too busy singing to notice the young couple disappear and David happily escorted Lily to the marram covered sand dunes out of sight of the parlour window.

'Sit you there, Lily,' the boy urged. 'The tang of the sea will make you feel better.'

'I feel better already,' said Lily, smiling up at the young soldier.

David squatted down beside her. He knew it might be a long time before he got another opportunity to have Lily all to himself, but he found he couldn't think of a thing to say to her. He searched desperately for a subject of conversation. His gaze fell upon her embroidered apron and he muttered in embarrassed tones, 'That's very pretty, Lily. Did Mrs Gillings make it?'

Lily laughed softly. 'No, of course she didn't. My mother-in-law's not one for fancy work. She can do plain sewing right enough but she leaves anything special to me. Haven't you seen all the pretty things I've made for the baby? I hang them on the line to air every time it's a nice day.'

'Yes, I had noticed. They're all lovely but I didn't think you made them. Annie's not that clever, though she does make a lot of the littl'uns every-day clothes.'

'Well, you can't expect her to do fancy stuff if she hasn't been trained. I first learned from my auntie – she was a dressmaker. You remember, David. I told you my auntie brought me up. She was my only family. She say, "Lily, you gotta have a trade. There won't be no-one to take care of you when I'm gone". When I was twelve, she took me to see her employer, Mrs Pringle. She had a shop in the centre of Norwich. That was a very high class shop, David. That served only the gentry from all over the county. My auntie used to do work at home for Mrs Pringle and take it to her when it was finished, but most of her workers lived in. When my auntie asked Mrs Pringle if she would take me as an apprentice, she say, "Yes, as a favour to you, Miss Hatton, because you've been a good worker to me all these years and I reckon Lily will take after you".'

'Didn't you mind leaving home, Lily?'

'That seemed strange at first, David. The shop was on the ground floor, the next two floors were work-rooms, and we all slept in the attic. I'd always wished I had brothers and sisters and all of a sudden, I had eleven sisters!'

David laughed. 'I reckon eleven sisters would be too many even for me.'

'That was a happy time once I'd settled down. Mrs Pringle was very good to us though she was strict. She'd take us all to chapel with her every Sunday and we were all Sunday school teachers. We weren't allowed out after dark and even light nights in the summer we had to be in afore half past eight – and we didn't finish work afore seven. But that wouldn't do to be a minute late home, or the lady that had charge of us would tell Mrs Pringle next morning.' Lily drew herself up and assumed a prim voice. '"That's my Christian duty to see you all grow up nice respectable girls. I've never had a girl go astray while she was under my roof and I'm never going to."

Then my auntie died. She'd always suffered with her chest every winter but she was taken very sudden. That was a blow; she'd been like a mother to me.'

'I'm sorry to hear that, Lily,' murmured David.

'Mrs Pringle was very kind and one day she say, "Lily, I think that would do you good to live in the country. You're pale and delicate looking just like your poor aunt. Country air might put some colour into your cheeks. Lady Meredith has asked if I can spare one of my girls to go and take up the position of seamstress at the Hall. I've told her ladyship I'll let you go because you're one of my best workers and you've no family or home of your own." So that's how I came to live at Haisbro, David. I tried not to let Mrs Pringle down – Lady Meredith was one of her best customers – and living at the Hall was like being part of a big family. Afore I left Norwich, Mrs Pringle say, "That's a pity her ladyship's not Wesleyan – she's Church of England – but that doesn't matter because she keeps a very proper household. I wouldn't let you go otherwise." And Mrs Pringle was right. We had to do as we were told and work hard, but we were happy. I mended all the household linen and repaired and altered her ladyship's clothes. When she saw how good I was at my trade, she let me make petticoats and some dresses for her and her daughters – just their every-day ones, of course – not their best.'

'That must have been quite an honour for you, Lily. But if you were so well thought of at the Hall, I wonder that you left. You must have been very young when you got married.' David did not dare to look at Lily whilst he waited for her answer; instead, he plucked nervously at the marram grass. He had always felt curious about Lily's husband but he had never found the courage to ask about him before. The girl was delighted to be given the chance to talk about him.

'I was just seventeen when I was wed,' she replied proudly. 'If I hadn't gone to work at the Hall, I would never have met Arthur. When he was off duty, he used to come up to the Hall to visit his lordship's head game-keeper. They're friends, you see. His lordship knows Arthur too – yes, he thinks a lot of Arthur, does Lord Meredith. When none of his proper friends are staying with him, he gets Arthur to go shooting and fishing with him for company. Anyhow, Arthur used to spend a lot of his spare time at the Hall, one way or another and he always took the trouble to speak to me. No man had ever bothered with me afore and I'd had nothing to do with no men – or boys – afore, so I was very shy. But Arthur was that nice to me I soon got over being shy of him. He brought me here to see his mother many times, so when he asked if I'd like to marry him, I say, "Yes", right away. 'Course, then Arthur wondered who he should speak to with my auntie being dead, so I say he'd better ask his lordship. Lord Meredith was so pleased he paid for the wedding and for all my things, and he let us have a party in the Servants Hall afterwards. There was some problem about me being under age and having no legal guardian, but his lordship, being a magistrate, soon sorted that out.'

Lily suddenly paused and turned abruptly away from David. 'What's the matter?' the boy asked anxiously. 'You ent sick again?'

Lily shook her head vigorously then gave a little sob. 'Talking about Arthur has made me wish he was here. If Arthur was here, I wouldn't be so frightened.'

'But what are you frightened of?' enquired the boy with genuine surprise.

'Of having the baby, of course. That's how Arthur's first wife died – in childbirth.'

Once more, David found himself at a loss for words. Then he said in as confident a voice as he could muster, 'You've got nothing to worry about, Lily – my mother and my aunties have had lots of babies and they haven't died. When you see the littl'un, you'll be so pleased you'll forget you were ever worried.'

Lily turned to face David again. Her skin looked white against her black hair and her eyes were still brimming with tears. The boy wanted to put his arms around her to comfort her, but instead he took her hand in his and tried to cheer her. 'You'll see, Lily. That's lovely having a baby in the house. The first thing everyone does when they come indoors – Father too – is go talk to the baby.'

'Oh, I want the baby, David, but I just wish Arthur was here. There's nothing that Arthur doesn't know about and when things worry me, Arthur explains them to me. I wish Arthur was here – that I do.'

David searched for words to console Lily. He decided he must try to make her laugh. 'Yes, Mother always say she'd rather have Father with her than anyone else when she's having a littl'un. She say he doesn't shout at her like Mrs Higgins does. Mrs Higgins is the old lady in our village that brings the young uns into the world and lays the old uns out. But Father say she's gotta have Mrs Higgins, so Mother books her and then leaves it too late to fetch her so Father has to help. The only thing is, Mother say he's so used to delivering horses and cattle that he forgets she's his wife and talks to her like she's a mare. He's a-saying, "Whoa there, gal!" and "Steady on, gal!" ....'

Lily's laughter told David that his little tale had had the desired effect. Someone else was also amused by the story. Both young people looked round, startled at hearing a low chuckling sound behind them. 'Dr Lambert!' exclaimed Lily. David leapt to his feet, red-faced. Seeing his discomfort, the doctor patted his arm.

'Young man, my wife would be most interested in what you've just said. She swears I think more of my horse than I do of her.' The doctor pointed to where his pony and trap stood near the perimeter wall of the Station. 'But then, you must bear in mind that that mare, although she is a nag, does not nag me like my other mare at home does.' The doctor chuckled anew at his own joke and his generous paunch quivered like a jelly. David and Lily looked at each other blankly. 'But to be serious, Lily, there's a moral in this young man's story. Kindness, Lily, can perform miracles. Now, boy, your father has discovered that when he treats his livestock with compassion the birth process is made easier for them – and so it is with your mother.'

At that moment, Ginny scrambled up the sand dunes towards the group. The doctor appealed to her as she approached. 'Ah! Ginny, my dear, won't you agree with me that of all human traits, there's none as important as kindness?'

Ginny smiled and answered without hesitation. 'Yes, I agree with you, Doctor. I reckon I could forgive a man anything if he was kind.'

'Well said, my dear. Well said,' muttered the doctor, taking Ginny's arm. 'And have you come to fetch me to some patient I didn't know I had?'

'No, Doctor,' laughed Ginny. 'I came to look for Lily because her mother-in-law was worried about her.'

'Then that makes two of us,' said Dr Lambert. 'I was visiting in this area and just stopped by to see how Lily was faring. I can see that she is perfectly well, so perhaps you will be so kind as to escort me to the festivities. My ears do not deceive me, do they? I do hear some form of entertainment emanating from Mrs Brewster's parlour, do I not?'

'You do, Doctor,' Ginny assured him. 'It's young James's birthday.'

'Well, well, how delightful! There's nothing I like better than a nice piece of birthday cake – and something to wash it down with, of course.'

'You'll be very welcome, Doctor. You know that. We're having a sing-song at the moment.'

'Then you will need my incomparable contribution. But don't let me get carried away and stay too long, will you, my dear? Mrs Lambert gets very upset if I'm late for supper – and come to think of it, the horse doesn't like to be late for supper either.'

VII

Tovell had covered less than a mile of his patrol when a familiar noise
made him look up. There, in the clear sky above him, was a tiny
biplane. It flew low over his head and the pilot leaned out of the
cockpit and waved to him. Tovell waved back. It was a routine which
had been established soon after the soldiers had taken over the
Coastguard Station. Tovell followed the biplane's course as it flew out
to sea. The water was sparkling in the bright sunshine. Tovell had to
shield his eyes against the glare. He watched as the pilot dipped his
machine so that he could inspect a group of fishing boats. Then he
returned to his original flight-path, hugging the coastline.

As the biplane disappeared from view, Tovell lowered his gaze and
was, at once, captivated by an even more wondrous sight. Ginny was
standing on Haisbro Cliffs staring into the distance. Her slim figure was
silhouetted against the cloudless blue sky, the gentle breeze tugging
playfully at her dress and tousling the curls of her dark auburn hair. A
field of golden stubble stretched behind her and Haisbro Lighthouse,
painted in wide bands of red and white, towered over her like some
giant Guardsman.

Tovell had not taken long to conclude that Ginny was the prettiest
woman he had ever seen. He felt no compunction about spying on her
– it was a habit he indulged at every opportunity and one which was
aided by the fact that the tiny cottage they shared was not designed to
allow the inhabitants privacy. Tovell slept in one corner of the living
room in the bed previously occupied by the children; the latter had
been taken into their mother's bed in the only bedroom the cottage
possessed. Tovell was careful never to draw the curtains which hung
around his sleeping quarters too closely together, thus making certain
that he would be able to watch Ginny at her early morning chores
through the peep-hole he had left himself.

Seeing Ginny now, away from the dark confines of her home, out in the open where the sunlight served to enhance her natural beauty, Tovell felt overwhelmed by her presence. He forced himself to break the spell; shouldering his rifle more securely he strode along the cliff-side towards her. He expected her to turn and greet him with her usual welcoming smile, but instead she tried to rush past him, deliberately hiding her face. He grabbed hold of her and forced her to look at him. The big expressive eyes, green with a hint of grey, which he admired so much and which were usually full of laughter, were brimming with tears.

'Whatever's happened, Ginny? Why are you crying?' Tovell demanded.

Ginny hesitated and then blurted out, 'My brothers .... They just came to say goodbye to me. They've gone to join up.'

'Poor Ginny,' murmured Tovell sympathetically. 'You're very fond of your brothers, aren't you?

Ginny nodded and continued. 'That was such a shock. They didn't say nothing about it last Sunday when I took the littl'uns to see them. They say they can't get work on the boats this year so they might as well join the Army.'

'The boats? I thought your brothers worked on the land.'

'They do – for most of the year – but they get stood off after the harvest. They always go down to Yarmouth and get berths as sharemen on the drifters for the Home Fishing season. Of course, they know they might not earn any money that way either – if the boat doesn't make her expenses there's nothing to share out – but at least they get fed. They've heard that this year there aren't many boats fishing because of the war. All the best drifters are being chartered by the Admiralty for patrol duties and minesweeping. I don't know, Tovell – maybe this war's going to affect us more than we'd bargained. There's hundreds like my brothers that depend on the Home Fishing for a living after the harvest. The roads would be full of them at this time of year walking to Yarmouth or Lowestoft – whichever port was nearest. The regular fishermen even have a special name for farm-workers that go part-time fishing – they call them joskins. I reckon there'll be a lot of joskins doing the same as my brothers and joining up. But everyone say the war'll be over by Christmas, don't they? So that'll seem like they've only been away for the herring season.'

'Perhaps, Ginny – perhaps they'll be home by Christmas. But try not to worry about them. From what I've heard about conditions on the drifters, if you can survive there you can survive anywhere.' Tovell hoped he sounded convincing. At least Ginny had stopped crying but he did not like the thought of her being alone when she was distressed. 'I wish I could stay with you, Ginny,' he said, 'but I've got to continue my patrol. Why don't you go back to the Station and go next door and talk to Mrs Gillings and Lily?'

'I'm alright really, Tovell. I only came up here because it was a special place for us when we were littl'uns. See that field behind us – after the corn had been cut we'd go along between the stubbles and glean what was left. Then we'd tie the corn we'd collected into bundles and go round selling it to people that kept chickens. Oh, we were up to all kinds of tricks to make a bit of money. And when the boys started going to sea every September, we'd come up here before they left and fill some sacks with straw for them.'

'What the heck did they want with sacks of straw?' asked Tovell in amused tones.

'For mattresses, of course,' replied Ginny. 'You don't think an old drifter's got mattresses, do you? Well, you'll not pass many joskins on the road carrying their sacks of straw this year…. I've gotta get back – I've done nothing about dinner yet. That doesn't do to go neglecting things just because of a little old war. I'll be myself time you get home, Tovell.'

Tovell caught hold of Ginny's hand as she turned to leave. 'You're a good girl, Ginny,' he said affectionately. 'I bet you never let anything get you down for long. You're like these poppies,' he pointed to the red flowers which grew in wild profusion all around. 'You can bloom anywhere in the roughest conditions – bright, cheerful, colourful – no matter what.'

Ginny laughed. 'Oh, Tovell, you can tell you're not a countryman. The farmers call poppies, "bloomin' old red-weed", because they choke up the cornfields. They thrive so well here that this area round to Cromer and Sheringham is known as Poppyland.'

'Well, I don't care what the farmers call them,' asserted Tovell. 'I think they're lovely and they'll always remind me of you.'

Ginny was embarrassed by the compliment and with a brief wave she hurried away, running lightly along the coastal path in the direction of the Coastguard Station. Tovell watched her go, thinking as he had done on several previous occasions, that her husband was a man to be envied. Strangely enough, jealousy was an emotion Tovell had rarely experienced and he had never before coveted another man's wife. He had been struggling to control his feelings almost from the first day he had set eyes on Ginny and was very thankful for the existence of the *Admiral Lord Nelson*. There he could numb the pain with his favourite medicine and be further comforted by the congenial company. Ted Carter had been as good as his word and because of his patronage Tovell had been spared the normal lengthy testing period accorded to strangers and had been accepted by the other customers in a remarkably short time. The fact that it was wartime and allowances had to be made and standards adjusted may also have played a part, and Tovell's own gregarious and generous nature stood him in good stead, but the soldier felt he owed a debt of gratitude to his friend for the welcome he received on every visit and he rewarded him with many a pint of his favourite brew.

That night, Tovell made his way to the public house at the earliest opportunity and launched into anecdotes about the war in the Sudan as soon as he had an audience. As usual, the group at Tovell's table included Ted and his friends from the Volunteer Life-saving Brigade, the lifeboat coxswain and Dr Lambert.

'Tovell, you're the biggest bloomin' liar I've ever come across,' declared Ted Carter as the first tale got underway.

'I ain't lying,' protested Tovell. 'It's the Gospel truth I'm telling you. These Dervish women lifted up their smocks and showed us everything they'd got. Hundreds of them there were, all naked underneath like the day they were born. But they didn't have any other choice. The Dervishes – the Fuzzy-Wuzzies – all dress alike in smocks – long robes – and if they hadn't proved to us that they were women, we'd have thought they were men and run them through with our bayonets. Atbara, it was. The Dervishes had dug trenches there for defence protected by prickly bushes six feet high. Their commanders had chained a lot of poor devils to the bushes by their ankles so they couldn't retreat. Some shells set fire to the bushes and – well, you can guess what happened – they were all roasted alive. I'll never forget that sight – or sound – either.'

Tovell shook his head and took another swig of beer. He was still looking morose when he replaced his mug on the table. Dr Lambert diverted him with a question, 'But were you at Omdurman, my boy?'

'I was indeed, Sir,' replied Tovell proudly. 'It was the same year – 1898. I'd have been eighteen – nineteen. I can remember it as though it were yesterday. *Reveille* sounded at four. We all stood to arms 'til daybreak. Sunrise in the tropics is always a marvellous sight but that day it was even more spectacular than usual. I reckon I must have been wondering whether it would be the last sunrise I'd ever see. But by six thirty that evening we marched into Omdurman and ate our breakfast, dinner and tea all in one! After thirteen years we'd avenged the siege of Khartoum and the death of General Gordon. That was a proud day. Her Majesty thought a lot of Gordon.'

Tovell stood up and raised his mug of beer aloft. 'Come on, boys. Let's drink a toast to General Gordon.' As his companions joined him, he quoted dramatically, *'His bones are dust; His good sword rust; His soul is with the Saints, I trust.'*

'To General Gordon,' proposed the doctor, 'may he rest in peace.'

'To General Gordon,' muttered the company assembled around the table.

'And to Her Majesty, Queen Victoria!' declared Tovell.

'To the old Queen, God rest her soul,' agreed Ted Carter.

At that moment, Tovell glanced up at the clock on the wall, abruptly finished his drink and walked rapidly to the door without a word to his friends.

'There he go – eight on the dot,' said Ted. 'He'll be back again on the dot o' nine, even more cheerful, and carry on drinking again like nothing's happened.'

Tovell was a man of strict habits but it was this evening routine which had aroused the most interest amongst the locals. How he passed the missing hour had not remained a mystery for long. He was sighted in back alleys, down quiet country lanes and behind barns and haystacks – always in female company. The faces of his partners were never seen – only their rear views – but it was reported categorically that he was never with the same girl twice. This had led to much hearty discussion in the public bar as to how he managed to find so many different young ladies to take the nocturnal air with him. Perhaps it was as well that this thought alone captured the imaginations of the drinkers or it might have occurred to them that Tovell's willing consorts were someone's sister, daughter, granddaughter, cousin or niece. As it was, they were content to speculate at length on what attributes Tovell had which normal male mortals did not possess. There had been some consternation when it was revealed that Tovell was billeted with Ginny. This concern, however, was short lived – the general consensus of opinion being that with so much sexual activity during the evening, Tovell would be 'spent afore he gets home'.

When the soldier re-entered the hostelry at nine, he went straight to the bar, returning to the table with drinks for everyone. 'Now where were we? We hadn't drunk to the victor of Omdurman. Raise your glasses, boys. Lord Kitchener!'

'And I propose Mr Winston Churchill – for being a master fine organiser,' insisted Ted.

When the roll-call of national heroes was exhausted, the friends turned their attention to local heroes. Every man for miles around who was known to have volunteered or been mobilised was duly toasted, and because Tovell's conscience was troubling him, he saw to it that the health of Ginny's husband, Robert Adams, was drunk no fewer than six times.

That night, Tovell staggered home wheeling Ginny's bicycle. He was singing at the top of his voice as he made his tottering way up the garden path which led to both the Gillings's and the Adams's cottage. Mrs. Gillings threw open her rear window and swore at him. 'Hold your row, you drunken devil!' she hissed. 'That's well past midnight. Do you want to wake up all the littl'uns?'

Mrs. Gillings's sudden appearance momentarily silenced Tovell. She had rolled up her hair in bits of white rag and the ends of the material quivered when she shook her fist at him. Tovell was mesmerized by the sight of little vibrating horns popping out of Mrs. Gillings's head. It was several seconds before the significance of the remainder of her night attire struck him: she was dressed in a voluminous white garment, high-necked and long-sleeved. Tovell began to laugh – so much so that he had great difficulty in communicating his thoughts. At last he stammered out the words. 'I know who you are – you're a Fuzzy-Wuzzy come to haunt me! C'mon – you've got to prove it. You know what I've got to do if you're a man and you know what I've got to do if you're a woman – and if you're a woman, Gawd help me! I'll break ranks! I'll be shot for cowardice!'

Tovell collapsed on the path convulsed in mirth. Mrs. Gillings glowered at him. 'You need sobering up, bor. I've got just the thing for you.' She promptly disappeared only to return to the window bearing a large chamber-pot in her hands. Tovell saw what she was holding just in time. He threw himself out of range and crawled thankfully through Ginny's scullery door muttering, 'Tovell's done it again; he's escaped the mad Fuzzy-Wuzzies.'

As he lay panting on the cold stone flags he became aware of a noise coming from the direction of the bedroom. It sounded as though some heavy object was being pushed across the floor. He considered the matter for a while and then decided that his fuddled brain was incapable of solving any riddles so he might as well go to bed. He dragged himself across the living room and fell asleep on his bed without bothering to remove his boots or clothes.

After a few fitful hours dreaming that he was fighting a Dervish army led by Mrs. Gillings in her curling rags, Tovell was awakened by a stern-faced Ginny. 'Here's your tea and you're on duty in forty minutes,' she snapped. The usual warm smile and cheerful greeting was missing.

Breakfast was not a happy meal either; the children were strangely silent and scarcely touched their porridge. Tovell would have questioned their behaviour had his head not been pounding. He spent his watch puzzling over the coolness of the entire family towards him. When he returned to the cottage he found Mrs. Brewster sitting with Ginny. The conversation ended abruptly as he entered. Tovell had had enough mysteries for one day and he asked without hesitation, 'What's the matter now?'

It was Lydia Brewster who replied. 'I'm sorry to say, Mr. Tovell, that you have caused Mrs. Adams considerable distress by your drinking habits.'

'My drinking habits!' exclaimed Tovell incredulously. 'She's never complained before and I go drinking every night I'm not on duty.'

'Not like last night,' retorted Ginny, looking up at Tovell with red and swollen eyes. 'You've never got roaring drunk afore. That's what I don't like. I don't begrudge you a drink, nor a few drinks, but not to get helpless drunk. That isn't right.'

Tovell suddenly remembered the strange noise he had heard. 'You barricaded your bedroom door last night, didn't you?' he said, stating a fact rather than asking a question. Ginny looked down at the table once more but did not reply. 'So that's it! That's what you're upset about. You think that when I'm drunk I'm going to break down the door and jump on you. Ginny, use a bit of sense; you have the littl'uns in bed with you. The minute I got into your room they'd be off next door. That old witch would be laying into me with her horse-whip before I'd even got my flies undone.'

Both women had difficulty suppressing smiles. 'That's not what I'm worried about,' mumbled Ginny, without looking at Tovell.

Mrs. Brewster intervened. 'All that matters is that Mrs. Adams should not be upset again. It seems to me that there is a simple solution, Mr. Tovell. We must control your excessive drinking by putting a time limit on your re-entry to the house. I suggest that Mrs. Adams bolts both doors promptly at midnight on the assumption that if you are later than that you have consumed too much alcohol.'

Tovell could scarcely believe his ears. 'Who are you to interfere?' he exploded.

Ginny was appalled by his reaction. 'Mrs. Brewster is the Station Officer's wife.'

'Does that make her your officer too?' Tovell demanded.

'Of course it does,' replied Ginny.

Tovell was flabbergasted but he realised he could not win the argument. 'In that case,' he conceded, 'I reckon I'm guilty of insubordination as well as …. whatever it is I'm accused of.' He saluted Mrs. Brewster smartly. 'Very well, Sir …., I mean, Ma'am! Twenty four hundred hours it is.' He marched out of the cottage by the front door and rushed round to the back door. By the time he crept quietly into the scullery, Mrs. Brewster had left.

Ginny was setting the table in the living room. She was obviously embarrassed by his presence; he was hurt that she should have complained about him to another woman. They sat down to eat in a strained atmosphere. Tovell, however, was not a man to bear a grudge for long and he was distressed to think that he had caused Ginny to weep. After a few minutes he put down his knife and fork and placed his hand gently over her hand. 'I'm sorry, Ginny,' he said earnestly. 'I didn't realise how much I'd upset you. It won't happen again. I promise I won't get roaring drunk again.'

Ginny said nothing for a few moments, then she looked up, eyes still watery and said, 'That does rile me to see a man pingle his food. Now what's the good of me cooking you a decent meal when you don't eat it?' They both laughed, the tension disappeared and their appetites returned. For once, Ginny did not protest when Tovell helped her to clear away the dishes. He knew he had been forgiven. He stretched out in the comfortable armchair beside the cooking range as Ginny took down all her brass and copper ornaments from the mantelpiece and arranged them on newspaper on the table, ready for cleaning.

'They don't need polishing,' Tovell chided. 'They're as bright as new pennies.'

'You're a one to talk,' replied Ginny, teasingly, 'Always brushing your uniform, polishing your buttons and cleaning your boots.'

Tovell laughed. 'Army training – Army discipline! It's drummed into you from the first day you join. Things have got to be done right – done proper. It's a habit I shall never get out of and you're the same, aren't you? Sure you've never been in the Army, Ginny?'

'Not your army but another very similar,' she replied. 'I used to work up at the Hall. You must have seen it – a big house in acres and acres of land just afore you get to the village. Lily worked there too but after my time. Mrs. Kemp, the housekeeper, ruled us with a rod of iron. There was only one way – the proper way – of doing any job. I can't do a thing now except Mrs. Kemp's way.'

'We've got a lot in common, Ginny,' said Tovell quietly.

Ginny smiled at him and seemed about to reply but changed her mind. She applied herself to the polishing with renewed vigour. 'That'll do for today,' she decided, somewhat abruptly. She hastily gathered up some of the ornaments and brought them back to the mantle-piece. At first she stood very close to Tovell's feet, her skirts brushing his legs. She stretched up on tip-toe to see if there was any dust on the shelf before she replaced the brasses. Tovell leant forward in the chair, his eyes centring on her tiny waist. The temptation to close his large hands around it and draw her down onto his lap was almost more than he could bear. He was about to succumb and reach out for her when she moved to the other end of the mantle-piece. Tovell rested his elbows on his knees and put his head in his hands. He found he was shaking slightly and his palms were sweating. The dog seemed to sense his distress. He came out from under the table and put a paw on Tovell's thigh. The soldier fondled the animal's head.

'What's the matter, Blackie? Want me to take you for a walk? Yeah, maybe the fresh air would do us both good.' Tovell got up immediately and made for the front door, the dog jumping excitedly around his heels.

Ginny was surprised by the sudden departure. 'I'm not forcing you out,' she said.

'I know you ain't,' answered Tovell from the doorway. 'We'll be back when the children get home from school.'

VIII

Ginny had noticed soon after Tovell's arrival that if the soldier happened to be off-watch in the mornings he could not settle until the newspaper boy had made his delivery. If the lad was late Tovell would repeatedly leave the cottage to see if he could spy him in the distance and when the familiar ring of his bicycle bell was heard at last, he would rush outside to meet him. Tovell had made a standing order for what Ginny called a London newspaper. She herself bought only a local newspaper, or rather she continued to receive the paper her husband had always taken. She did little more than glance through it, claiming that she 'hadn't got the time'. She was both amused and mystified to find that her lodger did not merely read his copy but appeared to devour every word of it, but she refrained from asking him where he had acquired all his schooling.

It was the war news which concerned Tovell the most and he followed the fortunes and misfortunes of the British Expeditionary Force on a daily basis. He delighted in reading extracts to Ginny whenever the Press praised the fighting prowess of the British Army but he could not hide his despair that they and the French 5th Army were falling back under the might of four German armies. He followed the retreat from Mons, which lasted a fortnight, in spirit every step of the way. Ginny knew he was torturing himself about the fate of his friends from whom he had been separated. When the news came in the first week of September that the German invasion had been checked at the Battle of the Marne, Tovell was jubilant.

Across the green, Lieutenant Collins was another avid reader of London newspapers. He too, discussed the progress of the war with his landlady. 'Do you realise, Lydia, that if we had the manpower to follow through our success at the Marne, we could end this war here and now?'

'Very possibly, Richard,' replied Lydia Brewster, putting aside her newspaper. 'But we haven't the manpower. We've been horribly outnumbered since the beginning.'

'There's no doubt about that. The Germans had vast numbers of men ready to put into the field. We, on the other hand, have always avoided the expense of a large military commitment on the Continent. As the greatest naval power in the world we've always assumed that our role in war would be largely maritime. After all, that was the policy of both Pitts – my God, I've drummed that fact into my pupils often enough – and I'm sure it's our policy now. The Royal Navy is expected to destroy, or at least contain the German battle fleet and then blockade Germany. On the assumption of speedy and total success at sea, a large land force would not be necessary. I fear such a policy won't work this time. I'd hazard a guess that the Germans have mustered a million and a half men already. They're steamrolling across Europe on an enormous front. The only way to stop them is with an equal number of men – not ships. If we don't make the most of our present advantage and beat them decisively now, we could be embroiled in a bloody conflict that could last for years.'

'Oh, Richard, you're being too pessimistic. The Government is quite certain the war will be over by Christmas.'

'I wish I shared their optimism. And I wish I didn't feel so impotent. Seeing the situation and knowing that I, personally, can do nothing about it ….'

'But you are doing something about it. You're setting aside a great deal of time for training. The new recruits are responding well to the lessons they're learning from Sergeant Harris and Private Tovell. Taking your argument to its ultimate conclusion, if the Germans were to invade this shore we are well prepared to defend ourselves.'

'Well prepared,' mused the lieutenant. 'You've given me food for thought, Lydia. I'm not at all sure we're well prepared; there's one aspect I'd overlooked completely. If you will excuse me, I shall attend to the oversight immediately.'

The officer got up from the table and crossed to the door at the far end of the parlour. He called up the narrow staircase to the Watch-room above. 'Sergeant, do you know which off-duty men are on the Station?'

'As far as I know, only Wilson is on site, Sir. He rarely leaves the

46

place,' replied the Sergeant.

'Yes, I had noticed,' muttered the lieutenant as he closed the internal door.

'David had his breakfast very early. I haven't seen him since.' Lydia called out.

'I'm sure he'll be easy to find,' said Richard Collins with a smile. With a wave of the hand to Lydia, he walked rapidly to the rear door of his quarters and headed straight for the little gardens which backed onto the cottages. The boy was there talking quietly to Lily. 'Good morning to you, Mrs. Gillings. I hope you are well,' said the officer courteously.

Lily blushed slightly and half curtsied as she replied shyly, 'Yes, thank you, Lieutenant Collins.'

'Perhaps you will excuse us ma'am, but I have an urgent job for this soldier.' Turning to the youth, he called out, 'David, I'd like a word with you, please.'

Tovell, who happened to come out of the back door of his billet at that particular moment, heard the last remark. He watched with interest as the pair walked slowly towards Mrs. Brewster's home. Lieutenant Collins had his arm around the boy's shoulder and was talking to him quickly and in an animated and persuasive fashion. 'It's time you spoke to young Davey,' said Tovell to himself.

A few hours later when Tovell was on duty in the Watch-room, he chanced to catch sight of David through a side window. He was about twenty five yards from where a mobile gun had recently been installed, and he was waist deep in soil. 'Jesus Christ!' Tovell exclaimed. 'Look at the boy: he's digging his bloody grave. It must be all that pining for Lily: it's gone to his ruddy head.'

'Stop fussing, Tovell,' said Lieutenant Collins without bothering to look up from his desk. 'Wilson isn't digging his grave: he's making an underground shelter to protect the women and children in the event of an enemy attack. We must not overlook the possibility of a bombardment from the sea. Better to be safe than sorry. And please exercise some restraint. There is no excuse for blasphemy or for your habit of constantly using swear words as adjectives.'

47

As soon as Tovell's watch was over and he had snatched a hasty meal, he joined David in the trench. 'Great idea Davey, making a dug-out for the families.'

'I didn't think of it,' admitted the young soldier. 'Lieutenant Collins did.'

At the mention of the officer's name Tovell asked, 'Does he always call you David when you're off duty?'

'Yes, he does,' replied the boy. 'And Mrs. Brewster – she does an' all. When I'm in the house they both treat me like a child.'

'What's he like – old Collins – when he's in the house?'

'He's alright, I reckon. He doesn't pay much regard to me. He reads most of the time. He likes to read out loud to Mrs. Brewster – poetry I reckon you'd call it. He even follows her round the kitchen when she's cooking he does, reading to her.'

'Gawd Almighty! She must want to stick a knife in him!'

'She doesn't seem to mind, but then, they were both schoolteachers. They laugh a lot at what he reads out, though what's funny about it I don't know. That sounds more like a foreign language to me – that that does. I can't understand a word of it.'

'What did you say, David? He used to be a schoolmaster?'

'Yes. Before the war he was a schoolmaster at some big school near Oxford. It's one of them ones where the boys live there and don't go home at night.'

'A schoolmaster at a boys' public school…. That would suit our Lieutenant Collins fine. Well, you'd better watch out, Davey. If he's partial to young boys he'll have a go at you. Has he tried anything yet?'

'Tried what, Mr. Tovell?' enquired David, wide eyed.

'You know, Davey. Your dad told you about women; he must have told you about men like old Collins. Has he ever asked you to go to his room with him when Mrs. Brewster wasn't there?'

David shook his head vigourously. 'Mr. Collins wouldn't do nothing like that.'

'Wouldn't he?' laughed Tovell. 'You can tell you haven't been in the Army long, son. I've seen high ranking officers – and I don't mean piddling lieutenants – risk everything for a pretty boy like you, Davey. You'd better watch yourself and if he so much as lays a hand on you, or says something dirty, you tell old Tovell. I'll soon sort the bugger out!'

At that moment, Fred Mannell arrived on the scene carrying a spade. 'I'll give you a hand, David,' he said as he jumped down beside Tovell.

'Thank you, Mr. Mannell,' replied the boy. 'Sergeant Harris and Mr. Westgate helped me earlier. They said they'd have another go tomorrow when they're off-watch and Mr. Jackson said he'd help an' all. We'll soon get it done.'

The proceedings had been watched from a discreet distance by three of the wives. They had been huddled together by the perimeter wall of the Station, whispering, for some minutes. Now, having reached a decision and carrying their youngest offspring in their arms, they approached the soldiers. They watched in silence for a few moments then Mary asked the question they all wanted answered. 'Why are you digging a bloomin' great hole? We're dying of curiosity.'

Tovell laughed. 'It's for you – all of you.'

'Well, it's big enough to bury us all in – that's for sure,' ventured Emily.

'It's a dugout to protect you,' said Tovell.

David elaborated. 'Lieutenant Collins say the enemy might attack us and we've gotta have somewhere safe underground for you and the littl'uns to hide.'

'It'll be a proper shelter when it's finished,' Fred assured the women. 'It'll be alright.'

'Well, that's very kind of you,' said Phyllis, the third member of the group, 'but I don't reckon that'll ever get used.'

Mary nodded in agreement. 'That'll all be over soon. Anyway, the Navy would never let the Hun get anywhere near our coast …'

Emily was suddenly afraid that they might have given offence so she interrupted her friend. 'But that's not to say we're not grateful. Thank you very much, boys, for thinking of us.'

The other two women hastily expressed their appreciation of the soldiers' efforts on their behalf before all three hurried back to their cottages to convey the news of what the soldiers were doing to their neighbours – Ginny, Mrs Ellis and the two Mrs Gillings. The reaction of those four was identical to that of the other three women; they were touched by the soldiers' concern for their welfare but amazed that the men should think such a precaution necessary. The opinions of the women regarding the likely time-span of the conflict, and the invincibility of the Royal Navy, were shared by the vast majority of the British people. It took just one man – a daring German commander – a little over an hour to shatter the illusions of a nation.

Tovell watched that fateful dawn rise – it had been his turn for the twelve hour watch, most of which he had spent out on patrol. He paused on Haisbro Cliffs for a last scan of the horizon. He was glad it was nearly six; he would not be sorry to be off-watch. It had been a rough night – what his friend, Ted Carter, called "rafty old weather". During the previous couple of days westerly gales had whipped an earlier ground swell into ten foot waves. The wind seemed at last to be moderating although the clouds were still scudding across the sky above Tovell's head. He remembered later thinking how strange it was that the weather had deteriorated so early – it was only the twenty second of September – and reflecting that, had he been a superstitious man, he might have interpreted the freak gales as a bad omen. He had taken a long final look at the murky depths before hurrying off along the cliff path, thinking to himself that if he had any choice in how he should die, he would not choose drowning.

The women of the Station afterwards remarked how strange it was that not one of them had had any premonition of the impending disaster. As it was, when the telegrams started to arrive the following morning, they came as a complete shock. Every family, without exception, received at least one. They brought news of a loved one missing at sea – a brother, a brother-in-law, a cousin, a comrade from a former coastguard posting. The telegram which the Gillings family received told of the loss of Arthur Gillings. It was apparent that a very large number of His Majesty's Coastguards had been wiped out with one blow.

IX

The concisely worded telegrams gave no indication of what terrible fate had befallen the dead coastguards. It was left to the Coastguard Divisional Officer to supply the details to the acting Station Officer and for Lieutenant Collins to pass on the distressing information to the grieving ladies afterwards.

Mr. Latham, the Divisional Officer, apologised as soon as he had taken his seat in Mrs. Brewster's parlour for the fact that he could not stay long and could spare the time only to visit the two Mrs. Gillings personally. 'Regrettably, I can express my sympathy to those who have lost their next-of-kin but to no-one else, simply because so many have been bereaved. I shall cause grave offence if I do not visit every station in my division either today or tomorrow. Yes, I am sorry to say that every station has suffered losses, such is the magnitude of this tragedy.'

'You look quite worn out, Mr. Latham. Let me get you some refreshment,' said Lydia Brewster.

'Thank you, ma'am, a cup of tea would be appreciated.' As Mrs. Brewster hurried to the kitchen the Divisional Officer continued his conversation with the lieutenant. 'What should have been my last day of service was the day war was declared. When I was requested to postpone my retirement I readily agreed. I was prepared to serve in any capacity required in the absence of my colleagues. But never once – never once, Sir – did it occur to me that I should have to undertake my present onerous task.'

'You have my sympathy, Sir, such as it is,' said Lieutenant Collins as Lydia joined them and handed Mr. Latham his tea.

'I shall come straight to the point – more than fourteen hundred men were killed yesterday morning and almost all of them were coastguards.' Mr. Latham paused and wiped his brow with his handkerchief. His hand was shaking and his voice was unsteady as he admitted, 'I've made that statement twice already at stations further round the coast but the words still stick in my throat.'

'I'm not surprised. To lose fourteen hundred men in a single action is almost unbelievable.' Richard Collins was momentarily stunned. 'I don't know what to say ....,' he stammered. 'They must have put up a tremendous fight. The German battle fleet ....'

Mr. Latham interrupted. 'They didn't encounter the German battle fleet – not even a single battleship – just one tiny U-boat.'

'A submarine!' exclaimed the lieutenant. 'But I thought those things were supposed to be more of a danger to their own crews than to other shipping.'

'That was the general assumption – until now. Do you know, Sir, what they call submarines in the Royal Navy? Little pig boats. It's difficult to find any man with a good word to say for them. Even on peacetime manoeuvres they're a confounded nuisance – always sinking. And of course, quite unhealthy to work in – dangerous too – so thin skinned. They'd been virtually discounted as an effective weapon because when a torpedo is fired, the sudden loss of weight forward more often than not causes the submarine to surface. She's a sitting duck then for the gunners on the enemy ships. Even if that doesn't happen – if the vessel doesn't broach the surface – the chances are that she'll be damaged by the force of the explosion from her own torpedo. It's reckoned that at a range of less than six hundred yards her bow would be damaged, and her diving planes, making her uncontrollable. Yet that did not happen on this occasion. From the evidence of survivors, the Admiralty thinks six torpedoes were fired and not once did the U-boat broach the surface. And it's calculated that she must have fired at considerably closer range than six hundred yards – without blowing herself up.'

'But what precisely happened?' asked Lydia.

'Three armoured cruisers were patrolling about twenty miles off the Dutch coast. The patrol had been maintained since the outbreak of war but the usual destroyer escort had been withdrawn because of the atrocious weather. It would have been ineffective anyway in those rough seas. Suffice to say, the three cruisers were steaming at ten knots in a triangular formation when the lead ship, the *Aboukir*, blew up astern and sank within minutes. The captains of the other two ships naturally assumed that she'd hit a mine. They immediately turned and came to the rescue. The *Hogue* reached the scene first but as she was lowering boats to pick up the men in the water, she too was struck and quickly sank. Even then, I've no doubt they still thought they were hitting mines. The *Cressy* was circling the wreckage, her lifeboats picking up survivors, when one of her crew spotted a periscope breaking the surface. They trained their guns on the spot at once and the captain ordered full power to evade the torpedoes and ram the U-boat. It was too late. One torpedo just missed the stern but the other hit the starboard side aft. Even then, although she was listing badly she wasn't done for, but the U-boat came back for the kill and finished her off with what must have been her last torpedo.'

'Three great battleships sunk by a single small submarine', said Lieutenant Collins sadly. 'The implications are too terrible to contemplate.'

'I agree with you, Sir,' replied the Divisional Officer. 'This event changes our entire concept of naval warfare. A great battle fleet such as ours was designed to fight and defeat other battle fleets – not to be destroyed by a tiny unseen enemy. If indeed the Hun has perfected the submarine then a dreadful new weapon has been born.'

'Did you get your letters written?' asked Tovell.

'Yes, eventually,' replied Ginny, 'but it was a struggle to find words of comfort to send my poor sister-in-law and my cousin's wife. What can you say that makes any sense?'

'I don't know, Ginny. I don't know.'

'We've been adding it up. The Admiralty's been running our numbers down the last few years. Mary reckons yesterday's disaster has wiped out nearly half of them.'

'That's a hell of a lot of trained men. The Admiralty will have a job replacing them.'

'How do you replace all those husbands and fathers? They were only in old reserve ships. You wouldn't have thought they'd be in any danger.'

'From what Lieutenant Collins told us when he came back to the Watch-room, the Admiralty had taken the same view. They didn't expect those particular ships to be engaged in combat or they would never have put the youngsters aboard.'

'You mean there were young boys on those ships as well?'

'Yes, young cadets from Osborne. They were being given sea-going experience.'

'Their poor mothers – that's terrible.'

'Talking of mothers, how's Mrs. Gillings taken the news?'

'She's a marvel – that she is. Arthur was her only child – she thought the world of him. I know she's suffering but she's doing her best to bear up for Lily's sake. She say, "You can't do nothing for the dead – you've got to think of the living". What she means is she doesn't want anything to happen to Arthur's child. That's all that matters to her now.'

'And Lily?'

'Poor little old girl – she doesn't know where she is or what she's doing. She doesn't speak – she just sits there staring at the floor. Lily had no family – her late aunt brought her up – so Arthur was everything to her. That's as well she's having the littl'un otherwise I don't reckon she'd ever get over Arthur's death. Dr. Lambert arrived just before you came home. Mrs. Brewster said she was going to telephone him.'

'She's been like that ever since we got the telegram, doctor,' explained Mrs. Gillings. 'She didn't respond to Mr. Latham or to Mr. Collins. Mrs. Brewster's been in, so has Ginny, Mary – all of 'em – but none of us can get through to her.'

The doctor walked over to the front window and stood for a few moments looking across the green to the beach and sea beyond. 'I think, Mrs. Gillings, in the circumstances Lily would be better off at the Cottage Hospital in North Walsham. As soon as I've finished my rounds I'll make the arrangements. It'll be the morning before she can go so in the meantime, you will make sure that she isn't left in the house alone, won't you?'

'Don't you worry, doctor. I shan't leave her. Anything I want Ginny will fetch for me. I'll have all Lily's things and the baby's things packed ready for the morning.'

Mrs. Gillings spent the next few hours sitting opposite Lily. When she saw her daughter-in-law closing her eyes she got up quietly and went into the bedroom. She was careful to leave the door open as she packed an old suitcase. Twice she checked that Lily was still asleep in the armchair before resuming the packing. The third time she looked the chair was empty. The front door was shut but the bolts had been drawn back. Lily had been so careful to make no noise that it was obvious to her mother-in-law what was in her mind. For the first time in her life the old lady panicked and ran screaming to the Watch-room. Within seconds the entire Station was roused and every man, woman and older child was involved in the hunt for Lily.

'Search the seashore first,' ordered Lieutenant Collins. 'She couldn't have chosen a worse time. Being dusk she won't show up very clearly against the dark sea.'

It was David who eventually sighted Lily; she was walking slowly into the water below Haisbro Cliffs. He cried out to her repeatedly as he ran along the beach towards her but she did not appear to hear his calls. Tovell, on the clifftop above, heard him and immediately scrambled down the cliffside. By the time he reached the water's edge, David had caught up with Lily. Tovell waded in after them. The girl was struggling fiercely to loosen the boy's grip on her.

'Let me go! Let me go!' she pleaded. 'I've gotta go to Arthur. He's out there. I've gotta go to him.'

'No, Lily! No! You mustn't do this. Don't fight me; let me bring you ashore.'

Making a superhuman effort, Lily managed to throw David off balance. As he momentarily disappeared beneath the breakers she hurled herself into deeper water. As Tovell reached her and made a grab for her she was carried away by the receding waves. David strove to regain his footing but once more the current swept him off his feet. Some sixth sense made Tovell leave Lily and go to David's aid. As he pulled the spluttering boy to the surface he said, 'You can't swim, can you, Davey?'

'No, I can't swim,' answered the boy, 'but that doesn't make no difference. Where's Lily? We gotta find Lily.'

Before Tovell could stop him, David lunged forward and caught hold of Lily's skirt as she floated past supported by an incoming wave. The boy hung on to the material with grim determination as the swell pounded over them both. The force of the water lifted them a few yards towards the shore then threatened to snatch them back into the depths again with the retreating tide. Tovell threw himself behind the couple just in time and knelt in the foam with an arm around each of them. He felt the surf sucking the shingle bed from beneath his knees, undermining his precarious grip, straining to pull him and his two young charges backwards into the hungry current. Summoning all his strength, he braced himself until he felt the surge lose its power. He waited for the next breaker to sweep the three of them landward. Timing his effort to coincide with the flow of the tide, he lifted himself and Lily and David, and propelled them forward until they reached the beach. There he relaxed his hold on them both and let them fall as gently as possible to the ground. Exhausted himself, he fell to his knees once more beside them.

Seconds later, Lily stirred and miraculously found the strength to pull herself around and begin to crawl back towards the sea. David and Tovell were after her at once. Still protesting, she tried to fight both of them. The boy, half-choking from all the water he had swallowed, endeavoured to reason with her. 'Lily, you've got no right to do this. Arthur wouldn't want you to kill the littl'un. You've got no right to kill him. If he lives then Arthur isn't completely dead. He'll go on living through the littl'un.'

Lily suddenly stopped struggling and lay quite still. Her only sign of life was the tears slowly trickling down her cheeks. David hugged her to him, rocking her in his arms as though she were a small child. His cheeks were wet too. Tovell struggled to his feet and looked anxiously around. Help was at hand. Other figures were running along the beach towards them and on the cliff-top, against the dim skyline, he could make out the unmistakable shape of Mrs. Gillings driving the horse and cart.

'C'mon, son,' he said kindly to David. 'We've got to get Lily back to the house before she catches cold.'

By sunrise the next day Lily's son had been born – not in the Cottage Hospital but in the bed where he had been conceived. When it was over Lily drifted into a deep sleep watched by her mother-in-law, Ginny and Dr. Lambert.

'Well, when it came to it, she felt no fear,' said Ginny, bending to stroke Lily's hair. 'I reckon she felt almost nothing she was so tired after her ordeal in the sea, poor little old girl.'

'And this young fellow seems no worse for his buffeting either,' said Dr. Lambert.

Mrs. Gillings gently lifted the tiny bundle from her daughter-in-law's side and placed him in his cradle beside the bed. As she did so she said to him quietly, 'The Lord gave and the Lord hath taken away; blessed be the name of the Lord.'

X

In spite of being several days premature, and being knocked around in rough seas only hours before birth, Lily's baby was in perfect health and was a comfort and a joy to his mother and grandmother from the very beginning of his life. Mrs. Gillings lost no time in lecturing Lily on the need to, 'pull herself together,' lest she find herself unable to feed the baby, but took the precaution of engaging the services of another mother from the village. The wet-nurse was not required; Lily had no intention of relapsing into her former depressed state and delighted in displaying her little son to all who visited her. Everyone agreed with her that the baby was the image of his father.

Mrs. Gillings felt she should publicly thank the men who had saved her daughter-in-law and indirectly, her grandson, and she made a formal visit to the Watch-room for that purpose. She was particularly generous with her words to David. 'I know I've been hard on you in the past, bor, and I hope you won't hold it against me. I'm in your debt and I don't know how to begin to thank you. Mr. Tovell told Mrs. Adams all that happened and she told me. That was brave of you to go into them seas when you couldn't swim and you could have been drowned yourself. And I appreciate what you said to Lily. She's taken your words to heart – that she has. She knows she done wrong and she's sorry, and she'd like to thank you herself – both of you.'

Tovell and David duly arrived to pay their respects to mother and child. The former politely declined the invitation to hold the baby but the latter nursed him throughout the visit and was reluctant to return him to his mother. He agreed to leave only after Tovell had glowered at him repeatedly and kicked him surreptitiously on the ankle.

'I hope you'll both be able to attend the christening,' said Mrs. Gillings as she showed the two soldiers to the door. 'That won't be for a few weeks yet, because of our bereavement, but my Arthur wouldn't want us to delay an important thing like that for too long.'

Perhaps it was because the birth of a baby was such a normal affair, and the arrival of Arthur junior seemed like a divine assurance that the future would proceed in the same manner as the past, or perhaps it was because no other family apart from the Gillings family had lost a next-of-kin, but life at the Station resumed its customary pattern in a remarkably short time. The wives convinced themselves within a few days of the disaster, that the combination of circumstances which had led to the tragedy would never be repeated and that their menfolk were, therefore, quite safe where they were. Everyone adopted Mrs Gillings's stoical attitude that life must go on, pushed doubts and fears aside and worked even harder and more dutifully than ever.

Tovell, on one of his days off had gladly assumed responsibility for Bobby and Lizzie while Ginny went to visit the family of her husband's late brother. He had taken the children and Blackie for a walk along the sand dunes. When they sat down to eat the food they had brought with them, he had entertained them with tales of the pets the regiment had adopted in Africa and India.

'Do you have kittywitches in India, Uncle Tovell?' asked Lizzie, pointing to the birds squabbling over the bits of crust she had thrown them.

'There are seagulls – or rather kittywitches as you call them – on the coast and for several miles inland, but not in the middle of the continent where I was for much of the time. When I see seagulls circling and diving and hear them screeching and squawking, I'm often reminded of the kites we had in India. Kites are what you call birds of prey and they would soar high up in the sky over the camp and circle until they saw someone carrying food, then they'd sweep down and grab it. The older men used to play a trick on the newcomers: without mentioning the kites, they'd tell some poor raw recruit to go over to the coffee-shop, get himself a plate of stew and bring it back to the barracks to eat. He'd be halfway between both buildings, thinking how good his meal smelt, when they'd be a swish of wings and his lump of meat would disappear, snatched up by the bird's claws, and all he'd be left with would be the gravy.'

'I'd have got my gun and shot any bird that stole my dinner,' announced Bobby.

'No, you wouldn't,' laughed Tovell. 'We were strictly forbidden to shoot kites because they served a useful purpose. They were the camp scavengers, you see. They always knew when it was mealtime and they'd fly down low around the bungalows where we lived and wait for the men to toss them scraps and bones. They could catch them in their claws before the bits reached the ground. Yes, they did a good job keeping the place clean so we never wanted to shoot them.

We had crows too and they were thieves as well. They'd sit on the bungalow roofs waiting for the native cooks to carry the men's dinners across from the cook-house to the barracks. At Bangalore the cooks used to use open baskets for transporting food. The old crow would watch for a moment when the cook was off-guard then down he'd hop and steal a piece of meat or a slice of pudding and fly with it back to the roof-top. We'd all have a laugh at the sight of the cook shaking his fists and cursing the bird and the old crow cawing back at him in between mouthfuls, just as if he were swearing too. We never used to kill them although some of the men would trap them, so that they could put a token on them. They'd insert a thin piece of wire through the holes in the crow's upper beak and thread a button or a metal disc onto it. Each troop had its own token – ours was a little bell, so we always knew which crows were ours.'

'Did it hurt the crows, Uncle Tovell?' asked Lizzie.

'No, Lizzie, it didn't hurt them. They seemed proud of their tokens. Our crows would sit in a row on our bungalow roof nodding their heads, making their bells ring and looking as pleased as an old soldier displaying his campaign medals.'

'I didn't think you'd have anything as ordinary as crows in India,' said Bobby. 'Didn't you have parrots? Our Uncle Billy brought a parrot home once when he'd been on a long voyage. That could talk.'

'Yes, Bobby, we had parrots and minah birds too. They're a bit like a starling and you can teach them to talk just like you can a parrot. I remember once this pal of mine taught his minah bird to shout out the nickname we had for our sergeant-major. He used to hang the cage up near the parade ground so everyone could hear the bird. I'm not going to tell you what the bird used to call out because it was rude, but the men loved it. The sergeant-major didn't think it was funny, naturally, and when he could stand it no longer he bought the minah off my pal for far more than the going price. We didn't hear any more of that particular bird.'

'Did the sergeant-major give it away?' asked Lizzie.

Bobby provided the answer. 'Of course he didn't, silly. He rung its neck so it couldn't shout out his rude name.'

Tovell was still thinking about exotic birds when he arrived at the *Admiral Lord Nelson* that night. He had not mentioned cock-fighting to the children but in answer to Ted's question, he agreed that cock-fighting was very popular in India. 'There are a lot of dry ravines around Bangalore and you could always find a match going on somewhere. I only went occasionally – when I'd nothing better to do – because I enjoy a gamble. I never owned a game-cock though some of my pals did. It would have upset me to see a bird I'd fed and cared for torn to pieces. To tell the truth, the reason I didn't go to cock-fights very often was that it seemed a crime to destroy such beautiful creatures. There can't be a bird anywhere as fancy as an Indian game-cock.'

'Now there I gotta disagree with you, bor,' announced Ted Carter. 'There int nothing to beat a cock pheasant – no, that there int. That's got lovely plumage and,' he added with a chuckle, 'that's got a lovely flavour an' all!'

'I have to agree with you, Ted' said Dr. Lambert. 'Surely you must have seen them, Tovell. Norfolk is renowned for its pheasants. The cock bird has a long brightly coloured tail. You see them in fields or at the sides of the road hopping out of hedgerows…'

'But not for much longer,' Ted interrupted. 'Come next week and you won't see one nowhere.'

'Why not?' asked Tovell.

'First of October! Them old birds know when it's the start of the shooting season and they go into hiding. Int that right now, doctor?'

'Yes,' agreed Dr. Lambert. 'It's quite uncanny really.'

Two men, who had been at the bar, sat down at the table and joined in the discussion about the pheasant's strong sense of self-preservation.

Tovell took the opportunity to leave as it was almost eight and time for his nocturnal jaunt. When he returned at nine, only the two men were sitting at the table. He asked what had happened to Ted and the doctor. 'Ted had to leave early. The master wants him to drive him to Stalham Station very early. Mrs. Lambert came for the doctor. He was needed urgent.'

The second man had a question for Tovell. 'You're lodging with Ginny, ent you? We're good friends of her brothers. Bet she misses them. Afore they went to sea with the Home Fishing they always used to stock her up with pheasants. She doesn't just roast them – she's got this here recipe for potted pheasant. Very nice that is for Sunday tea.'

'Pity she won't be able to make it this year,' said the other man, 'unless, of course, you'd like to come along with us.'

'Come where? Where are you going?' asked Tovell.

'Pheasant hunting! We know where there are loads of them. Been allowed to breed they have, ready for the shooting season.'

'How the hell are you going to find pheasants in the dark?' asked Tovell.

'We've got help,' replied the man. He put his hand under the table and fondled the head of a springer spaniel sitting at his feet. 'Toby here can sniff 'em out, can't you, boy?'

'Pity you haven't got Blackie with you. Ginny's brothers always bring Blackie along.'

'He's a funny old boy, int he?' said his friend. 'He'll sit quietly while you share out the birds but when you get to the last one he'll put his paw on it, snarl and bare his teeth at you. That's his prize. He'll pick that bloomin' bird up and carry it all the way home in his mouth and put it down at Ginny's feet.'

'Alright then,' Tovell decided. 'If it'll help Ginny I'll come with you. But let's have a few more drinks first.'

The three men were in high spirits as they stumbled noisily through the undergrowth. They stopped in front of a high wall. Tovell asked where they were and received the reply, 'Lord Meredith's estate.' Realisation suddenly dawned on Tovell. 'You mean we're going poaching?'

'What else did you think we meant?' asked his companion. 'His lordship won't miss a few old birds. He's got hundreds of 'em. He breeds them for his shooting parties. His friends'll kill plenty next week. We'll just get in first.'

The men were so drunk that they made several attempts before they succeeded in scaling the wall. They landed in a tangled heap of arms and legs in the grounds of the Hall. Toby circled them, crouching low and growling quietly, but they ignored his advice to take care and staggered into the woods supporting each other and making enough noise to disturb all life-forms, whether wild or human, in the vicinity. They had not advanced far before Tovell stumbled into a snare. To the dog's mounting consternation, neither the soldier himself nor the other befuddled trespassers could extricate him. Seeing that the situation was hopeless, Toby apparently decided to howl for assistance. Tovell's new friends promptly deserted him, blundered back the way they had come and disappeared head first over the wall, followed by the dog.

'Hey! Come back!' yelled Tovell as he lay on the ground. 'Don't leave me!'

A voice came out of the darkness. 'Don't you worry – I won't leave you, bor. You can rely on that.' Tovell found himself staring at a very large pair of boots and a shotgun.

Some time later, the village policeman, Constable Hadden, ushered a limping Tovell into the Watch-room. Bill Westgate grinned triumphantly at Tovell's obvious distress whilst the policeman addressed Lieutenant Collins.

'His lordship felt you should deal with the matter, Sir, according to military regulations. Lord Meredith was an army man himself, Sir. He isn't in no doubt that this soldier intended to do a spot of poaching – but as there was no harm done and being wartime an' all, his lordship isn't going to press charges and leaves everything to you.'

'Thank you, Constable,' replied Richard Collins. 'His lordship was kind enough to telephone me after you and Tovell left him. I'm sorry you had to come out here at this time of night.'

'So am I, Sir,' replied the policeman, glaring at Tovell. 'Some people have no consideration. Having me up all hours chasing miscreants who ought to know better …. Well, I'll be off now, Sir.'

After the constable had left, Lieutenant Collins turned to Sergeant Harris. 'Shouldn't Westgate be on patrol?'

'You're quite right, Sir,' replied the sergeant. 'Collect your gear, Westgate, and get out there.' Bill Westgate obeyed grudgingly and sneered at Tovell as he closed the outside door behind him.

Lieutenant Collins faced Tovell. 'Damn it, man! You know it's imperative we don't antagonise the local population. Whatever possessed you to go poaching? There's no shortage of food here – I'm certain you're being well fed. It's the drink, isn't it? You reek of it. Alcohol has impaired your judgement and induced a state of mind which has led you to embark on this foolish escapade. What am I to do with you?'

Tovell concluded that it would be wiser to confine his reply to, 'I don't know, Sir,' and to endeavour to look suitably contrite.

The lieutenant ignored his words and continued to rant. 'I can't reduce you in the ranks; you've hit rock bottom already. What can I say to you? You won't listen to reason. What can I do to you to make you see the error of your ways? I just despair of you, Tovell.' The officer walked away, sat down at his desk, laboured over the problem for a few moments and then snapped, 'You are confined to the Station for one week, fined one week's pay and you will, of course, pay for the damaged boots. Sergeant, have you noted the punishment?'

'I have indeed, Sir,' replied Sergeant Harris.

'Now get out of my sight, Tovell,' said the officer.

Ginny listened aghast to Tovell's tale of woe as she bathed his bruised foot and covered it with a cold compress to reduce the swelling. By her manner, however, she made it clear to Tovell that he was also in her bad books – not for the crime itself but for the inefficiency of its execution. 'Well, I've never heard of such a thing! Getting drunk beforehand! Just wait 'til I see them friends of my brothers – I reckon I know which ones they are. They'll get a piece of my mind – that they will.'

'Ginny,' asked Tovell tentatively, 'does that mean you knew your brothers went poaching?'

'I did tell you they weren't saints,' was Ginny's reply.

Richard Collins left the Watch-room via the internal door, still cursing Tovell under his breath. Mrs. Brewster's parlour was in darkness except for a candle burning in the centre of the table. The officer picked up the candle-holder and crossed the room. He listened outside a door on his left before opening the door quietly. David lay asleep in the bed. He stood watching the boy for a few moments before closing the door again. He crossed the parlour to the room opposite and went inside. The curtains had not been drawn and moonlight flooded the room. He blew out the candle and sat on the edge of the bed to take off his shoes. There was a movement behind him and a rustle of sheets.

'Is that you, Richard?' asked Lydia.

'You were expecting someone else?' he quipped.

'Don't tease. I think I must have fallen asleep waiting for you. You're late aren't you?'

'I had to wait for Constable Hadden to return with a prisoner.'

'Who was it?'

'Need you ask? Tovell, of course – caught poaching this time. Makes a change, I suppose, from brawling. He usually manages to pick a fight at least twice a week – more often than not with Westgate.' The officer stood up and began to undress quickly. 'When I think how I joined the Army immediately war was declared to escape the Tovells of this world – younger versions of course – I almost despair.' He climbed into bed and drew his companion into his arms. 'I tell you, Lydia, I do not know what to do with that man. He despises me. I can see the contempt in his eyes, just as I could in the eyes of my pupils.'

'You really mustn't let him worry you so much,' said Lydia soothingly.

'I've tried everything – appealed to his better nature and even dangled the carrot of promotion before him as an incentive to control his drinking.'

'I don't think he'll give you much more trouble. Ginny Adams does not approve of drunkenness and he seems genuinely anxious to please her.'

'Of course – he'll be sleeping with her.'

'As it happens, Richard, he is *not* sleeping with her. In fact, I think we can assume that you are the only soldier who has been taken into his landlady's bed. Now, not another word about Tovell…. Are you hungry?'

'Starving, my sweet! I haven't tasted you for at least twenty four hours.'

'Oh! Richard! You know very well what I mean.'

'The answer to your statement is "Yes" and to your question is "No". Have I not told you that the only conversation my wife will permit in bed is domestic chit-chat? Heaven forbid that you should acquire the habit.'

'I'm only concerned for your welfare and comfort,' murmured Lydia.

'And I share your concern so let's begin by getting rid of these bedclothes. There – now I can view my goddess at her most enchanting – bathed in lunar light. If I were an artist I would paint you exactly as you are at this moment, my love.'

'But you are an artist, Richard. You paint with words. They are your oils and canvas.'

'Perhaps... Now, woman-of-my-dreams, where shall your Pegasus take you tonight? Shall we fly to Mars, or if I really concentrate, shall we reach Jupiter?'

'Richard, you are quite mad.'

'Desire for you has made me so. We must delay no longer. Let me take you to the stars, my love.'

XI

Tovell, accustomed to harsh punishment, regarded the sentence Richard Collins had passed on him as far too lenient and instead of being thankful, proclaimed it as a further example of the lieutenant's poor performance as both an officer and a man. As time went by he changed his opinion and conceded that the punishment had been both apt and harsh since confinement to the Station, even for a week, deprived him of his normal intake of alcohol. Ginny watched his distress increase until she could stand it no longer. She heard him come in the front door one morning and sit down in the armchair by the cooking range. She peeped round the scullery door and saw that his hands were shaking and that he kept clasping his arms around his middle. She approached him – keeping one hand behind her back.

'Are you feeling worse this morning?' she asked.

'Yeah,' replied Tovell. 'I'm better off on duty when my mind's occupied. I'll go outside in a minute – dig up some potatoes.'

'I can't see you suffer any longer. I found this half bottle of rum – belongs to my husband.' Ginny offered the bottle she had been hiding behind her back to Tovell. 'It isn't full, so mind you water it down and make it last because there isn't any more.'

Tovell grabbed the bottle, uncorked it and took a long swig. 'Thanks, Ginny. You just saved my life – and I will water the rest down. It's been a shock even to me, how dependant I am on drink. I've made a resolution – you can smile but I mean it – to cut down the booze. I ain't promising to go teetotal – if this week's anything to go by it's too painful to stop altogether – but I'm going to cut down. And I'll replace your husband's rum as soon as I get paid again.'

Ginny's gesture cheered and comforted Tovell for a while but then his tobacco ran out. He had no money to buy more since the fine of a week's pay meant he had to wait another week to get paid and the cost of replacing his boots had taken every penny he possessed. His comrades, with the exception of David, would not finance him because they enjoyed seeing Tovell, the loud-mouthed braggart, reduced to a state of depression. The boy would gladly have lent his friend the money if he had had any, but he was in the habit of sending the lion's share of his pay to his mother. Bill Westgate, on the other hand, enjoyed telling Tovell, 'If I was the richest man on earth and you were starving, I wouldn't lend you a penny.'

'Spoken like a true Christian,' was Tovell's retort.

Once again, Ginny was moved to come to Tovell's aid. Seeing him so miserable during one of his off-duty periods, she disappeared without saying a word, rode into the village on her bicycle and bought him some tobacco with her housekeeping money. She apologised on her return because she could afford to purchase only a small amount. Tovell, for his part, was quite overcome with gratitude and showed his appreciation by making the children toy sailing boats and doubling his efforts to be helpful around the house. He paid Ginny back promptly the next pay day for both the rum and the tobacco.

Tovell's fondness for Ginny was increasing day by day and he was more determined than ever to control his drinking and not upset her again. One evening, however, the local beauty with whom he was strolling announced that she was afraid of the dark and expected to be escorted home. Tovell agreed without hesitation, only to regret his fit of chivalry when he discovered that "home" was a considerable distance on the far side of the village. By the time he arrived back at the *Admiral Lord Nelson* it was closed. His bicycle – Ginny's bicycle – was where he had left it earlier, in the back-yard of the public house. The gate was firmly bolted and when he scaled it he immediately attracted the attention of the two alsations kept by the landlord to patrol and protect his property. The dogs were delighted to have an opportunity to fulfill their true role in life and leapt at the woodwork with a will, eager to sink their teeth into Tovell's flesh. The soldier decided it was not the moment to be brave and scrambled hurriedly from his perch, falling heavily backwards into the road. He picked himself up, rubbed his bruised backside, and resigned himself to the fact that he would have to walk – or rather run – back to the Station. It was, nevertheless, past midnight when he arrived breathless at his billet. He prayed Ginny had not kept to her resolve. She had – both the front door and the back door of the cottage were locked.

Tovell was in a dilemma: he was longing for his comfortable bed but afraid that if he made too much noise he would wake Bobby and Lizzie, and worse still, Mrs. Gillings and her new grandson. He decided against rattling the back door or tapping on the bedroom window and settled for appealing directly to Ginny. 'Please let me in,' he called softly. 'I'm not drunk – honest, Ginny. Please let me in.' He tried twice more but his efforts did not meet with the desired response although he did fancy he saw a curtain move in the neighbouring cottage. A glimpse of rag curlers was enough to cause Tovell to retreat to the bottom of the garden. He was considering his next move when Bill Westgate, who was on patrol, caught sight of him. He laughed when he realised Tovell's predicament and diverted from the scheduled route so that he could come close to where the hapless soldier was leaning against the privy wall.

'Locked you out, has she? Good job too. I'd lock you out every night. You'll have to go sleep with the horse – two animals together.'

Tovell swore appropriately at Bill Westgate until the latter was out of sight and then weighed up the alternatives to sleeping with the horse. His first thought was to take refuge inside the privy but he dismissed that idea, not only because of the smell but because he did not care to sit upright all night. 'You must be getting old and soft,' he muttered to himself. 'You've slept out in the open on much colder nights than this. What's the matter with you?' Nevertheless, he continued to rack his brains to think of a warm shelter with room to lie down. Suddenly, he remembered Mrs. Gillings's fish-house. It had a fire of sorts and he could curl up in reasonable comfort. He made his way stealthily to the forbidden sanctum, all too conscious that he was trespassing on Mrs. Gillings's property. Till then, he had always kept clear of the smoke-house and even though his need was great, he took the precaution of holding his nose as he quietly unlatched the door. He crept inside and instantly felt the heat from the smoldering sawdust. He stood quite still letting the warmth penetrate his tunic. He had not worn his great-coat and until then had not realised how cold he was. Lulled by the glow into a daze, he looked upwards and saw, through half-closed eyes, not herrings impaled and hung in the curling smoke, but human beings. Shocked by this vision of a biblical Hell, he momentarily relaxed his grip on his nostrils. One whiff of the pungent aroma was enough to bring him to his senses. Suppressing an urge to vomit, he rushed out into the night air once more, slamming the door shut behind him. He started to shiver immediately the chill hit him. 'There's nothing else for it,' he muttered to himself. 'I'll have to sleep with the ruddy horse.'

Tovell's troubles were not yet over. The horse had by that time spent several hours shut up in his stable. When first he opened the door, the stench sent Tovell reeling but he forced himself to enter knowing that his queasy stomach was more accustomed to the odours of the stable than the odours of the curing-shed. The horse resented the intrusion and promptly pushed him out again. Uttering obscenities, the soldier picked himself up and renewed his assault. Once more the horse repelled him, determined not to share his already cramped quarters. Eventually, by crawling on all fours through the dirty straw, Tovell managed in the darkness to locate the cart at the back of the building. He climbed gratefully inside having at last achieved his objective – a bed for the night.

Tovell awoke next morning to find Lizzie and Bobby peering at him. 'Mother sent us to look for you,' announced the boy. 'Breakfast's ready.' Aching in every limb, Tovell emerged squinting into the daylight.

'You don't half stink, Uncle Tovell,' observed Lizzie candidly.

Her brother was more specific. 'You've got horse-muck all over your trousers – and your boots. Mother won't half mob you!'

Tovell glanced over his shoulder and then down at his feet. There was no denying the truth of Bobby's statement. Both children squatted down to watch with interest and to offer advice, while Tovell attempted to scrape his boots reasonably clean on the grass outside the stable. He could not think what to do about his soiled trousers. When at last he made his way up the garden path, flanked by the two children, Ginny was waiting for him at the back door.

'You're not coming in my house in that state,' she declared. 'You can change your mucky trousers and leave them there smelly boots outside.'

Tovell bent down and carefully removed his boots and placed them beside the doorstep. As he straightened up, he noticed Mrs. Gillings watching the proceedings from her scullery window. He felt sure Ginny must know they were being observed. He could not resist undoing the top button of his flies and asking with a roguish glint in his eyes, 'Shall I drop my trousers here, Ginny?'

'Don't you darst!' hissed Ginny with an anxious glance in her neighbour's direction. 'Go you down the privy and I'll bring your other pair of trousers there.'

Tovell retraced his footsteps to the bottom of the garden, accompanied once more by his young escorts. He had not gone far before he realised he was wearing only socks on his feet. He half turned with the intention of going back for his boots, but with Ginny watching him from the doorstep and Mrs. Gillings from her window, he had second thoughts. He continued on tip-toe down the path until he reached the lavatory, and while the children stood guard outside, he removed the offending trousers. Through the diamond-shaped cut-out in the door he saw Ginny approaching. He lifted the latch, put out one hand and took the clean trousers she proffered, her gaze studiously averted. She had also brought a pair of her husband's old boots and these she deposited on the ground with a deliberate thud. She then turned about and flounced back along the path, her skirts swaying vigorously from side to side. Tovell watched fascinated, marvelling that any woman could display so much displeasure through her posterior.

When he had dressed and reached the back door, Ginny was coming out bearing a bowl of water. She placed it beside the dirty boots where a cloth, soap and a knife were already in position. Tovell assumed this was a hint and was about to start renovations when Ginny snapped, 'Leave that 'til later. Your breakfast's getting cold.' He followed her meekly into the scullery and she pointed to the sink. 'Hot water's ready for you.'

He washed quickly but did not dare to stop to shave as he normally did before breakfast. Lizzie expressed her disappointment. 'Aren't you going to shave, Uncle Tovell?' she asked.

'I'd better not at the moment,' he replied quietly. It had become part of the morning ritual that unless Tovell had left the cottage for the first watch before they were awake, the children should form an attentive audience to watch him shave. He had been puzzled by their behaviour and had enquired whether they were accustomed to watching their father shave. Both children had become silent and wide-eyed at the question, and had only replied by a shake of the head. Not wishing to spoil their harmless fun he had not raised the matter again.

Tovell sat down uneasily at the table. He had no appetite for porridge and after a few seconds broke the silence with, 'Ginny, I didn't get drunk last night. I haven't broken my promise to curb my drinking. I was late because I found myself miles the other side of the village and by the time I got back to the pub it was shut and your bicycle was locked in their back yard ....'

'And what were you doing on the other side of the village?' Ginny demanded sarcastically. Before Tovell could answer she continued, 'Don't bother to tell me; I know what you were doing on the other side of the village.'

'Ginny ....?' Tovell could not bring himself to voice his fears but Ginny could not hold back her words.

'Do you reckon I don't know what you get up to of a night? We all know!'

Tovell was quite disconcerted. 'Ginny, I can explain,' he began.

'Explain? Why should you explain?' She paused and said in a much quieter and more controlled tone of voice, 'It's nothing to do with me and I had no right to mention it. I'm sorry.'

'But I want to explain, Ginny.'

'And I don't want to hear!' Her anger had returned instantly and her eyes blazed. 'I'm not interested in your women!'

'But Ginny ....'

'Not another word, Tovell!' She grabbed the children's arms, muttering, 'You'll be late for school,' as she bundled them into their coats. Both Lizzie and Bobby had followed the argument with bated breath and as her mother ushered her out of the door, the little girl escaped and ran back to Tovell.

She gave him a quick peck on the cheek and whispered in his ear, 'We told you she'd mob you.' Tovell smiled and stroked her hair affectionately. As she went out of the door he heard her say, 'That wasn't Uncle Tovell's fault; Prince is such a mucky horse.'

Ginny always escorted the children through the gate in the

perimeter wall of the Station to the cart-track which stretched across the fields. She would then watch and wave until they reached the road and turned right towards the village and their school. By the time she returned that morning Tovell had abandoned his breakfast and was outside cleaning his trousers. He looked up at the sound of her footsteps. She paused in front of him and said sheepishly, 'I shouldn't have shouted at you, Tovell. I've got a quick temper. I'm sorry. I'll go make you a fresh pot of tea.'

'That's alright, Ginny. It was my fault for getting back late when I promised I wouldn't. I don't mind you shouting at me – in fact, I'd rather you shout at me and get it over with than not speak to me. That's what I wouldn't like – you refusing to speak to me at all.'

Ginny stared at Tovell for a few moments as though she were trying to see in his eyes whether he was telling her what he truly felt. 'I just hope you mean what you say ….' she said at last.

'I mean it. You shout at me as much as you like,' Tovell assured her.

'Are you coming indoors then?'

'No, not yet – got a few things to do first.'

Still Ginny hesitated as though toying with the idea of saying something further, but eventually she contented herself with smiling at him somewhat wistfully before entering the cottage.

Tovell hung his damp trousers on the line to dry and cleaned his boots. He put them on with a sigh of relief – Robert Adams's boots had been crippling him. He then gave some thought to what he could do to please Ginny. With some reluctance he fetched the spade and fork and made for the vegetable patch. There was an area of ground which needed turning over; he had been putting the chore off for days. When he had finished, he dug up a row of potatoes for good measure. He was carrying them to the shed to store them as Ginny came out of the back door.

'I thought you didn't like digging,' she chided him gently.

'I don't! I hate it,' replied Tovell. 'The Army's always finding you something that needs digging. I've dug that many trenches in my time, I bet I've shifted more soil than Ted Carter. I'll put this sack in the shed then I'll fill the coal-scuttle.'

'That you won't!' said Ginny firmly. 'You've done quite enough good deeds for one day. You're wearing me out just watching you. Anyway, you're on duty at midday and you didn't get much rest last night. I've got you a bath ready – reckon you can do with it after being with the horse.'

'Thanks, Ginny. I'm grateful for the bath.'

'The water's a bit hot,' Ginny explained as he entered the living room, 'so you've time for the pot of tea I've just made you. I've put you something cold on the table to eat. You must be hungry seeing me and my sharp tongue put you off your breakfast. I'll bring you a hot meal over to the Watch-room later. Take your time; I shan't bother you. I promised to give Mrs. Ellis a hand with the nets this morning. She's been swamped with repairs. My father was a fisherman so my mother taught me to mend nets when I was a littl'un. Of course, I'm nothing like as quick as Mrs. Ellis ....' Ginny was about to close the back door when she had an afterthought. She called out to Tovell, 'Don't forget to close the curtains before you get started. You've given Mrs. Gillings enough shocks for one day. You should have seen her face when you pretended you were going to take your trousers down outside ....'

Once he was alone, Tovell realised his appetite had returned. He quickly ate the cold meal and drank one cup of tea. He poured himself a second cup and took it across to the bathtub by the fire. He removed his tunic and had extricated himself from the top half of his long-johns before he remembered Ginny's warning. He immediately went to the rear window and was reaching up to draw the curtains when Mrs. Gillings walked past. She blanched at the sight of his large muscular chest. Tovell promptly blew her a kiss and waved cheerily. He was still chuckling to himself as he took off the bottom half of his underwear and eased himself into the bath.

He lay back and let the warm water soothe his aching body. His uncomfortable bed in the cart followed by the gardening session, had taken its toll. The second cup of tea, sipped in the luxury of the tin tub, tasted even better than the first. He glanced up at the mantelpiece where Ginny's ornaments shone brightly. She had hung his clean clothes and a towel beneath the mantelpiece where the fire in the cooking range would warm them. He liked the feeling of being looked after; it was quite novel to him. He supposed his mother must have taken care of him when he was a baby but he was certain no-one else had – until now. He let his thoughts dwell on Ginny. It was a pity she knew about his nightly walks. The thought of her knowing gave him a queasy feeling in the pit of his stomach. He wished she had let him speak in his defence. He decided that something more than a spot of gardening was required.

Blackie chose that moment to amble over to the fire. 'What do you think I ought to do, old feller?' Tovell asked him. ''got to make amends somehow.' The dog came over to him, put his chin on the side of the tub, sniffed the water and promptly returned to the hearth-rug. Whilst Tovell continued to ponder on his problem, Blackie stretched out and was soon fast asleep. He only stirred momentarily when the soldier suddenly shouted, 'I know! I know what will please her. But don't tell her, Blackie. Make her wait 'til Sunday.'

XII

The following Sunday morning Tovell was careful to occupy himself as usual until Ginny and the children, dressed in their best clothes, had departed. He then sprang into action and by the time Ginny had seated herself in the back of the waiting cart alongside her neighbours, he appeared on the scene resplendent in his shiny-buttoned uniform. He marched to the front of the vehicle, came to attention, saluted Mrs. Gillings as she sat whip poised, in the driving seat and announced, 'Private Tovell reporting for Church Parade, ma'am.'

Mrs. Gillings was flabbergasted. Regaining her composure a little she turned round and glared at Ginny. 'You dint say nothing about this,' she accused.

'I didn't know nothing about it,' protested Ginny, adding tentatively, 'but he does look smart and that might do him some good.'

Mrs. Gillings looked back at Tovell and snorted. Clearly, she regarded him as long past redemption. This seemed an excellent argument to Tovell and he adopted it at once. 'The Army chaplains are always telling us that the good Lord is happy to see sinners among his congregation, but I can see that you must worship a different God at your church.'

Mrs. Gillings apparently conceded the point because, ignoring Tovell, she turned around in her seat again and spoke directly to Ginny. 'He do look smart, I'll grant you that, but will he behave hisself?' She employed the tone she would have used had she been asking the same question about one of the children. Having received the required assurance and still addressing Ginny, Mrs. Gillings gave her approval. 'Alright then – he can walk behind with the littl'uns.'

With a victory yell which earned him a withering glance from the driver, Tovell did a hop, skip and a jump to the rear of the vehicle where he was warmly greeted by David and the Station children. He was in an elated mood on the road to Haisbro village, playing games with the excited children and giving the smaller ones rides on his shoulders in turn.

Mrs. Gillings soon regretted her generosity in allowing Tovell to join the Station party. The group in the rear was getting further and further behind and she had to turn in her seat to yell back at them several times. 'I keep telling you all to hurry up. We hent never been this late for church afore. And calm you all down!'

Tovell's joviality vanished as soon as he entered the church. His presence caused the nearest thing to a riot that the little community had ever seen. The only vacant pews left were at the back of the church. The children were still in high spirits and were clumsy and noisy as they took their places. The parishioners in front turned round to ascertain the cause of the disturbance and soon the whole building was buzzing with the information that the notorious Tovell was in the back row. It seemed that the entire congregation was straining to catch a glimpse of him and to Tovell's horror, everywhere he looked he saw the familiar faces of the young ladies with whom he had shared his nocturnal jaunts. They were either smiling at him coyly or openly beaming at him, and every one seemed to feel the need to whisper something confidentially to her neighbour.

It had never occurred to Tovell that these brazen young things who lurked around corners to waylay him as he took his evening stroll would be members of staunch church-going families. It was obvious that they had told their younger sisters about him; many a girl of nine or ten giggled at him from behind a little gloved hand, only to be admonished by her mother who, from her backward glance, was also aware of his reputation. As the noise increased, Tovell began to feel more and more hot and uncomfortable. He risked a quick look at Ginny who was standing beside him. She was regarding the reaction open-mouthed. He felt sick and was about to bolt for the door when the vicar, who had been standing for several minutes in the aisle nearby, waiting to lead his staff and his choir to the front of the church, nodded to his organist and the processional hymn began. Tovell made a tremendous effort to control his wayward digestive system and somehow got through the next hour and a half.

His ordeal was not yet over. He failed to leave his pew in time and had to wait whilst the congregation, eager for another look at him, filed past him and out into the churchyard. Trapped as he was, Tovell had to acknowledge bashfully all the greetings of the young ladies who were prepared to risk a cuff round the ears later in order to establish their claim in the eyes of their peers that they were on intimate terms with the dashing soldier. Without exception, the matrons regarded Tovell with disdain but their husbands, all patrons of the *Admiral Lord Nelson*, did not appear to share their animosity. These sober gentlemen, Sunday bowlers held in proper fashion to their chests, gave Tovell a crafty wink as they passed. Ginny could not help but be amazed that her lodger had made so many male, as well as female friends, in such a short time.

Dr. Lambert chanced to leave the church at the same moment as the Station party. In spite of the lady on his arm exuding disapproval, he did not stoop to subterfuge but greeted Tovell jovially and insisted upon introducing him to his wife. The latter proffered her hand most reluctantly, so Tovell bowed and kissed it daintily. The action set the portly doctor off on one of his fits of laughter. For a moment it looked as if Mrs. Lambert was going to strike her spouse but she managed to check the impulse, no doubt because they had drawn level with the vicar who was standing in his customary place on the doorstep bidding his flock farewell. The doctor introduced his friend. The vicar announced that several of his parishioners had mentioned Tovell to him. He then magnanimously expressed the wish that he would see the soldier in his congregation again.

Tovell made this point to Mrs. Gillings as he helped her, in spite of her protests, into the cart. 'There you are – what did I tell you? The poor old vicar doesn't get many sinners around these parts. He's glad of a chance to get to work on an out-and-outer like me.'

Mrs. Gillings did not bother to argue; she was too busy smacking Tovell's wrists and hissing, 'Get your filthy plawks off me, bor! Them shameless mawthers may like the feel of 'em but I certainly don't.'

The nearer the little column came to home the more half-hearted became Tovell's attempts to play the fool with the children. Though he could not hear what was being said, it was perfectly obvious that Mrs. Gillings was giving Ginny the benefit of her assessment of the recent performance in the church, in no uncertain terms. The thought of how life would be with Ginny from now on brought back Tovell's nausea. As the cottages loomed in the distance his depression increased. Soon he became a straggler lagging some distance behind everyone else. Bobby and Lizzie went to his assistance, took a hand each and half-dragged him home. When they reached the back door, Tovell flopped down on the step and put his head in his hands. In answer to the children's questions he admitted that he did not feel very well. Bobby and Lizzie duly reported this fact to their mother and seconds later Ginny was standing over him.

'You can't be sick again,' she stated incredulously. Tovell nodded. 'I've never known a man have sickly innards afore!' she exclaimed in exasperation. 'I reckon when you were put together you must have got some female parts by mistake.' Then she added more kindly, 'Shall I fetch you some water?'

'Water!' Now it was Tovell's turn to sound incredulous.

'Yes, water,' confirmed Ginny. 'That's one of your troubles; you never have a good wash out with water.'

'Alright, I'll have some water,' agreed Tovell resignedly.

Ginny brought him a cup of water and he sipped at it without enthusiasm. She bent over him, felt his forehead and said gently, 'Sit you here awhile in the fresh air. You'll soon fare better.'

Her face was very close to Tovell's. He looked into her eyes and there was no anger in them. She was even smiling at him kindly. 'Ginny, ain't you angry with me?' he ventured.

'Angry? Why should I be angry?'

'You know – 'cause of what happened in church.'

'Oh, that! You weren't to blame for that. Making eyes at you and in church too – they should have been ashamed of themselves. Now you just sit quiet – dinner won't be for a while yet anyway.'

So saying, Ginny went back indoors taking the children with her and leaving behind a totally bewildered soldier. Tovell shook his head. How could she have been furious only two days ago at the very mention of his ladyfriends, yet now, when she had been confronted by them in person and in numbers, be not even remotely annoyed? It was beyond comprehension. Thirty minutes later Ginny returned and confirmed by her solicitude that he was not out of favour with her. Yes, he thought he might be able to manage a little dinner after all and he allowed himself to be escorted to the table by the children. The three welcoming faces restored his appetite and he found he was quite hungry.

Ginny at once put Tovell at his ease by stating, 'I didn't know you were Church of England.'

Tovell laughed. 'In my time I've been Church of England, Roman Catholic, Baptist, Methodist – you name it, I've been it!'

Ginny was amazed. 'Couldn't you make up your mind?'

'It's an old army trick,' Tovell explained. 'You have to turn out in full dress for divine service – well, I never minded that – but like most soldiers I hated the CO's inspection of barracks. That always took place on a Sunday, you see. When you were moved to a new station it was customary to find out the times of the services of the different denominations. You could change your religion then to ensure that you were in church or chapel at the time of the CO's inspection, you see.'

'Oh, I see alright,' replied Ginny in shocked tones, 'but I don't think that's right. Why, that's not …. reverent.'

'But you're worshipping the same God, aren't you, whether it's in a church or a chapel? What does it matter if the form of service is a bit different? Anyway, the services you have on a battlefield don't follow any particular denomination. They're meant to be a comfort to all the men, whatever their preference. To tell you the truth, Ginny, I can never understand what all the fuss is about. The way I see it, the people who worry about which way is the right way to worship and don't hold with any one else's opinion on the subject, are missing the point – they're all supposed to belong to the same religion – Christianity. People fear what's strange and unfamiliar to them so I reckon it should be compulsory to visit different types of churches and chapels. Everyone would know then that they have nothing to fear from other denominations. It might put an end to killing for religious reasons. Over the centuries, thousands – no, millions – of poor devils must have been slaughtered because someone else didn't like the way they said their prayers. Now to me that ain't right, Ginny. That's what ain't reverent.'

That afternoon, Tovell dozed intermittently in the armchair beside the cooking range and Ginny sat opposite him sewing. In spite of his drowsy state, it began to dawn on him that every time he chanced to half-open his eyes, Ginny was looking at him – and in a way she had never done before. Tovell could not stand mysteries and eventually he had to ask, 'Ginny, what's the matter? Why do you keep looking at me as though something is puzzling you?'

Ginny blushed, shook her head and applied herself more assiduously to her needlework.

'Hey, Ginny, it's me – Tovell! You can ask old Tovell anything.'

'Not this, I can't,' replied Ginny emphatically. 'I can't ask you this.'

'Why not?'

'Because that wouldn't be proper – that's why not.' The statement was delivered in a tone which indicated that no more was to be said on the subject and as though to confirm the point, Ginny cast aside her sewing and proposed, 'Why don't we go for a walk? Lovely sunny afternoon like this we shouldn't be cooped up here. Let's go down to the cut. You could help the littl'uns sail them boats you made.'

Before Tovell could reply, Bobby and Lizzie, who had been playing quietly on the hearthrug, leapt upon him, and Blackie, who had been asleep under the table, woke up and began barking excitedly. Tovell, always happy to assume the paternal role, cried, 'Alright, alright, the river it is!'

The walk to and from the cut was a joy in itself with the children happily singing rhymes, Tovell joining in wherever possible and Ginny giving assistance with the unfamiliar words. When they reached their objective, Ginny sat down on the river bank a little above and apart from the other three and watched them, smiling wistfully, as Tovell helped her children to sail their boats. Lizzie seemed oblivious to her presence and kept putting her arms around Tovell's neck as he knelt by the water's edge. Bobby, for his part, was in his element running up and down the river bank urging the craft along, accompanied by an enthusiastic Blackie. At one point Tovell glanced round at Ginny and she saw the look of total happiness in his eyes.

When the outing to the river had been proposed, Tovell had been so delighted that he had pushed all anxiety over the strange workings of the female mind into the back of his head. Next morning, however, he announced straight after breakfast that he was going into the village to fetch Ginny's bicycle. He was gone before she could suggest that he leave it where it was until the next time he went drinking at the pub. He returned a little later and entered the scullery somewhat sheepishly. Ginny, her sleeves rolled up, was doing some washing in the big stone sink. Tovell did not look at her as he spoke.

'Ginny – you know yesterday I was only trying to make amends to you by going to church – because of being late the other night?'

'I know. I know you were trying to please me – and you did.'

'But it all went wrong – turned sour, didn't it?' Then Tovell added hastily, 'So I bought you this.' From behind his back he produced a straw hat covered in trimmings which seemed to embrace all the colours of the rainbow. Ginny was speechless as he thrust the gift into her wet hands but Tovell had more to say. 'I'm sorry it's not a brand new one but it was all I could afford. The lady in the shop said it had only had one owner. Some of the flowers are a bit faded ….'

'It's lovely – I've never seen anything so lovely,' enthused Ginny. 'Nobody's ever given me anything like this before.' On an impulse she threw her arms, still dripping soapsuds, around Tovell's neck, kissed him briefly on the chin – she couldn't reach any higher – and was out of the back door before he could capitalise on her display of gratitude. As she ran she planted the hat on her head and yelled, 'I've gotta show the neighbours!'

Lily agreed with Ginny that it was the most beautiful hat she had ever seen and added that even her ladyship had no better headwear in her entire collection. Mrs. Gillings too was visibly impressed but had to qualify her approval with the observation, 'He would buy a thing like that. Only a tart would wear a hat with all that frippery on it!'

'Well,' declared Ginny, 'I shall just have to look like a tart then. He meant well and I'm not going to hurt his feelings by not wearing it.'

XIII

Kapitänleutnant Otto Weddigen's courage and achievement, in pushing his tiny U-9 to limits previously undreamt of, had hit the headlines and sent shock waves through every naval headquarters in the world. Military scientists and experts in naval warfare racked their brains to think of a means to combat this new deadly weapon, deliverer of destruction on an unparalleled scale. The coastguard families around the shores of Britain took a stoical attitude and comforted themselves with the thought that the Coastguard Service must have had its share of bad luck all in one go, but they had not reckoned with the good luck of Weddigen. After receiving the Iron Cross from Kaiser Wilhelm himself, the national hero had returned to his little pig boat to continue hunting his enemy in the North Sea. On the fifteenth of October, just three weeks and two days after his first triumph, he looked through his periscope and saw, yet again, three British warships in his sights. But Admiralty orders had been well heeded; the battleships zigzagged, changing course and speed so frequently that after chasing them this way and that for two and a half hours, Weddigen managed to torpedo only one of the three. This time the other two ships did not stop to lower boats but immediately steamed away before they too could become targets. *HMS Hawke* sank within fifteen minutes with the loss of five hundred men – most of them coastguards.

Sergeant Harris had just left the village when he was overtaken by the Divisional Officer on horseback. Mr. Latham waved as he galloped past in the direction of the Coastguard Station. Knowing the timetable as he did, Jack Harris was aware that the officer was not making a scheduled visit. With increasing concern, he quickened his own pace. When he reached the settlement the horse was tethered to the hitching post near the perimeter wall. There was no sign of Mr. Latham. The sergeant hurried to his billet, praying that his own kind landlady had not been the recipient of bad news. He paused in the doorway from the scullery when he saw that all the women were sitting around the living room table. Mary was counting a pile of money and Mrs. Brewster was working something out on paper. Mrs. Ellis was sitting beside them in an obvious state of shock. Mary looked up and he heard her say, 'That's a pity it's Edinburgh. I don't reckon we've got quite enough.'

'Mr. Latham was in no doubt,' said Lydia Brewster. 'All the casualties from the *Hawke* are being brought to Edinburgh.'

Sergeant Harris had heard enough. He immediately left by the back door. He returned a few minutes later and this time he walked straight into the living room and added more money to the pile in the centre of the table. 'All of us boys want to help. Will you have enough now?'

Mary quickly sorted the coins. 'Yes, thanks! Now we've enough for the train fare and several weeks lodgings, if need be.'

The sergeant turned to his landlady. 'Don't you worry, Mrs. Ellis – from what you've told me, your Wilfred's a tough one. He's a fighter. You'll have him home in no time.'

Mrs. Ellis tried to smile back as the sergeant put a comforting hand on her shoulder. 'You're a good man, Jack Harris. I'm truly grateful to you.'

'And please thank all your men,' said Lydia Brewster.

'Did Mr. Latham say what happened?' asked the sergeant. 'Was it a U-boat again?'

'Yes, unfortunately,' replied Lydia, 'off Scapa Flow. But there were survivors and, thankfully, one of them was our own Mr. Ellis.'

Mrs. Gillings gave a polite little cough. 'Sorry to interrupt you, Mrs. Brewster, but we ought to be getting to Stalham Station.'

'You're quite right, Mrs. Gillings,' agreed Lydia. 'We can sort out the duty rosters later for looking after Sergeant Harris and Peter.'

'And we'll take turns to see to your house, garden and livestock,' added Emily 'Don't you worry about a thing. You just concentrate on nursing Mr. Ellis.'

With all her neighbours voicing their agreement, Mrs. Ellis was soon reduced to tears. Ginny's suggestion that she should pack some clothes whilst they found some suitable food for the journey, gave her an opportunity to escape to the bedroom. By the time she emerged, she had her emotions under control and walked quite calmly with her friends to the waiting cart. Mrs. Gillings was already aboard and Sergeant Harris helped Mrs. Ellis up onto the seat beside her before loading the luggage into the back. Everyone stood by the perimeter wall to wave good bye and as the assembled wives watched the horse and cart disappearing into the distance, Phyllis spoke for them all when she said, 'I reckon we got off lightly. At least none of our men was killed. We were lucky.'

Fortunately, there was little time to philosophise; a spell of bad weather had resulted in a spate of ships in distress. As was the custom in isolated coastal communities, everyone – women and children included – turned out to do what they could to help. The most memorable of these incidents took place two days after Mrs. Ellis's departure. A schooner had run aground on a sandbank not three hundred yards from the shore and quite close to the Coastguard Station. It was late afternoon and with darkness closing in fast, it was clear that the crew must be taken off the stricken vessel without delay. The Volunteer Life-saving Brigade was duly summoned, as was Dr. Lambert and Constable Hadden. Mrs. Brewster took over the Watch-room to release all the soldiers for their recently learned drills. The Brigade volunteers could be seen hurrying to the spot along cliff-top and beach, accompanied by family, friends and neighbours, clearly visible in the light of their lanterns. It seemed that all members had been expecting their services to be required – it had been one of those days when storm clouds had been gathering menacingly and heavy seas had been building up since dawn.

Ted Carter was a leading member of the Brigade and he was the first to arrive on the scene. Others quickly followed and were greeted by Tovell by their first names. The company could have been called the Admiral Lord Nelson Volunteer Life-saving Brigade since every member was a regular customer at the hostelry. Tovell already had the rocket apparatus out of its box and the rescue operation was soon underway. He had a soldier's natural interest in all forms of artillery and had requested that he be made responsible for the Boxer Rocket equipment. Lieutenant Collins had granted the request and put him in charge of all launchings.

The first two shots fell wide of the ship – the strong wind blowing the missiles off course. Tovell, always a good marksman, took over from the Brigade member and succeeded in getting a line aboard. The shipwrecked mariners quickly hauled in the rope carrying the breeches-buoy which was to be the means of their salvation, and secured it high in the rigging of their vessel. The first two men were brought ashore without mishap but when the third crew member climbed into the harness and the rocket-party tried to haul him to safety, nothing happened – the breeches-buoy had jammed. Thirty minutes ticked by and the last glimmer of daylight faded. All attempts by the men on the beach to free the apparatus by manipulating the ropes failed, and if the men on the ship made any attempt themselves, they were unseen in the darkness and equally unsuccessful.

'There's only one thing for it,' declared Tovell at last. 'I'll have to go out to the ship myself and free the ruddy tackle.' He began at once to strip off his oilskins and heavy boots.

'One of us will go,' said Ted Carter. 'We're all experienced men and we know the sea and the equipment better than you do.'

Tovell looked at the eager faces all around him and shook his head. The average age of the members of the rocket-party must have been sixty years. 'You men give your services voluntary whereas this is part of my military duty. It's only right that I should go.' Before there could be any further argument he yelled for a rope. David brought him one straight away and he was tying it round his waist when Lieutenant Collins came hurrying over to him.

'Have you gone mad, Tovell?' he cried. 'You don't stand a chance in those seas. You'll drown for sure, man!'

'If someone doesn't free that bloody buoy,' Tovell retorted, 'those poor devils out there will drown for sure.' So saying, he pushed past the officer and made off towards the water. As he moved, the huge coil of rope which David had deposited on the shingle began to unravel.

'Who will be responsible for Tovell's lifeline?' called Lieutenant Collins.

'I will!' answered Bill Westgate without a second's hesitation. He stooped and caught the moving rope in his huge hand, jerking it as he did so. Tovell was immediately thrown off balance. He scrambled to his feet cursing and looked back to see what had happened. The sight of the ex-boxer leering at him, flexing his muscles and twisting the life-line around his massive arms and across his ample shoulders, made Tovell see red. He ran back up the beach shouting in protest.

'I don't want that man anywhere near my rope!'

'What's the matter with you, Tovell?' demanded Lieutenant Collins. 'Westgate's the best man for the job. He's by far the strongest and of course, the rest of us will back him up and help haul you in if you get into difficulties.'

'He knows why I don't want him holding my bloody rope,' snarled Tovell.

Bill Westgate laughed. He put his face close to Tovell's, knowing that no-one else would be able to hear his words above the noise of the storm. 'Think I'm going to let it go, do you? Think I'm going to let you drown? Well you're wrong, chum. I shan't let the sea have you because you're mine. You belong to me. And like the lieutenant says, I'm the best man for the job.'

Tovell still hesitated, glowering fiercely at Bill Westgate, but he knew he could delay no longer. Addressing everyone in general who was gathered round, he cried out, 'You watch him! You just watch this bugger!'

As he turned to run back to the water he almost fell over the tiny figure of Ginny. She had just returned to the beach after taking the children home and putting them to bed. 'Take care, Tovell,' she whispered as she reached up on tiptoe to put her arms around his neck. A quick hug and she jumped backwards away from him, but in that moment he had felt her soft baby-fine hair brush his cheek and her firm breasts press into his chest. As she stood at arm's length from him he saw the undisguised concern in her eyes. Instantly, his anger evaporated and was replaced by love – a totally overwhelming surge of emotion which flooded his senses and blotted out all other considerations. For that split second in time the world contained only Ginny. But as he moved towards her the tender expression on her face changed to one of alarm and he was suddenly made aware of his surroundings. He had to content himself with lightly touching the side of her face with his hand as he passed and then the chill water completed the process of bringing him back to reality as he waded into the sea. Not daring to look back, he raised an arm in acknowledgement as the cries of the well-wishers on the beach followed him. The last words he heard were those of Ted Carter exhorting his company of volunteers, 'Stand firm, boys! Keep the rope taut and take the strain!'

Tovell knew it was hopeless to attempt to swim out to the schooner – the strongest swimmer would have found it impossible to make any progress in such mountainous seas – but he did not think it would be too difficult to reach the ship using the rope which carried the breeches-buoy. Knowing that it was made fast to the vessel at one end and held tightly by the combined strengths of his drinking companions at the other, he confidently grabbed hold of the rope and made his way forward, hand over hand. His troubles began as soon as he was out of his depth and could no longer push himself along by digging his toes into the sea bed. Unbeknown to Tovell, he was only about fifty yards out from the shore when David arrived at the water's edge, yelling his name and gesticulating in his direction. The boy had had the foresight to run back to the Watch-room for a cork life-jacket, but it was too late.

The howl of the gale was, by that time, so intense that Tovell could not even hear his own laboured breathing. He kicked strongly with his feet, trying to use his legs to propel himself along and ease the strain on his arms. He was buffeted by wave after wave. Time and again he was completely submerged and came up spluttering and gasping for breath. The force of the water was much greater than he had expected and threatened to tear him from his precarious hold at any moment. His progress was painfully slow. The ache in his shoulders and limbs became agonising. As he heaved himself forward he felt that his arms were being wrenched from their sockets. To add to his torment, he had to contend with another enemy – the icy cold of the North Sea. With every minute that passed it seemed to penetrate further into his body. He could scarcely feel his fingers. Why, why, had he not thought to wear gloves? Twice his grasp slipped and he had to make superhuman efforts to seize the rope again before he was swept away. He began to wonder whether he would make it. Perhaps Mr. Collins had been right after all; perhaps it was a foolhardy attempt. How much longer could he hang on? He knew he must be reaching the limit of his endurance. Then, mercifully, he realised he was not so low in the water. For a brief moment the clouds broke and before they closed over again, the moon shone through for a few seconds. He was able to make out the lines of the ship. She resembled some giant whale floundering in the shallows of the sandbank. She was listing badly to one side and this was to Tovell's advantage for suddenly he felt the hull beneath his feet and he was walking up the side of the schooner, clear of the water.

As the exhausted soldier reached the ship's rail he was dragged aboard, clapped on the back and hailed as a saviour. He prayed he could do the job he had come to do. Fortunately, he did not have the breath to explain to the crew that he did not share their confidence in him. For a few seconds he hung onto the foremast to which the breeches-buoy equipment was attached, shoulders heaving as he gasped in air. The wind cut across the storm-tossed deck like a knife and he feared his sodden clothing would soon freeze to his flesh. Someone pulled him away from his resting place and forced his arms into a spare oilskin. He nodded his thanks, marvelling that the men gathered round him, their faces eager with hope and expectation, could have any strength left after their ordeal which by now, had lasted for several hours. Making a tremendous effort, Tovell yelled above the roar of the wind that he needed someone to hold a light for him while he worked. A crewman held up an unlit hurricane lamp and indicated that the waves swamping the foundering vessel had put out the light, but that he would attempt to get it going again. Tovell hung grimly to the rigging whilst he watched the man sliding perilously down the slanting deck – the whole area was awash with loose wreckage – in the direction of the cabin. He emerged several minutes later bearing the lamp triumphantly aloft. In its glow Tovell could see that he also held a coil of rope. There were more anxious moments as the man struggled to scramble back to Tovell. He made it at last and, miraculously, the lamp stayed alight. The seaman handed the coil of rope to Tovell and tried to explain something. The wind whipped away his words but his intention was clear – he wanted the soldier to lash the pair of them to the mast. Once they had climbed the mast rungs to where the breeches buoy was secured Tovell hastily complied. It seemed a sensible precaution given the violence of the storm, and without the need to hold onto the mast he would have his two hands free for the job ahead.

The task of freeing the jammed pulley and tackle was not an easy one and he suspected that the action which he and the members of the

Volunteer Life-saving Brigade had taken in trying to free the equipment from the beach had only made matters worse. He also feared that the icy temperatures had contributed to the trouble. Certainly, since the apparatus had been motionless tiny crystals of ice had formed in the twisted strands of the fibre. The ropes seemed fused solidly together and Tovell could not force them apart. He cursed his own weakness and endeavoured to blow some warmth into his frozen fingers. Even his brain seemed to be numb with cold as he tried to think of a possible solution. He knew that the pulley was always kept well-oiled but perhaps a more generous application of lubricant would help and it should also raise the temperature slightly – hopefully, enough to melt the ice. It was worth a try and anyway, he could not think of anything else.

Tovell called to the crewmen waiting on the deck a few feet below him, cupping his hands around his mouth to make his voice carry in spite of the gale. Someone apparently understood, disappeared from view and returned moments afterwards with an oil-can. The man passed the container up to Tovell and the latter renewed his attempts to unblock the apparatus. It was just as well that the soldier was so intent upon his task otherwise the violent pitching and tossing of the stranded vessel as it was assailed by the mountainous waves would have rendered him very sick indeed. As it was, the spray from the constant surge of water crashing over the ship and the wind, howling mercilessly, persistently trying to dash the two men from their perch on the mast, were hazards enough. The seaman could do nothing to help the soldier; he was occupied totally in trying to shield their meagre light from the elements.

Tovell swamped the pulley and the ropes frozen to it, with oil. He tried to force the lubricant into the fibres and then, for good measure, rubbed his greasy hand repeatedly over the strands leading to the pulley. When he had used up all the oil in the can, he threw the container away and using both hands, tore furiously at the ropes. Still they would not move. It was hopeless. Anger and frustration welled up inside him. He hurled obscenities into the gale and attacked the ropes again. Suddenly, they moved; the pulley was free. The two men laughed with relief. Tovell released them from the rope which had lashed them to the mast and they clambered thankfully down to the rolling deck.

The crewmen, one by one, climbed into the breeches-buoy and the Brigade, responding to Tovell's signals with the lantern, quickly pulled them to the beach. The evacuation was almost complete – only the man who had held the lamp remained to be rescued – when the ship gave a violent shudder. Rigging came crashing down onto the deck, narrowly missing the two men. Terrible groaning and cracking sounds reached their ears as though the very bowels of the vessel were being torn asunder.

'She's going! She's breaking up!' screamed the crewman.

Tovell glanced anxiously up at the mast holding the breeches-buoy rope. As far as he could make out in the darkness it was still intact. 'You've got time to get ashore,' he shouted back, 'but hurry!'

The man scrambled into the harness and then hesitated. 'What about you?' he yelled.

'I'll be alright,' answered Tovell. 'I've got a lifeline attached to my waist.' Tovell waved the hurricane lamp towards the beach. The oil in it must have been running out because the light only flickered for a few seconds before it died. It was enough – the breeches-buoy moved and the man was gone. Almost immediately, the foremast began to splinter. Tovell rushed to brace himself against it. When he heard rending sounds he looked upwards. As he feared, the mast was bending under the strain. He gripped the woodwork as tightly as he could with both arms and pushed with all his might. Thank God he would not have to prop up the mast for long. He knew how speedily the volunteer company worked. Ted Carter would have given the command, 'Haul ashore, boys!' and the Brigade would have gone into action following a drill as precise as any used by the Army. As Tovell strained with gritted teeth to support the weakening mast he felt it vibrate in time to the rhythmic movements of the beach-party as they hauled the last crewman to safety. When the vibrations stopped Tovell knew the rescue was complete and that he could relax his grip. As he straightened his back, the mast gave off a loud, harsh, creaking sound and toppled over. Then, like some giant tree torn up by its roots, it ripped up part of the deck and sweeping all that lay in its path before it, the mast slid over the side of the wreck in a mass of spars, ropes and cargo, taking with it a large section of the ship's rail. Tovell leapt for his life and hung on grimly to a capstan until the danger had passed.

Staggering to his feet once more, Tovell felt the vessel lurch ominously. Was she slipping off the sandbank? He must not delay – but he must not be panicked into jumping too soon. He must wait until the sea had carried away the jumble of wreckage caused by the falling mast otherwise he would be entangled in the debris. He threw off the borrowed oil-skin, made sure his life-line was still securely tied around his waist and stepped cautiously onto the sloping hull. He had made his way almost to the point where the body of the vessel slanted sharply towards the keel when the sky above his head was suddenly illuminated by a brilliant light. He looked up and followed the blazing trail of the rocket as it soared upward and then descended, exploding in a shower of dazzling sparks over the wrecked ship. It seemed he had underestimated Lieutenant Collins; he was proving to be quite a competent officer. Tovell made the most of the opportunity he had been given to show that he was still alive. Feet well spread to keep his balance, he waved frantically in the direction of the shore with both arms until the last glimmer of light from the flare was fading. He then took a deep breath and dived into the raging churning waters.

XIV

Mrs. Gillings had found herself a vantage point on top of a shingle bank and since she was taller than most people anyway, she had a clear view over the heads of the other onlookers. She was the first to sight Tovell after the skies cleared and the moon lit up the scene. He was hanging on to his lifeline with both hands and letting his comrades on the beach drag him through the water. When he was about one hundred yards from land she saw him engulfed by a series of gigantic waves. He struggled, striking out desperately with his arms to keep his head above water, but the breakers overwhelmed him and swallowed him up. The soldiers, conscious of the peril he was in, made furious efforts to haul him in quickly. When Mrs. Gillings caught a glimpse of him again he was much nearer to shore but no longer holding on to his lifeline. He was floating, face downwards with his arms and legs spread-eagled, on the surface of the water. She looked around for Ginny and hurried over to her.

'C'mon, gal!' she urged. 'We've got work to do. They'll be bringing him ashore any minute now. We've gotta get back to the house and get his bed brought over to the fire, and hot water bottles filled and warm blankets ready. C'mon now, Ginny!'

Mrs. Gillings was taking no chances. She was almost certain that Tovell was dead and she was determined to spare her friend as much distress as possible. She had also witnessed the adoration in Tovell's eyes during that unguarded moment on the beach. She had been standing behind Ginny so she had been unable to tell whether the feeling was reciprocated. Just in case it was, she wanted Ginny out of the way when the lifeless body was laid out on the sand lest she make a fool of herself in front of her friends and neighbours by throwing herself upon the corpse. And if Tovell were alive – and she prayed that he was – the preparations would be necessary.

Ginny was reluctant to leave; she wanted to be certain that Tovell was safe. Mrs. Gillings would have no nonsense and bundled her off in the direction of the Coastguard Station. When they reached the perimeter wall, the old lady risked a backward glance and was in time to see Bill Westgate wading out of the water with Tovell's limp form slung over his shoulder. Her heart sank but she continued to order Ginny about as though nothing was wrong. They busied themselves in anticipation of the soldier's imminent arrival but after they had completed every task which Mrs. Gillings could think of, he had still not appeared. Ginny's anxiety increased until she could contain her fears no longer.

'Where is he?' she burst out. 'Why haven't they brought him home? That doesn't make sense to leave him on that cold beach.'

'They've gotta clear up – and get the survivors away. That all takes time,' answered Mrs. Gillings as convincingly as she could.

'Maybe they took him to the Watch-room. I've gotta go see,' muttered Ginny, halfway to the front door.

'No!' cried Mrs. Gillings in alarm. 'That's best if you stay here and I go see what's happened.'

The matter was settled when the front door suddenly opened. Lieutenant Collins walked in with an apologetic nod to the women, and held the door whilst Bill Westgate and Sergeant Harris carried Tovell through, swathed in blankets. Dr. Lambert followed.

'Is he alright?' demanded Ginny.

'Well …. He's alive, just about,' replied the sergeant.

'Put him here, on the bed,' said Mrs. Gillings. The soldiers did as they were told and then quickly removed the rough blankets and the wet clothing from their unconscious comrade. Mrs. Gillings stood at the ready with a flannelette nightshirt which had belonged to her late husband. She and Ginny dressed Tovell in the nightshirt, placed stone hot-water bottles wrapped in flannelette on each side of him and under his feet, and covered him up with the warm bedclothes.

Ginny lingered, shaking her head 'Doesn't he look bad?' she murmured sorrowfully.

'He'll be alright once he's warmed up,' Mrs. Gillings assured her, but the look she exchanged with the sergeant said she was far from confident.

Dr. Lambert bent over the unconscious soldier and began to

examine him. The others moved away from the bed. Ginny asked in a whisper, 'How long has he been like this?'

'Since we took him out of the water,' replied the sergeant. 'There wasn't any sign of life that I could tell. We all thought he was dead. If it hadn't been for Private Westgate here, we might have accepted that he'd drowned and left him in peace.'

'Not straight away,' interrupted Lieutenant Collins. 'Coastguard regulations make provision for the resuscitation of the apparently drowned. However, I would agree that all credit is due to Westgate. I doubt whether the rest of us would have persevered for as long as he did.'

'I had to,' explained Bill Westgate to the women. 'I'd given him my word. I'd told him I wouldn't let him drown – so I couldn't let him, could I?'

'Good man,' said the doctor, looking up from his patient. 'In cases like this it never does to give up too soon. There's still so much we don't know about how the human body works or reacts ....' When the doctor had finished his examination, he removed his stethoscope from his ears and addressed his remarks to the lieutenant and Ginny. 'I wish I could say with certainty how he will be – but I cannot. It's only three months since he contracted pneumonia. That's why he's here, I understand, on light duties, so called. That won't help but, on the other hand, he's tough and he's been used to hardship. I'm sure he's survived where many others have gone under. If a man's got a lot to live for ....'

'But he hasn't!' cried Ginny in anguish. 'He's got nobody – no family – nothing.'

The doctor patted her arm comfortingly. 'Who's to say, my dear, what gives a man the will to live. All I can tell you is that Tovell must have a strong will to survive or he would never have lasted this long – not leading the kind of life he's lead. Now try not to worry. There's nothing more we can do tonight. I'll be back first thing in the morning and depending on how he is, I'll arrange for him to be moved to hospital.'

'To North Walsham?' asked the lieutenant.

'I think Norwich may be more suitable,' answered the doctor. 'It all depends on his condition and what treatment he needs. I'll have to see in the morning. Until then just keep him warm. Don't attempt to give him anything to drink whilst he's unconscious, of course, and I should mention that if he does come round, he may not be himself. We have no way of knowing how long he was under the water and, therefore, how long his brain was starved of oxygen. So don't be upset if he doesn't behave normally, Ginny. I'll be here early, my dear.'

As they were leaving, Sergeant Harris told Ginny to fetch him if she needed any help with Tovell during the night. She thanked him as she closed the front door behind the four men. Once they had gone, Mrs. Gillings suggested that she sit with Tovell while Ginny got some rest. 'No, I couldn't sleep,' protested Ginny, 'not whilst Tovell might be dying. But that's kind of you to offer.'

'In that case you may as well make us both a cup of tea,' said Mrs. Gillings. 'That never does to sit about moping.' She sat down at the table whilst Ginny prepared the beverage. They were drinking it when they realised that Tovell's breathing had become more laboured. They both rushed to the bed and Mrs. Gillings propped the soldier up higher with more pillows.

'That sounds like the death rattle to me,' said Ginny, half sobbing.

Mrs. Gillings grabbed hold of Tovell and shook him. 'Come you on, bor!' she shouted. 'Don't you darst peg out on us!' Still grasping the soldier by the collar of his night-shirt, she glanced over her shoulder at Ginny and ordered, 'Make him some hot rum – you know, rum, hot water and sugar.'

'But the doctor …,' reasoned Ginny. 'He say we mustn't give him anything to drink.'

'If he's a-going anyway,' argued Mrs. Gillings, 'that won't make a mite o' difference what we do, and if he int ready to go yet that might bring him round – with the good Lord's help. Do you do as I say, gal. Hurry, now!'

Whilst Ginny quickly prepared the drink, Mrs. Gillings positioned herself on the bed so that she was sitting behind Tovell with his unconscious form resting against her ample bosom. His head lolled and rolled about so Mrs. Gillings held it firmly against the crook of her neck with her left hand whilst she administered the steaming cup with her right. 'I won't let him choke,' she assured the distressed Ginny. 'I've got him upright.'

To Mrs. Gillings's annoyance, the liquid trickled from the corners of Tovell's mouth. 'Now don't you waste it,' she said. 'I reckon this is the only time I'm ever likely to pour booze down your gullet, bor.' She tried again and some of the drink must have found its way to Tovell's throat for he began to retch. 'Quick, put that bowl under him!' Mrs. Gillings called out. 'He's a-going to be sick. I reckon that's just what he needs. Get it off his chest – all that there sea water, oil and muck.'

Ginny, more distraught than ever, rushed to the other side of the bed convinced that she was witnessing Tovell's imminent demise. Mrs. Gillings was equally confident that the vomiting had ensured that he would not die. When she was satisfied that the bout was over, she instructed Ginny to deal with the bowl while she sponged the patient. When Ginny returned, both nurses agreed that Tovell's colour had improved considerably and so had his breathing. His coma did not seem so deep – in fact, he looked as if he was merely sleeping. The women seated themselves on either side of the bed and observed their charge intently for a further ten minutes – then Mrs. Gillings began to yawn.

'I reckon you were right,' said Ginny. 'He'll be fine now he's been sick. The danger's passed, thanks to you. Go you home now and get some sleep. There's not much of the night left. I can keep an eye on him 'til the doctor gets back.'

'Well …, I don't know.' Mrs. Gillings was reluctant to leave her friend in her moment of need but she suddenly felt extremely weary. 'He do look a lot better, I must say. And I've left Lily and little Arthur alone long enough – in fact, I hent never left them alone afore.'

'You get back – go on now,' urged Ginny. 'And I'm truly grateful to you.'

Mrs. Gillings allowed herself to be persuaded but not before she had fussed over her patient one more time. 'I'll just give you a hand to turn him over on his side. That way he won't come to no harm even if he is sick again and you just happened to have dozed off.' She tucked a pillow into Tovell's back and placed an old towel beneath his mouth. She departed only after extracting a promise from her neighbour that she would knock on their adjoining wall at the first sign of trouble.

Once alone, Ginny walked around the bed several times worrying whether they had overlooked some essential. Her thoughts centred on the problem of what would happen if she did fall asleep and Tovell rolled onto his back. A pillow positioned behind him was hardly an adequate preventative measure for a man of his stature. What if he did turn over; might he choke on his own vomit? Ginny had used all her spare pillows so she took the cushions from the two armchairs and propped those behind Tovell. His back still felt cold so she found more covers. She settled herself in her chair, but only for a few seconds. She got to her feet again, still apprehensive, still terrified that Tovell would lose his fragile hold on life. She hovered over him until, suddenly, she had the answer. Stepping noiselessly out of her dress, removing all the extra bed-linen and cushions she had wedged behind Tovell and taking their place, she curled herself around his still body and was soon fast asleep.

XV

Lydia Brewster climbed the internal staircase from her parlour to the Watch-room. The only light came from a lamp shaded sharply downwards onto the officer's desk. 'How is Tovell?' she asked.

Richard Collins looked up in surprise from where he was busily writing and answered, 'I didn't bother to come and tell you because I assumed you were asleep. He's still unconscious and the doctor plans to move him to the hospital in the morning.' The officer got up from his chair and walked over to Lydia. He glanced across at Fred Mannell who was standing at the main window of the look-out, his binoculars trained on the raging sea outside. 'I shall take a short break, Mannell,' he said. 'Call me if you need me.'

'Yes, Sir,' replied the soldier without looking round.

Lydia did not speak again until they were safely downstairs and the inner door firmly shut. 'You should have guessed I would wait up for you,' she chided, embracing him. 'The least I can do is get you something hot to eat and drink after all the time you've spent on that freezing beach tonight.'

'Ah – again you show excessive concern for my material comfort. You worry too much, my love. All I really need is a few hours ensconced in your bed, but I dare not take the risk. The gale persists – there could be another emergency before morning and I must return to the Watch-room.'

'Then let me get you some supper quickly.'

'I'm not hungry, but I can see that you will not be happy until I've allowed you to perform some menial task on my behalf. So be it – you may make me a cup of tea.'

'That was unkind, but I can see that tonight's events have affected you.' Lydia promptly withdrew to the kitchen. She returned shortly afterwards bearing the tea-tray which she deposited on the large parlour table. Richard Collins was slumped in an armchair staring in a disgruntled fashion into the fire. She poured the tea and placed his cup on the small table by his side. He looked up at Lydia, leaned forward, grabbed hold of her around the waist and pulled her onto his lap.

'I'm sorry,' he whispered, embracing her lovingly. 'A teacher, of all people, should never be sarcastic – such a destructive trait. But then, as you know, I have many faults.'

'And now you're inviting me to contradict you, but I shall not give you that satisfaction. Instead,' Lydia's voice softened, 'I shall assure you that I love you, faults and all.'

Richard Collins laughed. 'You're too perceptive; you understand me too well. And you're correct – the events of the night have put me in an ill humour.'

'What upset you?'

'You mean, who upset me? Who is the one person who always upsets me?'

'Tovell?'

'Of course!'

'David told me the whole story before he went to bed.'

'Did he tell you Tovell was magnificent? Once he realised he couldn't free the apparatus he decided instantly what to do. There was no mental struggle – no thought of what he had to lose. Damn him!'

'He did the right thing and so did you, Richard. As the officer in charge your place was on shore directing operations.'

'Ah – but if I hadn't been the officer in charge …. What then, Lydia? Would I have risked life and limb without a second thought? I fear I know the answer to that.'

'You cannot possibly know, Richard. If the onus had been on you, you would have done whatever was necessary.'

'I wish I had your confidence, my dear. My father would have been in no doubt. In his opinion I was always a coward – both a physical and a moral coward. How he would have loved to have had Tovell as a son. Backbone – that was the quality my father most admired in a man. That was the quality he told me repeatedly that I lacked. Tovell has it in plenty. He would have suited my father perfectly – an intellectual was the worst type of offspring he could have had. He hinted more than once that my mother must have gone astray. He had to. How could he accept that he had sired me? But Tovell, – he would have taken such delight in Tovell. He would even have enjoyed sharing his escapades ....'

'Why torture yourself, Richard? It's pointless to compare yourself with Tovell. There is no comparison.'

'And what of your husband?' demanded Richard Collins, ignoring Lydia's attempts to comfort him and pointing to the photograph of Station Officer Brewster, in full uniform, which sat on top of the piano. 'How would he have behaved in the situation we encountered tonight?'

'As the officer in charge, he would have behaved exactly as you did.'

'But when he was younger; when he was not in command,' persisted the lieutenant. 'What would he have done then?'

Lydia answered slowly. 'He would probably have done the same as Tovell. He has won several awards for bravery in the past.' She got up and moved to the other side of the hearth.

Richard leant forward, hunched over the dying fire and wrung his hands in despair. 'My God, Lydia! I wonder why you bother with me. Your husband is a proven man of courage, and if that picture is a good likeness, a handsome one too. How can you find me anything but repulsive?'

'Repulsive! That's the very last thing I find you, as you well know. You're the most attractive man I've ever met.' She knelt on the floor in front of him and took his hands in hers. 'Stop this torture,' she said earnestly.

'Then tell me something to console me. Tell me what first attracted you to me – if, as you would have me believe, I'm the most attractive man you've ever met?'

Lydia replied without hesitation. 'Your voice – your beautiful rich, vibrant, exciting, enticing voice attracted me. It stirred something deep inside me the first time you spoke to me; some memory, some passion long dormant. You've been blessed with a poet's voice, an actor's voice, an orator's voice. Without doubt, a politician would be eternally grateful for a voice like yours. Yes, it was your voice which cast a spell over me when we first met. Later, to my joy, I found we shared a love of literature and poetry. At last I could talk with a sensitive man who felt as intensely as I did about the creative arts. I cannot begin to tell you what satisfaction it gives me to be able to express my innermost thoughts to someone I know will understand. We're both romantics at heart, Richard dear, and we've found in each other the romance we've yearned for, secretly, all our lives.'

'And which I haven't found with my wife nor you with your husband,' added Richard. Lydia stiffened and would have withdrawn her hands had not her lover grasped them more tightly. 'I've stepped on sacred ground, haven't I?' he said. 'I've mentioned that which is unmentionable; the subject which is taboo between us – your husband. You're prepared to be unfaithful to him in deed but not in word. How strange. Perhaps speaking of him to me makes you feel guilty.'

'I did feel guilty at first,' admitted Lydia. 'I've never been unfaithful to him before, nor have I wanted to be, but that's not the reason I don't speak of him to you – it's because I don't need to. You tell me about your wife because you need to. You spit out the words and with them your profound sense of disappointment and disillusion. It's necessary for you to divest yourself of your intense feeling of bitterness. I've no such need because I feel no bitterness towards my husband. We've always been happy together in our quiet way and if I hadn't met you, I would have sought no other. And, of course,' Lydia paused and smiled at Richard, 'if I hadn't met you I would never have known how wonderful a relationship could be.'

'I suppose I must be grateful for that morsel. But why do you say you felt guilty, at first? Do you mean that you no longer feel guilty?'

'Yes.'

'What has changed?'

Lydia was silent and stirred uneasily. She turned her face away as Richard repeated the question. 'Why are you not answering? Do you think your reply will hurt me? Come, my dearest, we're nothing if not completely honest with one another. Why do you no longer feel guilty?'

'Because I know that you are not a real threat to my husband.' She looked up and met Richard's gaze. 'I know that when the war is over you will go back to your wife.'

'*Et tu*, Lydia! So it didn't take long for even you to see the coward in me. I wish I could deny it. I wish I had the courage to say run away with me, Lydia, and to hell with everything else, but I have not.'

Lydia moved closer to him and said softly, 'You misunderstand me. I'm not accusing you of being a coward. I don't think you are a coward, rather I think you are a man of high moral principles – even though you would deny this strenuously to yourself and to others. I think that, simply, your principles would never allow you to desert your wife. That is as it should be, and since we're being honest with one another, I should tell you that I could never desert my husband. He's done nothing to deserve such treatment and nor, in your wife's eyes, has she.'

'You are right, of course,' agreed Richard sadly. 'I'm certain Mildred regards herself as the epitome of a dutiful wife burdened with a wretched husband. So we understand one another, my love, in this as in so many other matters. We are to be but playthings to one another; toys to be cast aside in the nursery cupboard when we have outgrown them.'

'But think what sweet memories are aroused by recollections of the joy which was given by a much loved toy,' murmured Lydia.

Richard gathered her into his arms and whispered, 'We must make every moment together count, my darling – every precious moment.' They were silent for a while, both intensely aware of the futility of their love, but they could not remain entrapped in their despondency. Richard deliberately released them with his next remark, delivered in his customary flippant manner. 'What a pity I have to go back on duty. I should have delighted in playing romantic games with you tonight – or rather, this morning.'

Lydia replied in like vein. 'And I regret the need to part with my favourite toy, if only for a little while.' Then, more seriously, she stated, 'You will, of course, have a lengthy report to write.'

'I've already written it. I did it straight away while the details of the night's proceedings were fresh in my mind.'

'What about Tovell?'

'I've recommended him for an award. You look surprised, my dear, and in that you do me a disservice. You've just said that I am a man of principle and to some small extent perhaps that is true. Certainly, I would not allow my animosity towards a man to interfere with my sense of fair play. I hope my recommendation is upheld. Tovell is a brave man. His record shows that he has always been at his best in action. He should not be here; he's wasted. His place is with the British Expeditionary Force. By now he would be a hero – or dead.'

XVI

When Tovell awoke next morning it took him a long time to come to his senses, realise where he was and recall what had happened the night before. It then dawned on him that he was not alone in his bed. The warm body tucked in behind his own, the soft arm cuddling his middle, the small knees fitting snugly into the bend of his own knees, could belong to only one person. For several minutes he lay quite still luxuriating in the pleasure of Ginny's proximity, but the urge to take a peep at her was too strong to suppress and eventually, he gingerly lifted his head and glanced over his shoulder. He caught a glimpse of a cluster of auburn curls nestling against his spine. It was enough and he settled down on his pillow once more smiling to himself with contentment. He could not remain motionless for long. His hand moved to cover Ginny's hand. He caressed the small fingers – a fraction of the size of his own. His hand wandered further – downwards and backwards. He made contact with Ginny's thigh where it hugged his thigh. He stroked it tenderly – and woke her up!

'Tovell, you're awake!' she cried propping herself on her elbow and leaning over him so that she could see his face. Tovell decided it would be politic to assume the role of a man not responsible for his actions. He kept his eyes shut and made a few moans and groans. Ginny was not deceived by his performance. 'Tovell,' she repeated, 'do you answer me now. I know you're awake because I felt your hand on my leg.'

Tovell opened one eye and grinned at her. 'I'm not awake,' he asserted. 'I'm dead and in heaven. How else would I find you in bed with me?' Ginny gave a little gasp and leapt to the floor. 'Hey!' Tovell protested. 'My back's cold now – don't leave me.'

Ginny bustled to the other side of the bed, anxious to set the record straight. 'I only got into bed with you because I feared you were dying. I wanted to keep you warm and stop you rolling backwards in case you choked. I might have guessed it would take more than a drowning to finish you off. There was I worrying myself sick how you'd be when you came to. Dr. Lambert say you might not be yourself – you might not be normal. You're normal alright. Up to your old tricks as soon as you're awake – trying to molest me ....'

'Molest you! I was only stroking your leg while you were asleep. You can't blame me for that. You wouldn't let me do it while you're awake, would you? The way you're carrying on at me you're making me think you're sorry I'm not dead.'

Tovell sounded so hurt that Ginny was overcome with remorse. She immediately seated herself on the bed and bending over him, began to straighten his pillows, tidy his hair and talk to him in the same earnest, reassuring tones she used when comforting her children. 'I'm sorry for going on at you like that. I didn't mean nothing by it; that's just my way. You should know that by now. And of course I'm not sorry you're not dead. You shouldn't say things like that – no, not even in joke. You should have seen the state I was in last night when they brought you back. I don't know what I would have done without Mrs. Gillings's help. I was too upset to be much use. I didn't know whether I was coming or going – no, that I didn't. You'll have to thank her – that you will. I reckon you owe it to her that you're still here – and to Bill Westgate. They say he kept trying to bring you round on the beach after the others had given you up for dead. You'll have to thank him an' all. And no, I'm not sorry. I was praying and praying you'd be alright. If anything had happened to you ....' Ginny could say no more and she turned her head aside while she brushed away her tears.

Tovell's vast experience of life had not fitted him for this situation; no-one had ever cried over him before. For a few moments he was at a loss for words then, to cover his confusion, he muttered awkwardly, 'Blimey, Ginny! You don't half pick your moments. Here you are, friendly, showing me all you've got and I'm too weak to do bugger all about it.'

Ginny reacted as though she had been slapped in the face. She jumped off the bed, one hand clasped to her breast, the other to her flushed cheek. Until that moment, she had been quite oblivious to the fact that she had positioned herself across Tovell in such a way that he had had an uninterrupted view down the front of her petticoat. 'Oh!

You!' she ranted. 'That's all you think about. You ought to be ashamed of yourself; at death's door last night and having carnal thoughts this morning.' She searched frantically for the dress she had cast aside hours before and hastily scrambled into it, her back to Tovell but her angry voice still reaching his ears. 'And don't you darst tell Mrs. Gillings I was in bed with you – no, nor the doctor. Don't you darst tell anybody ....'

There was a peremptory knock on the front door and in walked Dr. Lambert. Ginny tried to finish doing up her dress with one hand whilst tidying her hair with the other. The fact that the doctor was quite obviously amused by her dishevelled appearance did not improve her temper. To hide her embarrassment she blurted out, 'There's nothing wrong with him, doctor. He's perfectly normal.'

'Now, now, Tovell, what's this? Upsetting our Ginny – what have you been doing to the girl?' As usual, the doctor managed to chuckle with every ounce of his corpulent frame.

'Nothing much to my way of thinking,' replied Tovell, a little wearily. 'You'd think she'd welcome back a man who's stood on the brink with open arms, but all she does is nag me.'

'I'm sure you deserved it,' concluded the doctor. 'And now to business; I'm delighted to see you conscious. How do you feel, my boy?'

'Awful,' answered the soldier in a tone which implied that he had decided to feel sorry for himself. 'Everything hurts – my head, neck, arms, chest ....'

'Yes, yes, I'm afraid that's only to be expected. The strain on your body from hauling yourself out to the wreck, plus all the seawater you swallowed .... However, when I examined you last night there appeared to be no breakages or evidence of internal injuries, but I'll look at you again now to make sure.'

'I'll go make some tea,' Ginny called out and she rushed into the scullery as the doctor lifted the bedclothes from his patient. It was not until she had filled the kettle with water that she realised she could not boil it unless she went back into the living room and placed it on the cooking range. The idea was unthinkable in the circumstances so instead, she applied herself to the task of completing her toilet before the doctor finished his examination. By the time the latter entered the small scullery Ginny was looking as neat as ever. 'I'll just go put the kettle on,' she greeted him.

'No, no, my dear – don't bother for me. I must get on. I've several calls to make in this area. I only wanted a quiet word with you before I leave. Don't be fooled by Tovell's apparent friskiness. I'm sure it was only his way of expressing relief that he was still in the land of the living.'

'Oh, I'm sorry, doctor. I do apologise. I shouldn't have carried on like that. I know Tovell doesn't mean any harm – it's just his way – but sometimes he does rile me with the things he say and do.'

'I understand, my dear. Don't give it another thought. What I really wanted to explain to you was that Tovell's courageous feat last night has totally exhausted him and it may take him a few days to recover. There is also, of course, the possibility of a recurrence of the pneumonia. There's no need for him to be moved to hospital but keep him in bed and I'll call again in the next day or two when I'm passing. If there's any deterioration in his condition, or you have any cause for concern, you will inform them in the Watch-room, won't you? They'll soon contact me.'

'Oh, yes, doctor, of course I will. But does that mean you fear he won't be alright?'

'I'm certain he'll be fine – given time. All I'm saying is don't expect him to recover overnight. I shouldn't be surprised if he's gone back to sleep again already, so we won't disturb him. You be a good girl and let me out of the back door. Just see he gets plenty of rest and as much as he can manage in the way of food and drink. Don't worry now.'

Ginny accompanied Dr. Lambert to his pony and trap, thanking him profusely for his kindness and was met by Mrs. Gillings on the return journey. The old lady was genuinely pleased to hear that Tovell had regained consciousness and would not require transportation to hospital. She almost ran through the scullery into the living room before Ginny could stop her, so keen was she to express personally her immense relief that he was better. Tovell woke up with a start and lay momentarily dazed as Mrs. Gillings told him noisily how concerned she had been for his welfare. Only when it looked as though she might be going to hug him did Tovell hastily pull himself up on his pillows and declare in most fitting and generous terms his appreciation of her efforts on his behalf the night before.

Mrs. Gillings accepted his thanks somewhat bashfully. Then, as a sudden thought struck her she turned to Ginny and demanded, 'Where are the littl'uns? You hent forgot about them, have you? They'll be late for school.' Ginny had forgotten. The children were still fast asleep in her bedroom. Ginny panicked; Mrs. Gillings took over. 'Go you see to the littl'uns and I'll attend to Tovell,' she commanded, rolling up her sleeves in an ominous fashion.

As Ginny fled into the bedroom she heard her lodger groan and caught a glimpse of him sliding under the bedclothes. When she emerged a few minutes later and hurried her offspring, now dressed, into the scullery he was protesting in no uncertain terms at the rough manner in which he, a bruised and battered wreck, was being washed. Ginny was certain he would regret having made any reference to his aches and pains. Her worst fears were realised when, after having set her children off on the road to school fortified with large chunks of bread and jam in lieu of breakfast, she returned to her cottage. She could hear Tovell yelling and howling even before she reached her back door and as she entered her living room, Mrs. Gillings was scolding him for behaving like a baby.

'That always amazes me the way you men do carry on. You go do something brave like last night and think nothing of it, but do you go catch a little old cold or something, and you'd think the end of the world had come. Do you hear him, Ginny? All I'm a-trying to do is help ease his pain, but he's a-hollering as though I'm killing him and working hisself up into a muckwash.'

Certainly, Tovell was sweating profusely and Ginny knew she must save him from Mrs. Gillings's heavy-handed ministrations. 'I reckon he's taken all he can for the time being,' she said anxiously. 'The doctor say he's still very weak and ought to get plenty of rest. You leave the liniment and I'll put some more on him when he's had a sleep. I know that'll do him good – everyone knows you make the best liniment going.'

'That I do,' asserted Mrs. Gillings. 'My grandmother gave me that recipe – swore by it. My family hent never used nothing else. There int an embrocation made that's better. I use that on the horse and I use that on myself. Nothing to beat it but you gotta rub it in proper – none of your mamby-pamby stuff.'

'Oh, I'll rub it in proper,' Ginny assured her neighbour.

'Alright then,' conceded the old lady, handing over the bottle. 'That's the only answer anyhow 'cause I've promised Lily I'd go into the village today and see the vicar to make the arrangements for the christening. Seeing as Tovell's much better that seems a shame to disappoint the little old gal.'

'Oh, I agree. Go you see to your arrangements. Lily and little Arthur are your first duty,' urged Ginny. 'I can manage fine now.'

When at last Mrs. Gillings had departed Tovell heaved a sigh of relief. 'Thank Gawd for that. She's the salt of the earth – no doubt about it – but she was literally killing me with kindness.'

'I know – she means well but she does overdo things at times. Anyway, it was my fault really – for oversleeping. That won't happen again,' Ginny promised.

As she approached the bed, Tovell stretched out and grabbed her hand. 'Nothing's your fault – everything's my fault,' he said quietly and earnestly. 'The only thing which matters is this – are we still friends?'

'Of course we are, you old silly. We can't go against our nature – it's too late for that now. I fly off the handle too easy and you .... Well, you're the way you are. We can't do nothing about the way we're made – just accept things. Now, I gotta get you some tea and porridge.'

'Ugh!' was Tovell's reaction. 'I couldn't face either of them. I've got a horrible taste in my mouth. I'll just stick to water for the time being.'

'Water!' cried Ginny in surprise. 'I can see I was wrong – you're not normal!'

XVII

Tovell would have been glad to sleep the rest of that day but he did not get a great deal of opportunity. Everyone on the Station – soldiers and Coastguards' wives alike – visited him. Lieutenant Collins was the first of the military contingent to arrive. He was very solicitous and told Tovell that in his opinion his action deserved recognition and that he had made a recommendation to his superiors to that effect. Next to put in an appearance was Bill Westgate. He accepted Tovell's expressions of gratitude as bashfully as Mrs. Gillings had done earlier. Both men seemed to regard the handshake which they exchanged as symbolic – an unspoken agreement to bury the hatchet. After his comrades and the Station families came Tovell's drinking companions – members of the Volunteer Life-saving Brigade, all of whom just happened to be passing. Ted Carter brought with him the good wishes and appreciation of the mariners from the wrecked schooner. He had been responsible for driving them to Stalham Station that morning and had needed little persuasion to dally awhile to give them the chance to show how grateful they were for the part played by his Brigade. From the colour of his face and the cheerfulness of his mode, it seemed he must have accepted a free drink on behalf of every single member.

'They left a couple of drinks for you an' all,' he advised Tovell. 'Proper gentlemen – that they were. Kath, she say she has put them on the slate for you, so don't you forget now, bor, to call in next time you're in Stalham.'

'He doesn't need any drink,' snapped Ginny. 'What he needs is his rest and he isn't getting any. The doctor say he's gotta have rest.'

'Alright, gal, alright! Hold you hard – I'm now a-going. I've got to anyway 'cause I hent done nothing for the master yet today. Still, he's a good old boy – he knows how important the Brigade's work is, that he do. See you later, Tovell. Fare ye well together.'

'I'm going to put a notice on that there front door,' threatened

Ginny as Ted Carter left. '*No visitors!*'

There were no callers for the next hour and Tovell managed to snatch a sleep but when the children arrived home from school his peace was ended. They were very excited because they had been the centre of attention all day. Everyone knew that Tovell was their lodger and they had been inundated with questions, not only about his exploit of the previous night but about the man in general. The fact that they had both slept through the entire episode of Tovell's part in the rescue, did not deter them. They had enjoyed holding court in the playground and had willingly given colourful accounts of other heroic deeds performed by him, such as his single-handed victories over the Dervishes.

'Oh Gawd,' gulped Tovel as visions floated before him of numerous families being entertained at the supper table by their younger members with glorious tales of his fictitious past. 'I wish you hadn't done that. Those stories were our little secrets. They were only meant for your ears, no-one else's. You see, a really brave man keeps quiet about what he's done. If he's going to go around boasting, well, it detracts from …. No, let me put it another way so you'll understand – he should act bravely because it's his duty and the right and proper thing to do. He shouldn't do it because he wants everyone to praise him afterwards.'

The children, whilst not fully comprehending, were extremely contrite – Lizzie had tears in her eyes. 'Sorry, Uncle Tovell,' said Bobby. 'We didn't know we were doing wrong.'

'I was the one doing wrong, Bobby. I shouldn't have told you those tales in the first place.' Tovell felt guilty – so much so that he was obliged to stay awake and divert the children until their mother had the evening meal ready. 'Don't be upset, littl'uns. Come and sit on the bed and tell old Tovell what you want him to make you for Christmas.'

'A doll,' cried Lizzie at once.

'Alright,' replied the soldier, 'a doll my little lady shall have, and I promise you that none of your school friends will have one like it. I'll make you a Hindu bride doll like some of the little girls have in India.'

"Hindu" made no sense to Lizzie but she was suitably impressed and delighted at the thought of possessing something which would be unique. She needed no encouragement to demonstrate her affection for the bestower of wonderful gifts and promptly smothered him in kisses. Tovell winked at Ginny over the top of Lizzie's head and said, 'She doesn't take after her mother, does she?' Ginny tried to scowl but grinned instead. 'And what about you, Bobby – what do you want me to make you for Christmas?'

'Will you make me a catapult? A really good strong catapult – please, Uncle Tovell. Tommy Stark's catapult killed six sparrows last Friday; I couldn't even get one with my little old catapult.'

'But why do you want to go killing poor little sparrows?' enquired Tovell. 'They aren't doing you any harm and it's not as if they're big enough to eat.'

'Sparrow pie,' giggled Lizzie.

'I'll tell you something, Bobby. In India no soldier ever kills a sparrow.'

'You've got sparrows in India?'

'Oh, yes, Bobby. We've got sparrows in India – as many as you have here, only they're much glossier and cleaner. No soldier would dream of harming a sparrow. They remind him of home, you see – of the British Isles. And the sparrows know this – that's why they're so tame. They come into the barracks and fly onto the table and eat the crumbs. They'll even perch on your cup while you're sitting there and have a sip of your tea. No, don't go killing sparrows. I'll make you a catapult if that's what you want, but only if you'll promise to use it for target practice – you know, seeing how many stones or cans you can hit – not for killing.'

'But you kill men, Uncle Tovell'.

'Ah, yes, I'm afraid you're right, Bobby. But I do have my own code of behaviour, if you like. I only kill when I have to – when it's my duty; when my officers order me to; when it's a case of self-defence – me or him. I can honestly say, Bobby, I've never killed for fun – for the pleasure it's given me. Killing never has given me any pleasure. There are some blokes who enjoy it but they're no friends of mine. Many's the time I've spewed up when I've seen what I've done. No, Bobby, being a soldier's not all glory and daring deeds, believe me.'

By the time supper was ready Tovell was feeling exhausted again. Ginny put some broth in a bowl and took it to him. She helped him to sit up and propped more pillows behind him. He managed a few spoonfuls but his eyes kept closing. 'I'm sorry, Ginny, but I just can't manage any more. I'm so tired ….'

'Yes, I can see that. You haven't had the restful day the doctor ordered. I won't let the littl'uns bother you any more.' She took the bowl and the extra pillows away and helped him to get comfortable. She turned and checked that the children, who were seated with their backs to the bed, were intent upon their meal. Tovell was fast asleep by the time she turned back. She bent over him to adjust the covers and kissed him lightly on the forehead before she returned to the table.

Ginny was careful not to disturb Tovell next morning when she woke the children. He was still slumbering when she returned from seeing them off to school. Quietly, she picked up the tub of wet clothes which she had washed the previous night and crept out of the scullery door. She had finished mangling the clothes and was wiping her washing-line, preparatory to pegging out the laundry, when she was joined by Mrs. Gillings.

'Well, now, how is he this morning?' she asked.

'He's still asleep,' replied Ginny. 'He's that worn out he worries me.'

'Now don't you start that. He's got more than enough worrying over him. He's a brave feller and the good Lord knows I've got every reason to be grateful to him for my Lily and little Arthur, and I don't mean to speak ill of him, but I'm telling you, gal, I'll never forget that day in the church. No, that I won't – not as long as I live. All them slips of mawthers, making sheep's eyes at him – well, I dint know where to look, that I dint.'

Ginny smiled and confessed, 'Yes, I know what you mean. I keep thinking about that an' all. But you've got to admit that the way they looked at him …., well, they were all happy to show they knew him. They all gave him what you might call, welcoming looks. They weren't afraid of him – no, not one of them. What I mean is …., well, whatever it is he does to them, he doesn't hurt them, that's for sure.'

Mrs. Gillings gave her neighbour a shrewd glance and seemed about to comment on her remark. Then she changed her mind and decided to assist her with the washing. The action of hanging up a pair of Tovell's long-johns and straightening out the crumpled crotch area, must have brought her back to the original thread of the conversation for she added, 'Well, whatever it is he do to them silly little mawthers, it can't be nothing like my Henry used to do to me. No woman in her right mind would have stood in line for what he had to hand out. But there, I mustn't run the old devil down. If he'd have been perfect he wouldn't have wanted nothing to do with me, would he now? He was a good old boy really and I still miss him. Yes, even after all these years I still wish he was here.' She sighed deeply and quickly pegged out the last garment. 'Well, I hent got time to stand here mardling and nor have you.' Showing that their little gossip was at an end, she turned abruptly to retrace her footsteps to her own cottage – and caught sight of Tovell stealthily tip-toeing down the garden path. 'Look at that,' she whispered, grabbing Ginny's arm.

Tovell, realising he had been spotted, almost ran the last couple of yards to the privy. Only when he had safely bolted the door did he call out, 'You're not carrying any more slop-buckets for me!'

Ginny appealed to Mrs. Gillings in exasperation but received no sympathy. 'What did I tell you? Stop worrying about him. There can't be much wrong with him if he can do that.'

Mrs. Gillings went into her cottage but Ginny hung around readjusting the washing until Tovell was ready and she could follow him through her back-door. He gave a further demonstration of his determination not to remain an invalid while Ginny was in the scullery drawing water for his breakfast – he dragged his bed back to its original position in the corner of the living room behind the curtain. Ginny found him collapsed across it when she brought the kettle and the porridge pot to the cooking range. She ran to him in consternation.

'Whatever are you playing at? I could have got the other men to do that if you'd have said.'

'I must be getting particular in my old age,' gasped Tovell by way of explanation. 'I didn't like being stuck in the middle of the room yesterday being stared at by everyone – me, who's shared one open room with twenty, thirty or more and not a curtain in sight ....'

'It's only natural you should want a bit of privacy. I'm sorry I didn't think of it myself. Now I reckon you've gone and pulled all those strained muscles again.'

'Yeah,' agreed Tovell, recovering rapidly. 'Looks like you're going to have to rub me down with Mrs. Gillings's horse liniment.' By the time Ginny had fetched the bottle, Tovell was back in bed displaying a bare torso.

'I see you managed to undress in spite of the pain,' commented Ginny archly.

'Didn't want to trouble you,' was Tovell's answer, 'but it was agony.'

'Turn over on your tummy so I can do your back.'

Tovell obliged and murmured with satisfaction as Ginny massaged his neck, shoulders, upper spine and rib-cage areas. As her hands moved rhythmically and progressively over his body he allowed himself to relax and wallow in the pleasant sensation. He had almost reached a state of total euphoria when the source of his gratification suddenly ceased operating. 'What have you stopped for?' he demanded irritably.

'I've finished,' she replied, ramming the cork back into the bottle and giving it a final loud slap to signify her resolution.

'But you haven't done lower down yet, or my front,' argued Tovell.

'You're quite capable of doing lower down and your front yourself,' Ginny retorted. 'I've only done the bits you couldn't reach easily. I'm not here to indulge your every whim, you know. Anyway, I've gotta stir your porridge. Here's the bottle – you get on with it.' Before Tovell could protest further she slammed the liniment on the floor beside his bed and skipped out of reach.

'You're a hard woman at times,' the soldier grumbled.

From the safety of the cooking range Ginny looked back and laughed. Pointing the wooden spoon at him she said, 'And you're a tricky man. I've gotta keep one step ahead of you.'

Tovell did not sulk for long and after his fast of the previous day, he ate a hearty meal. He earned another rebuke from Ginny when she found he had dressed while she was in the scullery doing the washing-up. 'You can nag me all you like,' he told her, 'but I'm not spending another day in bed – not unless you share it with me, that is.'

The last remark brought a scathing look but Ginny did not bother to reply. 'Sit you in the chair beside the fire then. You've gotta keep warm and rest, like the doctor say. Your paper's come; you can read that.'

Tovell whiled away the time until lunch with his national newspaper and Ginny's local one but the war news brought him little comfort and he was constantly shouting out critical comments to her as she went about her chores. By early afternoon he was really fretful and demanded that she sit with him and keep him company.

'I can't do that – I've got work to do. Sitting in the middle of the day – unless you're ill – is a sinful waste of time.'

'Yeah, I know – *the devil makes work for idle hands,*' quipped Tovell, quoting one of Ginny's favourite phrases. 'But please, just indulge me this once. Sit and talk to me – we may not have many more opportunities. From what I was reading this morning about the terrible losses, I could be recalled to my regiment at any time. Let me have a few happy memories to take with me – something to think about when I'm crouching in a cold damp trench, artillery shells bursting over my head ....'

'Oh, Tovell, you don't half know how to tug at a person's heart strings. Alright then,' there was a note of resignation in her voice as she flopped into the chair opposite. 'I'll sit and talk to you, but only until it's time to get the meal ready. It amazes me, that it does, that you're so fond of female company yet you've never been married.'

'Who'd have me?' Tovell gave his stock answer then elaborated on the subject. 'I did have hopes once upon a time but they didn't amount to much. You've got to remember that I've spent most of my army life abroad where there aren't that many women available – not to ordinary private soldiers. I've had two long spells in India and a lot of the NCOs out there had their families with them. Some of them had young daughters of course, and naturally they were in great demand, but what NCO would throw away his little darling to a waster like me?'

'You're a very kind man, Tovell,' said Ginny gently, 'and that counts for a great deal with most women.'

'I never got close enough to an NCO's daughter for her to find out what I was like,' said Tovell ruefully. 'I applied to an orphan school in Bombay twice, for a wife. I knew blokes who'd got wives from there – pretty half-caste girls they were. To tell you the truth, Ginny, it made you feel ashamed to visit the place. It was full of little children who must have been fathered by British soldiers. I reckon the families of the Indian mothers must have chucked the bastards out. At any rate, the poor little babies who ended up at that orphanage were lucky – the nuns couldn't have been kinder. They educated the children and made sure they were nicely brought up, so naturally, they weren't going to give the girls to just anyone. Any soldier wanting a wife had to convince those good ladies that he was a sober character, upright, steady and reliable, and that he had saved enough money to start providing for a family. I know some blokes lied, but when it came to it, I couldn't put my hand on my heart, look those good nuns in the face and swear that I was anything other than a drunkard.'

'But weren't any of your friends married?' asked Ginny.

'A few of them were. And of course, it's the nature of our trade that from time to time wives become widows, but as soon as a woman lost her husband she'd be surrounded by suitors like bees round a honey-pot. Things are different overseas, you've got to understand. The conventions which apply here don't apply thousands of miles from home where there's such a scarcity of white women. And it wasn't just soldiers pursuing them – in India there were a lot of white civilians working for the trading companies. They were always hanging around the camp asking if there were any soldiers' widows to be had. In the face of all that competition I never used to bother to enter the bidding.'

'Hasn't there ever been anyone special in your life?' Ginny asked tentatively.

'I thought so once. I was stationed in London – yes, I have had a few years in this country – and she was a lady's maid. She worked for some duchess and they lived in a big house overlooking Hyde Park. I wasn't a private then – it was the one time I'd made it to sergeant – and I thought I was going to be alright with her. She even took me home to tea twice – to her own home I mean, to Clapham Common where her father was an ironmonger. Her family seemed to like me and I was just plucking up the courage to propose to her when I had a relapse.'

'A relapse?'

'Yeah – you know what I mean. I got drunk, hit an officer and lost my stripes. She didn't want anything to do with me after that. She really rubbed salt into the wound when she told me the reason she'd gone out with me was because it was the only way she could get herself taken to the lavish dances we used to have in the Sergeants' Mess – and to the theatre. That's when I got to be an admirer of Marie Lloyd. After that, I suppose I just gave up trying to find a wife.'

'You were well rid of her,' Ginny stated vehemently. 'She wouldn't have been any good to you. But that seems a shame you haven't married when you like littl'uns so much. Look how well you get on with my Bobby and Lizzie.'

'Yeah – but I don't reckon I shall marry now – not after being here with you. Before, I didn't know what it was like – being a family man, I mean. I had no yard-stick to go by but from now on I'm going to be comparing every woman I meet with you, Ginny, and I can tell you that not one of them is going to measure up. If I can't have the best I'd rather go without.'

Ginny hastily rummaged in her pocket for her handkerchief and blew her nose loudly. 'Oh, Tovell, I do wish you wouldn't say things like that,' she mumbled as she searched for a way to steer the conversation away from the personal to the impersonal. 'And how can you think of us as the best – you, a much travelled man who's seen foreign lands and met all sorts of interesting people. You must find us, and this place, very boring.'

'Oh, I thought at first I was going to find it boring here,' admitted Tovell, 'but the place grows on you. Trudging through the marrams and over the sand dunes day after day, that bleak grey sea out there begins to fascinate you. And the marsh – I love to roam about the marsh. You can sit quite still in the reeds and more different birds than you've ever seen in your life before, will come and sit near you. You've got room to move and room to breathe here. I've always been used to crowded streets and crowded barracks. You'd think I'd feel lonely here in so much emptiness, but I don't. Fact is I've never felt less lonely in my life.

And then, of course, there's you Ginny – you and Bobby and Lizzie. I couldn't begin to tell you what living here with all of you has meant to me. No matter what happens to me in the future, I'll always look back on this time as the happiest I've ever known ....'

'Don't say any more,' begged Ginny, jumping up from her chair, handkerchief pressed to her face again. 'I've gotta go see to the food,' she called out as she disappeared into the scullery. 'And whether you like it or not,' she called back, 'you're getting peeled onions for a vegetable so as I've an excuse for a good howl!'

118

XVIII

Tovell reported for duty next morning. He explained to Ginny that he had never favoured swinging the lead, at least not in wartime, and much as he enjoyed her company his conscience would not let him turn malingerer. Lieutenant Collins promptly sent him back to his billet but conceded that he could have the middle watch provided the doctor, who was expected that morning, gave him a clean bill of health. Dr. Lambert reluctantly yielded under pressure and the afternoon saw Tovell patrolling towards Sea Palling. By dusk, however, the soldier was beginning to regret his hastiness. He was shivering with cold and aching all over. It was difficult to keep his mind from wandering to thoughts of the warm fire and comfortable armchair in Ginny's living room. He made a determined effort to concentrate and once more scanned the horizon. Something caught his eye. He blinked and stared harder. There was nothing – nothing but water. It must have been an optical illusion – after all, he wasn't quite fit yet, was he? There it was again – a tiny black speck bobbing up and down on an ever darkening sea. Instinctively, he fell to the ground, knowing that even in the half-light and at that distance, there was a chance he could be spotted against the fading skyline. He crawled on all fours to the edge of the marram hill, selected a convenient clump of grass to hide behind, and trained his field glasses on the area where he had last seen the moving object. Eventually, he found it. Now he was in no doubt; it was a rowing boat with four – no, five – men aboard. Instantly, a few words from Lieutenant Collins's first lecture flashed through his mind. 'You couldn't have chosen a better place to land,' he growled under his breath. 'Old Tovell's going to be waiting for you.'

He knew he had no time to lose; he must move to a better position before the boat was close enough in shore for its occupants to see him crossing the open sands. Without any further hesitation, aches and pains forgotten he dived head first over the top of the marram hill, rolled down the soft shallow incline and landed flat on his back on the beach below. He had been careful to hold his rifle in front of him, the palm of one hand protecting the barrel from sand, and now he struggled to elbow himself onto his chest. He lay still for a few seconds, peering into the gloom, trying to gauge exactly where the boat would land. He decided that it would probably be about two hundred yards to his right. As he began the long crawl he was thankful for the cover of approaching darkness and reflected that the enemy had chosen their landing place well. He estimated that the spot must be about five miles from Haisbro Lighthouse so there was no danger of the craft being caught in its beam. It was reasonable also to assume that the area would be deserted at that time of day, and perhaps most important of all the road, after it left Sea Palling, curved close to the shore-line at this particular point. At last he reached the shelter of the wooden groyne which he had calculated would be his best hiding place. He crouched there until he had regained his breath, then taking out his field-glasses once more he cautiously raised his head and searched for the boat. He had made the right decision; it was directly ahead of him. He squatted down again although he knew that there was little chance of being seen – the last streaks of daylight had almost disappeared from the sky. He rested his head against the wooden pile and tried to recall from his vast store-house of knowledge, any appropriate phrases of German picked up somewhere, sometime, during his travels. He looked up again – he had no need of the binoculars now – they were very close. Gun at the ready, he felt the excitement mounting inside him. He held his breath and waited, straining for the sound of the boat's keel crunching on the shingle. He heard the splashes as the men jumped into the water; listened as they dragged their craft up the beach. When they were about four or five yards from him, he leapt out in front of them and shouted, '*Anhalten Sie! Anhalten Sie!*'

All five men stopped dead in their tracks. One of the group whispered something but Tovell could not make out what was said. He did, however, distinctly hear the others gasp. The sound gave him a great deal of satisfaction – not only had he foiled their plans, he had given them a nasty fright into the bargain. He stepped to the left and gestured with his rifle that they should precede him up the beach. At the same time he ordered them to, '*Marschieren Sie!*' Still no-one moved. '*Schnell! Schnell!*' he commanded. His captives remained rooted to the spot. It then occurred to Tovell that in the darkness they may not have seen his uniform and could be unaware that he had a rifle trained on them. After all, he was having some difficulty in making out the mode of their dress although he was certain they were disguised as fishermen in calico slops and oilskin smocks. He wondered which of them had thought up the idea of smearing herring oil on their garments. He decided to give them the benefit of the doubt and assume that as he was standing with the marram hills behind him they could not see him – only hear him. He would let them know he had a gun – he fired two shots into the sand just in front of the group. As a man, they leapt backwards and the two in the rear fell over one another. It was all Tovell could do to control his mirth.

'*Schnell! Schnell!*' he yelled again. He got the effect he desired this time and his captives struggled along the beach in front of him as fast as their heavy sea-boots would allow. Knowing they must have rowed some considerable distance – he had seen no sign of the ship which had brought them across the North Sea – he found himself feeling rather sorry for them during the three mile hike back to the Coastguard Station. He had to keep reminding himself that this was not an occasion for showing compassion; that if he allowed them to walk on the marram hills where the going would be easier, he might lose control of the group and one or more of his prisoners might escape over the fields and marshes. He never had been partial to shooting men in the back, whatever the circumstances. Consequently, every time his captives showed signs of flagging, Tovell encouraged them, and himself, to greater efforts by repeated staccato commands accompanied at intervals by shots from his rifle. He was as relieved as they were when he was able to herd them up the wooden steps to the Watch-room.

'Private Tovell reporting with five spies and saboteurs I caught landing on Sea Palling beach, Sir,' he announced to an astounded lieutenant.

'Skipper, they speak English!' cried the youngest of the prisoners.

''Course they speak bloomin' English – they *are* bloomin' English,' growled the oldest of the men looking around at all the charts which adorned the walls of the Watch-room. 'This is a ruddy Coastguard Station. Where's that bloody idiot?'

All five rounded on Tovell, hurling abuse at him and pushing and pummelling him until he backed into a corner. He tried to explain and shouted repeatedly, 'I thought you were the Hun,' but his voice was scarcely heard above the clamour as they all cursed and swore at him. Eventually, Fred Mannell and Lieutenant Collins rescued him and were able to restore some measure of order. The officer attempted to defend his action.

'Private Tovell was only following my instructions, gentlemen. I realise you've suffered a most distressing experience but you must understand that if the enemy wished to land spies and saboteurs on these shores, these remote and largely deserted stretches of coastline would be ideal for their purpose. They would also most likely disguise their men as fishermen – it's the obvious thing to do – and would drop them in a small open boat from a warship under cover of darkness.'

'But he dint give us no chance to explain,' protested the skipper. 'He jumped out at us, hollering some gibberish that the mate say was German, and we thought *he* was the Hun. That looked like Norfolk had been invaded whilst we were at sea and we'd landed in occupied territory. And when he started shooting off his bloody gun at us that was my lot. That was bad enough when this here ruddy U-boat popped up alongside us at dinner-time – cor, blast bor, I nearly messed myself then – but to be met by this raving lunatic …. He int safe, y'know. You should have seen him run us along that beach – that must have been a good three mile – and heard him too, a-shooting off his bleedin' gun. That's a miracle I dint die of heart failure – a man of my age – that that is. You don't want to go letting him loose with a weapon again – he might kill someone next time.'

Lieutenant Collins refrained from commenting on the advice and instead tried to divert the skipper from his ranting by enquiring about the earlier incident. 'You say you were attacked by a U-boat, skipper?'

'That we were. Ruddy thing came up alongside us and ordered everyone into the little boat. While we watched, them bastards stole our catch and any other stores they fancied, and hopped it back to their pig-boat. After they were gone the *Mary Lou* blew up. They'd set a time-bomb down in the chain-locker, y'see. They dint want to waste a torpedo on a little old sailing smack, that they dint. Int that right, boys? The buggers always order the crew off then plant a bomb in the fish-hold or the chain-locker.' The skipper's statement was vociferously confirmed and he continued his story. 'Something will have to be done. There ent that many boats fishing – only old muck. The Navy's already requisitioned the best steam vessels. Only the old sailing smacks are left to go fishing and the way the Hun is carrying on, they ent going to last long. That's the same with the Yarmouth fleet and the Lowestoft fleet – the U-boats are sinking them hand over fist. I don't know what my owner's going to say; the *Mary Lou* will be the third boat he's lost. He had a devil of a row with the Navy blokes last time. He asked 'em if some of the boats could have a gun put aboard so they could protect theirselves and this here Navy Commander just laughed at him. My owner was wholly raw, that he was.'

'I think perhaps one can understand the Navy's reluctance to arm a fishing boat,' said the lieutenant gently. 'Once you have a gun aboard you become a warship and the Germans would feel justified in torpedoing you from a safe distance. I doubt whether they would treat you as they did today.'

'That may be so, Sir, but that can't go on like it is with so many boats being lost. What my owner's going to say I don't know and,' the skipper glared at Tovell once more, 'what he's going to say about the way we've been treated by them that should have helped us, I don't know an' all.'

Seeing trouble brewing again, the lieutenant acted quickly to dismiss the offender. 'Your watch was over some time ago, Tovell. You can report to me later.'

'Yes, Sir! Thank you, Sir!' replied Tovell who needed no persuasion to retreat from the line of fire. As he told Ginny minutes later, 'It was like facing a lynch-mob. What they wouldn't have done to me, given half a chance ....' He feared the episode would haunt him for some time to come. He was right; the news travelled fast. The very next occasion he entered the bar of the *Admiral Lord Nelson* he was greeted by cheers and a chorus of, 'Caught any more spies lately, bor?'

XIX

'*Rule Britannia, Britannia rules the waves ....*' Mrs. Gillings was in excellent form, Britannia personified, as she stood beside the piano in Lydia Brewster's parlour singing her heart out. Those particular lyrics were, perhaps, an unusual choice for such a party, but the entire christening had been unusual. Mrs. Gillings's relatives had travelled from Great Yarmouth to be present and the vicar, being a perceptive man, had decided to combine the christening service with what amounted to a memorial service for the baby's late father. In his experience, people needed to publicly mourn their dead. Since, in the absence of a body, he could not provide them with the usual means of expressing their sorrow – a funeral – he made an appropriate extension to the christening service. The proceedings had ended with a well-known hymn for those at sea, *Eternal Father, strong to save*, so it was little wonder that Mrs. Gillings, feeling that the gathering required an injection of patriotism to counter the depressing war news, chose to open the celebrations with a reminder of her country's invincibility on water.

The baby appeared to find nothing unusual and remained good humoured even when passed around all those who wished to admire him. He had been duly named Arthur David Alec Gillings after his father and his saviours. The latter had also been appointed his godfathers. David had been delighted but Tovell had regarded it as a dubious honour and had gladly deferred to his junior when the question had arisen of who should hold the baby at the font. It was David too who watched the little one's progress anxiously as he circulated from lap to lap at the party whilst Tovell, with a certain amount of relief, returned to duty.

The young soldier was unable to contrive a way of getting Lily to himself, surrounded as she was by her relatives, but he gained considerable comfort from the knowledge that he had a legitimate excuse for maintaining contact with her for years to come – the welfare of his godson. He did, however, manage a few quiet words with her at the closure of the celebrations.

'There, you see, I was right. I kept on telling you how happy you'd be once you had the baby.'

'Yes, you were right, David,' agreed Lily. 'I am happy now. I've got little Arthur and lots of relations too. Did you see them all? They'd come all the way from Yarmouth. They didn't come to my wedding – I can't remember why. You don't know what that means to me to be part of a real family.'

'I reckon I can understand, Lily. And I hope you count me as one of your family. You know I think a lot of you Lily, and of the littl'un. Thank you for letting me be his godfather. You know I'll do the job proper. Anytime you need anything – either of you – you've only gotta ask. I'd do anything for you, Lily – that I would.'

There was an embarrassing silence during which neither dared look at the other. Lily broke it by suddenly thrusting her infant into the young soldier's arms with the words, 'He say he hasn't had a cuddle from his godfather yet.'

David laughed. 'He's a little beauty, isn't he? I only wish I could take you both home with me. I know Mother and Father and Annie, and all the littl'uns, would love you just like ....'

This time Mrs. Gillings came to the rescue. Bustling into the parlour from Mrs. Brewster's kitchen she called out, 'Put that there child back in his crib for Lord's sake. The amount of attention he's having he'll be ruined, that he will. Come you on and give us a hand now. There's plenty of clearing up to do yet and I've got to drive the relations back to the station.'

David immediately made himself useful whilst Lily, cradling little Arthur in her arms, went outside to wave good-bye to the members of her family whom she had welcomed so eagerly for the first time, a few hours before. As they disappeared from view, Lily could hear her mother-in-law urging the horse along with a second rendition of *Rule Britannia*. She found herself humming the same tune as she returned to the house to assist her neighbours with the task of restoring the Station Officer's residence to the pristine condition it had enjoyed before the christening party. It was as well that they did not delay, for the very next day the parlour was required for a meeting of a quite different kind – a meeting which showed that in one part of the world at least, Britannia most certainly did not rule the waves.

'So here I am visiting you again to perform the same dreadful duty – to offer my condolences to the bereaved,' said the Divisional Officer as he wearily accepted the cup of tea proffered by Lydia Brewster.

'We commiserate with you, Sir,' stated the lieutenant sincerely. 'You have an unenviable duty.'

'I suppose this time I can offer some comfort to the poor widows,' said Mr. Latham. 'At least their loved ones have not come to an ignominious end brought about by some pig boat. They had the honour of engaging the enemy in battle.'

Richard Collins shook his head and for a moment, Lydia thought he was going to challenge the remark. To her relief, he controlled the urge to argue, commenting instead, 'The first of November, you say.'

'Yes, it happened on the first. They're calling it the Battle of Coronel. The action took place off a town of that name. As I understand it, Admiral Cradock was proceeding north up the coast of Chile hunting for a German squadron commanded by Admiral von Spee. Regrettably, our ships were technically inferior to those of the Hun. When the two groups met, Admiral Cradock's flagship, an old cruiser called, ironically, the *Good Hope* was hit by one of the Germans' more powerful battleships, the *Scharnhorst*. Our ship blew up and sank with all hands. As you will have guessed, a great many of the crew were coastguards. The other ship in the squadron which had many coastguards among her complement was the *Monmouth*. She too was hit but managed to limp away – only to be caught by the *Nurnberg*. She capsized in ten minutes and again, the entire company was lost.'

'And the battle itself?' asked Lydia.

'A total defeat for the Royal Navy,' answered Mr. Latham. 'Merciful, is it not, that Admiral Cradock went down with his ship?'

'It is indeed,' agreed Lydia.

'They'll be burning the midnight oil at the Admiralty tonight,' observed the lieutenant ruefully. 'First the totally unexpected scourge of the U-boats and now defeat on the high seas in a conventional battle.'

'Yes, there will be many questions asked and quite rightly so. We've always been so proud of our Navy,' said Mr. Latham. 'I suppose we've been guilty of over-confidence and of under-estimating the enemy. I'm thankful these issues are not my responsibility. My concern is if the Fates remain so unkind, will there be any coastguards left to return to our shores?'

Richard looked sharply at Lydia. She was clearly distressed by what the Divisional Officer had said. 'Let me accompany you to the homes of the widows, Mr. Latham. You were seen arriving, I've no doubt, and all the families will be worried.'

'Yes, you're right, Mr. Collins,' said the Divisional Officer as he pushed back his chair. 'We'd better go at once.'

Lydia was still sitting at the table, looking pale and withdrawn, when Richard Collins returned. She had not heard him enter the room and was startled when he sat down beside her and spoke to her. 'You must try not to worry, my dear,' he said gently. 'Oh, I realise it's easy for me to say but worrying is such a futile pursuit.'

'I know, but I can't help worrying,' protested Lydia. 'It's as though there's some kind of curse on coastguards for so many to lose their lives in such a short time.'

'Come, my love. An intelligent woman should not give way to superstition. It's not logical.'

'Logical! What has logic to do with it? I'm worried that it may be my husband's turn next. That has nothing to do with logic and everything to do with caring.'

'And with guilt. You tell me you no longer feel guilt, but I think that's what's eating at you now. You're overcome with guilt that your husband may be dying whilst you're romping with me. By worrying you hope to assuage your shame and, perhaps, at the same time to protect your husband by covering him with the shield of your worry.'

'Oh, Richard, those are harsh words.'

'Yes, but they're honest words. And honesty is the cornerstone of our relationship.'

Lydia nodded but said nothing. She continued to stare ahead of her, a look of despair in her eyes. Richard watched her for a few moments before getting up from the table. 'I think, my dearest, I'd better leave you in peace to continue your soul-searching. Indulge yourself – suffer agonies – so that when I return your torment will have purged you and your feelings of guilt, so inconvenient from my point of view, will have vanished. I'm certain, with just a little effort you'll be able to come to terms with your predicament.'

'At times you're so selfish and heartless.'

'How true, my love, but surely I've every reason to be selfish. Obviously, in your distress, another aspect of this sad business has escaped you. If the coastguards are being lost at an unacceptable rate, those remaining will be recalled and returned to their former posts to train another generation. Is it not possible that in a few weeks time, your husband may be standing where I'm standing now, and you may be worrying – dare I hope – what fate has befallen me in the trenches of Flanders?'

The first Tovell knew of the most recent tragedy was when he met Bill Westgate as he was returning from patrol. 'The lieutenant's waiting to speak to you in the Watch-room, Tovell,' Bill told him. 'Another two of the poor devils have had it – Mary's husband and Ginny's husband.'

Tovell's heart missed a beat. In his confusion, the only thing he could think of to say was, 'Those blasted U-boats. When are they going to do something about them?'

'It wasn't a U-boat this time,' replied Bill. 'Mr. Collins said it was the German fleet – off South America somewhere. I was covering the Sea Palling look-out for Fred, so I've only just heard myself. Mr. Collins said I'd better get back to my billet straight away and see how poor Mary and the children are taking the news.'

Tovell hurried to the Watch-room and when he left again a few minutes later, the lieutenant's words, 'Prepare yourself to face a household in mourning,' were ringing in his ears. When he entered the cottage he still had not decided what he was going to say to Ginny. He prayed that the correct expressions of sympathy would come into his head when he needed them. The children were playing happily in front of the cooking range so Tovell concluded that Ginny had not yet broken the news to them. 'Where's your ma?' he asked.

Bobby replied. 'She don't fare very well, Uncle Tovell. She's in there.'

Tovell looked towards the bedroom door which was ajar. He could just make out a form on the bed. He approached as quietly as he could. He had never set foot in the room before nor even seen inside. He could tell from the light filtering through from the living room that Ginny was in a deep slumber. Her face was half-buried in the pillow; in her hand she clasped a handkerchief. It was clear that she had cried herself to sleep. Tovell glanced around the room, found a bedspread folded on a chair, opened it and gently covered her with it. He closed the curtains and left the room, shutting the door silently behind him.

He noticed that the fire in the range had gone down and he tended that straight away. Lizzie came and stood beside him as he worked and said, 'I'm hungry, Uncle Tovell. Will Mother be getting up soon?'

'No, Lizzie – she's asleep. I think we ought to leave her – it will do her good. Old Tovell will get your supper tonight.'

Lizzie laughed. 'How are you going to do that, Uncle Tovell? You're not Mother.'

'Oh, you'd be surprised what I can do, Lizzie. Of course, it won't taste as nice as your ma makes, but it'll stop you going hungry. You come and help me look for the things we need.'

Bobby joined them and both children enjoyed the novelty of watching Tovell's culinary efforts. When they were all seated at the table Tovell remembered just in time to say grace. As they ate he considered whether he ought to ease Ginny's burden by telling the children about their father's death. He was on the point of doing so when Lizzie announced, 'You can stay here forever now, Uncle Tovell.'

'What do you mean, Lizzie?' enquired the soldier with some trepidation.

'You don't have to go away now,' the child explained. 'Before, whenever we asked Mother if you could stay always, she say, "Only till Father get back." But he isn't coming back now, so you can stay.'

'That's right, Uncle Tovell,' added Bobby enthusiastically. 'Mother told us afore she went to lay down that Father isn't coming back, so you don't have to leave us any more.'

The children went on eating totally unaware that their remarks had shocked Tovell by their apparent callousness. He had been struggling with his own conscience ever since Bill Westgate had informed him of Ginny's widowhood. He had been ashamed of himself for thinking immediately of how he might gain from the death of a fellow fighting-man. He felt compelled, therefore, to say some words of correction to the children. 'Now I know you're only littl'uns and don't really understand what you're saying,' he began gently. Before he could continue there was a rap on the back door and Mrs. Gillings strode into the living room.

Seeing the food on the table she said, 'Ah, I see Ginny's alright then. I wondered if she'd been up to getting your supper ....'

'Uncle Tovell got the supper,' declared Lizzie.

'Well I never did in all my born days!' exclaimed Mrs. Gillings. 'And here was I thinking that all he was good for was boozing and whoring.' A few weeks previously she would have meant her remark literally; now she intended it as a joke. Tovell accepted it as such.

'I'm not all bad, you know. I do have my good points, though not many.' He went on to explain in more serious tones, 'Ginny was asleep when I came off duty so it seemed better to leave her.'

Mrs. Gillings nodded her agreement. 'Well, if she int up on time in the morning you've only gotta knock on the wall. I'll soon come in and get your breakfasts. And if the littl'uns are any trouble in the night just do the same.'

When their neighbour had left both children were anxious to assure Tovell that he would not need her assistance. 'We won't be any trouble,' they promised. 'You won't have to get Mrs. Gillings to us.' As though to confirm that they intended to be on their best behaviour, they promptly cleared the table and showed such willingness to be helpful that Tovell could not bring himself to deliver the lecture which he had planned.

After the three of them had washed up and put away all the dishes and cutlery, Tovell supervised the ritual of getting ready for bed. Both Lizzie and Bobby were in their nightclothes, faces shining, hair brushed, when their mother, ashen-faced and swollen-eyed, burst through the bedroom door in a state of near panic. She took one look at the children and cried, 'Oh, my God, what's the time? I've gotta get your supper.'

'Uncle Tovell gave us our supper.' The honour of making the announcement was claimed by Bobby on this occasion.

'Oh no!' gasped Ginny. 'Oh Tovell, I'm so sorry. Bobby, Lizzie, you should have woken me. What a thing to do – you coming home and no supper ready.'

'What does it matter, Ginny? I'm not exactly helpless,' chided Tovell gently.

'I know you're not but that does matter. I was neglecting my duty. If it had been my husband ....' Her voice trailed off and she covered her eyes with her hand.

Tovell led her to a chair and said kindly, 'Don't let it bother you, Ginny. We managed alright. Lizzie and Bobby helped me. They were little heroes, weren't you?' The children ran to their mother eager to tell her how clever they had been. While she listened and wiped away her tears, Tovell poured her a cup of tea and brought it to her. 'We kept you some supper – it's on the steamer – but I don't expect you fancy it yet.'

'Not yet – perhaps later. But thank you, Tovell, for all you've done.'

'I haven't done much.'

'Well, you won't have to do it again – I'll be myself tomorrow. I shouldn't have given way like that.'

'I understand, Ginny, really, but since it means so much to you I won't argue.'

Ginny was as good as her word; she was up at her usual hour next morning. Over the next few days she went about her chores as normal although she was very quiet and withdrawn. If she cried any more it was not in Tovell's presence or hearing. Many times he caught her with a troubled far-away look on her face and he longed to take her in his arms and tell her not to worry for he would take care of her and the children. He stopped himself because he was convinced that if he made his move too soon she would be so offended he might lose her forever. Tovell told himself that he had been alone too long to risk spoiling his chances of future happiness by acting in a premature unseemly manner. He was, in fact, so afraid of saying the wrong thing that he reverted to his former habit of saying very little. He waited patiently for Ginny to recover and was surprised when only a week after her bereavement she resumed her customary quiet singing whilst engaged upon her favourite morning chore – the black-leading and polishing of her pride and joy, the cooking range. He was thus encouraged to speak to her about her late husband before he went on duty. 'Ginny, I've never said how sorry I was about your loss. I didn't want to speak too soon and upset you. I wanted to give you a chance to get over the shock.'

'I know, Tovell,' Ginny replied with a smile. 'You've been most considerate and I appreciate that.'

'I've wanted to ask if you think you'll manage alright.'

'Oh yes, we'll manage. The Admiralty won't kick us out of the house just yet. They told Mrs. Gillings there was no hurry when Arthur was killed. I reckon they'll want us to stay on while you soldiers are here – to look after you. After that – well, I've got plenty of relations I can go live with.'

'But what about money, Ginny? I'd be glad to help you.'

'You're a good man, Tovell – so generous – but we shall be alright. I'll get some sort of pension, I reckon, and if we can't live on that I can always go back into service. Like I say, I've got a lot of relations. One of them would be glad to look after the littl'uns for me while I work.'

Tempted by how well the conversation was going, Tovell pushed his earlier resolutions aside. 'Surely it won't come to that, Ginny. I expect after a while, when you've got over the initial upset, you'll maybe want to get married again.'

'Married! Me, wanting to get married again! That's something I'll never want to do. I've been married once and that's enough. No, that'll never be – we'll manage fine.'

To emphasise her displeasure at what was obviously an appalling suggestion, Ginny abandoned the polishing of her grate and withdrew to the scullery, slamming the living room door behind her. When Tovell found the courage to follow her she was pummelling the clothes which had been soaking in the sink with such vigour that he decided he had better leave. He paused briefly as he opened the back door. 'Sorry, Ginny. I didn't mean to upset you.' She did not look up or reply and sorrowfully, he made his way down to the sea-shore.

He still had thirty minutes to go before his watch and he spent the time throwing pebbles into the water with as much force as he could muster. He cursed himself repeatedly for his folly in not sticking to his intention. Why, why, had he mentioned the future so soon? And how had he misjudged the situation so badly? Obviously, Ginny was a long way from being reconciled to her husband's death, and by declaring so vehemently that she would never allow anyone to replace him, she had proved that she loved him much more than Tovell had anticipated. He could see now that she must have been concealing her grief for the sake of the children. He must be very careful not to tread on that ground again. He must say nothing further but concentrate on making himself indispensable to both Ginny and her young. It was his only hope. If they all came to depend on him, she might relent. He would have to keep trying however many rebuffs he received. There was no doubt whatever in Tovell's mind that more than anything else in the world he wanted Ginny as his wife.

After the third tragedy in six weeks it was difficult for the women of the Coastguard Station to throw off their despondency. Three of their number had been widowed and Mrs. Ellis was still in Edinburgh nursing her badly burned husband. From the one short letter which had been received from her, she was likely to remain there for some time. It was little wonder that the other two women, Emily Foster and Phyllis Bishop, whose husbands were still alive and well, should be thinking along the same lines as Lydia Brewster. No longer could they console themselves with platitudes; instead of, 'It can't happen again,' they were obsessed with the thought, 'Whose turn will it be next?' Emily and Phyllis, after a hurried consultation and knowing how trying and tactless small children could be, volunteered to take care of Ginny's two and Mary's three at any time. They could think of no other way to help their neighbours other than to provide them with the opportunity to mourn in peace, and no other way to help themselves other than to keep as fully occupied as possible.

There was no comfort to be found either in the way the war as a whole was progressing but indignation at what she was reading in her morning newspaper was enough to restore Lydia's fighting spirit the morning after Mr. Latham's latest visit.

'I really cannot believe this is happening,' she exclaimed to Richard at the breakfast table. 'First the U-boats take a dreadful toll of both naval and merchant vessels; yesterday we hear of defeat on the high seas and today, to add insult to injury, we learn that they have dared to approach our very doorsteps and fire on our homes. Are we totally powerless against the Germans? And as it says here, no-one would expect enemy battle cruisers to cross the North Sea and bombard an English town. What's the world coming to when the civilian population are made a military target.'

'I doubt the Hun saw it that way,' said Richard, looking up from his newspaper. 'Great Yarmouth is a military base so they were after the installations, and we know that the bombardment was a cover for mine-laying operations.'

Lydia would not be appeased. 'What about the Naval Air Station? It used to be the Coastguard Station until last year when the Admiralty decided to convert it for the Air Service. It's on Yarmouth beach itself with uninterrupted views out to sea. How could they fail to see the enemy ships approaching?'

'There was nothing they could do, Lydia. As you know, they ceased patrolling the coastline last month because they had no machines in service. I've spoken to the Station Commander; he only had a single *Longhorn* in the hangers on the third, and that was being overhauled. Had it been operational and on patrol then yes, it would have sighted the warships and been able to alert our fleet, but that would have been the limit of its action. You're suggesting they should have intervened, but how could they when they're not armed?'

'But they should be armed,' insisted Lydia.

'A reconnaissance aeroplane? My dear, you know how easy it is to speak with the benefit of hindsight, but this bombardment came as a complete surprise. But the Commander tells me that the Admiralty is so shocked that they've promised him more machines to restart the patrols and, from now on, they'll have a passenger as well as a pilot and the passenger will carry a rifle. And he also said that the Admiralty has ordered all Naval Air Units to mark their machines on the underside of each wing with a Union Jack.'

Lydia smiled. 'Well, that's a little victory in itself. And we must be thankful that the Germans are such poor shots. It says here that the shells fell mostly on the foreshore.'

Richard shook his head. 'It would be wrong to assume they were poor shots. Those who should know have come to the conclusion that the Hun took their range from the St. Nicholas lightship. Had the attack come a few days earlier the shells would probably have landed on target but what the enemy didn't know was that the light-vessel had recently shifted her moorings. It's safer to assume that Providence rather than faulty gunnery saved Great Yarmouth.'

'Well, we must be thankful for that,' conceded Lydia, 'although I see little other cause for rejoicing. It seems you were right – the war will not be over by Christmas.'

'There is no chance,' agreed Richard. 'This newspaper thinks that the system of trenches now stretches from the Channel coast in the north almost to the mountains of Switzerland in the south. How do you defend an unbroken Front of say, four hundred miles? How many millions of men will it take? No open land so no room for manoeuvre and no flanks, only the sea on one side and the mountains on the other, so no possibility of getting around or behind the enemy. What a situation ....'

'I suppose the only way to raise enough men is by conscription – as they've already done on the Continent,' said Lydia.

'It would be against the principles of a Liberal Government but they cannot rely on a call to arms forever – even if men are responding in their thousands,' observed Richard.

'Yes, their posters have appealed to the patriotic.'

'I doubt whether patriotism has inspired all the recruits – many of them, yes, but others will be escaping from something, whether it be hunger, unemployment or,' he added with feeling, 'a hated way of life. But I mustn't be cynical ....'

Ginny saw the war news from a much more personal point of view. With her husband dead, all her concern was for her brothers. 'You don't reckon they'll be home by Christmas then?'

'I can't see it,' replied Tovell regretfully.

'But everyone – everyone in power – said it would be over by Christmas.'

'Everyone but Lord Kitchener,' replied Tovell. 'He's always

maintained that we're in for a long bloody struggle. I was with him in the Sudan and again in South Africa. I know he's a good bloke, Ginny. If he says we're in for a long struggle, we're in for a long struggle. I'd rather take his word before the rest of them. And anyway, he's already been proved right, hasn't he? Both sides have dug in. They're facing each other from the longest line of trenches in history. They could still be there years from now. I reckon it will be a case of which side can hang out the longest. At the moment, I'm afraid our chances don't look too good. You know I got a letter this morning? It was from my old pal, Jim Wade. He's in hospital in London recovering from his wounds. He's with the Queen's Royal Regiment and he says when they crossed to France on the twelfth of August their total strength was nine hundred and ninety eight men, all ranks. What do you think they're down to now?' Ginny shook her head. 'They're down to two corporals and twenty seven men.'

'That doesn't seem possible!' gasped Ginny.

'I know but it's a fact – no officers, no other NCOs and only twenty seven men. I knew a lot of the blokes in that regiment – that's why I cleared off first thing this morning and took Blackie for a long walk. They weren't novices, Ginny; they'd seen plenty of service. If that can happen to one regiment – and remember, the war's only been going three months – it can happen to the rest. You could have a situation where all the seasoned soldiers are wiped out in the early months. That would leave only the raw recruits – the poor devils who are volunteering in their thousands at this moment – to man those bloody trenches.'

'So you don't hold out much hope for my brothers?'

'I can't say, Ginny. I wish I could sound more cheerful and give you hope but I don't know how things will turn out. I bet even Lord Kitchener doesn't know. There's never been a war like this. All I'm sure of is you shouldn't count on your brothers being home for Christmas. But don't despair – your brothers are tough – tougher than most. They'll have more than an even chance of surviving. You never know, I might meet up with them soon and I'll give them your love.'

Fortunately, there was little time for Tovell to become depressed, either at the thought of the many friends and former comrades he was losing on the other side of the Channel or at the thought that he could shortly be called upon to leave Ginny to replace them. The weather had once more deteriorated creating a manpower problem for Richard Collins as he strove to cope with the number of ships needing assistance. For a while, he was forced to confine everyone to the Station on permanent stand-by in order to make the best possible use of his meagre resources. Horrifying as the war being waged on the continent of Europe was, it was not for the moment as real or as urgent as the war being waged with the sea.

The lieutenant, in his opening address to the soldiers, had stressed that the coast to which they had been sent was subject to fierce storms. Haisbro Lighthouse, he had informed them, had been built to warn ships of the presence of what were reputed to be the most treacherous shoals off the English coast – the Haisbro Sands. These lay about nine miles from the shore and in places were covered by only a foot of water. Surrounded as they were by perilous currents, they had been the graveyard for hundreds of vessels. Lieutenant Collins had also explained that among the duties they had inherited from the coastguards was not only the responsibility for the life-saving apparatus but also the expectation that they would assist in the launching and manning of the lifeboat provided by the Royal National Lifeboat Institution. When it became clear that the soldiers' time as replacements would not be as brief as had been thought, he invited the local lifeboat coxswain to visit the Station before the bad weather set in, to give the men basic instructions.

Tovell was well acquainted with the coxswain, a large red faced man with a bushy white beard who was a frequent customer at the *Admiral Lord Nelson*, but his admiration for the man increased after he had listened to his lecture. 'The type of vessel we use hereabouts is called a Norfolk and Suffolk lifeboat. It's unique to these shores. It's what you call a sailing and pulling boat because it's got oars as well as sails. The Royal National Lifeboat Institution doesn't really favour sails and they're forbidden in most areas but they make an exception for us because of the distances we usually have to cover to reach a wreck. As you know, there are sandbanks several miles out along the East Anglian coast. In spite of the Haisbro Lighthouse on the cliffs and the Trinity House vessel, the Haisbro lightship out at sea, them bloomin' sands off here are a deathtrap. We'd never get to a stranded ship in time if it weren't for our sails.

But I've gotta be honest with you boys, she's a heavy boat – has to be – and she isn't self-righting. You won't find her very comfortable but she's safe enough. You've got ridge ropes to grab hold of along the gunwhales so you shouldn't go overboard. But I must tell you that the most dangerous time is at the launch. Generally speaking, we go off under sail but sometime that isn't possible and we have to use setts – that's long poles – to push the stern and haul-off warps – ropes on an anchor – at the bow. But if a heavy sea were to catch her broadside and overturn her, there wouldn't be anything anyone could do for the poor devils trapped underneath – not with a heavy Norfolk and Suffolk lifeboat on top of them. As I recall, that happened at Aldeburgh once and six of them lost their lives. Then again that happened at Caister and nine of them were trapped underneath. Forty four children were orphaned that night – I'll never forget that. At the inquest they said the crew shouldn't have gone out in such dreadful conditions, but a former crewman who'd lost two sons and a grandson in the disaster stood up and he say, "Caister lifeboatmen never turn back." Well, I reckon he was speaking for us all. The way we look at it, if we're freezing cold and frightened half to death, what state are the poor buggers in who are waiting for us to rescue them? What I'm a-trying to say boys is, unless you're prepared to stick it out whatever the weather, don't bother to come along in the first place.'

Lieutenant Collins was excluded from being a member of the lifeboat crew because he was not allowed to be off-station for long periods. He devised a rota for the other six men to ensure that no one person had an unfair share of the dangers and each soldier took his turn to either help with the launch or crew the boat. They were all thankful for the rota; no-one wanted to join the regular lifeboat volunteers who, for the most part were fishermen by trade, more often than was absolutely necessary once they realised what a gross understatement it had been to say that they would find the experience, "not very comfortable".

Tovell's worst experience of a rescue came in mid-November when a ketch ran aground on a sandbank some eight miles offshore. In spite of the fact that it was midday when the lifeboat set out visibility was bad and even though they were under sail it was hours before they reached the stranded vessel. The heavy boat had ploughed through the waves and plunged into the troughs safely enough but as the huge seas broke over the vessel the crew had been submerged momentarily and thrown from side to side against the hazardous assortment of gear which a lifeboat carried. Tovell had spent most of the voyage clinging grimly to the ridge ropes. He was protected well enough in regulation oilskins and cork life-jacket, except at the neck where streams of water, channelled by his sou'wester, escaped down his back. He shivered in the bitter wind and icy water and dreaded that when they reached the stricken vessel it might be deemed necessary to stand by and wait for the next high tide in the hope that it would float the ship off the sandbank where it had run aground. It did not matter whether the sea was merely undulating or whether it was so rough that the lifeboat pitched and tossed, all the soldiers suffered from seasickness in those circumstances, to a greater or lesser extent. In Tovell's case, he found it impossible when standing by to keep even a morsel of the iron rations which the lifeboat carried, inside him.

Tovell need not have worried; standing by was the last thing on the coxswain's mind as they approached the ketch. They had battled their way through horrendous seas and with a blizzard blowing, the coxswain, standing at the tiller, had had difficulty in locating the ship. Once he had sighted her, he shouted his orders above the gale. 'Sail straight ahead, boys! Maintain this course! Don't lower the sail!' Tovell was aghast and thinking that the man had taken leave of his senses, he glanced quickly round and saw at once why the coxswain was ignoring the standard drill. The plight of the crew of the ketch was desperate. The vessel was already waterlogged and the men were clinging to the mast and the rigging. They were chest high in water and the next big wave would overwhelm them. The coxswain had no alternative but to sail his boat right over the bow of the ketch if the men were to be saved.

Tovell braced himself for the collision with the wreck. As the keel of the lifeboat crashed onto the submerged deck of the ketch, the coxswain, hands cupped around his mouth, yelled to the crewmen, 'Jump boys! Jump!' The three men hurled themselves forward and grabbed hold of the ropes suspended along the sides of the lifeboat.

They were quickly dragged aboard – Tovell's reaction was only a split second behind that of the other rescuers – as the lifeboat hit the ketch's deck for the second time. Then a gigantic wave swept them up, swung the lifeboat around and dashed her against the already weakened forward main-mast of the ketch. The mast collapsed instantly and as it fell it caught the lugsail of the lifeboat, ripping it apart. Next the mast tore into the lifeboat's mizzen, entwining its ropes and spars around the mizzen-mast. The wave threw the lifeboat clear of the deck of the wreck but the ketch's broken foremast was carried along with her and its weight threatened to drag the lifeboat under. The coxswain called out, 'Hatchets boys! Clear the lot!' Tovell and the other men struggled to release themselves from the fallen rigging. They grabbed their hatchets and chopped furiously into the ropes until they had freed themselves from the ketch's mast. Then they turned their attention to their own mizzen-mast, splintered and leaning perilously over, still burdened by rigging torn from the wreck. They hacked into the wood until their frantic efforts severed their mast and they were able to hurl it into the sea along with its shredded mizzen-sail and tangled rigging from the ketch.

The danger was far from over; the lifeboat had been extensively damaged both from the impact of hitting the deck of the ketch twice and from striking the mast of the ship. Water poured in where the lifeboat had been holed and through the blinding snowstorm, the coxswain could see that the gale was driving his vessel back towards the sandbank. With no sail at all aft and the foremast damaged and its lug-sail in ribbons, the lifeboat was in danger of being grounded herself. 'To the oars, boys! Row, boys!' yelled the coxswain. It then became apparent that only six men, Tovell among them, were capable of rowing, the others having suffered injuries in varying degrees. Somehow, those six managed to summon up enough strength to heave the waterlogged boat away from the swirling currents. They took many minutes to row against the fierce gale to a safe distance away from the sandbank. Only then did the coxswain give the order to cease rowing and drop anchor.

The coxswain and the second coxswain then moved carefully around the boat, trying to assess the damage to both men and vessel. In the poor light they gave what little aid they could to the injured. The lifeboat was low in the water and listing to starboard so those who were able to, made every effort to lighten the load on that side. They also shifted the injured men to the port side. They accomplished this in spite of the furious gale, the blinding snowstorm and the mountainous sea which hurled the frail craft violently about as though she were already mere flotsam. Darkness fell – all hope of reaching the shore was gone. The coxswain knew his men could not go on. He himself was close to exhaustion having stood at the tiller for hours. He made his decision. 'We'll rest here at anchor until first light. Get what sleep you can, boys.'

Tovell, like the other rowers, slumped over his oar. As usual, whilst action was needed, he felt no nausea but now that they were anchored he was tormented by sickness. Although he had no solid food inside his stomach he retched repeatedly. He could not remember a longer or more bitterly cold night. As the sea became calmer, he dozed a little. The coxswain roused them all at daybreak. The storm had abated.

'We'd better have a roll call of sorts, boys. Tell me your condition,' said the coxswain.

'I'm alright,' replied the second coxswain, 'but one of the poor devils from the ketch has died during the night.'

'What a bloomin' shame. And after all that …. What about the other two?'

'They're alive but only half conscious.'

'We've gotta get them ashore quickly.' The coxswain turned to the rest of his crew. 'What about you, bowman?'

'When their foremast fell on us it busted my arm,' replied the bowman. 'Ernie and Derby are still stretched out here. It hit them an' all. I reckon they've got concussion.' Two more men reported injuries; one had suspected cracked ribs and the other had a gashed head and crushed fingers.

The coxswain addressed the oarsmen. 'Well, I can see you boys are covered in cuts and bruises but the other five are in a worse state, so there's nothing else for it – you're going to have to row us the eight miles to shore.' In low spirits they pulled for the distant coastline. After an hour of painfully slow progress with the second coxswain doing his best to plug holes and bail out water, the rescuers were rescued themselves. A steam tug sighted them and the skipper, realising their plight, diverted from his course, threw them a line and towed them to within a few hundred yards of their lifeboat shed. The six oarsmen took over again and rowed for home with renewed vigour, cheered on by the people crowded on the beach who had stood in silent vigil anxiously watching and waiting for their return. Thankfully, all Tovell had to show for his twenty hours at sea was some frostbite on his knuckles, broken blisters from so much rowing and sore muscles around his middle from ineffectual vomiting.

XX

Tovell may have hated standing by at sea but he had no objection to standing by on land. When the lieutenant confined him to the Station in his off-duty periods he no longer found it a hardship, rather he welcomed the opportunity to remain with the little family he now regarded as his own. Frequently, as his watch came to an end he would survey the sky hoping he could report the approach of storm clouds and put the idea into his officer's head that there might soon be ships in distress. He still liked to visit the *Admiral Lord Nelson* at least two nights a week but his dependence upon alcohol was gradually waning. He was also glad to exchange the company of the young ladies of the locality for the company of Ginny and the children.

He had always taken a keen interest in the children's education, asking them about their school work and helping with any problems they had. Now he felt entitled to increase his involvement and he encouraged them to sit with him for a while in the evenings practising their reading, writing and sums. They found this new turn of events somewhat irksome so Tovell bribed them with promises, which he always kept, that he would play with them or relate stories after they had completed their work. Always, he gave them the same explanation for his insistence that their schooling was of major importance. 'You don't want to grow up like old Tovell. I was a fool – never wanting to learn when I had the chance.'

On one occasion Bobby challenged this argument. 'But you've done alright, Uncle Tovell.'

'Only because I joined the Army,' answered Tovell. 'Where would I have been otherwise? I'd have turned thief to stay alive and probably spent most of my life in prison.'

'Did your mother want you to be a soldier, Uncle Tovell?' asked Lizzie.

Tovell smiled and shook his head. 'I ran away from home long before I joined the Army. No, it wasn't my mother who wanted me to be a soldier – it was a policeman. He was always catching me doing something I shouldn't and giving me a box of the ears instead of reporting me. His heart was in the right place and I reckon he must have seen some good in me. When he found out I was sleeping rough he gave me an ultimatum – either I went with him to see his pal and listen to what he had to say, or he'd take me to the Police Station and lock me up. I didn't have much choice, did I? Anyhow, it turned out that his pal was a recruiting sergeant and between the two of them they convinced me that the Army was the best place for me. There was one snag – I was barely sixteen but I swore I was eighteen and as I passed the tests for weight, height and measurement, they let me join. I've never regretted it. They were right; the Army was the best place for me. Everything I know I learned in the Army. Accepting the Queen's shilling – that's what they presented you with when you joined – was the cleverest thing I ever did.'

'The Queen's shilling? You mean the King's shilling,' stated Bobby.

'No, Bobby. It was the Queen's shilling. Queen Victoria was on the throne in those days. The Queen Empress she was – ruler of nearly a quarter of the world. Yes, I was proud to be a soldier of the Queen, helping to defend her Empire and keep the peace.'

'So did the Army make you learn to read and write?' asked Lizzie.

'In a way, Lizzie. I didn't learn at school – I was hardly ever there. I couldn't see the point of learning until I saw a lot of the old soldiers in my barracks paying this other soldier to read their letters to them and write their replies. Well, I thought, he's onto a good thing so I asked him if he'd teach me. He said he would since he'd be leaving the service in a few months and I could take over his trade. I had to pay for the privilege, of course, and it cost me dear. We used to get a shilling a day less three and a half pence for our food. As I was still growing then, most of what I had left went on buying more food. When he said he wanted six pence a day for teaching me, I knew I'd have to be a fast learner or starve. Fortunately, several of the men in our barrack-room were heavy drinkers – really heavy drinkers, worse than I've ever been – and they were light eaters. Booze can do that to a man – take away his appetite. Anyhow, it worked in my favour because at night, after lights out, I'd crawl around the room feeling along the shelves for anything uneaten. Even a dry crust was welcome!

And I made up my mind to help myself by getting as much practice as possible at reading. We had a regimental library and I spent as much time as I could studying there. Most of the books were on military strategy and past campaigns, so I must have been the best informed private in Her Majesty's Army. But I also got into the habit of reading newspapers – your ma knows it's a habit I haven't lost. I had this pal – he worked in the Officers' Mess – and he used to collect together the papers the officers left behind and pass them on to me. For the first time in my life I became aware of another world outside my own little existence. Learning to read will do the same for you, littl'uns.'

'I'd like to be a soldier when I grow up,' declared Bobby. 'I want to be like you, Uncle Tovell.'

'But not too much like me – I've done a lot of bad things that I've been sorry for afterwards. For one thing, don't drink like me – that can get you into all sorts of trouble – and as I keep telling you, learn all you can while you're still at school. You too, Lizzie ....'

'But I don't want to be a soldier,' protested Lizzie.

'Of course you don't. You're going to grow up as pretty as a picture, just like your ma, and all the boys will be begging you to marry them. But you still need to learn – if only so you can help your children with their school work.'

'Uncle Tovell's right,' said Ginny who did not normally intervene in such conversations. 'I've been glad that you've had someone to help you with your learning – I'm sorry I'm not much of a one for writing and reading myself.'

Tovell was encouraged by the remark; she was conceding that he was a benefit to the family in one respect at least. Perhaps his plan to make himself indispensable to them all would work – that is, if there were sufficient time left. He could only take each day as it came and assume as much responsibility for the family and the household as Ginny would allow. She was still at times very preoccupied, as though some worry was nagging at her and Tovell's efforts to persuade her to confess what was troubling her only served to irritate her – as did the children's high spirits. On such occasions he would take Lizzie, Bobby and Blackie for long walks, knowing that Ginny would strive to recover from her strange mood before they returned. His pleasure in such excursions had not diminished with the passage of time; he enjoyed the children's company as much in November as he had in August.

Bobby and Lizzie were happiest if they could trick Tovell into a state of reminiscence. They were fascinated by all he told them about his life in foreign lands and on one bright chilly day, as the three of them wandered along the coastal path towards Haisbro Cliffs, the dog running back and forth in front of them, Bobby said, 'Blackie doesn't half like you, Uncle Tovell. Have you always kept a dog?'

Tovell shook his head. 'I haven't had much to do with dogs, Bobby. I remember quite a few dogs marched with us in South Africa. They were strays which attached themselves to the soldiers so they could cadge food. They'd be adopted as pets by the regiment as a whole. No, I never got that fond of a dog but I'll tell you what I did keep as a pet in India – a mongoose.'

'A mongoose? What's a mongoose?' asked both children together.

'How can I describe it?' pondered Tovell. 'Something like a ferret but longer. It's about eighteen inches long and grey in colour with a very long tail. People in India keep them because they're so good at killing snakes.'

'Snakes?' said Lizzie with a shiver. 'Are there a lot of snakes in India?'

'Yes, Lizzie,' replied Tovell, 'and they're very dangerous. My little mongoose saved my life several times. I used to carry him around with me tucked in the top of my tunic. His little head used to peep out between the buttons and his bright eyes didn't miss a thing. He was an affectionate little creature and many a night he kept me from falling asleep on guard duty.'

'That's bad, is it, Uncle Tovell, to fall asleep on guard duty?'

'Bad – it's downright wicked, Lizzie. If you aren't keeping a sharp look out when you should be, the enemy can get close and kill all your pals. But it's not always easy to stay awake when you're tired from marching all day, so I was glad I had Brighty to keep me company.'

'Why didn't you bring Brighty home to England with you, Uncle Tovell?' Bobby asked. 'Lizzie and me would have loved him.'

'You'd have loved him alright, but I'm sorry to say he was killed eight months ago. It was a king cobra that got him – a huge snake fourteen feet long. They're so big and fierce that they live on other snakes. Of course, in his time little Brighty had killed lots of ordinary cobras and they grow to seven feet. A mongoose is very clever; he knows he's got to outwit the snake because the snake's bite is venomous – poisonous. In a straight fight the mongoose knows he couldn't win – the snake's got the best weapon – so he doesn't attack him head on. Instead, he races round the old cobra at top speed, keeping out of striking distance of that bite. The snake rears itself up and spreads its hood – cobras have something like a hood for a neck which can expand – and turns its head from side to side trying to catch the mongoose as it circles. After a time the snake gets tired, and dizzy I reckon, and it lowers its head for a rest. That's the moment the clever little mongoose has been waiting for; he leaps up, sticks his teeth into the back of the cobra's head and hangs on for grim death until he's won the fight.'

'But what happened to Brighty? How come he didn't win?'

'Well, like I said, Bobby, it was a giant king cobra that got him. It would have had me if Brighty hadn't seen it first. He went through the same drill as if it had been an ordinary cobra but I reckon he must have misjudged its reach. It bit him but it didn't stop him. He went on fighting till he'd killed it but a few minutes later he died himself. A lot of people had told me that couldn't happen – that a mongoose wouldn't be affected by a snake bite – but it certainly killed my little Brighty. He was such a brave and loving creature I couldn't bring myself to replace him.'

'You should have got a dog,' said Lizzie sympathetically. 'Dogs wouldn't have had nothing to do with snakes.'

Tovell laughed. 'Talking of dogs,' he said, looking around, 'what's happened to Blackie? He's left us.'

'There he is, Uncle Tovell,' shouted Bobby, 'down on the beach. He's found something.'

Instinctively, Tovell restrained the children. 'You two wait here while I see what it is that Blackie's worrying.' He slithered down the cliff-side and had only advanced a few yards across the beach when the dog danced out of his line of vision. He was then able to see quite clearly that something dark, metallic and rounded was half-buried in the sand. He approached very cautiously. He was almost certain that he knew what it was. Blackie was encouraged by his interest and apparently decided that a proper performance was warranted. He immediately began to attack the invader, running forward and giving it a little push with his two front paws accompanied by a loud yap, then jumping back, spreading himself low on the beach and growling, as though challenging the object to get up and fight. The soldier at once dropped to his knees and yelled to the children to flatten themselves. 'Here, Blackie,' he called as persuasively as he could. 'Here, boy – come to Tovell.'

The dog took no notice. Tovell called again and again. Blackie would not be diverted. Well aware of the risk involved if he made a false move, the soldier crawled on all fours until he was within reach of the dog, then lunged forward, pounced on the animal and dragged him under his body. He was able to hold the struggling dog there only by locking both arms around Blackie's neck and chest, and by gripping the animal's hindquarters between his thighs. By leaning to one side he was able to take a close, if brief, look at the object. He did not need to linger for very long – as soon as he caught a glimpse of a horn almost hidden in the sand all doubts vanished. Pulling the dog along with him, he retreated a few yards, still on all fours, before getting to his feet, both hands firmly grasping Blackie's collar. He scrambled back up the cliff-side, dragging the animal with him, and called to the children as he approached, telling them that they could get to their feet. Tovell could see from the fearful expressions on their faces that they had sensed danger and he tried to choose his words carefully so that he would not alarm them further. 'Bobby, have you got any string in your pocket?'

'Yes, Uncle Tovell,' replied the boy, surprised.

'Then tie it through Blackie's collar lots of times to make a leash you can get your hand through, while I hang on to him. We don't want him running off again.' Tovell did his best to appear calm while Bobby strove to carry out his instruction. When he was satisfied that the dog could not escape, he explained quietly what he wanted the children to do. 'Both of you are to go straight back to the Station taking Blackie with you. When you get there find Lieutenant Collins. He'll probably be in the Watch-room. No, on second thoughts, go straight to the Watch-room and give whoever is there this message. Say that we've found a mine on Haisbro beach just below the lighthouse. Tell them that Tovell is standing guard by the mine to stop people going near it but that he needs someone to bring him some tools so that he can make it safe. Now, have you got that, littl'uns? Tell them that we've found a mine, where it is and that I need some tools. Remember, you're on a very important mission and it's very urgent, so don't dawdle, will you?'

'No, Uncle Tovell – but what's a mine?'

'I haven't got time to explain now, Bobby, and anyway, you've got to hurry and deliver that message. Be careful, both of you. Off you go and whatever you do, don't let go of Blackie.'

Tovell waited impatiently a few yards from the mine, scanning the beach to the right and the left of him, and the cliff-top behind him, but no human and no animal came near. After about half an hour he began to worry whether the children had failed to follow his directions, or whether they had garbled the information to such an extent that they had not been understood. He was considering what his next move should be when he sighted three figures hurrying towards him. As they approached he saw that they were Mr. Collins, Ned Jackson and Fred Mannell. 'I was beginning to think the littl'uns had got the message wrong,' said Tovell when the group was within earshot.

'No, they were most explicit but I had to inform all the proper authorities before I left the Station,' explained the lieutenant. 'Gather round everyone and let's examine this find. Not too close, Jackson. Yes, it's quite definitely a mine – you can just see the outline of a horn resting in the sand. There are probably at least four of those horns situated around the top of the mine or any number projecting from various points on the casing. Pity the tide has buried the wretched thing so well. Until we've cleared away the sand we won't know what we're up against, but at least you men now have a better idea of what to look for when you're out on patrol. It could well turn out that this is the first German mine washed ashore anywhere. No doubt it's part of the batch laid by the enemy earlier this month when they bombarded Great Yarmouth. Something tells me that the highly speculative advice given by the Admiralty on this subject will not be of much use. However, I'm sure that they are correct in one aspect; the horns are the most dangerous part of this vile invention.'

Richard Collins paused for a moment and surveyed the area. 'I've endeavoured to acquaint the local constabulary with the presence of this hazard to life and limb but unfortunately, Haisbro's village policeman is not, according to his wife, at home. As substitute coastguards, responsibility for the safety of the public as well as responsibility for defusing the damn thing must, therefore, be ours. Jackson, you'd better stand on the cliff where you can see anyone coming from either direction. Remember to stand well back from the edge – just as a precaution. And you Mannell, position yourself about four hundred yards along the beach and stop anyone approaching from Haisbro. I'm not too concerned about the beach to the south of us – I left orders with those on duty in the Watch-room to keep a look out for pedestrians.'

'Excuse me, Sir,' said Fred Mannell. 'If this thing does go off, how far will the bits fly?'

'I've no idea, Mannell. Neither the Admiralty nor the War Office has any real idea how German mines are constructed or how they work. As I've already said, this may be the first opportunity that anyone has had to study a mine at close quarters. Let's pray that we live to pass on the information which we glean from this example. As for your personal concern, I think you can rest assured that you will be safe at four hundred yards. At that distance you would certainly hear the explosion and have time to flatten yourself before you were assailed by any fragments – human or otherwise.'

'Yes, Sir. Thank you, Sir,' stammered Mannell.

'Well, be off with you both and keep a sharp eye open.'

'Good luck to you, Sir, and to you, Tovell!' called both soldiers as they ran to take up their appointed stations.

The lieutenant looked sharply at Tovell. 'Can I assume that you have no objection to remaining in close proximity to this ball of destruction for a little longer?'

'I've got no objection, Sir,' replied Tovell.

'Good. Then let's get to work. The first step is, obviously, to dig away the sand.' The two men knelt down on either side of the mine and commenced to scoop away the grains with their hands. Whenever another horn was revealed they would use only their fingertips. Progress was, of necessity, slow and neither man spoke a word but concentrated totally on the difficult operation before him. The silence was broken only by the sound of their laboured breathing. When at last two thirds of the mine's surface had been exposed and they could sit back and rest, both men had beads of perspiration trickling down their foreheads.

Lieutenant Collins reached behind him for the canvas bag he had brought with him, saying as he did so, 'I fear the next stage will take even longer – but then again, it may end very quickly. I suggest, Tovell, that you take cover under the cliff. There's a section – there, man, you see where I mean – which juts out a little. It should afford you some protection and at the same time, you should be close enough to hear what I have to say. We've been specifically instructed to make notes and diagrams of what we find when dismantling a mine. I shall, of course, obey that order, but in case my literary and artistic efforts are blown to the four winds, I propose to describe to you exactly what I see.'

'I'd just as soon stay here and give you a hand, Sir.'

'That would not be logical, Tovell, and potentially it could be wasteful, but I appreciate the fact that you volunteered. And I do have the better chance of survival since I've studied the information, albeit largely hypothetical, put out by the Admiralty, whereas all you know about sea-mines is what I've passed on to you – namely, that you should watch for round metal objects with horns. No, you must take cover by the cliff.' Still Tovell hesitated. 'I'm giving you an order, man. Hurry up!' When Tovell was in position the officer called to him. 'Can you hear me clearly?'

'Yes, Sir,' answered Tovell. 'I can hear you.'

'First I'm going to try to loosen one of the horns manually.' There was a short silence before the officer continued. 'No, that doesn't work. I shall have to use one of the tools. I'm assuming that the horn was screwed on at the final stage of assembly …. The problem is I dare not apply too much force to turn the damn thing in case …. Ah, it moved …. Yes, it's definitely coming loose …. I'd better just use my fingers now – dare not apply too much pressure at this point …. I think it's almost free …. Must lift it off very very gently …. Ah, it's clear. Now I can see what's underneath. It's a glass tube, Tovell, a sealed glass tube containing some liquid. It must be an acid. I can understand the principle; if anything knocks against the horn – jars or bends it – the glass tube inside will be broken instantly. The acid will then be released and will leak through to the detonator, setting off the explosives. Simple but effective! I'm going to make a diagram and notes of what I've seen so far …. There, that will do.

I've a box in my bag, Tovell. I'm going to half-fill it with sand and place the tubes of acid in it as I recover them.' After a couple of minutes the lieutenant said, 'The box is ready. I'm going to remove the first tube ….It's clear of the mine …., and safe in the box.'

'The others will be easier, Sir,' shouted Tovell encouragingly.

'I hope you're right,' replied Richard Collins. Slowly, one by one he removed each horn and rendered its glass tube harmless. 'Just two more left, Tovell. Unfortunately, they're on the underside of the mine. I shall have to turn it over to get to them.'

Seconds later, Tovell heard the lieutenant cry out. He reacted involuntarily pushing himself into the cliff-side and protecting his face and head with his arms. Nothing happened. He peeped out and saw the officer stretched full length on the beach hanging on to the mine, a look of desperation on his face. Without hesitation, the soldier rushed to the officer's aid. He flung himself down on the sand so that his body was between the mine and the water and braced both hands against the metal casing. He was careful to avoid the two remaining horns which were only inches from the hard wet sand of the foreshore. 'It's alright, Sir,' he gasped. 'I've got the ruddy thing; you can let go.'

'Thank you, Tovell, thank you,' muttered the lieutenant unsteadily. He lifted himself up onto his knees and wiped his sweating palms on his trousers. 'I don't know how that happened – must have lost my grip.'

Between the pair of them they heaved the mine over so that the horns were pointing up towards the sky. 'I'll hold it steady for you, Sir, while you deal with the last two,' suggested Tovell.

'I'm grateful to you, Tovell, but it would be wrong for me to endanger your life so unnecessarily. All I need is for the mine to be stable. We could carry it back up the beach to where it was before and embed it in the soft sand, but I think that would be too risky. No, the answer is to pack wet sand around the abominable contraption so that it cannot move again.' As soon as he was satisfied that the mine could roll no further, Lieutenant Collins asked Tovell to fetch his tools, notebook and the box containing the tubes of acid. 'Thank you, Tovell. I can manage alright now. You go back to the cliff.'

Tovell, even more reluctantly, resumed his former position and waited anxiously while the officer completed the operation. They were both equally relieved when Richard Collins called out, 'It's done – finished. The thing is harmless.' Tovell scrambled down the beach to where the lieutenant was sitting, half-collapsed, with his head between his knees.

'Well done, Sir!' cried Tovell in congratulation.

'A nerve-wracking experience, Tovell, and one I should not care to repeat. Look at me – shaking like a leaf.'

'It's delayed shock, Sir,' Tovell assured him.

'Fear more like,' said the lieutenant. 'I've never been so frightened in my life.'

'But you still did the job, Sir.'

Richard Collins smiled to himself as he got to his feet. 'I must pull myself together before I call in Jackson and Mannell. They'll have to carry the mine back to the Station then the Admiralty can have it and take it to pieces. Where are my diagrams? Ah, yes .... I'm afraid I shall have to draw those again. Rather spidery, don't you think?'

XXI

Tovell had not forgotten his promise to make Christmas presents for the children and made the most of any free time he had whilst Bobby and Lizzie were at school. He had embarked on quite an ambitious programme, firstly because he wanted to make the children happy but secondly, because he wanted to ensure that he would be remembered when he was no longer part of the Adams's household. He had promised Lizzie a doll but then decided to give her a crib for the doll as well. He had promised Bobby a catapult, 'for target practice only', but then decided that that alone was not sufficient; he must have a fort and soldiers as well. Tovell turned out to be an excellent carpenter and wood-carver and Ginny complimented him on his skill. 'I've had plenty of opportunity to do this kind of thing,' he told her modestly. 'Time can hang heavy on your hands, especially on a troopship – thousands of miles to cover and nothing much to do. You'd have your drills and inspections and your duties, but most of the time was your own. A lot of the men belonged to gaming or card schools .....'

'I wouldn't have thought the Army would have allowed gambling,' commented Ginny.

'They didn't allow it – officially. Someone would have to be on guard keeping a look out for the provost-sergeant and his men. I like a game of cards generally, and a gamble occasionally, but I never went in for it much on board ship because the men played down below on the troop-deck, and you know what I am for seasickness. My main aim at sea was to get up on the top deck in the fresh air. I felt better there and if I could lay my hands on a bit of wood I was happy to pass my time whittling some figure or other. And there was plenty to look at. The rising and setting sun can be a grand sight and you've got dolphins and porpoises, flying fish and spouting whales to watch. Yeah, thinking about it, I reckon the sea always has had a fascination for me, even before I came here.'

'It always has for me,' agreed Ginny. 'I've lived by the sea all my life and I couldn't live anywhere else.'

Tovell thought of the picture he had of Ginny indelibly printed on his mind where she was standing on the cliff-top near the lighthouse against a backdrop of a sparkling sea and he wanted to say, 'I would never ask you to live anywhere else but by the sea. All I want is to live there with you.'

Ginny must have seen something in his eyes or sensed somehow that he was no longer thinking of wood carving for she suddenly put aside her mending and said, 'The basket's nearly empty. I should have brought some more fire-wood in before I started cooking.'

'You sit still,' Tovell said at once. 'Chopping fire-wood and logs and bringing it in is my responsibility. I should have noticed.' He put aside his handiwork, got up from the table, picked up the basket which stood by the cooking range and went out by the back door. Having filled the basket, he was about to return to the cottage when he saw Sergeant Harris with Peter, Mrs. Ellis's youngest son and the only child she had still living at home. From the rods on their back he could see that they had been fishing. He put the basket of fuel down and walked over to them.

'Where have you been to this time?' he asked.

'We tried further south from Eccles beach,' replied Jack Harris. 'We've been there since first light. I promised young Peter here that we'd have another go the first time I got a whole day off duty. He said the recent gales would blow up some cod, didn't you, boy? And he was certainly right.'

'Look what we've caught, Mr. Tovell,' said Peter. 'There's enough cod here to give everyone on the Station a good feed.' The boy opened up his sack and the one the Sergeant had been carrying. He held up the biggest fish to be admired.

'Well, that's a beauty,' exclaimed Tovell. 'And you've got enough there to open a market stall.'

'No, we always share things between the families,' replied Peter, taking him literally. 'We all do.'

'Well, we'd better make a start and get this lot gutted and cleaned,' said the sergeant. 'Then you can take them round to the other mothers. C'mon, son. Bye, Tovell.'

Tovell smiled as he watched Jack Harris lead Peter to the Ellis's back door with his arm around the boy's shoulder. He was still smiling a few moments later after he had gone back indoors and placed the wood basket beside the cooking range.

'What are you grinning about?' asked Ginny.

'Jack Harris,' answered Tovell. 'He's taken to being a family man with the same relish that I have. He's just come back from yet another fishing expedition with young Peter. They're full of it.'

'Peter used to spend a lot of time with his father. With his mother gone too he'd have been completely lost without Mr. Harris. He's been really good to him. To be fair, all you soldiers have helped with the littl'uns. Mary say she doesn't know what she'd have done without Bill Westgate – he's been marvellous with her three. They were very fond of their father …. And Mr. Westgate say that's just like being with his grandchildren, so I reckon they've helped each another.'

Tovell went into the scullery, washed his hands and then returned to the table to continue with his present making. After a few moments, Ginny put aside her mending once more, got up from her armchair and sat down at the table in front of him.

'Tovell, I don't know how to say this,' she began tentatively, 'because I don't want to cause offence, but I'm worried about the things you're making for Christmas. It isn't that I begrudge the littl'uns having presents, or that I'm not grateful to you for making them, but they just aren't used to having these kind of things. They do hang their stockings up Christmas Eve, that's true, but all I can afford to put in them is a bit of fruit, some nuts and perhaps a few sweets or something. They've never had anything big – none of the children have.'

'You're worrying about what's going to happen next year and the year after, aren't you? I can understand that,' said Tovell kindly, 'but I'm going to try to take care of it. I've made up my mind – from now on I'm not going to drink all my money away like I have in the past. You must have noticed – I've already cut down. I only go to the pub about twice a week now. I'm going to save as much as I can and send it to you. Perhaps you'll be able to put some aside to get the littl'uns something at Christmas. And I'm going to ask the Army to let me name you as my next-of-kin. That way when I do catch it, anything I've got coming to me will go to you.'

Ginny turned abruptly away from Tovell. As she wiped a tear from beneath her eyes she said, 'Who'd have thought a gentle man like you would make me cry so much. I don't know what to say …. You're too generous Tovell, but we can't accept your money – that wouldn't be right.'

'But I want you to have it,' Tovell insisted. 'I don't reckon I shall have much to leave, but whatever there is, why should the Army keep it when you can do with it?'

Ginny shook her head vigorously, her handkerchief covering her mouth to stifle her cries. As she struggled to control her emotions, Tovell lent across the table towards her and was about to touch her when she suddenly darted up from her chair and ran over to the cooking range.

'Now look what you've made me do!' she moaned, staring into the stewpot. 'Another minute and supper would have caught.' She reached for a wooden spoon and stirred the contents of the pot energetically. Without looking up from her labours she added, 'I do wish you wouldn't keep talking like you're sure you're not going to make it. I know you've lost a lot of your friends but that doesn't mean the same has to happen to you. In fact, the way you're going on is asking for trouble; that never does to tempt fate.'

'Alright, I won't mention it again, but whatever you say I'm sending you what money I can. You know I haven't got any family, Ginny, and all I'm really asking is that you allow me to look on you and the littl'uns as my family. If only you and I know, would that be so wrong?'

Still sniffing loudly, Ginny chanced a quick glance and a smile in Tovell's direction. 'You aren't half an old silly at times,' she said. 'You know very well that Bobby, Lizzie and I already think of you as family. No-one has ever been closer to the littl'uns than you, nor meant more to them – no, not even my brothers. Now why don't you stop upsetting me and get them things you've been making hidden away before that's too late. School must have finished half an hour ago – they'll be home soon.'

Tovell packed away the half-finished toys and hid them on the highest shelf in the darkest corner of the cupboard – all except the bride doll. 'I'll hide this in my kit bag,' he said to Ginny. 'I'll ride into the village when I get a chance and see if I can buy something fancy for the sari.'

'Oh, no!' cried Ginny in alarm. 'You don't want to do that.' Any reference to Tovell's efforts at needlework caused Ginny concern. For reasons which she did not understand herself, the sight of her lodger bent over the doll he was fashioning for Lizzie troubled her. She had offered to do the job for him but he had refused on the grounds that a promise is a promise. He had intended to buy all the materials in the village but Ginny had insisted that he use the calico which she always kept in stock, for the body, and that he stuff it with the scraps she had in her work-basket. Was this out of concern that he should maintain his manly reputation? She had told him that she wished to save him unnecessary expense, which was true as far as it went, and had thought that there was no longer any risk that he would be informing the local shopkeepers that he was making a doll. "Sari" she did not understand but "fancy" she did. 'They won't have anything fancy there. Your best bet's Lily next door. Lady Meredith let her keep some bits and pieces of material when she left the Hall. She'll give you something out of her treasure box – as she calls it. I'll take you next door now.'

'But I thought you were worried about the supper burning,' said Tovell in surprise.

'That'll be alright if I put it to one side of the hob. C'mon, now – before the littl'uns get back.'

Minutes later and Lily was displaying her precious collection of scraps. To Ginny's relief, Tovell quickly made his choice. 'This will do fine. Thank you very much, Lily. I'm much obliged.'

'You're very welcome, Mr. Tovell,' said Lily shyly.

Mrs. Gillings, meanwhile, had been admiring the doll which she had taken off Tovell as soon as he had entered her living room. He had dyed the calico a very pale shade of brown before painting the face. He had used black wool for the hair. The effect, as Ginny had been the first to admit, was quite beautiful. Mrs. Gillings was lavish with her praise. 'That's a master fine doll you've made – that that is. Young Lizzie will love it. I reckon you've tricolated it up a treat. All credit to you, bor, for having a go. I like to see a man that int dependent on a woman to do everything for him. 'Course, being on your own, you've had to turn your hand to anything and I must say, that don't matter what needs doing, you always make a good job of it.'

'Keep this up, Mrs. G and my head won't fit in my cap. I'd better go,' said Tovell laughing. As he made his way into the scullery and headed for the back door, Mrs. Gillings followed him, still singing his praises.

Lily suppressed a giggle. 'First he couldn't do nothing right and now he can't do nothing wrong.'

'How times have changed,' agreed Ginny. 'And I'm grateful to you an' all, Lily. He was threatening to go down to the haberdashers for the fancy stuff. Just imagine! That would've been all round the village in no time that my poor lodger has to do his own sewing.'

It was true; Tovell could no longer do anything wrong in Mrs. Gillings's eyes. What had begun the day he had gone into the sea to save Lily, had reached completion a few days before the incident with the fancy material. Mrs. Gillings had had the misfortune to slip on the ice outside her back door early one morning. It was still dark when Tovell came off duty just after six but he had heard her struggling to get up as he was about to enter his billet. He immediately went to her aid and with extreme difficulty – she weighed as much as he did – managed to get her off the ground and back into her living room. Lily was sitting by the cooking range giving the baby his first feed of the day. She was alarmed to see her mother-in-law, who never ailed anything, in obvious pain.

'Now, now, Lily,' gasped the old lady as Tovell helped her into her armchair, 'do you attend to the littl'un and don't worry about me. I'll be right as rain time I've got my breath back.'

'But you're hurt; I've gotta see,' cried Lily. Young Arthur let out a wail of protest as his source of sustinence was suddenly wrenched from his mouth. 'I'll feed him later,' Lily said as she hastily buttoned up her dress.

'That you will not,' declared Mrs. Gillings as her grandson asserted himself even more loudly. 'You do as I say, gal, or he'll fill hisself full of wind from crying and have colic all day. There int nothing wrong with me. I only slipped and twisted my foot.' She reached forward and eased her left leg off the hearthrug.

Tovell at once knelt in front of her, pausing only to say to Lily over his shoulder, 'Don't worry, Lily, I'll check and see what's the matter.' He unlaced Mrs. Gillings's boot and gently removed it. Even through the thick stocking he could see the ankle swelling up. 'I'll go over to the Watch-room and get them to telephone for the doctor,' he said.

'There int no need to trouble the doctor – that's only a sprain.'

'But you may have broken a bone.'

'There int nothing broke – that feels like a sprain. The white of an egg beaten to a froth and mixed with powdered alum, is all that needs. Remember that remedy, bor, if ever you get a sprain. Spread that mixture on a bit of old cloth, wrap it round tight and bandage it and that sprain will be cured in a few days. But afore I do that I gotta see to the horse ....'

'Oh no, you don't! Tovell's giving the orders now. You're staying here and I'm seeing to the horse.'

'What do you know about horses?'

'More than you think. I had my own mount in South Africa.'

'You never mentioned afore that you were a cavalryman.'

'I haven't mentioned it because I never was a cavalryman, as such. Do you remember the Boer War?'

'I remember. I lost a cousin at Ladysmith.'

'Well, you'll remember that after all the defeats in Black Week they sent out Lord Roberts to take command because he'd had experience of fighting guerrillas in Afghanistan. He raised units of mounted infantry to match the Boer horsemen. I volunteered straight away – having marched thousands of miles in my time, the thought of riding for a change was very appealing. Once I got used to it we made a good team, Rajah and me. I was very fond of that horse so you need have no fears for old Prince. I'll see he's fed, watered, groomed and mucked out the same as if you were doing the job.'

Tovell kept his word and the horse had first class attention throughout the following week. The soldier went even further and gave the stable the most thorough clean it had had in years, polished Prince's harness until it shone and gave the cart a fresh coat of paint. In addition, he took upon himself all the heavier daily chores which the old lady reserved for herself, such as digging the garden and carting coal. When she had recovered sufficiently to make a tour of inspection, Mrs. Gillings left Tovell in no doubt that he had finally been taken into the fold. 'We'll make a countryman of you yet, bor' she promised warmly.

XXII

Tovell chanced to be in Haisbro near lunchtime and since he had not seen his friends for several days he decided to pop into the *Admiral Lord Nelson* on the off-chance of any of them being present. Ted Carter was at the bar with three other members of the Volunteer Life-saving Brigade. All of them greeted the soldier cheerfully and loudly. It only took one drink to loosen Tovell's tongue and he was recounting another of his anecdotes. On his way into the public house he had passed a funeral procession going into the churchyard and this had reminded him of a frightening experience he had had whilst on guard-duty outside a mortuary in India.

'Cor blast, Tovell, you don't half talk some squit at times!' exclaimed Ted Carter.

'Squit! It's the gospel truth. It was a very nasty thing to happen to a bloke, I can tell you. No-one ever wanted that particular duty anyway because the mortuary was so far from the rest of the camp. It was downright eerie – at night. A ravine ran along the back of the building and it was full of cobras. You'd be standing there trying to cheer yourself up and a bloody great cobra would glide across the path in front of you. There were so many rats and bandicoots about you were under orders to bang on the mortuary door every so often with your rifle butt to scare them away from the body. On top of that there'd be the howling of the jackals. Oh, it was a weird place alright. The strongest character was believing in ghosts after a few hours alone there, so you can imagine the shock I got when this particular night the corpse got up and started hammering on the door and calling, 'Let me out! Let me out, chum.' Who'd think a doctor could make a mistake like that? It was lucky for the poor bugger that he'd been brought in near dinner-time. Had it been earlier in the day they'd have done a post-mortem on him straightaway and finished him off for good and all.'

'Well now, that's a pity we dint know you were a bloke that's partial to the supernatural or we would have told you afore about our local ghosts,' said Ted Carter with a wink at his companions. 'I reckon we were neglectful not to warn you considering all the night patrols you have to do, bor. Now let me see – there's the Eccles monster that rises from the sea, and Old Shuck, the dreaded ghost of a wolf-hound. Big as a calf he is, black as the night with eyes of fiery red. If ever you hear a hound padding behind you, run for your life, bor. His jaws are the jaws of death. They do say he was off a ship that foundered one stormy night. The villagers of Salthouse found him next morning lying dead upon the beach alongside his master, the ship's captain. The dog's jaws were still clamped to his master's jacket and his master was still clutching the dog's collar. Now had they known what was going to happen, them good people would have buried man and beast together, but that dint seem proper to them so they pulled 'em apart and buried the captain in the churchyard and the hound on the beach. Well, o' course, what else could you expect – that there old dog has been a-searching for his master ever since? Whenever that's bad out there, you'll hear Old Shuck's terrible howling above the raging storm. Wailing for his master he is.

Then on stormy nights you might come across the ghost of the Long Coastguardman an' all. He'll keep you company 'cause he still comes out to patrol the shore whenever there's a devil of a gale coming up ....'

'Tell him about the Legless Smuggler,' chorused the drinkers around the bar.

'The Legless Smuggler!' Tovell snorted with laughter, spilling his beer. 'Now who's talking squit?'

'Do you have a good laugh, bor,' said Ted. 'You won't be a-laughing if you catch sight of him. I wonder you ent seen him afore now, seeing as he haunts the road between this pub and Cart Gap near where you live. I'll tell you, bor, if you do set eyes on him he'll put the fear of God into ye. He's a hideous sight – that he is. They do say that was farm-workers that first saw him. He came gliding past them one evening – he had to glide 'cause he dint have no legs, y'see – and they saw that his head was nearly off an' all. That was hanging backwards, held on by a little flap o' skin. 'Course, no-one believed 'em, did they? There was a lot of smuggling going on in them days – rum and brandy and so on – and everyone thought they'd been at a few bottles. Anyhow, them there farm-workers decided to follow the thing. They lay in wait several nights running and that always acted the same. That would glide along the road from Cart Gap to Haisbro carrying this here sack upon its back. It was dressed like an old seafarer. Now in them days there used to be a well at the bottom of the hill – you know, the hill this pub stands on – and this here apparition wouldn't stop till he got to the well. Once there, he'd throw his sack into it and then hop in after it hisself. He did that night after night. Then one o' them farm-workers he say, "That's a rum old do. Tomorrow I'm a-going to get a ladder, put that down the well and see what I can find." So he did – and what do you think was down there? A sack with a pair of rotting legs in it. Well, that poor old bugger was in such a state o' shock he wouldn't go down no more but his pal, he say, "You've done your bit – now I'll have a try." A few minutes later, up he came with the rest of the stinking body, dressed in the same garb as the ghost was wearing and with its head almost cut off. In the finish, that turned out that they were the remains of a Sea Palling man – a smuggler that had fallen out with his comrades. They'd hacked the poor devil to pieces and dropped the pieces down the well. I reckon that must have been after that that they filled the well in. Cor, blast, who'd want to drink water that had had bits of body rotting in it? Not that that would have made a mite o' difference to me – never touch the stuff, unless that's boiled and in my tea.'

'Well, thanks for that most entertaining tale, Ted,' said Tovell, laughing. 'You should be on the music hall stage. I only dropped in on the off-chance, seeing I don't get here so much in the evenings. We're confined to the Station if the weather's bad.'

'Funny – I dint think the weather had been that bad lately.'

'Well, I'll have to be off. Won't your long-suffering master be wondering where you are, Ted?'

'Oh, he knows we had a meeting of the Brigade this lunchtime. Only me and these three turned up but we'll have another meeting next week, won't we boys?'

Tovell finished his drink and picked up the packages he had bought earlier. As he reached the door he called out, 'I'll think of you later – I'm on all night watch. I'll keep a look out for your ghosts. Bye all!'

Tovell was still chuckling to himself about Ted's ghost stories when he went on patrol and they remained a source of amusement to him throughout the long watch. He did, however, break out in a cold sweat at about ten in the evening when he realised he was being followed by an animal. Gun cocked, he leapt round and stood poised to fire in the direction from which the heavy panting was coming. But instead of Old Shuck he came face to face with Blackie, out for a last prowl round before sleep. 'Don't ever do that again, you daft dog,' he admonished as he fondled the animal. 'You could have got your head blown off creeping up on me like that. Off you go, home to Ginny. Wish I were coming with you.'

The night was a stormy one but Tovell met no ghostly Coastguard or Legless Smuggler and heard no noise save the howl of the gale and the roar of the waves crashing on the beach. He also, thankfully, sighted no flares from ships in distress. Mr. Collins had been forced to slightly rearrange the times of the watches to cope with winter sickness amongst the men and the need to provide support for the lifeboat. He had told Tovell that he must patrol an extra hour until seven. This had its compensation since finishing at six would have meant Tovell would miss the December sunrise. As it was, dawn found him standing on a sand-dune overlooking Eccles beach. He was staring intently out to sea, his gaze fixed on the horizon where water met sky, waiting for the first fingers of light to appear. The wind had dropped, the clouds were clearing. He had watched the day break on hundreds of occasions in different parts of the world but familiarity had never detracted from the excitement he experienced as the glow spread out before him. Momentarily dazzled, he lowered his gaze to the beach. His vision was blurred but he thought he saw .... No, it could not be. He shut his eyes tightly and told himself that what he was witnessing was a hallucination caused by the intense piercing light, or a creation of his imagination resulting from too much talk about ghosts.

He opened his eyes again. 'Jesus Christ!' he gasped. 'I'm not seeing things; they're really there.' The beach in front of Tovell was a hideous sight; it was littered with skeletons. He ran among them trying to count them but in his agitation he could not arrive at the same answer twice. He gave up, raced back to the Watch-room and reported to the lieutenant that there were, 'Between thirty and forty skeletons on Eccles beach, Sir.'

It had been a long night for Richard Collins too. The last thing he wanted as his watch was coming to a close was an emergency situation. 'You haven't been drinking again have you, Tovell?' he asked hopefully.

'No, Sir,' declared Tovell emphatically. 'I'm trying to curb the habit. Not a drop has touched my lips since yesterday lunchtime and that I swear, Sir.'

'Alright, Tovell – I believe you,' said the officer wearily. 'If they're skeletons they can't be from a recent shipwreck. Could you deduce anything from the scraps of clothing clinging to the bones?'

'There were no scraps of clothing, Sir. The bones had been picked clean – every damn one of them.'

'That doesn't make sense, unless …. Of course, you said Eccles beach …. What you've just witnessed, Tovell, are the ravages inflicted by the elements. You're aware, are you not, that Eccles was once a large village? Over the centuries the sea has encroached and on particularly stormy nights has flooded the land for miles around, claiming not only the dwelling houses but their inhabitants. I'm also informed that from time to time, a combination of easterly gales and scouring tides has resulted in parts of the village being uncovered. It may be that the strong winds which we've had to contend with lately have caused the original graveyard to be exposed – I understand that there have been gruesome sightings such as you've described on previous occasions. If that is the case we're faced with a problem. As part of the Coastguard Service, we act as Receivers of Wreck and as such we're responsible for anything which is washed ashore. I'm not convinced, however, that these skeletons come within the category of our responsibility. I shall inform the local constabulary. No doubt, Constable Hadden will wish to inspect the evidence for himself before advising his superiors. I suggest, Tovell, that you go to your quarters for some refreshment but I should be obliged if you would make yourself available, even though your watch is officially over, when the constable arrives. It will only be necessary for you to accompany him to where you made your find. You may then retire to bed and make out your report later.'

Two and a half hours later and Tovell was still sitting on the ground with his back resting against the perimeter wall of the Station, waiting for the policeman. At last he spotted him peddling his bicycle at a leisurely pace along the track from the road. He stood up as the man got off his bicycle and wheeled it over the marrams to the Station. He watched impatiently as Constable Hadden propped his bicycle against the wall, took off the clips around his ankles, put them carefully away in his pocket and straightened his trousers.

'Blimey, you took your time, didn't you?' said Tovell by way of greeting.

'There int no hurry,' returned the constable amiably. 'Skeletons ent likely to get up and run off, are they now?'

'No, but I might. I've been on patrol all bloody night and I'd have been snoring my head off by this time if I hadn't been waiting here for you.'

'Sorry to hear that, boy, but I had things to do. Just you lead the way and I'll follow.

'Course, to be honest with you, Tovell, I ent quite sure what your officer expects of me. I mean, what does he think I'm going to do with thirty to forty skeletons? Where am I going to put them for a start, and how am I going to get them there? I'll have to go around requisitioning horses and carts all over the place – that'll be a right to-do ....'

'You keep on like this and you'll have me apologising for having found the ruddy things.'

'Well, y'know boy, sometimes that's best to leave well alone. If these skeletons are from the village of Eccles they belong where they were afore – under the sea. If we do nothing and let Nature take her course, the sea will come in and reclaim her own – she always has done afore.'

'As far as I'm concerned you can do what you damn well like with them. I'm so tired I just want to hand them over to you and get back to my bed. There's the spot – over those dunes.'

The constable pushed on ahead of Tovell between the clumps of marram grass and scrambled onto the dunes. Suddenly he stopped, straightened himself and turned to face Tovell, grinning broadly. 'What was that you said you found? Skeletons? There ent no skeletons here, boy. Look for yourself.'

Tovell rushed past the policeman and stood open-mouthed surveying the empty beach. 'I don't believe it. I don't believe it,' he kept muttering. 'They were here, I tell you. I saw them with my own eyes – thirty or forty of them strewn all over the sands.'

'Well, they ent here now, boy. Perhaps I was wrong; perhaps they did get up and run off as soon as you were gone. On the other hand, perhaps they weren't skeletons at all but spies and saboteurs disguised as skeletons ....'

'I'm not in the mood for jokes. I know what I saw.'

'And I believe you, Tovell, even if you do have a flask sticking out of your back pocket ....'

'And I haven't been drinking either. I poured my second cup of tea into that flask to drink while I was waiting for you.'

'You dint let me finish, boy. I believe you because of what's in front of me. If you hadn't worked yourself up into a muckwash you'd have seen it too. Look boy – bones. Just odd ones lying here and there by themselves.'

Tovell stared hard at the beach. 'You're right!' he cried. 'There's one there – and another over here. And look at the sand itself; it's all been churned up and walked over. When I was here earlier it was smooth, just as the tide had left it. So where are the skeletons?'

'I wouldn't like to say. That must be three or four hour since you first sighted them. Some could be on their way to Norwich by now – or even to London. A complete skeleton is worth a penny or two to the right people – medical gentlemen, students and the like.'

'You're telling me they've been stolen?'

'I don't know what's happened to them any more than you do – I'm only guessing. But stolen – no, I wouldn't say they've been stolen. Nobody here abouts regards taking what's left by the sea as stealing. A lot of people come down to the water when it's ebbing to see what bounty's been left by the tide. When I was a littl'un, my mother used to send me down to the beach with a bucket every day, afore I went to school and when I came home again. I'd find all sorts – especially after a good old nor-easter had been blowing – coal, oranges, barrels of flour. That would all have been washed overboard from some ship or that might be jettisoned cargo or wreckage. Many a poor family used to depend on what they could pick up off the beach.'

'Now I know why you weren't in any hurry to get here. You knew if you delayed long enough all your problems would be solved.'

'What's this, Tovell? Are you making accusations against an officer of the law?'

Tovell sighed and shook his head. 'Well, what are you going to do? Are you going to make any attempt to trace these skeletons?'

'Well now, I can't rightly answer that at present. I shall have to report the matter to my superiors. They'll have the jurisdiction over what I'm going to do – or not do. You've gotta remember, Tovell, that I'm a man on my own trying to police a large parish. I've gotta have my priorities. That wouldn't make no sense for me to spend days making out thirty, or maybe forty forms, one for each skeleton that I hent seen and couldn't identify, while all my other duties were being neglected.

Let me give you a bit of advice, Tovell. We both know you're fond of frequenting the *Admiral Lord Nelson*. Why don't you do as I do and take a leaf out of the great man's book? What I'm trying to say is, that doesn't do no harm to occasionally turn a blind eye – and that'll save other people a hell of a lot of trouble an' all.'

XXIII

Lydia Brewster called the women of the Station to a meeting in the first week of December to discuss the arrangements for Christmas. Baby Arthur slept through the proceedings on Lily's lap whilst the toddlers played happily on the large parlour rug. Lydia's concern was that the three widows and Mrs. Gillings might feel that it was inappropriate to celebrate the festival in the usual manner when they had been so recently bereaved. The ladies did not agree and Phyllis summed up their opinion on the matter.

'Emily and I have already talked about this. We feel that's bad enough the littl'uns not having their fathers with them this Christmas without taking away the rest of their pleasure in Christmas. We think we should keep things normal, as far as is possible.'

'Very well, if that's how you all feel,' said Lydia. 'I have already explained to Mr. Collins that every year Mr. Brewster, as Station Officer, has hosted a party for all the families on Christmas afternoon and evening in this parlour. Mr. Collins said that he was happy to go along with tradition and do the same – if that was your wish. Clearly, that is your wish so I shall make the usual arrangements.

Now there's still the question of Mrs. Ellis and Peter. We know we can send food parcels to Edinburgh for her – Ginny has done a fine job with all the parcels she's already sent over the past weeks – but do we put Peter on the train as well to spend Christmas with his parents?'

'I took the liberty of mentioning that to him yesterday,' said Mary. 'He's been thinking about it but he's worried that Sergeant Harris will be left on his own. He say the sergeant's been so good to him that he feels he ought to spend Christmas with him since that might not be long afore Mr. Harris is sent to the trenches.'

'Yes, Peter told me the same thing,' agreed Ginny. 'He'd rather stay at home.'

'Well, that seems to be settled too,' said Lydia.

Emily leant forward in her seat. She and her friend, in keeping with their proposal to work rather than worry, had a suggestion to make. 'There's one other thing Mrs. Brewster, that Phyllis and I have been wondering about. Wouldn't that be nice if we let the married soldiers have their wives to stay with them over Christmas?'

Lydia was so aghast at the idea that she was momentarily speechless. No-one noticed her reaction because they were too busy enthusiastically agreeing with the proposition.

'That's a master idea,' said Mrs. Gillings. 'I reckon they've been good old boys to us. They've treated us well and they deserve the comfort of their own womenfolk around them at Christmas. I know Lily and me have had it easy, Mrs. Brewster, since you very kindly took David into your home — for reasons we won't go into — but we'll help with all the extra cooking, won't we gal?'

'Oh, yes!' cried Lily. 'And that'll be nice for the littl'uns too. They'll think they've got lots of extra grandmothers.'

'Well,' said Lydia, hastily regaining her composure, 'since you're all in favour, I'll put your proposal to Mr. Collins.'

Richard Collins was as appalled as Lydia had been at the idea. 'My God, you're not asking me to invite Mildred here, are you? For the first time in my married life — nay, in my entire life — I was looking forward to Christmas.'

'If you do invite her, my dear Richard,' Lydia retorted, 'I shall leave. For the first time in my life, I shall disobey Admiralty orders, leave the Station and their damn telephone, and go to stay with my daughter in Oxford.'

The matter was soon settled. 'In that case,' said Richard with a dramatic bow and a flourish of his hand, 'I shall exercise the privileges of my command and decree that the men may do as they please but I, because of the magnitude of my responsibilities — to the Service, of course — must make the sacrifice and deny myself my conjugal rights.'

A few days later there was something else to celebrate when news broke, at long last, of a British victory at sea. Admiral von Spee had

171

finally met his match. On the eighth of December, Admiral Sturdee had caught up with the German force just off the Falkland Islands and had destroyed almost the entire East Asiatic Squadron. Those coastguards who had lost their lives at the Battle of Coronel had been avenged. The news restored confidence in the Royal Navy, but that confidence lasted a mere eight days. On the sixteenth of December, the Germans decided to repeat their exploit of the previous month and once more crossed the North Sea with a force similar to the one which had bombarded Great Yarmouth. This time they were supported by their High Seas Fleet and their targets were Hartlepool, Whitby and Scarborough.

'I just don't understand how we could allow this to happen again,' said Lydia despairingly. 'It's unthinkable that the enemy should be able to shell our towns at will and then return home safely. Where was Admiral Jellicoe? I thought our Grand Fleet was supposed to cruise the North Sea to prevent any intervention like this.'

'Be reasonable, my dear,' said Richard Collins soothingly. 'The North Sea is a very large expanse of water and this time the Hun attacked much further north. Given the kind of weather we've had lately it wouldn't be too difficult for an entire fleet to move around undetected. However, if our main policy is still to blockade Germany, then I would agree that we're showing little sign of success. Have you seen today's papers? They're full of criticism, both of the Admiralty and of Churchill personally. I fear his days as First Lord of the Admiralty may be numbered.'

Mary was jubilant about the Battle of the Falklands but Ginny took the news strangely. Tovell expected her to find some comfort in the victory but as soon as he read the account out to her, she resumed her former depression. She remained dejected for a number of days and several times he came across her sitting or even standing at the sink or the cooking range, in a trance like state. He knew she was worried about her brothers – she had finally accepted, in the face of repeated newspaper reports of the stalemate which existed in Europe that she would not see them for a very long time – and he suspected that she was also dreading the thought of Christmas without her husband. Matters came to a head one suppertime. Tovell had been on duty all the previous night and had been woken at midday after only five hours sleep to take over Ned Jackson's watch when the latter collapsed with influenza. By the time he returned to his billet soon after six, Tovell was feeling very weary and out of sorts, and his usual patience with Ginny's moodiness had deserted him. When, towards the end of the meal Lizzie asked for the third time if she might take another slice of bread and received no answer from her mother, Tovell banged on the table in exasperation and shouted, 'Ginny!'

The effect of the outburst was instantaneous and totally unexpected. Both children and their mother leapt to their feet and took cover – Lizzie and Bobby behind the larger armchair and Ginny in the corner by the cooking range. There they cowed, white-faced and rigid with fear.

Tovell was flabbergasted, but then realisation dawned. 'How could I have been such a fool?' he cried. 'Everything makes sense now. The answer was staring me in the face and I didn't see it.' Pushing back his chair he went over to the children and taking them by the hand he said coaxingly, 'C'mon, littl'uns – it's only old Tovell. I wouldn't hurt you for the world – you know that. I didn't mean to bang the table so hard – in fact I don't think I did really. It was the clattering of the cutlery and crookery which made it sound so loud. I'm sorry – I didn't mean to scare you.' He drew the children to him until he could put an arm around each one and then he looked at Ginny. 'I'm sorry I shouted at you. I didn't mean that either – it's just that it's been such a long day and I'm so tired. C'mon out of there and let's all go back to the table and finish our supper.'

Slowly Ginny left her refuge and all four took their seats again. 'We'll talk about this later,' said Tovell quietly. He spent the next three-quarters of an hour restoring normal relations with Lizzie and Bobby and by the time the pair went to bed they were as happy and carefree as ever. When Ginny returned to the living room she sat down in her armchair beside the fire and for once did not take up some handiwork. Tovell, sitting opposite, reopened the conversation. 'I should have guessed, you know. My father was always beating us up – all of us. That was the reason I left home. My mother encouraged me to go because she knew one day I would have killed the bastard.'

'I couldn't tell you,' whispered Ginny. 'I couldn't bring myself to tell anyone.'

'You don't have to explain – my poor old ma was the same. She used to invent the most involved stories to explain to the neighbours how she got her black eyes and cuts and bruises.'

Ginny nodded and smiled slightly. 'I've always done the same. It was a matter of pride that no-one should know the truth.'

'I'm surprised Mrs. Gillings didn't guess.'

'I think maybe she did but, of course, she didn't say anything. Well, she couldn't could she? One thing you must never do is interfere between husband and wife. But she never liked Robert and she made that quite clear to him.'

'What about the litt'uns? Didn't their teacher suspect?'

'Littl'uns are always falling over anyway, aren't they? And I did try my best to protect them – to draw his anger on to me. Anyway, most of the time it was me that upset him. You know what I'm like with my quick tongue, always speaking afore I think. It didn't take much to rouse him and when he was drunk ….' The words tailed away as Ginny wrung the corners of her handkerchief in anguish.

'That's why you barricaded your door the night I got roaring drunk, wasn't it?' asked Tovell gently.

Ginny nodded. 'I couldn't be sure, could I, that the drink wouldn't turn you into a monster? I didn't know you very well then.'

'So why have you looked so sad and tormented since his death? In your place I'd have been rejoicing.'

Ginny did not reply straight away but continued to twist and turn the material between her fingers. Suddenly, she blurted out her confession. 'It seemed like I'd killed him. You see, I was glad when he got his call-up just like I was always glad when he got sent away on training exercises. But I did something wicked; I prayed the war wouldn't be over too soon. I prayed he wouldn't come home too soon. I just wanted a little peace from him – a few weeks, or perhaps a few months, when we wouldn't have to be afraid all the time …. When we wouldn't have to watch our step – be so careful of what we said and what we did. Like I say, he got upset so easy – the slightest little thing and he'd be in a rage. But I didn't wish him dead – I'm sure I didn't …. Yet ever since he was killed I've been going over it all in my mind – again and again and again – wondering what I was really wishing and praying. When I hoped he wouldn't come home too soon was I really

174

hoping he wouldn't come home at all? That's what's been torturing me; the guilt – the feeling that I wished him dead. I keep trying to put it out of my mind but that isn't easy when I'm surrounded by things that remind me of him and when people keep saying things – like that newspaper report of the battle you read out to me – things that bring it all back. I reckon there isn't anything I can do to ease my conscience – I'm going to have to live with my guilt ….'

'Telling me may have helped more than you realise. They say confession is good for the soul and if the Catholics I've met in my time are anything to go by, there never was a truer saying. I'd talk it over with someone who knew you both; someone who'd keep your confidence and because of his experience of life would give you sound advice. I'd go to Dr. Lambert or the vicar.'

'But that would seem like betraying him – especially now he isn't here to defend himself. I feel bad enough about telling you. That seems downright disloyal.'

'Disloyal! Ginny, your husband forfeited his right to loyalty the first time he ever struck you. I've attended one or two weddings in the past and though I'm no expert on the form of service I remember there's a lot of talk about loving and cherishing one another. I don't recall any mention of violence being part of the deal. I'm supposed to belong to a violent profession but I've never once hit a woman or a child, and never felt the need to. That's the point, Ginny – no amount of provocation could justify beating up a tiny little thing like you, or terrorising defenceless children like Lizzie and Bobby. He was just a bully who enjoyed making your lives a misery. If he walked through that door now I'd tear him limb from limb – and I'd suffer no pangs of conscience afterwards. He didn't deserve to go on living, Ginny, and whether or not you in your heart of hearts wished him dead doesn't matter a jot. If he'd have come back he might have killed you during his next attack. It seems to me that justice has been done – he's been killed before he could kill you. I wouldn't waste another thought or another tear on him – he doesn't deserve it and he never deserved you.'

Tovell's prediction proved to be correct and Ginny did feel better once the truth about what had been troubling her was out in the open, and there was the added advantage that Tovell was able to intervene as soon as she showed any signs of lapsing into melancholy. 'C'mon, Ginny,' he would say, 'remember what I told you – you've got nothing to reproach yourself for.'

Undoubtedly, the additional work entailed in preparing for Christmas also acted as a balm. The already spotless house had to be given an extra special clean, 'because you never know who might call,' and adequate time given to the making of festive foods. Some preliminary cooking had already taken place: the cake had been maturing in an air-tight tin for weeks and a dozen puddings, boiled initially all together in the copper which normally accommodated the heavy washing, sat on a shelf in the pantry alongside the home-made mincemeat.

As the holiday approached the children's excitement increased and it was infectious. Tovell entered into the spirit of the occasion with a will. 'I've never had what you might call, a family Christmas, and I mean to make the most of it,' he told everyone repeatedly. True to his word, he helped to decorate the cake and made several trips to the village to purchase nuts, fruits, sweetmeats and other delicacies which he paid for himself. He searched the woods with Lizzie and Bobby for holly, mistletoe and fallen branches which he could chop into logs. They piled all they had collected into a wooden box suspended on old perambulator wheels and dragged it home between them with the rope harness around their waists, jubilantly singing carols.

Ted Carter had assured Tovell that he knew where to acquire a 'master fine tree' from an acquaintance who owed him a favour but, as it was very big, the soldier would have to help him fetch it in 'the master's hoss and cart.' This simple procedure took a number of hours, partly because Ted's acquaintance lived the other side of Stalham, and partly because the old man could not bring himself to drive through the town without stopping to give the season's greetings to Kath, the landlady of the *King's Head* public house. 'I've always had a soft spot for that gal,' he admitted and proved the point by demonstrating considerable reluctance to leave the lady's presence. In the convivial atmosphere Tovell's resolve wavered somewhat and he was in a cheery mood on the journey back to the Coastguard Station.

Ginny had advance warning of their arrival and the state they were in because they were singing carols as loudly as the children had, but off key. She held open the front door and watched in amusement as the two men made a number of attempts, assisted by Lizzie and Bobby who had been waiting anxiously for their return, to bring the tree into the living room of the cottage. When they finally succeeded she reserved her only comment for Ted Carter. 'You're a bad influence on him – that you are to be sure.' The old man nodded his agreement and then tucked into the large plate of boiled ham and home-made pickles which she had prepared and managed to down twice as many hot mince-pies as Tovell.

The children brought out the box of trimmings and tiny ornaments carefully preserved from year to year and after the two men had with difficulty, planted the tree in a large tub, they enjoyed themselves adorning its branches. They had trouble reaching the highest branches and so did their mother. They turned to Tovell who had sobered up as soon as he had eaten and dragged him from his armchair where he had been sitting contentedly watching the blissful scene. Under their direction he completed the dressing of the tree and still following their instructions, went on to decorate the room with the greenery they had collected earlier. Christmas could now commence.

Over several days Tovell was introduced to an increasing number of Ginny's relatives. He had assumed that she only had the three brothers she spoke of so often but older brothers and sisters made brief visits accompanied by their offspring, as did numerous uncles, aunts and cousins. Now he understood why she had brewed so much ginger wine and baked so many tins of mince-pies. No-one came empty handed; they brought a bottle of some favourite recipe, a jar of preserves, a fowl, or a sack of vegetables grown in their own back garden. Christmas dinner was provided by the uncle and aunt Ginny had often spoken about warmly to Tovell – Uncle William and Auntie May. They worked a smallholding near Whimpwell Green and because they were elderly and childless it had been Ginny's custom for many years to give them a hand at particularly busy times in the horticultural year. In return for her services they had always presented her with a goose, plucked, singed and drawn ready for stuffing, as a Christmas present.

'Do you always have this number of visitors at Christmas?' asked Tovell.

'No,' replied Ginny, 'but I knew I would this year. They've all felt obliged to make the effort because of our bereavement. They all wrote to me at the time but they didn't visit then – except for Auntie May and Uncle William and my sister-in-law – the one I went to see when her husband was killed. I didn't expect my other relations to make the journey then because they live so scattered about, but I felt sure they'd make a combined visit at Christmas. It was kind of them to bring little gifts of food, wasn't it? I reckon that was instead of wreaths.'

Christmas Eve was a busy time for Ginny but as Tovell had had the middle watch he was able to assist her in the evening. He wrapped up the presents he had so carefully made for the children and placed them under the Christmas tree. When their mother was certain that they were asleep, he crept into the bedroom and helped her to fill the stockings that Bobby and Lizzie had hung on the bed-knobs with oranges, apples, nuts, sweets and two pennies apiece which he had polished until they shone.

'I'd better get on with making the sage and onion stuffing,' said Ginny after she had closed the bedroom door. 'I'll have to be up extra early in the morning to get that old goose in the oven. Dinner will need to be ready by the time we get back from morning service. I've asked Mrs. Gillings and Lily to share our Christmas dinner seeing as you're on duty. I would have asked young Peter too but Mary had already asked him. Her eldest boy is only a year or two younger than Peter. We'll bring plenty over to the Watch-room for you and Sergeant Harris, of course.'

When Tovell saw that the preparation of the sage and onion stuffing for the goose was going to be a lengthy procedure, he immediately volunteered to deal with the vegetables. Ginny was amazed. 'That's very kind of you – very kind indeed. I don't know any other man that would make such an offer, but would there be any sprout and potato left time you finished, seeing as you're not used to peeling vegetables?'

Tovell grinned and answered, 'I've got more talents than you give me credit for. I bet I can do as good a job as you can and I bet I've had as much practice – look I'll show you.' He picked up Ginny's small sharp vegetable knife and attacked the sprouts. 'Whenever I've been short of money – which has been quite often the way I've drunk it in the past – I've been in the habit of hanging around the cook-house asking them to let me do any of the jobs they hated. On the way back from South Africa I peeled spuds every ruddy day for six thousand miles. Mind you, I was desperate that time because I was literally penniless and didn't have anything I could sell. I'd been wounded, though only slightly, and then I went and caught a fever so they sent me down the line and eventually I ended up at a convalescent hospital in Cape Town. The night before I was due to board a transport ship for Portsmouth I was feeling really sorry for myself – you know, being parted from my regiment and all my pals – so I hopped it when the orderlies weren't looking and went out and got drunk. I passed out in some back alley and when I came to I'd been robbed of every penny. The bastards had even cut off all my tunic buttons and taken my cap badge. They were worth a few shillings, you see – the civilians would buy anything military as souvenirs. By the time I got to the ship I was a sorry sight, I can tell you, and with no money at all I'd got no hope of making any – from gambling I mean. The funny thing is, once I got to sea I suddenly felt hungry enough to eat three men's rations. They starve you when you've got a fever and your body's telling you to make up the loss. So there was nothing else for it but to peel spuds all the way home in return for as much food as I could eat, and to make sure I didn't lose my hard earned extras as soon as I'd swallowed them, I lugged every sack of potatoes and every bucket up onto the top deck where I could work in the open.'

'Oh, Tovell,' said Ginny sympathetically, 'drinking really has been your downfall, hasn't it? I'm so glad you're beginning to beat the habit and from the way you're tackling them sprouts, I've gotta agree with Mrs. Gillings – that doesn't matter what needs doing you always make a good job of it.'

Tovell felt a little guilty at the compliment for he had had an ulterior motive when he had suggested assisting Ginny: he had had in mind that if the work were completed quickly she might consent to sit with him and take a quiet Christmas drink or two, and that the romantic atmosphere created by the sweet-scented logs burning in the grate and the festive decorations all around the room, might induce in her a state of favourable intimacy. She dashed all his hopes with one yawn and the curt statement, 'I'm going to bed. Thank's for your help, Tovell.' Before he could attempt any form of persuasion she had disappeared. With a sigh he resigned himself to sleep and knew nothing more until Ginny woke him next morning. He opened his eyes to find her bending over him, smiling. He stretched out his arms towards her but she darted to the other side of the curtains and closed them behind her.

'I've left your tea beside you,' she called out cheerily. 'You wanted a proper family Christmas so hurry up and get dressed before the littl'uns wake up. I'll be in the scullery when you're ready.'

'Hey, Ginny,' he shouted, 'you haven't given me a chance to wish you Happy Christmas.'

'Sorry,' she replied. 'Happy Christmas, Tovell.'

He could hear her humming a lullaby as he dressed and when he had finished he pushed open the scullery door and watched her lovingly for a few moments until she realised he was there. She turned away from the sink and wiped her hands on her apron. As she brushed past him she smiled warmly up at him but she crossed the living room quickly and then tentatively opened the bedroom door. Tovell followed closely behind her and they could both see from the door-way that the children had already found their stockings in the half-light.

'Look what I've got,' cried Lizzie, 'two new pennies and sweets and nuts and things!'

'So have I – I've got the same,' shouted Bobby.

Both children jumped off the bed and ran to hug first their mother and then Tovell. He carried them, one under each arm, into the living room and set them down in front of the tree. 'Look – you've got more presents under the tree! Open them up!'

The children pounced upon the parcels, hastily un-wrapped them and beamed with delight at their contents, eagerly spreading them out on the floor. Suddenly, they remembered their manners and fell upon Tovell hugging him, expressing their thanks and assuring him that they would be the envy of all their peers.

'I'm glad you like your presents,' he said as he tried to disentangle himself from their embrace, 'but now I've got something for your ma.'

He managed to reach over to his armchair and extract a package from behind the cushion. Bashfully, he placed it in Ginny's hands and explained as she un-wrapped it, 'I don't know why I bought this. At the time I didn't have anyone to give it to so I must have been secretly hoping that one day I'd meet you. Even the colour is perfect for you. I reckon you'd call it pale apricot and gold.'

'It's like you made for the doll,' said Ginny as she spread out the flimsy material, her eyes shining.

'Yes, it's a sari,' replied Tovell, 'I bought it on impulse one day in an Indian bazaar and I've been carrying it around with my kit ever since.'

'Beautiful – that's what it is – beautiful. But how do I put it on?'

'Well, the bit with the sleeves is simple enough – you wear that on your top half – but the bottom half's not so easy to manage. It's got yards and yards of material as you can see. You have to wind it round your middle to form a skirt and then the tail end goes over one shoulder or over your head like a veil. Trouble is, I don't know when you're going to be able to wear it.'

'I'll find an occasion to wear it – don't you worry. Thank you, Tovell, thank you. I'll always treasure it, that I will.' She darted forward and gave him a quick peck on the cheek then dodged out of reach before he could touch her and ran to a cupboard. 'I made something for you,' she said, rummaging around on the lower shelf. She found the parcel she was searching for and thrust it in his direction. 'That's an oiled wool gansey. I thought perhaps you could wear it on cold nights underneath your tunic to keep you warm.'

Tovell set aside the paper and string and held the jersey to his chest. 'Just the right size and a lovely thought. Thank you, Ginny. Come here and let me thank you properly.'

Cheeks flushed and eyes sparkling, Ginny stretched out her hands to push Tovell away. 'Whatever will the littl'uns think,' she protested.

Tovell grabbed hold of the outstretched hands and pulled her towards him. 'What do you think, Lizzie and Bobby? Should I give your ma a Christmas kiss?'

'Yes, Yes!' cried both children in unison, tugging giggling at their mother's dress.

'There, I have the littl'uns permission,' said Tovell.

'Alright, alright!' said Ginny laughing. 'But hurry up else we'll be late for church. We haven't had breakfast yet.'

Tovell bent down and placed his hands around her waist. Effortlessly, he lifted her up until their faces were level. As he inclined his head towards her he felt her body stiffen and caught a fleeting glimpse of fear in her eyes. His lips scarcely brushed hers before she turned away from him. Gently he sat her back on her feet. 'I'm sorry,' he whispered. 'I got carried away.'

The children, oblivious to any tension between the adults, called out excitedly, 'You're coming to church with us, aren't you, Uncle Tovell?'

'That depends on your ma,' answered the soldier quietly. 'I'll come if she wants me to.'

'Of course I want you to come,' said Ginny at once, taking care not to look at Tovell. 'You wanted a family Christmas and going to church all together on Christmas morning is part of that. Anyway, Auntie May and Uncle William will be there. They want to meet you. They were sorry they missed you yesterday when they brought the goose, and they were sorry they missed your last visit to church. Uncle William had gout but their neighbours told them all about it. My auntie say, "I hope he's not too much trouble to you, Ginny" ...'

Tovell swallowed hard and glanced at Ginny nervously. 'What did you say?' he ventured.

Ginny looked up at him and grinned. 'Oh, I say, "He's no trouble to me, Auntie. You don't want to pay any regard to all them stories; he isn't as black as he's painted."'

At the appointed time, everyone except Lydia Brewster, Richard Collins and David, assembled outside for the journey to church. After exchanging cheerful salutations with the other families, Ginny climbed onto the cart alongside Mrs. Gillings. The latter whispered to her before they were joined by the other Station wives. 'You were right to bring him; a few more weeks and he could be at the Front. But I'm telling you, gal, that if any of them silly little mawthers play up like they did the last time he went to morning service, they'll get a piece of my mind, that they will.'

With four of the ladies in mourning dress and five of the children wearing predominantly dark clothes appropriate to the recently orphaned, the party which set out for Haisbro should have been a sombre one, but it was not. The three visitors declined the invitation to ride in the cart, preferring to walk arm in arm with their soldier husbands and holding the hands of the younger children. Sergeant Harris walking with Peter Ellis and Tovell, walking with Bobby and Lizzie, brought up the rear. The little group chattered together and sang all their favourite carols until they came within earshot of the village. Decorum then dictated that they should arrive in the churchyard in a subdued and dignified manner. Though no rehearsal had taken place, even the smallest child managed to behave with the propriety demanded by the social conventions of the day.

Seasonal good wishes were exchanged with other parishioners and the Station party took their places in the crowded church. The news that Tovell was once more present was rapidly conveyed among the younger female members of the congregation but his arrival did not cause the stir it had done previously. Certainly, a number of young ladies ventured a quick glance in his direction but this was invariably followed by an anxious look to see if parents had witnessed the action. Obviously, harsh reprimands for unseemly behaviour had not been forgotten. Also to Tovell's advantage was the fact that there were so many new faces present – relatives staying with local families for the holiday – which aroused the curiosity of the regular worshippers.

During the service Tovell realised that he was being scrutinised by a well-dressed lady he had never seen before. 'Who's that peering at me over the top of her spectacles?' he asked Ginny quietly during the vicar's sermon.

'That's Lady Meredith,' replied Ginny, whispering. 'You were on patrol the day she came to see me after I was widowed. You were on duty before that when she came to see Lily. She always has taken an interest in all her staff, past and present.'

After the service, Lady Meredith's interest was sufficient to keep two carriages of visiting relatives waiting outside the church whilst she was introduced to Tovell. 'I'm so glad we've met at last, Mr. Tovell,' she said, beaming at him. 'I believe his lordship has had a brief encounter with you but I have only heard of you by reputation.'

'I hope you don't trust all you hear, ma'am,' replied the soldier.

'Now don't disappoint me, Mr. Tovell. If you are in point of fact a saint, I don't want to know – sinners are so much more fun. When I was a child I longed to misbehave but little girls are rarely given the opportunity. I had to be content with listening to my brothers recounting their wicked exploits. And now I'm too old to be naughty myself but not too old to enjoy hearing about other people being naughty. Gossiping has become a much more interesting pastime since your arrival so please don't allow Ginny to reform you too much.'

'You can tell she likes you,' observed Ginny with a laugh when Lady Meredith had departed. 'But you don't want to be fooled by all that she says. When I worked at the Hall she always behaved very properly and we had to do the same.'

'She must have been quite a beauty when she was young,' commented Tovell. 'I bet she led his lordship a merry dance.'

'That may be so but she's been a good wife and mother. Of course, she's had nurses and governesses to help her but she's always looked happiest surrounded by her children and grandchildren. She had nine littl'uns altogether.'

'His lordship must have been of the same opinion as you – *the Devil makes work for idle hands* – and he saw to it that she didn't have time to stray from the straight and narrow.'

'There's some here just longing to stray,' said Ginny archly. 'Look behind you.'

Tovell looked – and cringed. Peeping at him from behind gravestones and the buttresses of the church were several of the sweet young things with whom he had dallied. Each one was smiling at him encouragingly, some were even daring to beckon and all were dangling sprigs of mistletoe in his direction. Tovell turned abruptly back to Ginny and offered her his arm. 'Come, m'lady,' he said. 'Let me escort you to your carriage.'

'But what are you going to do about that lot?' asked Ginny.

'I'm going to take Constable Hadden's advice,' replied the soldier. 'I'm going to turn a blind eye.'

Lieutenant Collins had decided that the three men – Westgate, Mannell and Jackson – whose wives had joined them for the holiday should have

Christmas day free of duties, barring emergencies, and he rearranged the rota accordingly. He particularly wanted to eat his Christmas dinner with Lydia and to be at the party in the afternoon. He felt sure that David also would want to spend the afternoon in Lily's company so he had allotted the middle watch to Sergeant Harris and Tovell. This meant that the two of them had to report to the Watch-room as soon as they returned from morning service. The lieutenant had agreed that Tovell need not begin his shore patrol until after he had eaten and promptly at one Ginny, assisted by Mrs. Gillings, arrived at the top of the Watch-room steps bearing trays laden with Christmas fare for the two men.

Neither Tovell nor Sergeant Harris minded eating their Christmas dinner together. They spent a very pleasant hour reminiscing about the Christmas dinners they had eaten in the past, provided as tradition decreed by their officers, the quality dependent upon the generosity of the individuals concerned. David on the other hand, minded very much having to eat his Christmas dinner with Lydia Brewster and Richard Collins. His officer managed to call to mind even more literary quotations than usual and seemed to be thoroughly enjoying himself, as did Mrs. Brewster. It was all a far cry from the kind of family merry-making which David had been accustomed to at home. At no time had he missed his parents and brothers and sisters more. He had secretly hoped that the Gillingses might invite him to their house for Christmas dinner but no such invitation had materialised. For a while there had been a possibility that the Gillings family might spend Christmas with their relatives at Great Yarmouth but at the last moment the old lady had decided that her bereavement was no reason to alter the habit of a lifetime – she had always spent Christmas under her own roof and always would. Lily hardly dared to admit her relief at this decision to herself, let alone to her mother-in-law. The one concession Mrs. Gillings made was to accept Ginny's invitation for the remaining members of the Gillings family to share Christmas dinner next door with the remaining members of the Adams family.

By three in the afternoon everyone on the Station, with the exception of the two soldiers on duty, had assembled in Lydia's parlour for the

185

traditional Christmas Day party. David cheered up at once at the sight of Lily and her offspring and he devoted the rest of the afternoon to entertaining them both. If Mrs. Gillings noticed she made no comment although she did make a point of telling the boy how pretty the knitted jacket was which he had given to little Arthur. The remark was particularly pleasing to David as it gave him an excuse to tell the old lady about his favourite sister, Annie, who had made the outfit for him. When he had sent the money home for the baby's present he had considered asking Annie to make something for Lily too but in the end he had dismissed the idea, fearing that what would be acceptable between godfather and godson would cause offence between godfather and godson's recently widowed mother.

A similar sense of propriety pervaded the gathering and although the traditional games were played with the children and the usual carols and Christmas songs sung, the unabashed gaiety which the Station wives associated with the occasion was tempered by thoughts of those who were missing from this year's festivities. The children, of course, were untouched by such reflections and delighted in the merriment as much as ever. The newcomers also, the soldiers and the three soldiers' wives, none of whom had any previous Christmas parties in Lydia's parlour to make comparisons with, enjoyed themselves immensely. The lieutenant, who had cheerfully paid for all the food and drink which had had to be brought in for the celebration, threw himself into the role of host with a will, conversing jovially with everyone in turn, joining in the games and singing, and constantly pressing refreshments upon his guests. At one stage he expressed concern that the preserves were running out and immediately picked up the two near-empty dishes with the intention of retreating to the kitchen to replenish their contents. Mrs. Gillings intervened at once, offering to do the job for him.

'My dear lady,' he replied. 'I would not dream of allowing you to perform such a chore on this day of all days. Throughout the year you wait upon us; on Christmas Day, therefore, it is only fitting that men should wait upon ladies.'

'Such a gentleman,' murmured Mrs. Gillings as the door to the kitchen closed behind the officer. Her neighbours all agreed with her and not one of them was indelicate enough to make any observations on the fact that it was a full ten minutes before the gentleman returned with dishes brimming with fruit. After all, what else could be expected from someone so unused to dealing with domestic matters?

As it happened, it had taken Richard Collins just one and a half minutes to locate and open the jars of preserves and eight and a half minutes to lure Lydia into the pantry and seduce her. She had been busily engaged at the kitchen table, a fact of which he had been well aware, refilling plates with mince pies and fancy cakes. She had looked up in surprise as Richard had rushed past her into the pantry but had returned to her own replenishing when she had heard him noisily moving jars around and fruit plopping into dishes. Once he had completed his task he called to her. 'Lydia, can you come here a moment, please?'

'What is it you're looking for?' she asked as she entered the pantry.

'You!' he cried gleefully, slamming the door shut behind Lydia and standing with his back pressed against it, barring her escape.

'Oh, Richard, this is no time to play games; we have a house full of guests.'

'I know – isn't it exciting?'

'You are depraved.'

'I cannot deny it, my love, for it is true. But come – we must not delay.'

'Not now, Richard, and not here.'

'Yes now, my sweet. Have pity on me for I shall be denied your loveliness tonight; I am on watch. It will not take long to gratify my desires, I promise. You must blame all the jollity for rousing my lust. And here is a perfect place.'

'But there's no room.'

'There's just enough room for us to stand face to face. What more is required? Remember your Chaucer – the Merchant's Tale? Not a composition you read aloud with your pupils, I trust. If Chaucer's hero could perform whilst perched with his beloved in the branches of a pear tree then surely I can perform here. Come, my dearest, see what surprise awaits you.' With a theatrical flourish Richard threw open the jacket of his uniform and revealed a sprig of mistletoe wedged into the top of his trousers. At once Lydia was convulsed with laughter and collapsed helplessly against her lover's shoulder. 'Ahah! Got you at last – and I shall not let you go until I've achieved satisfaction. Keep still woman – I'm getting lost in petticoats.'

'Oh Richard,' gasped Lydia. 'Christmas Day will never be the same again.'

Lydia's sentiment might well have been echoed by Tovell. His six hour watch passed quickly and he and Sergeant Harris were able to join the party. They both ate with a relish in spite of the generous helpings of goose and plum pudding which they had devoured only a few hours earlier. They also drank enough to compensate for their abstinence whilst on duty. Tovell then allowed Bobby and Lizzie to involve him in their games and later danced with every lady present. He honoured Ginny more often than anyone else but was careful to preserve her reputation in public. By the end of the evening he was convinced that no Christmas Day could equal this one and he told Ginny as they returned to her cottage of the joy he had experienced in sharing the day with her and the children. His only regret as they bid each other goodnight in the living room was that he could not fold her in his arms and tell her of his love. He had taken the unfortunate incident of the morning as a timely warning; he must not attempt any form of physical contact again. It was not too difficult to imagine the horrors to which she had been subjected by her brutal husband, and little wonder that she feared a man's touch. No, he must be patient and wait for her to come to him and in the meantime, he must hope and pray that such a miracle would come to pass.

1915

I

In the days following Christmas each household was *at home* to its
neighbours. With so much socialising going on the week passed quickly
and pleasantly and almost before anyone realised it another year had
dawned. The women looked back on 1914 with mixed feelings; so
many of their loved ones had been killed or wounded that they felt sure
no year could bring with it more ill-fortune, yet for Lydia, Lily and
Ginny there was the thought, shared with no-one, that 1914 had
brought them some good fortune as well – namely, the men who now
meant so much to them. For those men and the other four soldiers
there was the fear that all their good fortune was behind them and all
their ill-fortune ahead of them. All of them knew but would not admit
that they had thrown themselves into the Christmas celebrations so
enthusiastically because they feared that they might never see another
Christmas.

Ill-fortune had not yet finished with the inhabitants of the tiny
community. Mr. Latham arrived on only the second day of 1915 with
more bad news. Richard Collins could scarcely believe what he was
hearing. 'Yesterday, being New Year's Day, I visited each household to
wish them a happier 1915. Every one of the ladies was optimistic. 1914
had been such a dreadful year for them that they were glad to see the
back of it and confident that the new one would be better. Yet even as
we spoke, more of their men-folk were drowning.'

'Yes, I'm afraid that was so,' agreed the Divisional Officer. 'My
signal said that *HMS Formidable* was sunk west of Portland in the
Channel, with the loss of almost all hands, on the first of January 1915.
I'm sorry to say that the pig boats triumph again.'

'We'd better go to the widows without delay.'

'Yes, let's get it over with,' said Mr. Latham sadly. 'I should be finding the words come more easily with practise and repetition, but that is not the case.'

Lydia looked up and said, 'Tell them I'll be over later.' She remained seated at the table after the men had left and was still there when David entered the room. When he saw her he thought she too had been widowed. The boy had secretly marvelled that someone as old as his landlady – he was certain she must be at least ten years his mother's senior – could be so handsome. Everything about her was, in David's opinion, rather grand – the way she spoke, the way she walked and the way she held her tall curvaceous frame. Although her hair piled high upon her head was silver grey, it always shone. Her eyes sparkled and her complexion was as clear as a young woman's. But today for the first time she looked her age. She was sitting hunched at the table, her head resting on one hand, staring into space. She glanced up wearily as the boy approached, her fine high cheek-boned face gaunt and wan. He noticed wrinkles around her eyes and on her forehead which he was certain had not been there before.

'Has something happened to Mr. Brewster?' David asked anxiously.

'No, I'm thankful to say,' answered Lydia.

'You look so ill and worried, I was afraid ....'

'I am worried, David. I've been sitting here thinking that a mere five months ago there were seven coastguards working and living at this Station. Now all but one of them has fallen victim to this hideous war. Five are dead, Wilfred Ellis is horribly burned and only my husband has survived – so far. Mr. Latham tells us that it's the same story at all the other stations. One, maybe two, is still alive but at some establishments every single man has been killed. Such a tragedy, David – such a dreadful loss. The ships don't matter; they were old reserve ships just meant for training exercises, not modern warfare. No-one will mourn their passing but the men, almost all family men, how can we justify their loss? Such a waste, David. All so futile ....'

'But your husband's still safe, Mrs. Brewster. That must be a comfort to you.'

'Yes, he's still safe, but for how long? It can only be a matter of time and it's that thought which torments me. It's like having the sword of Damocles hanging over my head.' Lydia saw the puzzled frown on the boy's face and smiled. 'You must be hungry, David. Sit down. I've been keeping your food hot in the steamer. I hope you won't mind eating alone but I really should go and see if there is anything I can do for poor Mrs. Bishop and Mrs. Foster.'

That night after he had removed his tunic and trousers, Tovell was reluctant to leave the glow of the hearth. He stood in his long-johns at the cooking-range with his hands and forehead resting against the mantelpiece, staring into the embers. A slight noise startled him from his reverie and turning his head slightly, he saw the bedroom door slowly opening. Ginny emerged hesitantly, closed the door quietly behind her and then pressed herself against it as though afraid to leave the shelter of the familiar woodwork. With a tremor in her voice she said, 'I wondered if you were still cold – if I should make you some soup.'

Tovell straightened and turned around to face Ginny. He shook his head not daring to speak lest he broke the spell and the vision before him disappeared. Bare-footed, in a long high-necked nightdress like the ones which Lizzie wore, she looked tinier and more vulnerable than ever. As she stared at him from across the room her eyes told him that the miracle for which he had prayed was about to materialise. She was deathly pale. He wanted to stretch out his arms towards her but instead he clenched his fists at his sides, held his breath and waited. Then it happened – she gave a little cry and ran towards him. He caught her in mid-air and held her crushed to his chest. They laughed and cried and smothered each other in kisses, all their love and all their longing overflowing. When Tovell could support her weight no longer he collapsed into his armchair still holding her tightly.

'Oh, Ginny, Ginny,' he murmured, 'I thought you'd only ever come to me in my dreams.'

'You're not dreaming – I'm really here,' whispered Ginny. She reached up to stroke his face and looked at him with such tenderness that he could have wept with joy.

'The times I've wanted to reach out for you, tell you how I worship you. I've never felt this way before, Ginny. I swear no woman has ever had this effect on me. I didn't know what it was to truly love someone before I met you. I'll never love anyone else – you're the only woman in the world for me. Without you I'll be what I've always been – nothing.'

'You'll never be nothing to me – you'll always be everything. In years gone by when I've felt so wretched I've pretended to myself that I was married to a kind, gentle, loving man who'd never shout at me, or fly into rages, or hurt me …. Someone who'd make me laugh – make me glad to be alive – and someone who'd want all the love I can give in return. Oh Tovell, you're everything I've ever wanted in a man. When you came here that seemed too good to be true. I kept asking myself how it could be that of all the men who might have been sent here, they sent you – the one person I'd always dreamed about but never thought existed. It seemed like the hand of the Almighty …. Yes, I reckon I've loved you from the beginning.'

'But you never gave me any hint – in fact, you always seemed to be running away from me.'

'Well, I had to, didn't I? At first I was married and that wouldn't have been right, and even after …., but you know how afraid I was ….'

'But you're not afraid now, are you? You know I'll never harm you or the littl'uns. I'll love you and cherish you 'til my dying breath.'

'Oh Tovell, that's why I had to come to you tonight. The news about Emily's and Phyllis's husbands …. I've been tormented all day with the thought that you could be in the trenches soon and all I've done is push you away and never told you I love you. I want us to be happy for the time we have left.'

'The time we have left – that's the rub. It'd be a comfort if we could be married before I leave.'

'This isn't India, my dear. Widows can't remarry straight away in Norfolk, and from what I know of you, you'd want to do what was right and proper. We'll have to wait at least a year. I'm right, aren't I? You do want everyone here to accept you and respect you?'

'You're right, my little darling. I wouldn't want you to do anything to spoil your reputation or your standing in the community and as for myself, I do want to be accepted and respected here. This is a good place, Ginny, and even if I hadn't met you I think I would still want to come back, settle here and put down roots – and I've never felt that way before either.'

Once more Ginny reached up to stroke Tovell's face. He kissed her

– a long lingering kiss. Then he embraced her gently, cradling her body against his, caressing her tenderly. She purred with pleasure and after a few minutes she whispered, 'I would never have thought that a man could have such a soft and gentle touch. Now I know why all them girls in the village ….' Ginny hesitated then said abruptly, averting her eyes as she spoke, 'Tomorrow I'll move the littl'uns back into the bed in this room and you can share the big bed with me.'

Tovell kissed the top of Ginny's head and the palms of her hands before he replied. 'That wasn't easy for you to say, was it? But it's alright, Ginny, I don't want you to do that. I know I used to tease you about sharing a bed, but it was only talk. I can wait until we're married.'

'But you can't wait. Like I'm always saying, we can't help the way we're made. We can't go against nature and we both know what your nature is. I'm not being generous, Tovell; I'm being selfish. I couldn't bear it if you went with another woman – not now.'

'But I won't, Ginny. I promise you. I don't want any other woman; I love you. Anyway, I haven't been near any of the village girls for weeks and weeks. I haven't needed to because I've been able to spend more time with you.'

'But we aren't talking about companionship, Tovell, but about your bodily needs. I'm not judging you. I know you can't help yourself so please, let it be me.'

'Ginny, Ginny, I thought we were supposed to be safeguarding your reputation in the community ….'

'But I'd risk anything rather than have you stray to another woman.'

'I won't stray, believe me. You're wrong about me, Ginny. I'm not like you think. It's my own fault; I know I give the impression …. I'm no tom-cat, Ginny.'

'I want to believe you but I think you're only trying to put my mind at rest. Share my bed and then ….'

'No Ginny. No. All I ask is that you come to me when the littl'uns are asleep and sit on my lap and let me cuddle you, kiss you and caress you as I've done tonight. That will be enough, my little darling – that will be enough.'

Ginny rested her head against Tovell's chest and was silent for a while. Then she observed quietly, 'There's more, isn't there? Something you haven't told me.'

Tovell sighed deeply. 'Yeah – there's more. I'm supposed to be the biggest lecher going yet I'm harmless as a gelding. There'd be no sense in sharing your bed and risking the littl'uns saying something to someone when I can do no more to you there than I can sitting here. Talk, Ginny. That's what I'm good at. I even had you thinking I'd rape you if you gave me half a chance. As for the girls in the village, all I've ever done is kiss and cuddle them – and not, I hasten to add, the way I have you tonight. I love you but they meant nothing to me. So why did I bother with them? Well, that really was because I couldn't help myself. If ever I've been stationed near women I've been after them. It must be something to do with being shut up in barracks with men all the time. I've never been able to pass up an opportunity to be near a woman …. But all I ever do to them is kiss and cuddle them. I couldn't do anything else even if I wanted to.'

'Why? Is it all the fighting you've been in? Did you get injured?'

Tovell smiled. 'No, sweetheart, nothing like that. I've got all the necessary equipment as you should know, seeing you're sitting on it. No, it's not that. It's difficult to explain. I don't expect you've ever come across this word but I'm what you call – impotent.'

'Does that mean you've never been with a woman – all the way?'

'I'm ashamed to say I've been with plenty of women but they've all had one thing in common – they've all been prostitutes. That's my dark secret, Ginny; I can't do it with anyone who isn't a prostitute.'

'But that doesn't make sense.'

'I know it doesn't. I've come to the conclusion that the Army's to blame. You said yourself once – and come to think of it you said it again tonight – that I like to do things right and proper. Well, it's true, I do. It's the way the Army's trained me and to me it's right and proper to go to a prostitute and pay for her services. Once I've asked her how much and handed over the money I'm alright …. But even then I've got to admit that I'm hoping she'll let me stay a while afterwards and talk to her. Many's the time I've paid double for the chance of talking to her. Talking to a woman's so different from talking to a man. When I'm with men I'm another person. I can't stop bragging and boasting – telling them how great I am. I'm not like that with a woman. I don't feel the same need to put on an act. That's why I've been so happy here, Ginny, being around you all the time – being able to talk to you whenever I've wanted – it's been like living in paradise.'

'Oh Tovell – paying to talk to a woman – I'm going to want to cry every time I think about that. How lonely you must have been. Life just isn't fair. No man as kind and generous and thoughtful as you should ever have to be lonely – should ever have to pay for a bit of company. But you'll never need to again – you'll always have me to talk to. As for your other problem, I don't see how I can help you short of becoming a prostitute myself.'

'It won't come to that, my little darling. I'm sure I'll manage fine once we're married because then it will seem right and proper to me. Once it's legal I'm sure I'll be able to perform as often as you'll have me.'

'I shan't worry even if you can't. I'll still consider myself the luckiest woman alive knowing that I'll be spending the rest of my life with you.'

All the women on the Station rallied to the support of the two new widows. Since neither Phyllis nor Emily had any skeletons in their cupboard and had enjoyed a normal happy relationship with their husbands, they were beside themselves with grief. For the first twenty four hours after receiving the news they were inconsolable and their neighbours assumed responsibility for their offspring, their homes and their lodgers whilst they sobbed their hearts out in the privacy of their bedrooms. When they had no more tears left they slept the sleep of the exhausted, and awoke resolved to carry on for the sake of their children – and because fortitude in the face of adversity was the expected and the only option.

Two weeks later, Lydia was brought to the Watch-room to answer a telephone call from the Admiralty. It was clear to the onlookers from her reaction that she was being given momentous information. When the conversation was finished she said in a serious voice, 'Could I have a word with you, Lieutenant Collins, please.'

The officer followed her down the internal staircase to the parlour and once the door was closed behind them he demanded, 'What is it? What's happened?'

'You were right,' she replied. 'At long last someone at the Admiralty has realised that there are hardly any coastguards left alive. Those that have survived are being recalled from their ships and returned to their stations. The dead coastguards are to be replaced by retired men, young Sea Scouts and new recruits. In other words, my dearest, the soldiers are to be withdrawn and reassigned.'

'When?'

'As soon as possible. I was given no details on that score. As the officer in charge you are to be contacted very shortly by the Army and given fresh orders.'

Richard, white faced, walked over to the armchair by the fire and sat down, his expression grim. 'I was certain it would happen but now that it has I'm stunned. Of course you must be very happy.'

'My mind's in a turmoil. Yes, I'm happy and very relieved that my husband is no longer condemned to death, and glad that he and the other remaining coastguards will be coming home, but the thought that you ....'

With a cry of anguish Lydia rushed across the room and threw herself at Richard's feet. He took her in his arms and for a few seconds they were locked in a silent embrace. Then he whispered, 'I don't know how I shall bring myself to leave you, sweet love-of-my-life.'

Lydia was shaking with emotion as she said, 'I'm so frightened for you, my dearest. Promise me that you'll not deliberately endanger your life. Remember you no longer have anything to prove – not to your father, your wife, your pupils or yourself.'

Ginny reacted in much the same way as Lydia when she heard the news. Clinging to Tovell, tears rolling down her cheeks, she begged him not to take any chances. 'I know you – always wanting to be in the thick of things. Remember you're not on your own any more; you've got us – me and the littl'uns – and we want you to come home safe and sound.'

Lily's words to David contained a similar argument though she delivered them much less positively. They met briefly near the bottom of the outside steps from the Watch-room as the youth came off duty – by chance as far as he was concerned, by design as far as Lily was concerned. Cradling her son against her breast and not taking her eyes from his face, Lily said, 'I'm really sorry to hear you'll be leaving soon. We shall miss you – little Arthur and me. I do hope you'll be careful. We'll be counting the days 'til you come home, that we will. Don't forget now that you're little Arthur's godfather. He's going to need you when he's growing up and so shall I.'

The next few days passed very quickly. There was a great deal of clearing up to do since all the widows were moving out to make way for their late husbands' replacements. The soldiers, preferring not to have too much spare time to dwell on what was about to befall them, gladly assisted their landladies. The families were to remain on the Station until their lodgers had departed, but any furniture and effects which could be spared was transported to the new homes in advance, whilst the men were still there to lend a hand. Emily, Phyllis, Mary and Ginny had all elected to move in with relatives; Mrs. Gillings had other ideas.

'Yes, I've made up my mind for definite,' she told Ginny one morning. 'We ent going to go and live with my brother at Yarmouth after all; we're going to accept Lord Meredith's offer of a cottage. He told his agent he was mindful of the happy times he'd spent in the company of my Arthur and he wanted us to live rent free. 'Course, I wouldn't hear of nothing like that but we finally agreed on what I must admit is a very low rent. He gave us the pick of his vacant cottages but we've settled on one in Haisbro' village, hent we Lily?'

'Yes,' replied Lily, 'that's best for my trade.'

'Are you taking up dressmaking again?' asked Ginny.

'The pension isn't much,' replied Lily, 'and we've gotta live. I'll soon get customers.'

'I've told Lily she mustn't do nothing around the new house,' said Mrs. Gillings. 'Rough hands would snag people's fine materials. She'll earn the bread and I'll look after her and little Arthur. We'll manage fine. But what about you, Ginny?'

'I've decided too,' Ginny replied. 'We're going to go live with my aunt and uncle near Whimpwell Green. They'll be glad of a hand with the smallholding and the littl'uns will help an' all.'

'So that means we all stay in the area,' cried a delighted Lily. 'Mary, Emily and Phyllis all popped in today to see what we'd decided, didn't they, Mother? Mrs. Ellis and poor Mr. Ellis will be back soon and Mrs. Brewster say she'll always be on hand if we need her, so maybe that won't be so bad after all.'

'The Admiralty still moved mighty fast once they'd made up their minds,' commented Mrs. Gillings. 'The soldiers leave Thursday and we've gotta be out the same day.'

'I don't mind,' said Ginny. 'The men say Mr. Latham's arranged for temporary replacements to start that same afternoon. I know I don't want to be here when they arrive.'

'I know what you mean, gal,' agreed Mrs. Gillings. 'A lot's happened to us here and we want to remember the place as it was.'

Tovell was pleased about Ginny's decision to set up home with her uncle and aunt. He knew she would enjoy helping the old couple to work their smallholding and he would have the satisfaction of knowing that she was not alone. He was pleased also that none of the other women was leaving the district so their comradeship would continue and they would sustain and cheer one another during the bleak days ahead.

Inevitably, a certain gloom descended upon the little community – time was running out. By the preceding Tuesday, which was the nineteenth of January 1915, Ginny was in a state of despair. When Tovell entered the house shortly after six, having completed his watch, she whispered to him, 'We've only got two nights left. I'll get the littl'uns to bed early.'

After they had eaten their supper together, Tovell took Bobby and Lizzie over to his fireside chair and cuddled them whilst he told them a bedtime story. He kept it as brief as he could without upsetting them, conscious as he was that he would be telling them only one more story before this simple pleasure would be denied him – and them. He then hurried Blackie outside for his walk as Ginny organised the children for sleep.

It was a cold, slightly misty night but there was little evidence of the snow which had covered the landscape so picturesquely over the

Christmas period. Tovell took his favourite route towards Haisbro Cliffs. The dog was so certain that that was where they were going that he led the way. The soldier was painfully aware that these walks would soon be no more than a pleasant memory. Knowing that he must keep the outing short, he paused as soon as he was within sight of the lighthouse. Once he could see it in the distance he recalled that sunny day when Ginny had been standing on the cliff-top. After a while his gaze drifted upwards to the sky above the beacon. He watched the movement of the clouds for a few seconds and was about to turn round and head for home when it suddenly dawned on him that one cloud was behaving quite differently from all the rest. It was high above the lighthouse and it seemed to be altering course, leaving its fellow clouds behind and following the line of the coast. Strangely, there also appeared to be two stars moving with the cloud. At that moment the moon obligingly put in a brief appearance enabling Tovell to see that his particular cloud was a perfect cigar shape. He lingered no longer but calling to the dog to follow, he ran back to the Station as though all the ghosts in the neighbourhood were after him. He crashed through the Watch-room door yelling, 'There's a Zeppelin headed this way!'

Sergeant Harris who had been writing at the desk, leapt to his feet. 'Fetch Lieutenant Collins from his quarters,' he shouted to Ned Jackson. 'Tovell, you get the women and children into the dug-out and I'll man the gun.'

In the next few minutes pandemonium broke loose. As Tovell ran to the cottages he bumped into David who had been lurking around the Gillings's home in the hope of catching a glimpse of Lily. He grabbed hold of the boy and told him, 'There's a Zeppelin coming. Find one of the others and go to the gun emplacement and help the sergeant. Move, Davey, move!'

The shocked youth hesitated. 'Lily and the baby ....'

'I'll take care of them,' cried Tovell as he dashed away across the green. 'You do what I tell you – and hurry.'

Tovell raced along the row of cottages banging on every front door. Then he ran back throwing each door open in turn and ordering the startled occupants to take cover in the shelter. He was soon joined by Bill Westgate. The two men rushed between the houses and the dugout carrying the younger children, all in their nightclothes, and exhorting the older ones, most of whom were clinging to pets, to make all speed. Their mothers followed behind clasping their smallest offspring, swathed in blankets, to their breasts. Ginny and Mrs. Gillings, having no babies or toddlers to carry, rounded up the stragglers. To everyone's credit, all were safely under cover before the Zeppelin came into range. The screaming then began in earnest as the terrified children covered their ears against the noise of the firing and felt the vibrations as the nearby gun went into action.

Tovell hated deserting the families but he knew his place was not inside the pitch black shelter. He shouted as loudly as he could above the din of crying children, shrieking babies and barking dogs. 'No time to get you a lantern. Huddle together and keep your heads down.'

He emerged from the dugout to hear his officer yelling, 'There are still some lights showing. Put out every lamp!' Two figures ran past him to obey so Tovell felt free to dash up the steps to the Watch-room to retrieve his rifle. Even in the darkness he knew exactly where it was. He was outside again in seconds. The entire site was now blacked out. He knelt down on one knee and aimed his rifle at the sky. He knew it was hopeless; that the chances of scoring a hit must be nil but he fired just the same. He had to make a stand against the enemy even if it were only a token one. He was aware of flashes of light around him and heard the crack of other rifles; his comrades were apparently of like mind. To his left the mobile gun belched fire and the ground shook at its every recoil. The huge airship was almost directly overhead now. No bombs fell from its belly. There was no returning gunfire – no retaliatory action at all. He had seen the craft begin to rise out of harm's way when the first volleys had left the ground and now it glided high over the frustrated defenders as though they were of no consequence whatsoever.

'Cease firing!' commanded the lieutenant.

'Bastards!' Tovell swore. 'I bet they're laughing at us. They know we can't touch them.'

'They seem to know where they're going.' It was Fred Mannell speaking.

Again Richard Collins's voice came out of the darkness, closer this time. 'Undoubtedly they do. They must have set a course for Haisbro lighthouse and now they're following the coastline round. Once more, I fear Great Yarmouth is the target. They must be after the port's military and naval installations. There's nothing more we can do except warn them. I'll telephone the Naval Air Station. Mannell, Jackson, Wilson – fetch lanterns and guide the families back to their homes. They've suffered enough for one night.'

Tovell and Bill Westgate followed the officer into the Watch-room. When they had relit the oil-lamps Bill nudged Tovell and inclined his head towards the lieutenant. Tovell turned round and saw what Bill had noticed – that their officer was bare-footed and appeared to be clad only in his dressing gown. Once he was engaged in earnest conversation on the telephone Bill whispered to Tovell, 'Poor chap. He must have been feeling properly done-in to take to his bed so early.'

No-one noticed Lydia, also wearing her dressing gown, slip away from the shelter and disappear into the night before the all-revealing lanterns arrived on the scene. As she scuttled back to her quarters she heard Mrs. Gillings's unmistakeable voice. 'That's what you call a narrow escape,' observed the old lady to her neighbours – more significantly than she knew.

The following afternoon Lieutenant Collins assembled all the men in the Watch-room. 'At ease everyone,' he began. 'An hour ago I received our orders for tomorrow. We shall all travel to London by train, then the sergeant and Tovell will proceed to Southampton and board the first available troopship to France to rejoin their respective regiments. The rest of us are to report to Richmond Park where we are to be absorbed into a London Regiment.'

'I'd better get on with arranging the transport to Stalham Station, Sir,' said Sergeant Harris.

'No need, sergeant,' replied the officer. 'I've had a telephone call from Lord Meredith's agent. It seems his lordship has been impressed by the good work we've done here and thinks we deserve to leave in style. He's sending his two motor cars to transport us to the railway station.'

'That's very good of him, Sir,' said the sergeant with a certain amount of relief in his voice. With so little notice of the details of their actual redeployment, he had had visions of resorting to Mrs. Gillings's horse and cart as a means of transport.

Lieutenant Collins continued his address. 'I should also like to echo

Lord Meredith's sentiments. I too think that you've done an excellent job. I should like to thank you all for your diligent attention to your duties and, of course, to wish you luck.'

The sergeant responded. 'Thank you, Sir. And if I might say on behalf of the men, we all feel it's been a privilege to serve with you, Sir, and we wish you luck too.'

Richard Collins was so embarrassed by the chorus of 'hear, hear' which followed that he could not end the meeting quickly enough. 'Thank you, Sergeant! Thank you men!' he muttered. 'And now if there are no further questions ....'

'There is a question, Sir. All of us were shaken by what happened last night. Have you any news about the Zeppelin?' asked the sergeant.

The lieutenant relaxed. Being told he had earned the respect of his fellows had been like sailing in uncharted seas but answering a factual question was familiar territory. 'Yes, I have,' he replied at once. 'I've been in contact with the Naval Air Station, of course, but I also sent for the late edition of the local newspaper. I felt sure it would carry an account of the raid and it does. It seems that a second airship followed the first across the North Sea. You didn't catch sight of it, did you, Tovell?'

'No, Sir,' replied Tovell, 'but then I didn't hang about either. As soon as I realised what it was I'd been watching I was off like a shot from a gun.'

'It seems the second one veered right and followed the north Norfolk coast to Kings Lynn. Their bombs killed two people there but others fell harmlessly in countryside outside Sheringham and Hunstanton, although the newspaper is sure the target was Sandringham. They mention the indignation of the civilised world that His Majesty should suffer, without actually saying whether he was in residence. And you'll be pleased to know, Tovell, that the entire county is now convinced that enemy agents have been landing on our beaches for weeks. Every other man and his dog reports seeing spies in brightly lighted motor cars assisting the airships with signals.

But I must not jest,' said the officer altering the tone of his voice, 'it's a very serious matter. The airship which passed over our heads dropped nine high explosive bombs on Great Yarmouth, killing two people and damaging many homes. The newspaper, quite rightly, makes the point that at that moment the world experienced the first aerial bombardment in its history. It's bad enough that the Hun has transformed the submarine into a lethal weapon but now that they appear to have developed the Zeppelin to deliver death from the skies, the implications are even more hideous.'

'What about the Air Station, Sir?' asked the sergeant. 'You warned them.'

'They were powerless to stop the attack. They had three machines in operation but by the time they were ready to take off the airship had gone. The Station Commander admits that his aeroplanes could not have matched the height and speed of the Zeppelin and their only armament is still the single rifle carried by the passenger. Any attempt at attack would have been as ineffectual as our own puny efforts.'

'That means there's nothing to stop them dropping their bombs anywhere,' observed Ned Jackson, 'even where our families live.'

'I've no doubt,' said Lieutenant Collins, 'that last night's attack was something of a test – a trial run, if you like.'

'They could hit London next,' cried Fred Mannell, his voice rising.

'Or Birmingham where my missus is,' added Bill Westgate.

Lieutenant Collins could see that the subject of airships was far from being safe ground. He sensed a feeling of panic spreading amongst his men. David also looked about to open his mouth and voice his fears. He must calm the situation. 'Gentlemen, gentlemen, I understand your concerns for your families. We are totally unused to an enemy attacking in an indiscriminate manner so that unarmed civilians can be harmed. But please rest assured that the significance of last night's raid will not be lost on our leaders. They set up naval air stations like the one at Great Yarmouth all along the east coast before the war – admittedly only for reconnaissance purposes then – but undoubtedly their role will change and they will become the first line of defence against the Zeppelins.'

'It seems to me,' said Tovell, 'that the biggest worry is that the initiative is always with the Hun. They invent something or they think of a way of doing something which has never been done before. When are we going to come up with a first that will shock them?'

'I agree,' replied the lieutenant. 'Germany is a great industrial nation but we, thank God, have our scientists and engineers too. They are going to need luck as much as we shall in the coming months and inspiration too.'

Tovell was able to escape from the *Admiral Lord Nelson* that evening after only thirty minutes. As he told Ginny, 'Everyone in the bar was so preoccupied with the Zeppelins that I don't think they noticed me leaving. That headline, *Dropping bombs on babies' cribs,* had really made for heated conversations. Still, I promised to go and say goodbye and I kept my promise. Did Mrs. Gillings hear from her brother?'

'Yes, thank the Lord,' replied Ginny. 'She was worried sick but he sent her a telegram to say they were alright.'

As Tovell took off his coat he said to Ginny, 'Don't forget that I'm on duty at six in the morning so you'll bring the littl'uns to see me before they leave for school, won't you? If I can't delay going out on patrol I'll double back so I can give them a hug and a kiss goodbye.'

They spent their last evening together in the armchair beside the cooking range with Ginny curled up on Tovell's lap. They were both strangely silent. They had lamented again and again that they had had so little time together. They had confided to each other over and over their hopes and fears for the future. All that needed to be said had been said and said repeatedly. They watched the flames flickering in the hearth in a state of despondency until Tovell, just before midnight, suggested as tactfully as he could that they should try to get some sleep.

'I reckon you're right,' agreed Ginny. 'But I don't care what you say I'm not leaving you tonight. This once I'm going to take a chance on anyone finding out and I'm going to get into your little bed with you. We haven't got long with you being on duty at six.'

'I'm not going to argue with you,' said Tovell, hugging her affectionately. 'I don't want to be parted from you either. Remember the last time you climbed in with me? You must have cuddled me for hours and I didn't know a thing about it. What a crime.'

They clung together in the darkness sleeping only fitfully until it was time to get up. When Tovell had left the house Ginny lay on his bed once more and drenched his pillow with her tears. She took the children to see him before they left for school. Their sad goodbyes distressed her so much that she cried uncontrollably for most of the morning. She forced herself to prepare a meal for when Tovell came off duty at midday, but neither of them could manage to swallow so much as a mouthful.

Lieutenant Collins had instructed that the cars must be loaded and ready to leave at thirteen hundred hours. All the men except the lieutenant gathered outside at the appointed time and the two drivers helped them with their kit. The women and the youngest children came out too to give their former lodgers a farewell embrace and to wish them well – all except Lydia. They crowded round exchanging last minute messages. Mrs. Gillings was too misty eyed herself to notice Ginny's swollen tear-stained face. She did not see David take Lily's hand either as he kissed baby Arthur; nor did she hear him extract a whispered promise from Lily that she would write to him. Lieutenant Collins was late. He apologised, blaming the heavy cold from which he was suffering for confusing him. It was necessary for him to blow his nose loudly and often whilst his luggage was loaded. He also passed on Mrs. Brewster's apologies, explaining that she could not come out to see the soldiers off because she could not leave the telephone and the Watch-room whilst it was temporarily unmanned.

The time had come and the women all shook Lieutenant Collins's hand and gave each of the other soldiers a final hug in turn. Mrs. Gillings favoured Tovell with a quick peck on the cheek as well. 'Do you take care and mind you come back to us. Your place is here. Ginny and the littl'uns need you.'

'Thanks Mrs. G,' replied Tovell warmly. 'And you take good care of yourself too.'

Tovell paused in front of Ginny – neither dared to speak. A tortured look, a quick hug and he climbed into the car. The women, carrying the toddlers and babies, gathered at the perimeter wall as the cars drove out through the gate and onto the track to the main road. They waved until their arms ached. Then they returned sadly to their cottages, already stripped bare of many of their treasures, and completed their packing whilst they waited for their relatives to arrive with carts which would take them and the remainder of their belongings to their new homes. Within the hour, they too had made their departure.

Tovell, Sergeant Harris and Lieutenant Collins were in the lead car. The officer huddled in one corner, a handkerchief to his nose. 'I'll try to keep away from you. Don't want you to catch my heavy cold. You won't mind if I don't socialise, will you? I'm not at all well.'

'We don't mind, Sir,' replied the sergeant. 'We're not in a talkative mood ourselves, are we, Tovell?'

'That's right, Sir,' agreed Tovell. 'For the first time in our lives we know what it feels like to be leaving home.'

As they drove into Stalham, Tovell was reminded of that hot August day when he had first arrived. Could it be only five months ago? It seemed more like a lifetime ago. Once again, elderly men touched their caps as the soldiers drove by and many of the townspeople stopped and called out good wishes. As the cars drew up in front of the railway station Kath, the landlady of the *Kings Head*, was standing on the opposite side of the road on the steps of her establishment. She waved to the soldiers and bade them good luck as they unloaded their kit and went into the station. Once they had reached their platform, generously decorated with posters of Lord Kitchener proclaiming that, *Your country needs YOU*, they were joined by Ted Carter and two Brigade members. 'We thought we'd just come along and see you boys off,' said Ted as he embraced Tovell.

The train was on time and none of the soldiers was sorry. They had all had their fill of goodbyes. Lieutenant Collins took the opportunity whilst the final handshakes and good wishes were being exchanged with the members of the Volunteer Life-saving Brigade to wander off and find the first class carriages. He was thankful that the privileges of rank allowed him to travel apart from his men. He longed to close his eyes and succumb to the feeling of utter hopelessness which had threatened to engulf him ever since he had taken a painful and emotional parting from his beloved. As he climbed morosely into the carriage, shoulders bent, eyes downcast, he almost bumped into an officer in naval uniform who was leaving the train. As he mumbled his regrets he found he was looking into a familiar face. Those features had passed judgement on him every day from the photograph on Lydia's piano. He threw his luggage onto the rack and sat down in the empty carriage determined not to look back, but as the train shuddered preparatory to moving off he could not resist one glance out of the window. Any doubts he might have had about the identity of the man were dispelled at once. Ted Carter and the others were greeting him excitedly and pointing to the carriage where Richard Collins assumed the soldiers must be gathered. His last glimpse of the officer was of him waving and smiling to his men.

He slumped back in his seat. It was too much to bear – it was the last straw. They would be together within the hour. He was condemned to pass this miserable journey in agony, tormented by the picture of Lydia's husband taking her in his arms. Lydia – his Lydia whom he would never see again. What was left for him now? He could only pray that he would be sent to the Front quickly and that the enemy would put an end to his torture for him. Life no longer held any purpose. He had found his soul-mate and lost her again. There was no reason to go on living.

II

In the days following Tovell's departure, Ginny could not eat properly, could not sleep and could not rid herself of a pounding headache. She knew she had to rise above this overwhelming feeling of despondency because she must prevent her uncle and aunt from realising that she was pining for Tovell. She must also try her hardest to lift the children's depression. Bobby and Lizzie missed the friend who had lavished so much time and attention on them and it was no easy task to raise their gloomy spirits. The need for all three of them to establish a new routine to suit their changed lifestyle helped, and they were cheered when they each received a loving and encouraging letter from Tovell, posted just before he boarded his troopship.

Lily did her share of pining too and had to be even more careful not to let her mother-in-law guess just how dejected she was feeling. One day about four weeks later, David turned up unexpectedly on the doorstep of the Gillings's new home in Haisbro. Even Mrs. Gillings was pleased to see him and with baby Arthur on his knee he told the two women all his news. The Army was now satisfied with his standard of training and had given him forty eight hours draft leave prior to embarkation for, *an unknown overseas destination*. He had spent the previous day with his parents and brothers and sisters, but had left them early so that he could return to his camp via Haisbro. As he told the Gillings family, he could not go back without seeing his godson.

'I've got some really good news,' he blurted out as soon as they were all seated. 'They lined us all up one day and this officer came along and he say he's looking for specialists. He had this great long list that he read out and when he say, "Do any of you men hold a Red Cross Certificate?" I say, "I do, Sir." That's funny how these things happen, isn't it? That was only last spring that our vicar he say, "I reckon I can hear the rumblings of war. If that does come, and heaven forbid, that's our Christian duty to be prepared. My brother's a Red Cross man and he say he needs volunteers to train so as they'll know how to look after any casualties." Then he say, "I'm a-calling on as many of my parishioners as can, to enroll with the Red Cross." Well, my mother and a lot of the other mothers were wholly vexed. They say the vicar hadn't got no right and that he was talking a war up, but Father he say, "That won't do no harm to learn first aid and that might come in handy on the farm anyway." So I joined and did two evenings a week first aid instruction and stretcher drill and soon got my certificate. Now Mother's that pleased because they made me hand in my rifle straightaway. They say, "You won't need no gun, boy, if you're going to be a stretcher-bearer.'"

'I know how your mother feels,' cried Lily happily. 'That's a great relief to her – and to all of us – to know you won't be in any danger. If you haven't got a gun you can't be in any fighting.'

Mrs. Gillings said nothing. Worldly wise as she was, she watched the young couple chattering cheerfully together and could see no point in shattering their illusion and spoiling the hour or so they had in one another's company. She would also do anything to protect her Lily from any more anguish. Suddenly, she said, 'That's a nice bright, dry day – why don't the pair of you take little Arthur for a walk? I'll have a bite to eat ready time you get back.' Both Lily and David looked at Mrs. Gillings in astonishment.

Lily had dressed herself and the baby in their outdoor clothes faster than she had ever done before, and with David carrying his godson they hurried to Haisbro Cliffs. Once there, they decided the wind was too strong and chilly for the little one and they scrambled down the town gap until they were on the beach. They found a reasonably sheltered spot underneath the cliff, sat down and huddled shyly together against the cold with David still cuddling the baby.

They sat in silence for a while then David, in an attempt to overcome their mutual embarrassment at finding themselves for once alone, referred to the fact that Lily had been sewing when Mrs. Gillings had invited him into their small parlour. 'Yes, I've taken up my trade again,' said Lily proudly. 'I'm not clever at anything else and that did seem a shame to waste the skill that the good Lord had given me. I don't just make things, of course; I do repairs and alterations and anything people want. Lady Meredith has been very kind. She sends me work from the Hall and she's recommended me to a lot of her friends. Once I'd got a letter from you I was going to write back and explain what I was doing – if it wasn't too difficult, that is. Like I say, David, I'm not very clever – except at sewing.'

'I know what you mean, Lily. I tried several times to write to you to tell you about being a stretcher-bearer but when another soldier told me we'd get leave before we sailed that seemed easier to come and tell you. But when we get to wherever we're going, I promise to write to you and I hope you won't think badly of me if the spelling and so on isn't quite right.'

'I won't think badly of you, David, and you've gotta promise me that you won't think badly of me because of my poor letter-writing.'

'I could never think badly of you, Lily – not for anything. And as for your work, you won't take on too much, will you? If you can't manage I could always send you some money. As you know, I send most of my wages home, but I've told Mother and Father all about you and the baby, and I know they wouldn't mind if I gave some of it to you.'

'That's kind of you David, but I couldn't do anything like that. My mother-in-law would never let me anyway – she's always drumming it into me that people should take pride in being independent and standing on their own feet. And another thing – with all them mouths to feed your mother must be glad of every penny you can send her. That wouldn't be right to take anything away from her.'

'But I don't like to think of you working so hard, Lily.'

'That isn't hard work, David, because I love it, and my mother-in-law doesn't let me do anything else. She won't let me do housework, or gardening and she won't let me put my hands in water at all except to clean them. She does everything for little Arthur and all the cooking and washing herself. She say I can't afford to let my hands get rough.'

'Well, I reckon Mrs. Gillings knows what she's about but I still say you shouldn't overdue things and make yourself ill.'

'Don't you worry, David, I'm never ill. I haven't been ill since ….,

since that time I lost control of myself and went in the water. Do you remember that? It wasn't far from here – just a little further down the beach. If it hadn't been for you we wouldn't be sitting here now – baby and me. I reckon I can never thank you enough for that.'

'You don't have to thank me, Lily. If anything had happened to you I wouldn't have forgiven myself. You must know what you and little Arthur mean to me. I think about you every spare moment I have and I always make sure you're in my mind just afore I go to sleep so as I'll dream about you.'

'That's the same with me, David, only I have to try not to think of you during the day. I can't concentrate on my work with you in my mind – but at night when I'm in bed I think of you for hours.'

'You've never said how you feel before, but of course you couldn't – that wouldn't have been right. I reckon you wouldn't have said anything now if I hadn't been going off to war.'

'That's right, David. I wouldn't have said anything if you hadn't been going to war.'

'I know I shouldn't ask this when you haven't been a widow for long but I don't know when I'll get another chance ...., Lily, will you wait for me?'

'I'd have waited for you even if you hadn't asked. I loved Arthur – he was so good to me – but I love you now he's gone. I don't reckon he'd mind, in fact I think he'd be thankful I'd met someone who'd care for the baby and me just like he would have done. I'll wait for you, David, 'til you come home. There won't be no-one else, I promise.'

'Oh Lily, I'm so happy I think I'm going to burst. I've wanted to speak afore but I didn't darst in case I caused offence and you didn't want anything more to do with me. I want to put my arms around you but I'm afraid of dropping little Arthur.'

'You can put one arm round me and I'll put one arm round you and one round the baby. See, that works. He likes being cuddled by both of us at once. And I can also put my head on your shoulder.'

They held one another rather stiffly, David being even less relaxed than Lily. He had never been in such a situation before and was unsure of what was expected of him next. He was sitting so rigidly that his position soon became uncomfortable but he could not move for fear that Lily might think he did not enjoy being so close to her. He was further disconcerted to find that his left arm, the one encircling Lily, was twitching and shaking involuntarily. All his efforts to control the nerves and muscles failed. Then Lily, sensing his distress and partly misinterpreting it, lifted her head and gazed up at him red-faced. 'Oh, David,' she began rather self-consciously, 'I don't know what's come over me – being so forward, I mean. I do hope you aren't going to think ill of me for speaking out like that – saying I love you.'

Now that Lily was looking abashed David was able to regain some measure of composure. 'I could never think ill of you Lily – never. I'm glad that you spoke out and like I say, I know I've got to thank going overseas for that. You would never have said anything normally.'

'That I wouldn't,' said Lily emphatically. 'I'd have waited for you to speak first at the proper time.' Anxious to allay once and for all any suspicions that David might have that she was a wanton hussy she added, 'I reckon we ought to be going. That's none too warm sitting here and that wouldn't do for someone to see us.'

The young couple retraced their footsteps towards the gap in the cliffs but then instead of continuing on to the Gillings's cottage, they turned right by mutual but unspoken consent and wandered through the churchyard. They stepped carefully between the graves, many of them the last resting place of seafarers whose bodies had been washed ashore after their ships had fallen victim to the dangerous shoals nearby. They paused briefly at a large green mound, the communal home of the earthly remains of one hundred and nineteen of Nelson's men, the crew of *HMS Invincible* which had been on her way to join the fleet at Copenhagen when she had perished on Haisbro Sands. Lily gazed sorrowfully at the inscription on the tombstone and murmured, 'All those poor men – drowned.'

David looked at her anxiously. He touched her hand and suggested quietly, 'Let's go inside and say a little prayer.' They walked slowly towards the imposing structure of the church of St. Mary the Virgin, built in a commanding position on the sloping cliff-side where it could keep watch on the treacherous seas to the east whilst at the same time guarding the rich acres of farmland to the west. They looked up at the tower stretching high into the sky, buttressed to its parapet against the furious winds which lashed the wild exposed coastline, passed beneath the statue of Our Lady which resided above the porch door and entered the church where they had worshipped together every Sunday that David's duties had permitted.

They stopped beneath the ornate octagonal font and the boy playfully lifted the baby up and showed him where he had been christened. Then they crept down the main aisle trying to make as little noise as possible, not wanting to disturb the tranquility of the empty building. They felt rather overawed by their surroundings which appeared strangely unfamiliar now that the church was no longer crowded with parishioners. They sat towards the front in pews much closer to the High Altar than those they usually occupied and Lily glanced around her at the beautiful stained glass windows. She leaned closer to David and whispered, 'I've always liked this church – that isn't dark and gloomy like some churches. Even if it's dull outside – it's always bright in here.'

David nodded his agreement. 'I reckon that's because of being high up – nothing to stop the light.' The boy looked down at the infant on his lap. Little Arthur was contentedly chewing his mittens and raised no objection when the young soldier, still carefully cradling him in his arms, learnt forward and began to pray in a voice just loud enough for the child's mother to hear. 'Dear Lord, I know a lot of people must be asking you favours now there's a war on, but as I'm going away and can't look after them myself I'd be right glad if you'd keep a particular eye on Lily and baby Arthur here. Please take good care of them, Lord, and when it's all over I promise I'll be back to do the job myself. That wouldn't be fitting for us to tell anyone else now but Lily and me love each other and we wanted to tell you. When I come home and when Lily's time of mourning is over, we'll be married, and I promise that we'll bring up little Arthur and any other littl'uns that you bless us with, to be good and true Christians. And though I've thanked you many times afore, Lord, I'm thanking you again now for letting Lily and me meet. She means the world to me and I'll be forever grateful to you, Lord.'

Lily had left her seat and knelt on the hassock in front of her as soon as David had begun his prayer. When he finished speaking she began her own petition. 'Dear Lord, what David say is true – we do love each other and I promise, here before you, that I'll wait for him till we can be wed. So please, dear Lord, I beg you to watch over him and protect him from all harm and all evil while he's away at the war. Thank you, Lord, for all the good things you've given me and especially for David and little Arthur.'

Lily paused for a moment and then began to recite the Lord's Prayer. David at once joined in and after the final "Amen" Lily sat back in her seat and smiled at David. 'I reckon,' said the boy softly, 'that what we've just done is what you call, plight our troth, with the Lord as our Witness. Perhaps we ought to seal our vow with a kiss – if that's alright to kiss in church.'

'That's what a bride and groom does to seal their vows during the wedding service so that must be alright for us,' murmured Lily, eyes modestly downcast.

Inwardly trembling, David edged closer to Lily and timidly kissed her on the lips. He would have drawn back but the girl placed her hand behind his head and pressed her lips harder against his. For a few seconds he was conscious of the depth of her feelings for him. Desire welled up inside him and he responded eagerly. A thump in the chest from a tiny fist and a wail of protest from the fist's owner put an end to David's sudden burst of passion. 'Poor little mite,' said the youth soothingly. 'I forgot he was there. I must have been squashing him.'

'Perhaps he doesn't like us kissing,' suggested Lily. 'You don't have any cause to be jealous,' she told her baby with a laugh. 'We both love you an'all, don't we, David?'

'That we do,' agreed the young soldier. 'We'd better both give him a kiss too, so as he'll know.'

The display of affection had the hoped for effect and little Arthur stopped crying. 'It must be getting late,' declared his mother. 'We'd better be going before you miss your train.'

They hurried to the porch door but before they passed through it, David hesitated. Lily looked at him questionably. 'I've never kissed a young lady afore – except Annie,' he confided shyly.

'You were a long time,' remarked Mrs. Gillings after David had left. 'I hope you and the baby dint catch cold.'

'We didn't catch cold,' Lily replied. 'We went into the church and said a few prayers.'

'That was a lovely thing to do,' said her mother-in-law. 'There's no time in a man's life when he needs a woman's prayers more than when he's going off to war. What you did today should be a great comfort to David.'

Lily had the grace to blush and applied herself more diligently to her sewing. Mrs. Gillings considered for a while before deciding that the occasion demanded further comment. 'Put your work down a minute, gal, and listen to what I have to say. You've had a lot of trouble heaped on your young shoulders with my Arthur getting killed and I hope you won't have no more. I don't want to see you get hurt again, Lily, but you've got to understand that in wartime a lot of nasty things happen. You may say why does the good Lord let them happen? That int an easy question to answer. Just remember that the Lord's got his reasons and He doesn't always see fit to reveal them to us. Try to keep in mind the words of that there hymn we sing of a Sunday – *God moves in a mysterious way His wonders to perform. He plants His footsteps in the sea and rides upon the storm.*

Now you've gotta think of this here war as a storm and like all storms, that'll pass eventually. That int a mite o' use a-worrying about what might happen; you gotta get on with the business of living your life for little Arthur's sake. You've gotta ride that little old storm, gal. You've gotta sit up there on them storm clouds alongside of the Lord. Do you remember the third verse of that there hymn – the one that tells you, *fresh courage take*? Don't you forget that the rest of that verse say, *The clouds ye so much dread are big with mercy and shall break in blessings on your head.*'

III

Ginny's aunt believed in strict observance of the Sabbath and she would allow only the most essential work to be carried out on that day. As a result, Ginny always retired to her room after she had put the children to bed and spent every Sunday evening writing to Tovell. At first she was dissatisfied with her efforts; she had previously had little reason to put pen to paper and even her few letters to her husband or brothers had been undertaken as a duty rather than a labour of love. She wanted her letters to Tovell to express her true feelings but when she read them through the words sounded stilted and the overall effect was, to her mind, inadequate. This was not the case with Tovell's letters to her and eventually she realised it was because Tovell wrote exactly as he spoke. She immediately adopted the same method, and pushing aside all her worries about spelling and grammar, she would pretend that he was sitting opposite her and she was telling him what the children had been doing and bringing him up to date with the local news. When she reached the final paragraph of the letter she would conjure up a mental picture of herself sitting on Tovell's lap by the fireside, and the words of love would flow spontaneously.

Tovell, for his part, noticed the difference but made no comment. Now when he read her letters he could hear Ginny speaking to him and the miles which separated them vanished and they were together once more. His own letters to her contained little factual detail since censorship prevented the communication of any news calculated to convey information to the enemy should the mail be intercepted. For all that the letters were never short – they had often been written over a number of days – and were a repeated confirmation of his devotion. He was careful, however, always to include at least one anecdote which Ginny could recount to the children. Almost always, these referred to some incident or to some aspect of their former daily routine which showed that Tovell remembered every tiny detail of the time he had lived with the family.

Once he wrote, *Tell Lizzie and Bobby they'd laugh if they could see me shaving now — it's so cold here that I save the last few drops of my tea and shave with that!*

Even Blackie wouldn't be able to stand the smell of my feet these days. It's an offence to get trench foot so we have to rub our feet every day with whale oil — yes, whale oil!

Another time he described what life was like during the short spells he was given away from the fighting. Once more he demonstrated that wherever he might be, his thoughts were with those he loved. *Spent a few days in a rest camp but didn't get much rest. We slept ten to a bell tent and the other nine blokes snored louder than I do!*

Drank plenty of cocoa while I was there — you could buy it from the Y.M.C.A. tent — but you can tell the little ones that it didn't taste as good as their ma's cocoa.

A concert party called the Follies came to entertain us one evening. We had a good laugh and the show ended with a singsong. I thought of Mrs. Gillings and the singsongs she used to lead in Mrs. Brewster's parlour.

And there were references to established rituals. *The battalion marched seven miles today — for a bath! We hadn't had one for months. I bet Bobby and Lizzie envy me getting out of a weekly bath but you can tell them that two minutes under a spray of hot water which turns cold without warning, will never compare with a soak in their old tin bath in front of the cooking range.*

The food parcels which Tovell received from Ginny invariably prompted him to call to mind some happy occasion. *It was lovely getting some more home-cooking from you yesterday, sweetheart. Only thing is, I worry that you're sending me food you could do with yourselves. You won't ever do that, will you? I couldn't bear to think of you and the little ones going short because of me.*

You can be sure that all the stuff you've sent already has been really appreciated. We usually share our food parcels; it would be a crime to leave them lying around uneaten for the rats to get. I thought India was the place for rats but the trenches are full of them. Some are nearly as big as the bandicoots I used to tell the children about.

That last cake you sent — with all the fruit and spices in it — brought back memories. I shut my eyes as I was eating it and pretended it was Christmas again. We had a marvellous time together, didn't we, my little darling?

One letter especially comforted Ginny and lifted her spirits. *I had to write straightaway, my little love, to give you this piece of news. Yesterday I had a half-day pass and as there was a town about five miles away I went there for a meal. I found a cheap coffee-house and was eating away when I realised that the three men at the next table were speaking in Norfolk dialect. I asked them where they were from and they said, Haisbro. You won't believe it, Ginny, but it turned out that they were your brothers. Needless to say, we talked our heads off. They wanted to know how you and the little ones were getting on and all the news from home. They send their love and told me to tell you that they're sorry they don't write much but that doesn't mean they don't enjoy the food parcels you send them.*

You'll be pleased to know that we went out and found a photographer's shop and had our picture taken together. We gave the man your address and he promised to send it on to you. Hope you like it. We were all sober – at least we were when that was taken. They're all good lads, Ginny. No wonder you're so proud of them.

Ginny's delight when she received the promised photograph knew no bounds. She showed it to everyone who might have the slightest interest in the four soldiers and then she bought it the most elaborate frame she could afford. She cleared the little table beside her bed of all other possessions and placed the picture there where it would be the last thing she saw before going to sleep and the first thing she set eyes on when she awoke.

The letter describing the meeting which had led to the taking of that special photograph she kept apart from the rest. It was tied up in a separate piece of ribbon together with another letter which she wanted to read over and over again because it held a particular meaning for her. She received the second letter in the summer of 1915 and in it Tovell referred to the day he had seen Ginny standing near the lighthouse on Haisbro Cliffs – the day her brothers had left to join the Army. *Do you remember, my little darling, that I compared you to the poppies? I said I thought they were lovely because they were bright, cheerful and colourful – like you. The red poppy grows wild here too, Ginny. The fields are full of them – just like they are at home. So you see, sweetheart, I have in front of me a constant reminder of you. The sight of all these flowers gives me hope – hope that one day I'll be back in our own Poppyland with you, my only love.*

Shortly after Ginny received that letter, news came of the first casualty among the seven soldiers who had manned the Coastguard Station. The three wives who had spent Christmas 1914 at the Station had all kept in touch with the women with whom they had stayed, and Mrs. Mannell wrote to Phyllis to tell her that Fred was dead. Then, at the end of that summer, Mrs. Ellis received an official notification from the Army regarding her former lodger. She had returned to the Station as soon as her husband had been fit enough to make the journey and Wilfred Ellis, his scarred face a testimony to his suffering, had resumed his duties as a coastguard. Their son Peter had become a Sea Scout and was also employed at the Station, undertaking a routine which he regarded as preliminary training until he was old enough to enlist in the Royal Navy. Sergeant Harris had written to Peter regularly since he had left to join his regiment. When his letters suddenly stopped coming Ginny had assured Mrs. Ellis that the same thing had happened a few times with Tovell's letters. She had worried unnecessarily because then several had turned up at once. In Jack Harris's case the letters had not been held up and the Army informed Mrs. Ellis that she was the sole beneficiary of his will.

Sergeant Harris had lost contact with his relatives long ago and for him, as for so many others, the Army had been a substitute wife and family. A premonition that Gallipoli would be his Waterloo had prompted him to make a will in favour of the lady who had made him most welcome in her home, who had gone out of her way to make life comfortable for him and shown him every kindness. Like Tovell, he had never been made a fuss of before and like Tovell, he had felt that she deserved his savings rather than the State or some distant relatives who had never bothered with him. He had been saving for the day when he would retire from the Army; Mrs. Ellis now gratefully set aside that money for her husband's retirement. She also received Jack Harris's personal effects. His gold watch and chain she gave to Peter; the other items she kept in a little polished inlaid box. Throughout the remainder of her life she would open the box at intervals and shed a few tears over its contents – a letter from a long-dead mother, a farewell note from a faithless sweetheart, a few faded photographs of comrades, medals and ribbons of campaigns past and a small tattered bible with a sprig of honeysuckle pressed inside.

Christmas 1915 and the annual Christmas Day party was in full swing in Lydia Brewster's parlour. Peter Ellis was in charge of the children's games and there were many new faces amongst the adults. In one corner, however, sat Mrs. Gillings and all her former neighbours; Lydia had persuaded her husband to invite all the women and their children, firstly because she could not imagine a Christmas party without them and secondly because she was desperate for news. She had endured more pain in the intervening year than either Ginny or Lily for she did not have the balm of comforting letters from her loved one. At the first opportunity Lydia joined the little group. 'I'm so glad you could all come,' she said, for the second time, as she sat down.

'That was very good of you to invite us,' replied Mrs. Gillings. 'We dint expect to be invited now you've got the replacement people to feed.'

'It wouldn't be the same without you,' Lydia assured them all.

'I reckon we ought to call ourselves the Old Crew,' suggested Mary with a laugh.

'Mr. Brewster and Mr. Ellis are on watch now. They'll join us at six,' explained Lydia. 'In the meantime, why don't we all pool our news?'

Lily, shyly, opened the proceedings. 'We've got a picture to show you, haven't we, Mother? We got it yesterday with a letter from David. He say his Commanding Officer had the picture taken so his men could send copies home. It shows all thirty members of David's medical unit.'

The picture was passed around the group and duly admired. Then Phyllis spoke up. 'I had another letter from Mrs. Mannell the other day. She's found out how Fred died. She went to see his pal who'd been invalided out after Ypres. A bullet didn't kill Fred; that hideous stuff the Hun invented killed him – poison gas.'

'Poor old Fred,' said Emily. 'Good job he and his wife had a nice Christmas together last year, here with us.'

'I keep telling myself that when I think of poor Jack Harris,' said Mrs. Ellis. 'Peter say they had a lovely Christmas last year. You know I asked Mr. Latham if he could find out what happened to Jack, well he wrote back to me last week. It wasn't a bullet in his case either – it was cholera. He'd been a soldier all his life. He wouldn't have wanted that kind of death.'

'Mr. Latham told Mr. Brewster that the regiment was sent to the Dardanelles,' added Lydia sadly. 'They say as many have died on the

Gallipoli peninsula from heat, thirst and disease as from battle wounds. Poor Sergeant Harris – such a nice man. Lieutenant Collins thought highly of him. Er …. I don't suppose anyone has any news of Lieutenant Collins, do they?'

'Almost forgot!' shouted Mary. 'I brought this postcard to show you all. It's from Bill Westgate – lovely isn't it, with all the lace and embroidery and gold thread? On the back he sends his good wishes to all of us and he say he's looking forward to the Christmas dinner which is being provided by their new company officer – Captain Richard Collins! Look, see how he's underlined the last bit so as we'll know.'

The card was eagerly passed around. Lydia could not trust herself to take it because she was shaking so much but she leaned over and read it as Ginny, who was sitting next to her, held it in her hands. When she could contain herself no longer, she jumped to her feet exclaiming, 'Gracious, the preserves bowl is empty. Must excuse me – soon refill it.' Lydia fled to the pantry and took refuge there where she had hidden from her guests in quite different circumstances twelve months before. She leant with her back against the door where Richard had stood, shut her eyes and saw his laughing face. Then she repeated softly to herself again and again until she was composed, 'He's alive. He's still alive. Thank God, oh, thank God.'

1916

I

1916 began badly for Ginny; at the end of January she was informed that her youngest brother, Ben, had been killed. This news was dreadful enough but a few weeks later when another young man returned on leave to the village and told her how needlessly he had died, her distress was compounded. She learned that her brother had been in the forward trenches where, during the hours of darkness, sentries were posted at intervals along the high firing-step so that they could see over the top of the trench and keep watch for any of the enemy daring to cross *no man's land*. There was, of course, an element of risk to any soldier standing on the firing-step – the risk that the moon might suddenly shine brightly through the clouds, or signal rockets and star shells – tracer flares – might light up the night sky, making the soldier visible to the sentries in the German trenches opposite. The danger was greatest for the men who had the final two hour watch of the night; the ones who had to hold their position until their officer gave the order to stand down. Ginny's brother was one of the unlucky ones. Perhaps daybreak came a little early that day, or the officer was a minute or two late giving the order to stand down, but the boy was seen by an enemy sniper and killed instantaneously by a single bullet.

The only solace Ginny could find in the way her brother had met his death was that he had not suffered. She clung grimly to that one consolation, telling herself night after night as she gazed at his photograph beside her bed, that if he had to die at all he would have wished it to be that way. He had been such an active lad, such a mischievous little boy, that he would have hated being crippled or an invalid dependent upon others. This thought, however, was of no help to her when a voice inside her head kept shouting, 'Why? Why all the years of growing up? Why all the years of caring and hoping? For what? For nothing? What good has his death done? What purpose has it served? Why did he have to die – so young? Why?'

Ginny searched for the answers in the woods and the fields where they had walked together; in the church where they had worshipped; in the house, now empty, where they had once lived. Reconciliation to his death was slow in coming and never came totally, but at the end of April she set aside her grieving to welcome home her other two brothers.

They had a surprise for her – both were getting married while they were on leave. They had been writing to childhood sweethearts in the village for months they told her, but the decision to marry had been recent. Ginny, wisely, made no comment other than to congratulate them and wish them well. She knew they had had no such plans when they had left home and no special relationships with the young ladies they were now intending to wed. Obviously, the death of the baby of the family following hard upon the loss of other friends and comrades had had a profound effect. Ginny could understand that in those circumstances a man might ask himself, 'What if I die next – what will I leave behind me? Will it be as though I've never lived?' By marrying a man ensured that he would be remembered – at least for a while – by his widow, and if he also left behind a child he would be remembered for even longer. Ginny, therefore, did not raise the issue of whether it was appropriate for the family to be celebrating marriages whilst still in mourning for Ben, and when her aunt's neighbours expressed mild astonishment she replied, 'It's different in wartime.'

In spite of the rush to make the arrangements the double wedding was a cheerful affair, free of mishaps, and Ginny was delighted to see her brothers so happy. Their brides displayed the correct combination of coyness and pride as they stood beside their uniformed grooms, and Ginny found that she wholeheartedly approved of her new sisters-in-law. She was also encouraged to think that having attended two weddings she would soon be attending a third – hopefully, her own. Being from seafaring stock, Ginny was by nature superstitious and like her parents before her, she firmly believed that life's main events came in threes. Had there not, sadly, been three deaths since Tovell had left? Now there would be three marriages.

Tovell, also, was quite hopeful that he would soon be given leave and had said as much in his letters. He had first made an application stating that he wished to get married in November 1915, when Ginny's year of mourning had come to an end. He was confident that his turn would soon come but he had reckoned without the fact that his officers were reluctant to dispense with his services, even for a short time. Since rejoining his regiment promotion had been rapid, not only because of his undoubted ability, experience and personal courage, but because in many instances he was the only NCO to survive an attack virtually unscathed. He had climbed the ladder from private to Company Sergeant Major and because of his new-found soberness he had never faltered in his climb. As each promotion came he wrote to Ginny that he owed his new position in life to her, but after numerous requests for leave had been turned down, he began to wish he was still an ordinary private.

Towards the end of June 1916, Tovell made yet another request and as he made his way to his officer's dugout he hoped and prayed that this time he would be successful. He had his answer as soon as he looked at Major Webb's face. The officer, who was some years younger than Tovell, was a career soldier who had joined the Army straight from public school. Unlike many of his fellow officers he was quite emotional and had not learned to conceal his true thoughts.

'I'm sorry, Tovell, I really am,' said Major Webb with feeling. 'I know you first applied for leave to get married last year but I'm afraid, once again, it's cancelled. When I saw the old man this morning he was appalled. "What! Lose an experienced man and a Company Sergeant Major to boot, at a time like this? Never!" he said.'

'So can you tell me what's so important this time, Sir?' asked Tovell despairingly.

'This is to be the great break through – the battle to end the war,' explained the major, his eyes alight with excitement. 'Mark my words, Tovell, it's nearly over. You'll soon be getting married. I know you'll keep this to yourself,' he added in confidential tones, 'but the old man says the front will be forty miles wide and starting tomorrow there's to be the biggest and longest artillery bombardment ever known. It'll go on for a full week. Nothing will survive it. There won't be a single German left alive when we climb out of our trenches. We'll march uphill towards their positions like we're on a ceremonial day out.'

On the appointed day, the first of July 1916, Tovell waited expectantly in the trench with his men until the bombardment suddenly ceased, the whistles blew and they climbed over the top. As Major Webb had described, they marched uphill in broad daylight, weighed down by a hundred and fifty pounds of equipment. There the officer's fairy tale ended; the Hun too had been waiting for the bombardment to cease. They had been trapped for a full week in their deepest burrows, deprived of food, drink, warmth, light and fresh air, driven half crazy by the relentless pounding of the guns above their heads. As soon as there was silence they cried with relief, rushed out to embrace the light of day – and to set up their machine gun posts. They faced the allied soldiers as they marched towards them, shoulder to shoulder, wave upon wave, and mowed the lines down as though they were fields of corn. On that first day of the Battle of the Somme, the Allied front gained barely a mile of enemy territory. The price they paid for it was sixty thousand Allied casualties. By the time the offensive finally petered out in November, the price had risen to six hundred thousand casualties and the territory gained to seven miles. When Tovell finally arrived home in mid-December the conflict was still being waged inside him.

'I know I shouldn't keep on about it,' said Tovell to Ginny as they wandered hand in hand along the shore-line with Blackie ambling happily along beside them, 'but I can't seem to get it out of my head. You'd think after all my years in the Army I'd be hardened to death and destruction, wouldn't you? I suppose it's because I've never seen death on such a colossal scale – but then, who has?'

'I don't mind you talking about it,' answered Ginny kindly. 'We've got a couple of days before we're married – talking about it will help you to clear it out of your system before the wedding.'

'I'll never know how I survived the Somme. Day after day men were falling all around me yet all I suffered was cuts and grazes.'

'My prayers must have been protecting you,' said Ginny gently.

'Reckon so, sweetheart,' replied Tovell releasing her hand and putting his arm around her instead. Ginny immediately put her arm around Tovell's waist. They walked along for a few moments in silence, enjoying each other's closeness and oblivious to the tiny flakes of snow falling on their heads. When Tovell spoke again it was in a lighter vein. 'There's something I mustn't forget to tell Lizzie and Bobby. You know I've always been lamenting that only the Hun seem to come up with new inventions, well, on the Somme we had a new weapon – the tank. The first time I saw one I was sheltering beside a small outcrop when this big machine rumbled to a halt almost beside me. A little cover on the side of the tank opened, a hand came out holding a carrier pigeon and released the bird to fly back to Allied territory. Tanks may be the latest invention but they still have to rely on the oldest means of communication! That must have been the only time I smiled during the whole five months that awful battle lasted.'

Ginny laughed. 'Well, I reckon one bright moment is better than none. And I've a bit of news to cheer you up. Mary had another letter from Mrs. Westgate the other day. I wrote and told you that Bill got wounded in October – he'll have the same hideous memories of the Somme that you have – but now he's been brought to a hospital in Birmingham. She's pleased that she'll be able to visit him. She told Mary that the doctors reckon he's going to be alright even though he's lost a kidney.'

'I'm really glad to hear that,' replied Tovell earnestly. 'I owe my life to Bill. We didn't get on at first but he turned up trumps when it mattered. It's funny how wrong you can be about people. I misjudged Lieutenant Collins too, didn't I? You couldn't help but be impressed by his efficiency and, of course, his bravery. Any men who get him as a commanding officer should think themselves lucky. Have you heard anything of him?'

'No, we haven't – not since Bill's card last Christmas. No-one hears directly from him. Mrs. Brewster's always asking if anyone has mentioned him in a letter. I reckon she must have got quite fond of him – but then, he was such a gentleman, wasn't he? Last time Emily heard from Mrs. Jackson, Ned was fine and you know what happened to poor old Fred. Have you come across David, yet? Lily's always hoping you'll meet up.'

'Not yet. Poor Davey – he'll have grown up fast after what he's seen.'

'At least he isn't involved in the actual fighting – Lily's relieved about that.'

'Is that what he's told her? Ginny, that couldn't be further from the truth. Before an attack stretcher-bearers are assigned to every company and then they go over the top with that company. They're so busy seeing to the wounded they can't look out for themselves – they're like sitting ducks. They say runners – the poor devils who carry messages and orders at the front – have the shortest life expectancy but stretcher-bearers must come a close second.'

'You'd better not tell Lily that. She seems to think he spends all his time in the Aid Post. I reckon he must have deliberately given her that impression so she wouldn't worry.'

'Well, if that's the way he wants it …. But what about you, my little love? I've been a selfish devil ever since I got home last night. Apart from asking you about Ben I've scarcely enquired about how you've been managing. Today we've walked from Whimpwell Green to Haisbro Beach and almost back again and all I've done is go on about my war. What about your war?'

'I told you, my dearest, I don't care how much you talk about the war if that'll help you to get some peace of mind.'

'But now I want to hear about how you've been managing.'

'We've managed alright. You don't want to worry about us. I haven't had to touch that money you insist on sending us. It's all gone into the Savings Bank for when you come home for good – all except that bit I took out last year and this to buy the littl'uns Christmas presents, like you told me. We get almost all our food off the smallholding and being in mourning for Ben we haven't needed much in the way of clothes. In some parts of the country people are short of food because of the war. Them U-boats have been sinking our merchant ships and stopping the food getting through but they say the Americans have made the Hun give up that campaign now because of what happened to the *Lusitania*. Let's hope they don't start again. As you know, the fishing fleet has suffered enough from the U-boats round here and now the naval authorities have let a few of the Lowestoft sailing smacks have a gun and they've sunk one or two U-boats already. Imagine that – a little old sailing smack sinking a submarine!'

'I hope they let the skipper I arrested have a gun; he couldn't wait to have a go at the U-boats. Mind you, Mr. Collins had a point when he said as soon as you arm a fishing boat you turn it into a man-of-war and the U-boats could sink it with all hands aboard.'

'That hasn't happened yet as far as I know and pray God that it won't happen but the Hun sent their fleet over again last April to bombard Great Yarmouth and they had a go at Lowestoft an' all that time. They don't care anything about civilians.'

'It's a worry that this coastline is so close to the Continent. Are the coastguards keeping up the patrols?'

'Mr. Brewster's managing alright and we still see a few soldiers sometimes. Men from a Cyclist Battalion are billeted in the Holt area. They say they're a Territorial Unit from Fulham. That's London, I think. They've been patrolling the coastline on cycles. Ted Carter say that's part of their training so maybe they won't be here that long.'

'Ted Carter – yes, it was good to see the old devil again yesterday. On the journey from Stalham Station he was still smarting over the fact that his favourite, Churchill, had been forced to resign from the Admiralty, but when you have a disaster like we had at the Dardanelles someone's head has to roll. And I told Ted a good organiser like Churchill is what you need in time of war, so I'm sure he'll be back in government before long. Churchill rejoined the Army, you know. He was at the Front; I met some blokes who'd seen him. But all that isn't any comfort to Jack Harris and his pals left behind at Gallipoli. Poor old Jack – a good soldier and a good bloke. If he had to go it was a pity it wasn't in battle. You could say the same about Lord Kitchener, of course. I've served under him so many times I felt sorry when I heard he'd drowned on his way to Russia. That's no way for a soldier to meet his end either. But here I go again – talking about the war. I'll be better tomorrow, I promise, because then I'll only have one more day to wait before I wed you, my little darling.'

In accordance with her principle of not tempting fate, Ginny made no advance preparation for her wedding. She waited instead until she had Tovell's letter saying, *My leave has been granted and by the time you get this I shall be on my way home*. She then rushed to the Gillings's cottage and hoped that Lily could somehow magic a suitable outfit from thin air. Fortunately for all concerned Lily was entertaining another customer at the time – Lady Meredith. Ginny would not have intruded but her ladyship saw her coming up the garden path and insisted that Mrs. Gillings invite her to join them in the parlour. All four ladies sipped tea together whilst Ginny shared her good news with them. Lady Meredith was as pleased and excited at the prospect of the forthcoming nuptials as she would have been if one of her own daughters or granddaughters had been the bride.

'I agree that your biggest problem is your apparel,' said Lady Meredith, 'but since you have only a matter of days to make all the arrangements I suggest that you concentrate on the church, the special licence, the wedding breakfast and so on, and leave your dress to Lily and me. I bought a quite beautiful outfit in London some time ago which I have never worn. The fact is, it was far too young for me and I have put on a little weight as well since I bought it – I'm afraid I worry so much about my boys in France that I eat to comfort myself. I'm sure you would look perfect in it, Ginny. It's a matching dress, jacket and hat in beige, trimmed with fur – lovely against your auburn hair and green eyes. Lily would have to make a few adjustments, of course.'

Knowing that Lady Meredith was not only a head and shoulders above Ginny but probably nearly twice as broad, Lily hastily intervened. 'Your ladyship, I ought to point out that as Ginny isn't nowhere as tall as you, the alterations would have to be drastic and I don't know as I could put the dress back right for you again afterwards.'

'Oh, my dears, I don't want the dress back. Ginny may have it as a wedding present. There's one condition – I shall expect to be invited to the ceremony.'

'Lady Meredith – I'd be honoured, and so would Tovell, if you'd come to our wedding. And as for the dress – that's so kind of you I don't know what to say.'

'Then it's all settled,' decided her ladyship.

For Lily it was far from settled. Hours of hard work lay ahead of her but the result was magical. Not only did she provide Ginny with an elegant flattering outfit but Lizzie as well, using the material she had skillfully taken out of the original garments, supplemented by a few well-chosen scraps from her treasure box. She even managed to save enough of the beige cloth to make a fancy shirt for Bobby.

Ginny's wedding day dawned crisp and bright and she drove to the church in a borrowed pony and trap, accompanied by the children and her uncle and aunt. As they sped along the country lanes, carpeted with a light covering of snow, only two things were worrying Ginny. Firstly, she was concerned as to what kind of spread the publican at the *Admiral Lord Nelson* would provide as a wedding breakfast. Tovell had insisted in his letter that she book the reception at the inn near the church, arguing that Whimpwell Green was too far to transport the guests after the service, and that he did not wish to give her and her aunt the trouble of preparing the food. Since he was paying for the meal, she could not object but she had her reservations about the arrangement.

Her other worry was over Tovell himself. He had spent the night at the home of his best man – Ted Carter. The idea had come from Ted. 'That's unlucky for him to set eyes on you afore you gets to the altar, gal. He'll be alright along o' me. You hent got nothing to worry about.' After such an assurance, gravely given, Ginny could do nothing else but worry. She had, however, reckoned without her future husband's strength of will. He had kept his promise not to drink his money away as he had in the past and apart from the occasional lapse, such as the time he had met Ginny's brothers, he had been almost teetotal in France. Knowing how upset his bride would be if he were anything but completely sober for their marriage service, he had resisted all attempts by Ted and his associates to get him drunk. When Ginny walked up the aisle on Uncle William's arm and saw that her fears were unfounded, she glowed with happiness.

Tovell, beaming, turned to watch their progress to the strains of the Wedding March. As the procession got closer he leant to one side so that Lizzie and Bobby, looking important as bridesmaid and page, could see his face. He winked at them and they giggled back. Once Ginny had taken her place at his side, he whispered to her, 'You look radiant, my little beauty.' Ginny wanted to return the compliment but Tovell's appearance had rendered her speechless. Ginny was not surprised to see the King's Crown above the three bar chevron on his sleeve or the rows of coloured ribbons on his chest, but she was surprised to see these decorations emblazoned, not on his drab working uniform, but on a new full-dress uniform. Seeing her astonishment he straightened his tunic with deliberate care and whispered once more, 'Never realised how much I spent on booze till I started saving for this.'

Ted Carter, the epitome of well-brushed, well-polished respectability, took the opportunity as the notes of the organ faded away to lean forward, wink at Ginny and say, 'Told yer he'd be alright along o' me.'

The vicar frowned, coughed politely and tapped his Prayer Book. Old Ted took the hint, positioned his brand new bowler hat in the crook of his arm, threw back his shoulders, fixed his eyes on the high altar and the service began. 'Dearly beloved, we are gathered here in the sight of God ....'

By the end of the ceremony not a single member of the congregation could doubt that he was witnessing the solemnization of a perfect love-match. Both Tovell and Ginny made their responses with such feeling and sincerity in their voices, looking at one another with so much tenderness and affection, that not a woman present remained dry eyed. When Tovell placed his ring on Ginny's finger, saying, 'With this ring I thee wed, with my body I thee worship ....' Lily lost her self-control completely and the tears flooded down her cheeks. Handkerchiefs were much in evidence as the throng of friends and relatives filed from the church and even the stalwart members of the Volunteer Life-saving Brigade and the lifeboat crew, who had hurried outside ahead of the bride and groom to form a guard of honour, were heard sniffing loudly as they held an archway of oars above the happy couple's heads.

The bells peeled out and everyone crowded round to offer their congratulations. The photographer had extreme difficulty in restoring order so that he might perform the task for which he had been engaged, but as he disappeared beneath his black cloth he was almost drooling with delight. When had handsomer subjects ever stood in front of his camera – the bride a picture of delicate femininity; the groom a splendid example of military manhood? When he was satisfied that he had taken enough photographs in front of the porch and in the churchyard he gladly carried his equipment into the *Admiral Lord Nelson* and called the wedding party to him again once he was ready.

The photographer was well pleased with the results of his labours and he placed his favourite portrait – one of Ginny and Tovell flanked by Lizzie, looking daintier than ever, and Bobby, bright-eyed with excitement – on permanent display in the front window of his shop in Stalham. It remained there, fading with the passage of time, for years to come and had the photographer kept watch he would have realised that his establishment had become a place of pilgrimage for many a young lady who, even after she became a young matron with babe-in-arms, could not pass the shrine without pausing to heave a sigh of regret.

Ginny's anxiety regarding her wedding breakfast was dispelled as soon as she entered the hired room. A smiling landlord stood waiting to welcome the guests and Tovell told him, 'You've done us proud, pal.'

Ted Carter, in his official capacity as best man, echoed the opinion. 'That's the best looking table I've seen in many a year – that that is.' In spite of disapproving expressions and reproachful remarks from Mrs. Carter, old Ted did justice to the landlady's excellent cooking and washed his generous helpings down with ample supplies of free beer. Consequently, when called upon to deliver his much-rehearsed speech he had difficulty in standing, let alone addressing, the crowded room.

After a few moments of muddled oratory Tovell came to his aid. Standing up and towering over his friend, the soldier patted him on the shoulder and said in perfect Norfolk dialect, 'Sit you down, bor, afore you fall down.' Everyone laughed, clapped and cheered. Once Ted was safely seated and a hush had descended upon the gathering, Tovell spoke movingly of the joy he felt in his new wife and family. He gave praise where praise was due and expressed his profound gratitude to all who had made this the happiest day of his life. When he had finished the applause was long and loud. Ted managed to recover sufficiently to propose a toast to the bride and groom and the formalities were complete.

Lady Meredith, who had been accompanied by her housekeeper, the formidable Mrs. Kemp, was the first guest to leave and her parting wish was that the couple should find as much felicity in their marriage as she had found in her's. The call of duty meant that Station Officer and Mrs. Brewster, together with Mr. and Mrs. Ellis, were the next to leave. Both husbands declared exactly the same hope as Lady Meredith. Soon afterwards, Dr. Lambert was dragged away by his wife who feared that he might become incapable of dealing with any emergency which might arise during the rest of the day. After the Lambert's departure the remaining guests drifted away.

Mrs. Gillings had the last word. 'That was the most beautiful service I've ever attended and a real good celebration after. You know I wish you both well. You've got yourself a fine wife, Tovell, as I'm sure you know and Ginny deserves you after what she's had to put up with afore. As for you, gal, this one won't be no trouble to you. He's a proper family man through and through. He'll take to matrimony like a duck to water – just see if I ent right.'

The journey back to Whimpwell Green passed pleasantly and quickly. Uncle William sat in the driver's seat, Auntie May beside him whilst the bride and groom reclined in the back of the carriage with the children between them. Lizzie nestled against Tovell, her hand in his; Bobby, not to be outdone, managed to stretch one arm across his sister so that he could hold Tovell's free hand. At the same time, Bobby tucked his other arm under his mother's elbow so that he could hold her hand too. Both children had made it abundantly clear from the first moment that Ginny had told them of her plans to remarry that they welcomed the match. All the way home they competed with one another for the novel privilege of calling Tovell, 'Father'.

The night air was frosty and they were glad to huddle closely together under warm blankets. At first, the stars twinkling in the clear sky inspired the children to chant nursery rhymes and songs from their babyhood but gradually they became drained of their last vestiges of energy and were content to lay back and listen, bemused, to the crunching of the pony's hoofs and the crackling of the trap's wheels as they travelled over the frozen snow. By the time they reached the smallholding both children were heavy eyed and raised no objection when their mother hastily made them a hot drink and prepared them for bed. Lizzie recovered sufficiently to demand that her stepfather carry her up the narrow winding staircase to the room she shared with her brother. Tovell, enjoying his new role of parent, was glad to oblige and lingered to see the children snugly covered for sleep. He then sat on the edge of the bed and began to tell them a story. Seeing their eyes closing he did not bother to finish the tale but instead leant over Bobby and Lizzie and spoke softly and secretly to them for a few minutes. A goodnight kiss and he was gone, allowing their mother to hear their prayers in private.

Tovell returned to the living-room and was soon joined by Ginny. They sat awkwardly together on a small upright wicker settee. Auntie May and Uncle William were already settled in their chairs either side of the cooking range with Blackie stretched out on the hearthrug between them.

Auntie May broke the silence. 'That was a lovely service,' she said warmly.

'And that was a lovely spread afterwards, an' all,' chuckled Uncle William.

'Oh! William,' Auntie May laughed. 'Pay no regard to him. He found the service moving too. He's a-teasing.'

'Well, go on then. Get upstairs,' urged Uncle William. 'Don't waste time.'

Both Ginny and Tovell looked shocked at the old man's remarks. Auntie May was anxious to explain but was laughing so much she had difficulty in speaking at first. 'What your uncle meant to say is, whilst the two of you were putting the littl'uns to bed, he slipped up to your room and put a match to the fire he laid before we left for the church. We reckoned you ought to have a bit o' time to yourselves seeing as Tovell's due back at the Front in a matter o' days, and that's enough to freeze yer in that there bedroom.'

'Uncle William, Auntie May,' said Ginny looking from one to the other, 'that was so thoughtful of you – wasn't it, Tovell?'

'Very thoughtful indeed and we appreciate it,' agreed Tovell.

'Well, off you go and make the best of it,' urged Auntie May.

'If he doesn't mind,' said Ginny, somewhat nervously, 'I'd rather Tovell let me go up on my own first.'

Tovell smiled. 'You take your time. I'll be up in a few minutes.'

Auntie May spoke again as soon as she was certain Ginny was safely out of earshot. 'This gives us a chance to tell you how pleased we are that you've got together with our Ginny. I know you shouldn't speak ill of the dead but Robert was not a nice man.'

Uncle William joined in. ''Couldn't stand the bugger – biggest bloomin' know-all going.'

Tovell was gratified to find that his new relatives approved of him but discussing the demerits of his predecessor was not a line of conversation he wished to pursue. He was relieved when Auntie May suddenly changed the subject.

'Oh, there, I nearly forgot! I told you to remind me, William. Do you have a nightshirt?' she enquired anxiously. 'I should have asked you that afore.'

'Well, no …., I don't' replied Tovell hesitantly. 'In barracks we just wear our long-johns.'

'There, what did I tell you, William? I knew he wouldn't have no cause to own a nightshirt. That's a good job I thought o' that. I've got William's best striped one here a-warming for you over the cooking range. That wouldn't do for you to have no nightshirt on your wedding night – no, indeed.' As Auntie May got up from her chair and reached for the nightshirt hanging on the line beneath the mantelpiece, Tovell and Uncle William exchanged amused glances. She gave the warm garment to her new nephew-in-law and told him, 'Off you go now. She's had more than enough time to titivate herself up. See you in the morning.'

Tovell thanked her and bade both old people goodnight. As he reached the staircase in the corner of the room he glanced back and was in time to see Auntie May give her husband a playful slap across the knee. Uncle William grinned and went on puffing at his pipe.

Tovell entered the bedroom holding the nightshirt in front of him and chuckling quietly. 'Hey, Ginny,' he called out. 'Look what your

Auntie May says I've got to wear.' The curtains were drawn, the bedclothes turned back, the lamp lit and the fire burning brightly behind its brass guard, but there was no sign of Ginny. 'Where are you, love?'

'I'm hiding,' came the reply, 'and I'm not coming out 'til you promise to shut your eyes.'

Tovell laughed. 'Alright – my eyes are shut tight. Come out.'

There was a faint rustling noise and then Ginny spoke again. 'You can open them now.'

Tovell looked, caught his breath and the nightshirt slipped from his grasp.

'Didn't I say I'd find an occasion to wear it?' asked Ginny enticingly. Tovell did not answer but continued to stare, entranced by what he saw. Ginny, barefooted, was wearing the sari he had given her. She had covered her head and the lower part of her face so that only her eyes were visible. She was looking at him beguilingly. 'Is this how Indian women wear their saris?'

'It is,' answered Tovell weakly. 'But you look like a princess – an Indian princess – my golden princess.'

Ginny lowered her veil and smiled at him rapturously. 'Come over here,' she invited. 'Let's look at ourselves in the long mirror – standing side by side.' Tovell complied and with their arms around each other's waists they gazed at their reflection. 'Don't we make a handsome couple?' murmured Ginny, 'you in your fine new uniform and me in my silks and gold.' She turned to face him, her body close to his and said in a teasing voice, 'Do you realise, Sergeant Major, you haven't so much as kissed your wife since we left the church?'

Tovell grinned. 'What have I been and gone and done? I haven't married a woman I've married a temptress – a little enchantress. What a lucky bloke I am. But then, you always have bewitched me – even when you weren't trying. And as for not kissing you ….' He folded his arms about her, bent down and kissed her long and tenderly. Then, lifting her up effortlessly he carried her to the armchair by the fire. 'It's almost two years since you last sat on my lap and that's the next thing we're going to remedy.'

When they were seated, Tovell reached over to the chest-of-drawers in the alcove beside the fireplace and turned down and blew out the lamp. 'We don't need that,' he said. 'It'll be nice and cosy sitting here in the firelight....'

Ginny finished the sentence for him, 'cuddled up together like we used to be. Oh, Tovell, I have missed you.'

'I've missed you too, my little sweetheart. God knows I've missed you. Two long lonely years, night after night, I've pictured us together and prayed that I'd live to see the day. I meant what I said at the wedding breakfast – this has been the happiest day of my life.'

'I feel the same, my dearest. I began to fear that you'd never get your home leave – that the Army would never release you long enough for us to be wed. But here we are at last – husband and wife.'

'And just look at you. When I bought this sari it never entered my head that my wife would wear it on her wedding night.'

'I'm glad you're pleased. I wanted to please you. And I thought ....' She paused then continued rather timidly, 'I thought perhaps that would help if I wore the sari. You've spent so many years in India and in all that time you must have visited lots of prostitutes and they must have worn saris ....'

Tovell hugged her closer to him, kissing the top of her head. 'My little darling, there's no way I could mistake you for a prostitute. For a start, you're far too beautiful ....'

'But you could pretend. And you could tell me what you paid them to do and I could do it.'

'I don't need to pretend ....'

'Did they take off all their clothes for you?'

'Not for me. They might have for an officer but I've never had the money to ....'

'Tonight you *are* an officer – a general.'

She slid from his lap and stood in front of him on the far side of the hearthrug. As she reached up to undo the fastenings at the back of her neck Tovell made a half-hearted attempt to protest. 'Ginny, love,' he said gently. 'You don't have to do this.'

'But I want to,' she replied. 'We ought to have music. In India I expect they do this to music – strange music. Or perhaps they sing. I only know a lullaby. I'll sing you that – I'll sing you a lullaby.'

She began to hum a melody which was familiar to him – he had heard her singing it to Lizzie when the child could not sleep. He should have found it incongruous – his Ginny disrobing herself before him to the strains of Brahms's *Cradle Song* – but he did not. He found it disturbing, then sensuous – erotic. He could not take his eyes from her. He watched, fascinated, as she swayed to and fro to the rhythm of the tune. As he listened he fancied the notes took on a haunting quality – like the music of India. Her hair was still piled high upon her head but she discarded the pins, one by one, and let the tresses fall about her shoulders. She finished unfastening her blouse and let it slide slowly down her arms. In the darkened room the rosy glow from the fire accentuated her breasts. She took the edge of the sari between the fingers of one hand and held it aloft. Still singing quietly she began to dance in a circle, unravelling the material from around her waist. With every twirl more folds of the skirt became loosened. The delicate fabric wafted around her like a cloud. The tiny air currents which the movements produced caused the fire to flare, illuminating the scene of what had become for Tovell, an exquisite fantasy. Spellbound, he saw the final layer of the sari unfurl and slip from her hips. She lowered her arm and let the silk she was holding float to the floor. She stood quite still and silent, the sari clustered about her feet. The flickering flames cast an image on her naked body and deepened the hue of the pastel material which still clung to her ankles, creating the illusion that she was some mythological goddess rising from the eternal fires. Utterly captivated, Tovell gazed at the slender perfectly proportioned figure until Ginny stretched out her hands to him and called his name. In an instant he was at her side, his arms about her.

Ginny clung to him and there was apprehension in her voice as she said, 'You're so quiet. I hope I haven't given offence. I was only trying to ....'

'I know what you were trying to do and I love you all the more for it. But I've been trying to tell you that it wasn't necessary. You had me roused from the moment I opened my eyes and saw you in the sari. And earlier – in the church when the vicar pronounced us man and wife – instead of kissing you I could have taken you there and then. Fancy you thinking of this ....'

'I'm so relieved I haven't offended you. That isn't like you to sit and say nothing.'

'What could I say, my little darling? You took my breath away – I was overcome .... And you will get cold.' As he spoke, Tovell lifted

Ginny up and placed her between the sheets. She watched him from her pillow as he hurriedly undressed and she laughed when he said, 'You must excuse me, ma'am, for not singing and dancing during this performance but matters have reached a state of urgency.'

When Tovell was as naked as she was, Ginny threw back the bedclothes and he climbed eagerly into bed beside her.

1917

I

Tovell left Whimpwell Green two days before New Year to return to his regiment. The good-byes were even more poignant this time; the pain of parting had assumed a new dimension. Ginny and Tovell had shared seventeen happy days with the children, relatives and friends, and fourteen glorious nights with each other in the private intimate sanctum of their bedroom. It was little wonder that they felt so keenly the loss of each other's company and in particular, after two weeks when they had with much caring and inventiveness helped one another to reach constantly the heights of ecstacy, the loss of physical fulfillment as well. From then on their letters emphasised the overpowering sense of yearning they felt for each other – a yearning which did not diminish with the passage of time.

1917 saw little change on the Western Front as the fighting waged back and forth over the same ground. Early in the year the Germans withdrew north of the Somme to the Hindenburg Line and some Allied successes followed. The April offensive captured Vimy Ridge but the losses among the French troops were so horrendous that mutinies broke out among their ranks. In June, Tovell was part of the British force which captured Messines Ridge and he was in the attempted advance fromYpres to the coast – the Passchendaele offensive – which began in July and was to drag on, unsuccessfully, until November.

During 1917 Ginny scoured the newspapers for anything which might have some direct bearing on her husband's safety and welfare but other world events scarcely touched her. She was far too occupied with what was going on inside her own body. Her concern that Tovell should be able to consummate their marriage had stemmed not from any desire for sexual gratification for herself – she had expected none and had been astounded when she had found it – but from her wish to be the instrument whereby he achieved such sublime satisfaction that he would never again resort to the services of prostitutes, and perhaps even more importantly, from her longing to give him a child of his own. Almost from the day of his departure she was sure she was pregnant but she waited until Dr. Lambert had confirmed her diagnosis before she told Tovell. He was as overjoyed at the news as she had expected him to be, but for a man whose devotion was based on his instinct to protect and support his beloved, to be separated from her at such a time was mental and emotional torture.

Ted Carter and the other patrons of the *Admiral Lord Nelson* followed the world events of 1917, and momentous local changes, very keenly. Ted was jubilant in February when the Dardanelles Commission praised the original plan of his hero, Churchill, and exonerated him from blame for its failure. He was even happier in May when Churchill was made Minister of Munitions. 'You'll see – he'll come up with weapons to defeat the bastards,' he confidently predicted to his drinking companions. By the summer, the manner in which the war was affecting the local way of life was a nightly topic of conversation in the public bar.

'I tell you, boys, I ent never going to get used to it – working in the fields along o' female labourers.'

'There int no other choice, Ted,' said Constable Hadden. 'Take a look around this bar. Half the usual faces are missing. Since that there Coalition Government took over last year conscription's really started to bite. Good thing the women are filling the gaps.'

Dr. Lambert joined in the discussion. 'I was reading yesterday that they're putting us to shame in some factories. They're producing twice as much as the men ever did. Of course, Lloyd George has said we have three enemies – Germany, Austria and drink. They say that's why the King decided that he and the whole Royal Household would abstain for the duration of the war – as an example to the men who weren't producing armaments for the Front quickly enough. I've tried to cut down myself but I'm afraid I'm a bit weak willed in my old age.'

Ted was not sure he liked the tack the conversation was taking. 'You'll never guess what I heard today,' he added hastily. 'His lordship's two unmarried daughters have joined up – one to the Army and the other to the Women's Royal Naval Service – and to make matters worse, two of the maids have gone and followed their example.'

'That's a rum old do to be sure,' agreed the lifeboat coxswain. 'But going back to what the constable was saying, when Tovell was here last Christmas he say conscription had to come 'cause we weren't putting anything like as many men into the field as the French. He say them poor devils were sacrificing themselves in their thousands just to gain a few feet of land. Maybe we'd feel the same if we had the Hun occupying our soil. Poor old Tovell – just two weeks of wedded bliss then back to the trenches.'

Ted chuckled. 'By the look o' Ginny, two weeks was long enough to hit the bull's eye. I'll go get us some more drinks. We can wet the baby's head in advance.'

'I'll give you a hand, Ted,' said the coxswain.

'Just get your own,' Constable Hadden called out. 'The doctor and I'll get our refills in a minute. An officer of the law can't be seen breaking the law. It's still illegal to buy a round of drinks, though how I'd police that one without standing beside the landlord day and night, I don't know.' Once his two friends had left the table and were standing at the bar out of earshot, the constable asked the doctor if Ginny was alright.

Dr. Lambert smiled. 'At the present time I'd say Tovell is suffering more than she is – if the number of letters I receive from him is anything to go by. I keep telling him I'd have kept an eye on her even if he hadn't asked, but he still worries.'

'I suppose he's worried about the other littl'uns she's lost,' suggested the policeman.

'She hasn't told him,' replied the doctor, 'and I see no reason to worry him further. And anyway, I'm sure no medical condition was to blame.'

Constable Hadden pondered for a moment before commenting wryly, 'Funny thing the law. You ent supposed to step in whilst the poor woman's alive but once she's dead, you can hang the bastard. Not a lot of help to her then, is it?'

At that moment Ted and the coxswain returned to the table carrying their brimming mugs of beer. 'Talking of children, is what I hear correct, Cox?' asked Dr. Lambert. 'Has your son qualified as an aviator?'

'He has indeed,' answered the coxswain. 'And when I got home last night we had more news. The missus would scarcely let me get in the door she was so pleased. She'd been worrying that he'd get sent to France to fly scouting missions over enemy territory, but he's coming to the Air Station at Yarmouth. 'Course that place has got bigger and bigger every year, hasn't it, ever since that first Zeppelin came over here and the sods realised they could bomb London? And they get all the newest aircraft and equipment. Yes, my boy's proud as punch that he's going to be a Zeppelin Hunter and go after the buggers while they're still over the sea.'

'Pity they can't go after the U-boats an' all now the Germans have resumed unrestricted submarine warfare,' said Constable Hadden with feeling. 'The way they're sinking our merchant ships they must think they can starve us into surrender.'

'But the convoy system seems to be working,' the coxswain pointed out. 'They haven't sunk so many of our vessels this last month or two.'

'We won't be a-surrendering here,' Ted chuckled. 'Everyone's got more bloomin' back garden put to vegetables than ever afore and there's chickens under yer feet wherever you go.'

Dr. Lambert shook his head. 'It's not here, Ted, but in the towns and cities that they're short of food. As you know, I sit on the local Food Committee and so does the Constable here – and so does your master, come to that – and we're going to have to send more produce to the urban areas. We've already got sugar rationing but we'll soon have meat and dairy produce rationing as well.'

'Cor, blast!' exclaimed Ted. 'Don't remind me about the sugar rationing. I always like to have a bottle o' cold tea with me in the cart for when I ent near a pub, and that tastes like horse piss without sugar.'

By the latter part of September, Tovell's regiment was still entrenched near Ypres, having made no progress at all in their planned offensive. To the commanding officer, Lieutenant Colonel Bradshaw – the "old man" in Major Webb's jargon – morale was everything and never more than when things were not going well. Rumour had it that the colonel could have had promotion to the general's staff but that he had turned down the offer of a comparatively safe job at headquarters to stay with his men. He was regarded by all as a true line officer who believed in being seen by his men and in leading by example. It was his custom to wander along the trenches at some point every morning, pausing at intervals to speak to his troops. On one such tour he stopped in front of a very young soldier who had his hands tightly clamped over his ears, his eyes shut and his face screwed up in anguish.

'What's the matter with this soldier?' demanded the officer. 'There isn't even a bombardment going on. Take your hands down, man.'

The soldier tentatively took his hands away from his ears and looked warily around. At that precise moment a loud wailing and howling noise was heard coming from the nearby dugout. At once the young soldier put his hands back over his ears and cringed in terror against the wall of the trench.

'What in heaven's name is that dreadful noise?' asked Lieutenant Colonel Bradshaw. No-one answered and all the soldiers looked uncomfortable. The officer looked around and saw a corporal. He turned on him at once. 'Answer my question, corporal. What's that noise?'

'It's RSM Tovell, Sir,' replied the corporal reluctantly.

'RSM Tovell?' repeated the colonel incredulously.

'Yes, Sir. His missus is having a baby soon and he keeps having nightmares about it.' The noise continued and the young soldier was still cowering against the trench.

'Wake him up at once!' ordered the officer.

'We don't like to do that, Sir, in case it's harmful to him,' explained the corporal.

The colonel's face reddened. 'Wake him up at once, I say, and send him straight to me.'

A few minutes later Tovell, somewhat dishevelled and still bathed in sweat, stood hesitantly at the entrance to Lieutenant Colonel Bradshaw's dugout. The officer glanced up from his writing and saw him. 'Come in, Tovell. You look dreadful, man. You'd better help yourself to a drink. Bottle's over there.'

Tovell saluted and then hesitated. 'Thank you, Sir, but I promised my wife I'd curb my drinking.'

'Ah, yes …. Your wife ….' The colonel tapped his pen on the table for a few moments and then the words flowed. 'This won't do, Tovell. It's bad enough the Hun putting the fear of death into the men without you wailing like a banshee. You've been Regimental Sergeant Major ever since RSM Blake was killed and up to now I've never had cause for complaint. You've been an excellent RSM. Your ribbons testify to your bravery and to your past campaigns. They bring the men comfort. You're a hero to them. They look up to you. If you, of all people, go to pieces how can we expect them to stand firm?'

Tovell looked so distressed that his commander relented a little. He pointed to a chair. 'Sit down, Tovell. Now, what's all this nonsense about your wife? Women have been giving birth since time began.'

Tovell leant forward in the chair, resting his elbows on his knees and wringing his hands. He could not look at the officer – instead, he stared at the floor. 'With respect, Sir, you don't know my wife. She's a tiny little thing – I'm a giant by comparison. I'm truly sorry that I'm upsetting the men but the nightmares have got worse the nearer it gets to her time. I try to force myself to stay awake but when I do drop off to sleep, the nightmares always start. I see her writhing in agony because the child is too big for her. I see her in her death throes.' Tovell put his hands over his eyes. For a few moments he struggled to speak. Then he continued, his voice broken with emotion. 'If I could put the clock back and have my leave over again, I wouldn't touch her – I wouldn't go near her, Sir.'

As Tovell covered his face with his hands once more, the colonel got up from his chair and paced up and down whilst he considered what he should say. He was the epitome of a British officer, one who would do his best not to betray to others how he felt, but Tovell's situation had moved him. He knew what he could say, but was in a dilemma as to whether it would be fitting and appropriate to say it. He respected and admired Tovell as a soldier and in the end this outweighed any considerations about propriety. 'Tovell, this may be of some comfort to you,' he said quietly. 'My wife is from a celebrated military family. In her opinion, it is the duty of every soldier's wife to ensure – I say, *ensure* – that her husband has offspring. In this way she buys him some measure of immortality should he not survive the battlefield.'

The words penetrated Tovell's tortured brain. A vision of that wonderful first night – of Ginny dancing in the firelight, the sari floating around her – flashed before him. Realisation dawning, he slowly lifted his head and looked at the colonel. 'On reflection, Sir, I think my wife may be of the same opinion.'

'Good! That's very good ....' said the officer with relief. Now he could return to formality. 'When is the child expected?'

'Next week, Sir,' said Tovell, getting to his feet.

'We shall be out of the line in two days,' said Lieutenant Colonel Bradshaw. 'As you know, it's our turn for five days at a relief camp. Let us hope that the birth will coincide with our rest days and that the news will be good. But, Tovell, I must stress that when we return to these trenches, no matter what the outcome, I shall expect you to know *your* duty. Men's lives will depend upon it.'

As the summer progressed, Ginny felt increasingly uncomfortable and at times swore she was about to burst apart. In spite of this, and the debilitating heat, she insisted upon accompanying the rest of the family to morning service every Sunday and once there, she managed to forget her bloated appearance and aching back. Auntie May was not fooled by her seemingly stalwart attitude and by the time they got towards the end of September was determined that enough was enough. She, Uncle William and the children were all dressed in their Sunday best, ready to leave for church, when Ginny came down the stairs. 'Say good bye to your mother, littl'uns and get in the cart.'

'Go you outside like Auntie May say,' Ginny instructed. Then she added, 'I'm coming with you.'

Auntie May waited until Lizzie and Bobby had closed the door behind them before she turned to her niece. 'Oh! No, Ginny! Hent you made them girls suffer enough, flaunting your belly in front of them Sunday after Sunday? Don't think I haven't seen that look of fiendish delight in your eyes when you see them staring at you in envy.'

'Oh, Auntie May,' laughed Ginny. 'You don't miss much, do you? But it isn't that …. It's just that I want to come with you.'

'But you're so close to your time,' reasoned her aunt. 'What would the good Lord think if you gave birth in the middle of his church?'

Uncle William had been watching Ginny's expression closely and he had detected the apprehension in her eyes. He intervened, chuckling. 'Don't reckon the Lord would give two hoots. Verger might though. He'd have to clear up the mess.'

His wife glared at him. 'Oh, William – at times you ent much help. Ginny's best off here.'

'Don't talk squit,' replied her husband. 'You don't want to be left alone here, do you, gal?'

'No, Uncle William, I don't,' answered Ginny, looking at him gratefully.

'Then you're coming along o' us,' decided her uncle. 'Anyhow, what's wrong with the vestry? Better than a stable. Come you on, gal, and I'll hoist you and that sack o' potaters you've got hidden up there, into the cart.'

Two hours later and Ginny was very thankful that morning service was over. The congregation spread out into the churchyard and, as usual, people chatted together in groups before dispersing to their homes. Mrs. Gillings, accompanied by Dr. Lambert, came up to where Ginny was standing with her relatives. 'You're looking a mite sickly, gal,' said Mrs. Gillings.

'I told her not to come,' explained Auntie May. 'She would insist and William here, wasn't no help. We'd better get home quick.'

'Mrs. Gillings is right,' said Dr. Lambert. 'You don't look well, Ginny. Have you any pain?'

'Yes, doctor,' Ginny replied. 'It started during the service but I didn't like to say anything. We'd best get off home.'

'I don't think jolting over country roads in a farm-cart is such a good idea,' observed the doctor in concerned tones. He looked pointedly at Mrs. Gillings. That good lady took the hint at once.

'Come you stay with Lily and me,' she urged. 'I was with you when you had Bobby and Lizzie. I'd be disappointed if I weren't with you this time.'

'What a good idea,' enthused the doctor. 'I only live a few doors from Mrs. Gillings. It'll be easier for me to keep an eye on you here than at Whimpwell.'

'Alright, then,' Ginny agreed. 'Thank you. I need to sit down. I don't feel well.'

Auntie May and Uncle William looked around for the children who were talking to their school friends. They beckoned them over as the doctor and Mrs. Gillings took Ginny's arms and assisted her across the churchyard. Lily, carrying little Arthur, saw what was happening and immediately left the group of coastguards' widows and joined them.

'Give your mother a quick kiss,' Auntie May instructed the children. 'She's going to visit Mrs. Gillings and Auntie Lily for the night.'

'I want to stay too,' Lizzie said excitedly. 'I can play with little Arthur.'

'Mrs. Gillings hent got room for you an'all. Anyway, we've gotta bake a cake.'

'But Auntie May,' Bobby protested. 'You always say we mustn't do nothing that isn't essential on the Sabbath. You never bake cakes on the Sabbath.'

'That's true, Bobby, but that int what you'd call a hard and fast rule. I can change it at times.'

The children did as they were told and gave their mother a peck on the cheek. Lizzie was then content to take Auntie May's hand but Bobby hung back. He was suspicious. He looked anxiously at his mother. She was stooping forward and he could see that she was in pain even though she was doing her best not to let it show in her face. Something dreadful which he did not understand was happening. The fear brought tears to his eyes. His great-aunt was ushering his sister towards the cart but he remained rooted to the spot, watching with increasing trepidation as his mother was led away by the doctor and their former neighbour. Then he felt a hand on his shoulder and he looked up into the kindly eyes of his great-uncle.

'We'll let the women make the cake,' said Uncle William, guiding him towards their vehicle. 'How about if us men rake around in the compost heap until we find some nice juicy brandlings – juicy enough to tempt that big old carp out of his hiding place down at the lake?'

In the two days that they remained in the front line, the division saw heavy fighting, but by the time they reached the relief camp all thoughts of the battle were banished from Tovell's mind. He could think only of home and, with increasing dread, of what might have happened to Ginny. During the daylight hours he avoided the company of his fellows and at night, he was plagued by the nightmares. One afternoon he was sitting dejectedly on the grass at the edge of the camp, away from all the other men. A football match was going on a short distance from him but he took no notice. He became aware of a messenger boy standing in front of him.

'Telegram for you, Sir,' the boy said politely.

Tovell's throat suddenly became so dry his 'thank you' was scarcely audible. His hands were shaking as he opened the envelope. He glanced at the paper inside. In a daze, he got to his feet, stuffed the telegram in his pocket and walked down the lane from the camp to the nearby town. He stopped at the first church he came to and went inside. He did not know how long he sat hunched in a pew, leaning forward with his forehead resting on the back of the pew ahead, his hands clenched together. When at last he sat back, tears trickled down his cheeks. He wiped them away, got up and retraced his footsteps back to the camp. As he passed the Sergeants' Mess he paused, hesitated for a few moments and then went inside. As he entered, the comrades whom he had shunned over the preceding days stopped talking and turned around to face him. He put his hand in his pocket, retrieved the telegram and held it aloft. His face broke into a grin. 'I'm a father!' he shouted ecstatically. 'I'm a father! Drinks all round! Drinks on me!'

The next day Tovell wrote five letters; a long and loving one to Ginny expressing his joy and also his relief; individual ones to Bobby and Lizzie so that they should be in no doubt that he still loved them as much as ever; a sincere thank you to Mrs. Gillings for her kind ministrations and a message of heartfelt gratitude to Dr. Lambert for the safe deliverance of his wife and child, and for sending him the telegram which had put an end to his misery and torment. His letters crossed with Ginny's letter to him. She told him that his son, Alec Benjamin, weighed eight and a half pounds and was a healthy baby who was the image of his father. Her only reference to her long and painful labour was, *That was the hardest day's work I'd done in a long time.*

II

Six weeks after the birth of Tovell and Ginny's son, Lily was awakened by her own son, a sturdy toddler of almost three years, who was banging on the side of his cot and calling his mother. Lily jumped out of bed when she saw from the bedside clock that it was nearly seven. She dressed herself and little Arthur quickly. 'Your grandmother must have overslept,' she said to the child. 'That'll do her good. We can make her a cup of tea for a change, can't we, Arthur?'

Some time later Lily pushed open the door to her mother-in-law's bedroom with her bottom and backed into the room holding a tea cup in one hand and clasping her son with the other. 'Morning, Mother,' she called out. 'Little Arthur has brought you a nice cup of tea.' Mrs. Gillings did not reply to Lily's cheerful greeting. When the girl turned round and approached the bed she saw that her mother-in-law's face had a strange pallor. She was also very still. Lily put down the cup on the bedside table and released Arthur's hand. Tentatively, she touched her mother-in-law's cheek. It was cold. Lily pulled her hand away quickly. With an increasing sense of foreboding she shook her mother-in-law gently. There was no response. A look of horror, and then panic, spread across Lily's face. She grabbed her son, struggled down the narrow staircase with him and rushed, screaming, into the street. Mrs. Lambert heard her coming and opened the front door as Lily ran up the garden path. Dr. Lambert accompanied the girl back to her cottage straightaway. Once there, he examined Mrs. Gillings, but as he had feared as soon as he had heard Lily frantically calling his name, the old lady was dead.

'I'm very sorry, Lily,' he said gently as he removed his stethoscope. 'I know this is a terrible shock to you, my dear, but to me it is not entirely unexpected. Your mother-in-law has been ill for some time. It was her heart. I warned her repeatedly to take things more easily but she'd been a hard-working woman all her life and it was not in her nature to rest or be idle.'

'But why didn't she tell me?' Lily sobbed. 'I could've taken the heavy work off her hands. She wouldn't let me do anything.'

'That was the way she wanted it, my dear,' replied the doctor. 'She was so proud of you, Lily – proud of the beautiful work you produced, proud of the way you've pulled yourself round after Arthur's death and proud of the way you've taken upon yourself the role of breadwinner. She felt you had enough to cope with and she wouldn't burden you further.'

'But now she's dead. If she'd have let me do more she'd still be alive.'

'Not necessarily, Lily dear. Her heart may have been in a worse condition than I thought, and she was a big woman. She had a lot of weight to carry around and that must have been a strain on her heart.'

'It seems like everyone I love is taken from me ....'

'You have young Arthur. You must bear up for him. That's what your mother-in-law would have told you. Now, why don't you take your son downstairs and I will go to the next street and tell your friend Mary what has happened. I'll also telephone Mrs. Brewster, of course. I'm sure they will be glad to help you with the arrangements. I'll drop the certificate off to you later.'

Dr. Lambert's real concern that given her past record Lily might, in a fit of extreme loneliness and despair, attempt once more to take her own life and that of her son, was shared by Lydia Brewster and her former neighbours. Even though Arthur was a normal boisterous and demanding child, they felt that they could not rely on him alone to keep his mother from lapsing into the kind of total despondency to which she had succumbed after her husband's death. They agreed that it would be unwise for the girl to be alone in the house, especially at night, until she had recovered from her bereavement. They also felt that it was essential for her mental, as well as her financial state, that she continue with her work and so they did not argue when she refused to leave her cottage on the grounds that she must remain there for the sake of her customers. The only answer was for the six women to take it in turns to stay with her. Ginny had taken Mrs. Gillings's death to heart much more than the other five friends. Over the years she had become very fond of Mrs. Gillings and it was only a few weeks since she had stayed in her house for several days. Ginny was acutely aware that the hours that the old lady had sat with her whilst she was in labour, and the loving care and attention which she had lavished on her and baby Alec afterwards, could have contributed to her decline in health. Ginny was glad, therefore, to take her turn on the rota, accompanied by her new baby, as a way of helping to assuage her sense of guilt.

Lydia Brewster gave much thought to what should be done since the arrangement could only be regarded as a short term solution, given that the six of them were already weighed down with responsibilities and duties of their own. Ginny, Mary, Emily and Phyllis also had to work to a greater or lesser extent to contribute towards their keep and that of their children. All four were living with relatives so were in no position to offer Lily and little Arthur a permanent home. Mrs. Ellis had considered the matter but as she told Lydia, her Wilfred still suffered such terrible bouts of pain from his burn injuries that she could not ask him to put up with other people in the house when he needed peace and quiet. Lydia asked her husband but he refused on the grounds that he was getting too old to have a youngster around all the time, and that the Service would not approve anyway.

The members of the Gillings family from Great Yarmouth, when they attended the funeral, invited Lily and Arthur to live with them, but the girl declined the offer. She told them at great length that she was now used to living in the country and could not bear the thought of living anywhere else. She was sure it was best for little Arthur as well, and that his grandmother would have agreed. She turned down the entreaties of Lord and Lady Meredith with equal resolve. They had proposed that she resume her former position at the Hall and that her son should live with her until such time as he was old enough to go to school when they would pay for him to be educated in the same manner as their own sons.

'I know they were being kind,' Lily told Lydia Brewster, 'but I wouldn't want Arthur to go away to boarding-school and I'm sure he wouldn't be happy.'

The problem of Lily's future remained unresolved until a letter fell upon the front door mat on a morning when Lydia happened to be on duty. The girl immediately got up from her work and ran eagerly to pick up the letter. One glance at the writing and she announced excitedly, 'It's from David.'

From the way Lily reacted – her hands shook visibly as she took the sheets of paper from the envelope – it was clear that parting had only increased her affection for the young man. Once she had finished reading, Lydia was prompted to enquire, 'Does he write to you often, Lily?'

'Oh, he writes regular – always has done since he went away.'

'He must be very fond of you.'

'He is that – or so he say.'

'And you, Lily – are you fond of him?'

Lily nodded bashfully. 'There hasn't been anyone else since Arthur died.'

'Is David the real reason you didn't want to set up home with your relatives in Great Yarmouth, or with the Merediths?'

'Reckon so,' mumbled Lily.

Lydia hesitated then felt she must ask more. 'I've no wish to pry, Lily, but you know I'm concerned for you – we all are. Has David ever made you any promises – for when the war is over?'

Lily did not answer at first but when she did, her words came tumbling out. 'Yes, he did. I know that it wasn't right at the time, Mrs. Brewster, but he was just going off to war so he couldn't wait. That day he came to see me – before he sailed – we went into the church. We did what David called, plight our troth. He promised he'd marry me when he came back and I promised I'd wait for him. We said prayers for each other and ...., we kissed – but only to seal our vows, you understand – like they do in the marriage service. I know we were wrong, seeing Arthur hadn't been dead that long, and I felt ashamed at promising another man so soon .... It wasn't that I didn't love Arthur – I did very much – but I hoped he'd understand, seeing as David was going to war ....'

'I'm sure he would have understood, Lily. You did nothing wrong, my dear. You have no need to feel shame. In those circumstances you acted most correctly. Now tell me, did David ever mention you to his family?'

'Oh, yes. He say he told his mother and father all about me and little Arthur, and his sister Annie. She makes all the presents David gives to little Arthur.'

'Then would you have any objection if I wrote to them on your behalf?'

'Objection? No, I wouldn't have any objection. I'd be glad. I've felt I ought to write before but I'm not very clever at putting pen to paper – not to strangers anyhow.'

Lydia wrote the letter whilst Lily continued with her sewing and little Arthur played on the floor beside her. When Mary arrived at the appointed hour, claiming that she just happened to be passing, Lydia was able to leave and she posted the letter before returning to the Coastguard Station. It had taken her a long time to compose, so carefully had she chosen the words. It was the longest communication Mr. and Mrs. Wilson had ever received and they did not bother to reply.

The following Sunday morning, Lydia was sitting next to her husband in Haisbro church when she felt a tap on her shoulder. She looked round to find Emily and Phyllis sitting behind her.

'Sorry to bother you, Mrs. Brewster,' said Emily, 'but Lily isn't here and the service is about to begin. She's never late for morning service.'

'Who is on watch?' asked Lydia.

'Mary,' replied Phyllis, 'and she isn't here either.'

Lydia glanced anxiously at her husband. He turned to face the other two women. Seeing how worried they looked, he said, 'Perhaps we'd better go and check.' As they left their pews, Mr. Brewster raised his hand in apology to the vicar.

The four hurried to Lily's cottage, dreading what they might find when they got there. To their astonishment, a large wagon pulled by two shire horses stood outside. The wagon was piled high with furniture and a man, assisted by a dark-haired buxom young woman, was lashing ropes over the load. At that moment, Lily emerged from her front door carrying little Arthur. She was followed by Mary and Dr. and Mrs. Lambert, all carrying boxes and cases. Lily rushed up to the Brewsters, her face aglow with excitement. 'David's father and his sister Annie have come for us. They say our home's with them from now on.' Lily grabbed Lydia's hand and dragged her forward to the wagon. 'Mr. Wilson, Annie, this is the lady that wrote to you – Mrs. Brewster.'

Mr. Wilson turned, touched the peak of his cap in Station Officer Brewster's direction and nodded to the women. He wiped his right hand on the front of his jacket before offering it to Lydia. 'I'm much obliged to you, ma'am. We dint bother to answer your letter 'cause we knew we'd come the first Sunday to fetch 'em. You must excuse us for rushing off but Annie and me left at dawn and we've got a fair way to go to get to the other side of Fakenham afore dark. This here's my daughter Annie.'

Annie hurried forward and shyly offered her hand to everyone. 'David told us about all of you. That's lovely to meet you at last. I wanted to come after David wrote that Mrs. Gillings had passed on but Father, he say, we mustn't interfere unless we're asked. I'm truly glad you asked because now I've got another sister.'

'And so have I,' echoed a happy Lily. 'Oh, I almost forgot. I've taken everything with me and I'll post all the orders back to my customers as soon as they're finished.'

Everyone crowded round to hug Lily and little Arthur before they were helped onto the seat of the wagon by Mr. Wilson. As the magnificient pair of shire horses, more accustomed to trailing a plough than transporting furniture, pulled the big wagon away from the kerb, Lily had another thought. She called back, 'Oh, I haven't locked up!'

'Never mind, Lily,' Dr. Lambert shouted back. 'I'll do it and return the keys to his lordship's agent when I'm on my rounds tomorrow. Good luck to you both. Take care!'

Everyone waved to Lily, shouting good wishes, and she waved back until the wagon turned a corner and was out of sight. Lydia heaved a sigh and admitted to feeling somewhat dazed by what had just taken place. 'I hoped, of course, that the Wilsons would offer Lily and Arthur a home when I wrote to them,' she confessed, 'but I never expected events to move so fast. Just think how many letters of explanation I shall have to write.'

III

Tovell was shocked and saddened when he read Ginny's letter about Mrs. Gillings. In spite of living so close to death he was not hardened to it and he mourned as he would have done had he been at home. He realised how much Ginny would miss her. In the few months he had lived next door to Mrs. Gillings he had come to respect her and to admire her spirit. Whenever he had chanced to think about her since leaving the Coastguard Station, it had been with warmth and affection. He wrote to Ginny of the sorrow he felt and tried to find words of comfort for her. This was not easy for him to do; at the time of Alec's birth, he had experienced a surge of emotion and feelings of elation, but this high had been followed by a corresponding low. First he had felt frustration that he had missed being with Ginny at such a time and that he had not seen his son and had little hope of doing so in the foreseeable future. Next he had felt despondency and fear that he would never see Alec and never return to Ginny, Bobby and Lizzie. Throughout these weeks he had to keep these demons to himself and never betray for a moment in his letters home that he was in a state of despair – was beginning to give up hope.

The news of Mrs. Gillings's death did not help Tovell's state of mind but the weather was a contributory factor too. Autumn had given way to winter very quickly and by the middle of November the soldiers had suffered weeks of heavy rain. There was little respite other than the opportunity, taken in turns, to go to a drying-out dug-out in the support trenches and enjoy the warmth from the charcoal braziers. The pleasure was short-lived; the men were soon drenched again once they went back outside and the trenches were perpetually knee-deep in mud. Everywhere the smell of dampness was made worse by the smell of decay – the stink of rotting corpses somewhere beneath the mud. Only the rats seemed to be thriving in the conditions – they had a full larder of human flesh to feast upon. Many of the men declared that they hated the lice more than the enemy – and this was understandable as baths became more and more infrequent, some unfortunates having only one a year – but Tovell was in no doubt that what he hated the most was the mud. After what he saw at Chateau Wood near Ypres, mud became his new nightmare.

Tovell had been summoned by Lieutenant Colonel Bradshaw and to reach his command post he had to make his way through what was left of Chateau Wood. The scene was one of utter desolation – charred trees, bare of foliage, most of them mere stumps – the result of years of warfare waged back and forth across once-verdant woodland. A thick mist hung over the whole area which had been reduced to swamp by the weeks of incessant downpours. Tovell was careful to keep to the wooden duckboards and was thankful when he could climb to slightly higher ground. Three soldiers on horseback passed him. They descended to the water-logged ground and began to cross via the duckboard. Suddenly, Tovell heard shouting and the neighing of horses. He looked back and saw that the duckboard had tipped up and the lead horse had fallen into the quagmire, throwing his rider in the process. The other two riders struggled to keep their mounts steady on the wobbling duckboard but they too fell into the mud. As Tovell and several other soldiers scrambled back to the bog to help, the men and their horses thrashed about in a desperate attempt to reach firm ground. Tovell waded in but the soggy bed gave way under his feet. The mire was engulfing both men and animals before his eyes, swallowing them alive like some giant monster which had risen from the depths of the earth. Tovell felt around beneath the surface and located the reins of one of the horses. He tugged with all his might, throwing himself backwards as he did so. The soldiers behind him caught hold of him and hung on. Tovell yelled to one of the riders who had half-surfaced at that moment. 'Grab the stirrup or something!'

The man lunged forward and managed to get a hand under the saddle strap. Tovell and the others heaved until they had dragged the horse and the man clear of the morass. They both collapsed on the drier ground and the soldiers undid their water bottles and cleared the mud from the eyes and the nostrils of both the horse and the rider. The animal got up almost immediately and tried to shake off more of the mud. A soldier led the horse away. After a few more moments the rider recovered sufficiently to sit up but he was distraught when he saw that only he had been rescued.

Tovell turned to a sergeant. 'It's quiet at the moment. The Hun can't see us for the mist. Send someone for grappling gear. At least we ought to give them a decent burial.' He then proceeded on his way, shaking the mud from his clothes as he trudged back up the incline. When he reached the derelict cottage which served as a command post, he found several officers standing outside holding field glasses. 'You did your best, Tovell' said Lieutenant Colonel Bradshaw. 'At least you saved one of the poor chaps. Get cleaned up. Williams will help you,' he added, indicating his batman who was standing close by with a tin bowl and towel at the ready. 'Then come inside.'

Several minutes later, Tovell entered the cottage. He exchanged salutes with some officers who were leaving. Major Webb was with the colonel – the two men were pouring over a map which was spread out on the table. They beckoned to Tovell to join them.

'The general staff have finally accepted, after five months, that the Passchendaele offensive is a failure,' explained Lieutenant Colonel Bradshaw. 'You'll be glad to learn, Tovell, especially after what has just happened, that the regiment is to be redeployed to near here – Cambrai.'

Tovell looked at the spot on the map indicated by the colonel. 'Cambrai – looks like it's a road and rail centre, Sir.'

'Exactly, Tovell. The new plan is to tear through the Hindenburg Line and capture Cambrai. It's the break-through we've been waiting for.'

'I hope so, Sir,' said Tovell wearily.

The colonel permitted himself the trace of a smile. 'Yes, I know there have been a lot of promised break-throughs, but this one is different. We shall be using the infantry in a totally new way – in support of tanks. It's never been done before.'

'*Winston's Follies* – ever heard of them, Tovell?' asked Major Webb.

'I've seen them, Sir,' replied Tovell. 'The first time was last year on the Somme and more recently, I saw them at the third Battle of Ypres. Mostly they were either broken down or stuck in the mud.'

'But you haven't seen the Mark IV version, Tovell, and nor has the enemy,' said the colonel. 'As Major Webb has indicated, we have Winston Churchill to thank for ignoring the derision of others and promoting the development of the tank. And the land around Cambrai is ideal – chalk based and well-drained. It also has long stretches of woodland where we shall conceal the tanks – over four hundred of them – and five infantry divisions. There will be four cavalry divisions poised in the rear, ready to rush forward once *we* have made the initial breakthrough. This is a quiet sector. No-one will be expecting an attack in force here.'

'Well, I'll admit it's different, Colonel, but are we still going to warn the Hun that we're coming, with yet another useless barrage?'

'Not this time, Tovell. Everything has been prepared in the utmost secrecy and General Byng has ruled out the use of a preliminary artillery barrage. The element of surprise will be total.'

On the twentieth of November 1917, the early morning silence was shattered at a given moment by the thunder of a thousand guns along a ten mile front. Simultaneously, tanks emerged from their hiding places among the trees and advanced in groups of three in triangular formation, their infantry behind them, across *no-man's-land* towards enemy lines. So shocked were the Germans by this totally unexpected and awesome sight that many of them turned and ran.

As each group of three reached enemy territory, the lead tank crushed and flattened the first of the Germans' wire barricades, passed over it and swung left. The gunners inside the tank then fired down the length of the enemy's front line trench. The second tank followed the first through the gap in the barbed wire, dropped its fascine – a beamed crib-like device – into the front line trench, crossed over the trench and swung left so that it could rake the second line support trench with its gunfire. The third tank then followed the path of the other two but pushed forward until it had crushed the second of the enemy's wire barricades, dropped its fascine into the support trench, crossed over and positioned itself to defend the following infantry with its guns.

The soldiers ran closely behind the third tank, operating in two files, two platoons to a trench. The first group of men acted as *cleaners* and with the help of the stationary tanks, they cleared the enemy trenches. The second group was responsible for securing the lines and for widening the gaps in the barbed wire so that the reserve forces could pass through easily and quickly using the fascines as stepping stones over the trenches.

This systematic deployment of tanks and troops was a success. For Tovell, it was the kind of military action which would stand out in a professional soldier's memory. Tanks were being used in battle on a large scale and, as the colonel had emphasised, it had never been done before. At long last, the Allies had come up with a first which had shocked the Hun. Even better, Ted's hero, Churchill, had had a hand in this success. The old man would be jubilant. The answer had been found. A sense of elation spread through the ranks. Tovell felt he could almost smell victory.

As they pushed forward towards Cambrai, Lieutenant Colonel Bradshaw, on horseback, rode up to Tovell. 'Good morning, Sir,' Tovell called out cheerily. 'Looks like you were right – this really is the breakthrough we were looking for.'

'Yes,' agreed the colonel. 'We've torn a six mile gap through the Hindenburg Line in a matter of hours. Wonderful achievement! Unfortunately, there's one sector, right in the centre where things have not gone according to plan. It seems there was an error of command and the infantry was not allowed to follow closely behind the tanks as it was along the rest of the ten mile front. As a consequence, Flesquieres hasn't fallen and we've lost thirty nine tanks in that sector. However, the general is certain that that setback will not prejudice the final outcome of the battle, which will surely be ….' The colonel did not complete his sentence because at that moment, Major Webb hurried over to them.

'I've been looking for you, Sir,' the Major said, distress evident in his face and in his voice. 'Bad news, I'm afraid. Damn Bolsheviks!'

'Bolsheviks – what about the Bolsheviks?' demanded the colonel.

'The news has just come through, Sir,' explained Major Webb. 'The Bolsheviks apparently seized power in Russia days ago. They've overturned the Liberal Government which has ruled since the Revolution, and they've made an immediate peace with Germany. We no longer have a Russian ally and more to the point, the Hun no longer has an Eastern Front to defend. Our spies in Cambrai say that the first train-load of German soldiers has just arrived from Russia. If more follow, they'll be able to hold out against our offensive. What unbelievable bad luck, Sir.'

Thus the Allies were to be robbed of what had seemed certain victory because their well-planned offensive had coincided with the second revolution to take place in Russia in a year – the second a mere eight months after the first. Throughout that first day of the Battle of Cambrai, reinforcements continued to arrive from the Eastern Front. Although the Germans abandoned Flesquieres late on the first night, they were strong enough to hold out against the British attack for the next seven days. On the twenty seventh of November, the Commander-in-Chief, Sir Douglas Haig, gave the order to General Byng for the offensive to cease. Once more there was deadlock – but not for long. By the thirtieth of November, the troops from Russia had swelled the German forces to twenty divisions and they were able to launch a sudden counter-attack. They too had some new cards up their sleeves.

By the sixth of December, the Allies were still retreating. Above the noise and chaos of battle, shouts of, 'Pull back, pull back!' could be heard. Men took cover as best they could. Tovell, Major Webb and a crowd of soldiers were sheltering in a previously abandoned trench when a runner came to them. 'Sir, the colonel is a hundred yards to the right,' the runner said, addressing the major. 'He requests that you join him.'

The major thanked the corporal and then, turning to Tovell said, 'You'd better come along too.' Keeping low, the two men ran along the broken trench to their commanding officer.

'You'll be pleased to know,' announced Lieutenant Colonel Bradshaw without waiting for them to get their breath back, 'that the general staff are of the opinion that the Hun's counteroffensive is running out of steam.'

At that moment, German aircraft flew low over the trench, raking it with machine-gun fire and forcing the three men to take cover. 'Perhaps the general staff should visit this sector, Sir,' commented Tovell wryly.

The colonel almost smiled. 'Yes, I agree there's still some action in these southern sectors but it is quietening down. We should soon be able to dig in.'

'How far do the general staff think the Hun has pushed us back, Sir?' asked Major Webb.

'They think we've lost two thirds of the ground we gained on the first day – and forty four thousand men.'

'In seventeen days – God help us,' said Tovell sadly.

'We must concentrate our minds on what we've achieved at Cambrai,' said the colonel tersely. 'We've proved that surprise brings greater gains at cheaper human cost and that infantry supported tanks are a most effective new weapon.'

Just then, two of the low-flying German aircraft returned to strafe the trench once more. As the men ducked to take cover against what was left of the wall they could see the enemy infantry advancing towards them through the gloom, accompanied by a creeping artillery barrage. 'It's a pity we didn't think of that new idea as well,' observed Tovell looking up at the sky, 'infantry with close tactical support from the air.'

'That reminds me,' said the colonel, training his field glasses on the advancing forces. 'Tell the men they must stay vigilant even as things slow down – as I'm sure they will. We've reports that the enemy is still employing its new infiltration tactics. This attack could be a diversion by their reserves while their stormtroopers go around and creep up behind us. Tell every man to continue to watch his back.'

Three miles south of Tovell's position, David and a fellow stetcher-bearer were carrying a wounded corporal through the maze of inter-connecting trenches to the aid-post in the rear. As they travelled along a communication trench, David stopped suddenly. 'I can see Germans,' he whispered. 'Go back, Bert! Go back!'

'Oh, blimey!' gasped his partner. 'Quick, David, we'll have to turn round. We passed a dugout a couple of minutes ago.'

They hurried as fast as they could back the way they had come, carrying their heavy load, until Bert called out, 'Look – there it is!'

The dugout was an ideal hiding place. It was filled with boxes of stores and the piles were covered with tarpaulins in an effort to keep out the damp. David and Bert quickly carried the unconscious man behind the boxes, made him as comfortable as possible and then covered him and themselves with a large tarpaulin.

After a few minutes David said, 'We haven't heard the Germans come this way yet. I'd better run back to the front line and warn our boys that the Hun's behind us.'

'Alright,' said Bert, 'but you be careful, lad.'

David crept warily out of the dugout and to his relief, no-one was about. He hurried off in the direction of his front lines. Suddenly, he felt something hit him in the calf. He looked round and saw that the enemy was coming after him. He hobbled on as fast as he could, turned a corner of the trench and stumbled over a dead man. He fell face down, into the deep mud.

IV

Another Christmas – Christmas 1917 – and still the war was not over. Ginny had her new baby to console her but nevertheless, her thoughts kept drifting back to the previous year when Tovell had been home at Christmas. She also found herself thinking increasingly of Mrs. Gillings. The old lady had been living at the Coastguard Station with her son and his first wife when Ginny had moved there. From the beginning, Mrs. Gillings had taken her young neighbour under her wing and had always been on hand whenever she was needed. After her death, the immediate problem had been to safeguard Lily so Ginny had not mourned for Mrs. Gillings then as deeply as she might otherwise have done. The old lady had been part of Ginny's Christmas for the previous eleven years and the celebrations could not be the same without her. Memories of happy times past came rushing back and Ginny grieved for Mrs. Gillings as for an adoptive mother.

There was no Christmas Day party at the Coastguard Station that year. There was, however, a brief meeting after the congregation had spilled out into the churchyard after Christmas morning service. Ginny's uncle and aunt had gone over to their neighbours to exchange the greetings of the season, leaving Ginny and her children to join Mary, Emily and Phyllis and their families. Soon afterwards, the Brewsters crossed the churchyard to speak to them.

'Happy Christmas to you all, ladies!' said Mr. Brewster, 'My apologies for not inviting you to the usual Christmas Day celebrations but we felt that, in the circumstances, we couldn't have a party this year.'

'Don't apologise, Mr. Brewster. We all understand,' Mary assured him. 'How is your poor daughter?'

Station Officer Brewster shook his head and turned to where his elder daughter and her three small children were talking with Dr. and Mrs. Lambert. Lydia Brewster answered for him. 'She's trying to bear up for the sake of the children, just as you all did, but having her husband home, thinking he was going to recover from his wounds and then he did not …. It's left her devastated.'

'We're hoping that a few weeks with us with Mrs. Brewster taking the children off her hands to a certain extent, will help her to recover,' explained Mr. Brewster.

Lydia felt it was time to change the subject. 'Has anyone any news?' she asked.

'I heard from Mrs. Jackson the other day,' announced Emily. 'Ned's alright – he's been made a corporal now.'

'That's good news,' said Mary. 'I heard from Mrs. Westgate and she had good news an' all. She say Bill's as right as rain although they've discharged him from the Army. I reckon they had to seeing he's only got one kidney now. She say they might come to Yarmouth for a holiday next summer and if they do, they'll come and see us all.'

'Let's hope they do,' agreed all the women. Phyllis added, 'Last time I wrote to Mrs. Mannell I reminded her that we'd all be pleased to see her anytime. She took Fred's death hard and she's had one illness after another ever since. I haven't heard from her lately – I hope she's alright.'

'I haven't heard from Lily lately. Has anyone else heard?' asked Ginny.

The others shook their heads. 'She seemed very happy when last she wrote,' said Lydia Brewster, 'and she mentioned having acquired a sizeable clientele in the Fakenham district so perhaps she's been busy completing orders in time for Christmas. Any other news?' she added hopefully.

No one had any other news so Mr. Brewster was able to close the little meeting. 'Well, let's hope next year will be a better one for us all. In case we don't see you before next week, let me take the opportunity to wish you all a Happy New Year for 1918.'

1918

I

Lydia had hoped that someone would have information about Richard Collins but with her husband standing beside her, she had had to refrain from interrogating her friends further on Christmas morning. On the way home from church that day she had wondered whether she would ever be released from the torment of not knowing what had happened to her lover. Four weeks later she was supplied with the answers to all her questions – by her husband.

Harold Brewster was reading the newspaper one morning and Lydia was watching him nervously. She was trying to appear busy with her dusting. In her anxiety she knocked over a small ornament. The noise made her husband look up.

'Doesn't Mrs. Hendry do that?' he enquired.

Lydia blushed slightly. 'We don't employ her to come every day,' she replied quickly, 'and anyway, she's been overloaded with laundry to do whilst Julia and the children have been staying with us.'

Her husband nodded and resumed his reading, commenting as he did so, 'Seems very quiet now they've gone home, doesn't it?'

'Yes,' agreed Lydia. 'I feel quite lost. Have you nearly finished with the paper?'

'Won't be long, then you can have it,' he replied. Suddenly, he saw something of interest, scanned it quickly and then called out to her. 'Just look at this, my dear. I caught sight of the name, *Richard Collins,* and read on in case it was about the man who was here. I think perhaps it might be.'

Lydia's heart missed a beat. She dropped the duster and rushed over to where her husband was sitting at the table. She stood behind his chair and looked at the newspaper over his shoulder, thankful that he could not see her face. 'Where is the reference?' she asked, trying to keep her voice steady.

'There, under the Court News,' replied her husband. '*Major Richard Collins received his country's highest award for valour from His Majesty the King ....* There's a note that the full story is in column four and if you read that you will see what I mean. It must be the same man – too many coincidences otherwise.'

The print danced before Lydia's eyes. Through the blur she strove to make out the gist of the report as she read it aloud. '*During the final stages of the Passchendaele offensive, so incensed was the major by the relentless slaughter of his men .... He charged up the incline towards the machine-gun outpost .... Though caught repeatedly by enemy fire, nothing could stop him from reaching his objective .... He stormed the enemy position single handed .... Through his heroic assault, many lives were saved and a valuable piece of land at a commanding site, won ....*

Major Collins's selfless action must not be forgotten .... Although he is recovering well from his wounds, he has lost the use of his left arm and will carry to his grave the deep scars to the left side of his face ....

Pupils at his old school ...., are planning a hero's welcome for their former master when he returns to spend a few weeks recuperation with his wife ....

His appointment to the War Office, where he will head a department which co-ordinates and disseminates information on sea and land mines, is particularly appropriate since in the early days of the war, when little was known on the subject, he defused one of the first German mines to be washed up on our shores.

It is hoped that he will be able to take up his new command, with the rank of lieutenant colonel, by the end of February.'

Lydia gripped the back of her husband's chair to stop herself from swaying. She felt weak with relief. Richard was not dead; he was alive and never again would he be called upon to dice with death in the front line. Thank God, oh, thank God. She took a deep breath and said calmly, 'Yes, I'm sure you're right – it must be the same man. Certainly, the public school they mention is the one where Mr. Collins taught and they would never have two masters with exactly the same name. And, of course, his personal courage was never in question – particularly after he dealt with the mine.'

'I've decided what I shall do, Lydia,' declared Harold Brewster. 'I shall write to him and address the letter to the school. I did wonder whether I should do that when I first came home. I wish I had now.

He'd kept everything here in such perfect order. He'd even left me a copy of every report he had made, every letter he had written, so that I would know what had been going on in my absence. Obviously, the man's a first class administrator and just right for his new job. Yes, I'll write and thank him for the good work he did here and at the same time, congratulate him on his award and wish him a speedy recovery. There's no doubt my Station was in good hands when he was in charge – and so were you, my dear.'

Lydia smiled to herself but confined her reply to a request. 'When you write, perhaps you would pass on to Mr. Collins my kindest regards. Tell him I hope he soon feels strong again and that I pray the quality of his life will be improved because of his brave deed.'

'The quality of his life? That's a strange remark to make to the man in the circumstances, isn't it?'

'Oh, he will understand. You're forgetting, Harold, that we had the teaching profession in common. We talked about it a great deal. Mr. Collins had taught both English and History in his time and he loved both subjects – literature in particular – but he could not instill much enthusiasm into his pupils.'

'You mean he couldn't keep control of the young devils.'

'Well, I suppose that's what it amounted to. My point is, they can hardly ignore him now, can they? What boy could fail to admire a scarred war hero?'

'Very well, my dear; I shall convey your sentiments as you wish. You never know – we may get to meet the Collinses one day. I shall be retiring in the not too distant future and we shall have much more time for socialising. His school isn't far from Oxford – we might be able to pay him and his wife a visit when we're staying with Muriel.'

Lydia had not trusted herself to comment further but had retreated to the pantry on the pretext that she needed to rearrange the shelves. Once her husband had returned to duty at midday, she read the newspaper account of Richard's heroism over and over again. Whatever happened now, whether her husband established a correspondence with him or not, whether she ever saw him again or not, her torment was at an end; no more harm could come to Richard because of the war and he could only benefit from what had already happened to him. Once and for all, he would be able to cast off the burden of guilt he had shouldered since childhood – guilt that he was not the kind of son his father could be proud of – and the burden of fear that his father's low estimation of him might be the correct one.

Perhaps, too, he would stop hiding behind a veil of sarcasm and cynicism. His relationship with other people must then improve – even his relationship with his wife – but Lydia did not want to dwell on that. It was too painful to think of her Richard in the welcoming arms of another woman. She knew she was being unreasonable. What agonies he must have suffered knowing that as he left, Harold was on his way back to her. Yet, for a few moments, she was overwhelmed by the jealousy she felt towards Mildred. She found herself weeping again, just as she had that morning in the pantry, but this time the tears were not tears of relief that he was safe, but tears of frustration and sorrow that he could not come back to her.

Eventually, she managed to overcome these harsh thoughts and concentrate instead on the most positive outcome of all – the respect Richard would enjoy from now on from his pupils. This respect would ensure that they listened to him and so he would have the opportunity which had eluded him before, to plant the seeds of his knowledge into receptive minds. He would be rewarded by the arousal of interest where none had existed before. He would be able to feel that he had been an inspiration to his pupils – a teacher in the true sense of the word. Yes, Lydia hoped they would meet again one day. She wanted to see for herself a happy and fulfilled man.

As for her own life, now that she no longer had any cause to worry over Richard, she might be able to get her affairs into perspective. He had been the centre of her existence for the last three years. The highlight of her day, every day, had come when her husband left their quarters and she had been free to scan the newspaper for any word of Richard. She had read every account of every battle; searched through all the casualty lists; trembled over the obituary columns. Until she had satisfied herself that his name was not mentioned anywhere, she had found it impossible to settle down to perform the simplest domestic chore. How she had missed the original report of his courageous action she could not imagine. The only possible explanation was that it had appeared in the Press at the end of November. At that time she had hurried to Kings Lynn to comfort her daughter when her husband, on recuperation leave, had died suddenly. There had been a few days leading up to the funeral, before she had brought Julia and the children back home with her, when she had not had an opportunity to read a newspaper. Richard must have been headline news then.

Now she would have to establish a new routine – find another *raison d'etre*. Richard no longer needed her or the shield of her worry. He had the prospect of a full life ahead of him; a life which would not include her. If she were to retain her sanity and find some purpose in her existence she must push him from the forefront of her thoughts. She must find a place for him in the back of her mind – a safe and secret place. In moments of quiet solitude she would be able to take him from his hiding place like a treasured toy from the nursery cupboard and relive again their joyous moments together. They had been fortunate – so few people have the chance to realise their dreams, even for a short time. Hand in hand, they had walked through Elysium and climbed the heights of Mount Olympus – such memories would sustain her in her old age. And she still had the love of her husband; she must not forget that she had a debt to repay to him. She would make restitution for her unfaithfulness by her solicitude for his well-being. She had been blessed with the love of two good men – how many women could say that? And she had her books. They would mean so much more to her now. All those favourite passages read aloud and shared …. Perhaps she would try to write herself. She had reached a new maturity; experienced such depth of feeling. Could she express those feelings in words? Words – they had both set such store by words. Could it be that each was destined to immortalise the other in words – he in verse, she in prose? At least there was solace to be found in the speculation.

II

Lily and Annie stood very close to one another as they waited by the barrier at Thorpe Station, Norwich. Both were shivering – more from nervousness than from the cold. The Red Cross train had shunted to a halt some minutes earlier and the volunteers who had been waiting on the platform for the train to arrive had climbed aboard.

'Why's that taking them so long to unload any of the wounded?' asked Lily.

'I reckon they've got a lot of sorting out to do first,' suggested Annie. 'They've got to decide which men are going to which hospitals.'

'Yes, that's right – but I wish they'd hurry.' A few more minutes passed then Lily exclaimed, 'Look, Annie – here they come!'

The crowds who had congregated in the hope of catching a glimpse of a loved one began to jostle for a better view. The two young women found themselves carried forward until they were pressed against the barrier. They watched anxiously as stretcher after stretcher was carried along the platform. They peered at every face which passed them until Lily began to lose heart.

'Perhaps he isn't on this train after all. The vicar's brother might have got his name mixed up with someone else's.'

'We mustn't give up yet,' said Annie, taking Lily's hand in hers. 'The train isn't empty yet; he might still be on it.' More stretchers, more stretcher-bearers, more wounded passed until Annie too began to despair. Then suddenly, she gripped Lily's hand more tightly. 'I think that's him coming now. That's his blond hair colour anyway.'

Lily hardly dared to look as the next group of Red Cross workers approached. 'Let it be him,' she whispered. 'Oh, please God, let it be him.'

'It *is* him,' cried Annie. 'It *is* him!'

The young man on the stretcher did not hear and did not open his eyes. 'Oh, doesn't he look ill?' gasped Lily. 'He's so white and sickly.'

'We'll soon get him right once he's home,' Annie assured her. 'Don't you worry, but first, we've gotta find out where they're taking him – c'mon, Lily.'

Although many in the crowd had dispersed by then, the young women were still jammed against the barrier. Annie, however, was determined not to be trapped or to be deterred from her intention. She forced her way through the mass of people, dragging Lily along behind her. At last they were outside in the station fore-court where a fleet of motor-ambulances was lined up waiting to transport the wounded to their allotted hospitals. Annie ran from one vehicle to the next, peeping inside at the occupants. She was about to call out to Lily that she had found David when she felt a heavy hand on her shoulder.

'Now, now, young lady,' said the policeman. 'You mustn't go making a nuisance of yourself, disturbing these poor fellows and getting in the way of all the good work that's being done.'

'I ent being a nuisance. I won't get in the way. Please let me see my brother. That's my brother David in there.'

Lily ran up and began to plead in like fashion.

'Quiet, young ladies, quiet,' admonished the constable. 'Now which one did you say was your brother?'

By now David had recognised the familiar voices and had struggled to prop himself up on one elbow. 'Lily? Annie?' he called in a weak voice. The two began to climb the steps of the ambulance and the policeman, seeing it was useless to protest further, helped them inside.

'You can only speak to him for a minute or two,' the constable warned. 'As soon as they load the last man into this vehicle, that'll have to be off. And mind you don't get him too excited or I'll be for it.'

'Thank you, officer, thank you,' said Annie and Lily in unison before turning their attention to David.

'I couldn't believe that was true when I heard your voices. I thought I was delirious again,' explained David as he gazed with shining eyes at the two young women leaning over him. 'How did you know I'd be on this train? How did you get here? Where's little Arthur?'

'Give us a chance to answer you,' said Annie, laughing. 'We asked the vicar if he'd speak to his brother about you. He's an important man in the Red Cross now. He has the jurisdiction over the train loads of wounded. He has to find enough beds for them in the local hospitals. He must have boarded your train just now but I reckon you were too weary to notice him. Anyway, he told the vicar he'd let him know as soon as your name appeared on one of his passenger lists. He telephoned yesterday, the vicar sent word to Father and we caught the train for Norwich this morning.'

'And we're going to stay with you till you're well enough to come home to Fakenham,' added Lily. 'You remember I told you about Mrs. Pringle – the lady I was apprenticed to as a girl? Well, she's agreed to let us stay at her shop. We'll be sleeping in the dormitory where I used to sleep, and in return for our keep I'll be working for her again – just till the hospital discharges you. Mrs. Pringle say she'll be glad of a bit of help because her girls keep leaving to do war service.'

'But what about little Arthur?'

'You don't want to worry yourself about little Arthur,' said Annie. 'Mother's taking care of him. He took to her right away, didn't he, Lily? He plays with young Henry all the time – there's not much more than a year between them, if you recall – and Amy drags the pair of them everywhere with her.'

'That's right, David,' agreed Lily. 'You couldn't find a happier little boy. He thinks all the littl'uns are his brothers and sisters, so there isn't any reason why we shouldn't stop in Norwich and visit you every day.'

'That's enough about us. You haven't told us how you are,' Annie pointed out.

'Oh, I'm alright – especially now I've seen you two. I had the fever bad but that's going now,' was David's off-hand reply.

There was no opportunity for further questioning. Red Cross volunteers carrying more stretcher-cases appeared in the doorway of the ambulance. They were annoyed to find their way blocked by the young women. Apologising profusely, Lily and Annie hastily climbed down from the vehicle. They waited patiently whilst the wounded were made as comfortable as possible then Annie ventured to enquire where her brother was being taken.

'To the Norfolk and Norwich Hospital,' the helper answered brusquely.

'We'll see you tomorrow then,' Lily and Annie called to David as the doors of the ambulance slammed shut.

True to their word, both young women were waiting outside the hospital ward when visiting time came next day. 'First Father had a telegram to say you were missing in action and then, a few days later, he had another telegram to say you were wounded,' explained Annie.

'We didn't know what to think,' said Lily.

'Well, they were telling you the truth. I was missing at first – I got trapped behind enemy lines.' The statement brought such looks of horror to the faces of his listeners that David hurriedly continued. '.... So you could say that dead man saved my life. The Germans just ran straight past thinking we were both dead bodies. That was a good job they didn't waste any time else I'd have suffocated. I couldn't breathe face down in that there mud.'

'Oh, poor David,' cried Lily, stroking his hand.

'But what happened next?' Annie demanded.

'Well, once I'd made sure the Hun had gone I made my way back to the dugout. I knew that was too late to warn anyone by then. I didn't half give old Bert a shock – covered head to toe in mud. I tried to clean my leg up as best I could but it was only a flesh wound so I didn't worry. The corporal had got some bad injuries so I didn't want to waste too much of the stuff from our first-aid bag on myself. 'Course, if I'd realised how long we were going to be stuck there ....'

'How long were you there?' asked Lily.

'Three more days and nights,' David replied. 'We had to stay hidden all the time 'cause the Hun was up and down the trench. There was a lot of firing at first but that was soon over. I reckon they must have killed all our blokes or taken them prisoner. Over the next three days, they kept coming into the dugout to get the stores. It was lucky for us that they didn't take all the boxes or we'd have been seen.'

'But what did you live on?'

'We had water in our canteens, Annie, and we had emergency rations so we were alright. After three days everything went quiet. We couldn't hear the Germans talking no more and no-one was walking up and down the trench outside. Then my pal, Bert, remembered that all the trenches thereabout were low-lying and he reckoned the Hun had abandoned them and retreated to higher ground. They'd done that afore. So out he goes to have a look round. He was gone so long I thought he'd copped it but then he came back with stretcher-bearers from another company. Was I glad to see them?'

'Reckon you were. But what happened about your leg?' asked Lily.

David shifted uncomfortably in his bed and did not look at either Lily or Annie as he replied. 'The medical officer agreed that that hadn't been a serious bullet wound at first but what with getting mud and filth in it and no proper attention …. It had been hurting me and I'd felt feverish but that was no more than I'd expected. There's a stink with gangrene, of course, but that there dugout stunk anyway after we'd been stuck there three days, and I didn't know if the corporal's wounds were stinking. As that turned out, he wasn't as bad as we'd thought, but they had to take my leg off.'

There was a shocked silence until Lily recovered sufficiently to say sympathetically, 'Poor David. That must have been dreadful for you.'

Annie, who had momentarily been as stunned by the news as Lily, blurted out, 'But you're not going to let that make any difference to you, are you?'

'Hope not,' mumbled David.

'You'll soon get used to having one good leg,' Annie assured him. 'Remember old Bill Partridge? He lost a leg in a farming accident. Can't recall now how that happened but it was one harvest time. Then there was Tom Cooper. He used to go as a joskin every autumn on the Yarmouth boats. I remember he got caught in the rope when they were hauling the nets and that took him round the capstan. He lost a leg an' all. You've gotta admit that didn't make a mite of difference to either of them. They still used to hobble down the pub most nights.'

'They weren't young men,' replied David quietly. 'They'd had their life.'

'And you'll have yours,' Annie retorted, 'and that's more than you can say for a lot of the boys we grew up with. They won't have any life 'cause they're dead. You aren't dead, David, thank the Lord, and you aren't blind and you aren't without any limbs at all. A few weeks from now and you'll be rushing around the farm almost as fast as you did afore.'

Annie's heavy-handed attempt to help David to come to terms with his disability was unsuccessful because he was not primarily concerned with her reaction. He needed to know how Lily felt about his mutilation. Fortunately, the couple had ample opportunity to talk to one another privately during successive visits because Annie was increasingly occupied with cheering the young soldier who occupied the bed next to her brother.

'I feel sorry for that poor lad,' Annie explained. 'He's got no-one to visit him – except on a Sunday – 'cause that's a long way from his village, Winfarthing, to Norwich. It's the least I can do to chat to him while you keep David company.'

Lily did not dispute Annie's claim that she was acting out of charity but accepted gratefully that the pair had taken a fancy to one another and that meant she had David to herself. 'You mustn't pay no regard to what Annie say,' she told her fiancé at the first opportunity. 'She doesn't mean to sound hard; she's as upset as I am really that you lost your leg but she reckons we've got to encourage you to overcome your loss. And there's another thing – a lot of the young men she knew, and some she was sweet on, have been killed or badly wounded, and that's upset her more than she'll admit.'

'You don't have to make amends for Annie,' David replied. 'I ought to know her by now. Anyhow, I'm not too worried about what Annie thinks – what matters to me is what you think. Ever since they told me they'd taken my leg off I've been worrying whether you'd still want me.'

'Why shouldn't I still want you?' asked Lily, aghast that David should have had any doubts. 'What difference does a little old leg make? You're still my David and I still love you just the same. We promised ourselves to each other in Haisbro church. You haven't forgotten, have you?'

'Forgotten? How could I ever forget? I think about that day all the time. The Lord's been good to us, Lily. He took care of you and little Arthur like I asked ….'

'…. and watched over you like *I* asked,' said Lily taking over the theme, 'and sent you home safe so we could be wed like we promised. That day after you left, Mother likened the war to a storm cloud and she reminded me of the hymn, *God moves in a mysterious way*. Then she say to keep in mind the third verse – *The clouds ye so much dread are big with mercy and shall break in blessings on your head*. She was right. When the war took Arthur that was terrible. Then you got sent to the Front. Next thing, Mother was dead. Everyone I loved was gone. But then, suddenly, there was your father and Annie, come to fetch us and now, there's you. I'm part of a big happy family like I always wanted to be and with you back safe, I've got everything I've prayed for. Truly, those clouds have broken in blessings on my head.'

III

On the twenty first of March 1918, at about the time that Lily was taking her promised walk up the aisle to David, the Germans began what they intended should be their final offensive to win the war. Once more they made effective use of infiltrating storm-troopers and of aircraft in close support of their ground troops. So successful were they that they pushed the Allies back relentlessly, day after day.

When Tovell entered the command post in a war-damaged house near the River Marne, Lieutenat Colonel Bradshaw was writing a letter. The officer turned the sheets of paper over as the soldier approached the table. He got up from his chair. 'Morning, Tovell. I've asked you to come here instead of just sending you the Order of the Day, and when I read it to you, you will see why.' The colonel picked up a piece of paper from the table and looked at it for a few moments before reading it aloud. *'With our backs to the wall, and believing in the justice of our cause, each one must fight on to the end. Signed, Sir Douglas Haig, Commander in Chief, ninth day of April, 1918.'* The colonel looked up at Tovell. 'I think you will agree that that is the most chilling Order we have received yet. And no wonder. The Germans' progress is nothing short of alarming. Here we are, driven back almost to the Marne, only a few miles from Paris. If the German offensive continues, and with so many troops released from the Russian Front it is sure to, we shall be back to where we started in 1914. In three years and eight months not an inch of ground gained – only millions of French, British and Empire casualties.'

The colonel's voice had been getting louder, betraying the anger he felt. He paused and when he continued his tone was controlled, quieter – and sorrowful. 'When you pass this Order on to your NCOs, Tovell, I want you to instruct them to arrange for any man who has not already put his affairs in order, written letters, made a will or whatever, to be allowed the time to do so. We also have a duty to those we leave behind.'

'Yes, Sir, I'll certainly do that straight away. But is there nothing else I can tell them?' Tovell asked. 'Some ray of hope?'

Lieutenant Colonel Bradshaw considered for a moment. 'Yes, as a matter of fact there is.' He shuffled around in a pile of documents until he came to a newspaper. 'The Times has published a copy of a letter which His Majesty the King has addressed to all the American troops now arriving in England. I'll read it to you. *Soldiers of the United States, the people of the British Isles welcome you on your way to take your stand beside the Armies of many Nations now fighting in the Old World the great battle for human freedom. The Allies will gain new heart and spirit in your company. I wish that I could shake the hand of each one of you and bid you God speed on your mission.* His Majesty never spoke a truer word. Fresh troops, coming now, will indeed put new heart and spirit into us.'

'Do we know when, Sir?'

'June, Tovell. The High Command expects American troops to be fighting beside us in the trenches by June. In other words, we have to hang on for two more months.'

'We've hung on this long, Sir. Another two months should be possible.'

'Let us hope so. Now you'd better get your NCOs together.'

When Tovell had gone, the colonel sat down and read through the letter he had been writing. Satisfied with the contents, he folded the pages carefully and placed them inside an envelope. He addressed the envelope with the words, *Lady Edwina Bradshaw. To be opened in the event of her husband's death.* He then took a wallet from inside his jacket, removed a photograph and looked at it for a few moments. The photograph was of his wife and four children. He replaced the photograph with the letter behind it, in his wallet and put the latter back into his jacket. He stood up, flicked a speck of dust from his highly polished riding boots and crossed to the small mirror on the back wall. He stared at his reflection for a while with glazed eyes, his thoughts far away from the tumble-down house which had been his base for the last few days. Then his eyes focused again, he straightened his cap, smoothed his moustache, picked up his cane, threw back his shoulders and marched through the door, calling to the major, 'Come along, Webb, we're late for visiting the men.'

Now that he knew that even the colonel considered their situation was hopeless, Tovell felt worse than he had the previous year in the weeks following Alec's birth. When he addressed his NCOs, however, he was careful to emphasise that they would soon be supported by their new ally, America, and played down the real reason that the men should put their affairs in order, claiming that this instruction had been issued on the grounds of efficiency. He could see from the look in their eyes that he had not fooled all of his staff. But he would not betray the colonel. He had the feeling that during their brief meeting he had come closer than anyone to seeing the man behind the uniform.

When his NCOs had left him, Tovell took his collection of photographs from his pocket. Ginny, realising how despondent he must feel at times had sought to sustain him by keeping him in touch with every stage of the children's progress. Desperate though he was for any form of contact with his family, the photographs had also saddened him because they demonstrated only too clearly how long he had been away. Bobby and Lizzie were taller and sturdier in each picture and Alec had grown from baby to toddler. He resented bitterly that he had been denied the chance to share the years with them. And as for Ginny, he had no need of photographs to remind him of his constant yearning, his painful longing for her, his little darling.

Tovell had no need either to put his affairs in order. He had done that long ago just as he had written individual farewell letters to the four members of his family. He carried them on him, together with the photographs. His problem now was the same one he had had in the latter part of the previous year – how to write home without the sense of hopelessness which was engulfing him spilling over, creeping into his letters. He decided that the only solution was to fill them full of factual detail but not, of course, detail about the progress of the war. During his time in France he had met many soldiers who had sailed from the far-flung continents of the Empire to come to the aid of the motherland. Tovell's innate quest for knowledge had led him to interrogate these men and they, happy to have an opportunity to talk about their homeland, had provided him with a wealth of stories to tell the children. Many titbits he had already conveyed to Bobby and Lizzie but he racked his brains to think of any he had omitted. He filled his missives with information and drew maps too of the countries these men called home; maps showing the relative positions of Canada and Newfoundland, Australia and New Zealand, India and Ceylon.

Lizzie and Bobby were happy with this turn of events and particularly pleased to have so much to relate, suitably embellished, to their impressionable class-mates. Ginny, however, was concerned that these geography lessons meant that Tovell was trying to pass on as much of his knowledge as he could in a short time, fearing that he would never have another chance to help the children with their education in person. She too had become an avid reader of newspapers and it was obvious that the war was almost lost. After she had filled her letters with any tiny bit of news about the children or the smallholding, she had difficulty in finding words of comfort to impart to Tovell. She was relieved in the spring when at last she had something to relate which she hoped might cheer him. She told how pleased Station Officer Brewster was about the successful raids the Royal Navy had made on the Flanders coast to block the two U-boat bases at Ostend and Zeebrugge. *Mr. Brewster say he reckons we won't have any more trouble from U-boats now. The old joskins who used to fish before the war with the Lowestoft fleets are glad. As you know, the U-boats sunk two of the Lowestoft smacks last August and a lot of fishermen died. Mr. Brewster also reckons that as the German fleet has stayed in port since we beat them at Jutland, we can claim to have won the war at sea. He say we should be able to strangle Germany into giving in with our blockade.*

Tovell tried to take heart from Harry Brewster's convictions but it was not easy to rejoice at the vindication of the Royal Navy's honour, or to believe that the enemy was on the point of being blockaded into submission, when day by day the Allies were being driven back towards Paris. Life in the confines of the trenches was anyway so unique, so oppressive, that anyone who endured it found his dulled brain could not envisage any other form of warfare. U-boats and Grand Fleets were too far removed from the squalor and decay of the trenches.

In April the Allies, in desperation, decided to appoint an Allied Supreme Commander over all their forces. They chose General Ferdinand Foch. The situation changed little and April faded into May. When June dawned the Allies were still being pushed back but the end did not come; still they hung on and then, as promised, the Americans took up the sword and entered the lists. With these fresh reinforcements, General Foch felt strong enough by the middle of July to launch a counter-attack on the Marne.

Once they were moving forward again instead of retreating, Tovell's attitude changed. His inherent fortitude came to the surface once more and with his spirit restored, hope pervaded his letters. His cheerfulness and confidence was infectious; it was easier now for Ginny to write to him. She was pleased, nonetheless, when in the first week of August the Westgates took their long-awaited holiday. She would have something different and more interesting to report in her next letter to Tovell.

IV

Mrs. Westgate sent Mary a postcard as soon as they arrived in Great Yarmouth. She told her which day they would be coming to see her and the train they would be catching. Mary was, therefore, able to invite Ginny, Lydia, Mrs. Ellis, Emily and Phyllis to join her on that day, and to arrange for Ted Carter to meet her guests at Stalham Station. The old man was as pleased as the rest of them to see Bill again and he gladly stayed to hear the news and to partake of the tasty refreshments which Mary had prepared.

The proceedings opened with everyone congratulating Bill on his healthy appearance. He assured the company that he was fit as a fiddle and had plenty of good years left in him yet. The conversation then turned to a discussion about those who were not present. They remembered Fred Mannell and Jack Harris and Mrs. Ellis told of the latter's generosity. The Westgates were shocked and sorry to hear of Mrs. Gillings's death but delighted to learn that David and Lily's story had a happy ending. Emily was able to tell them that Ned was alive and well and Lydia proudly described the last heroic battlefield encounter of Bill's former company commander. She was also happy to confirm that Mr. Collins was recovering well from his wounds although he had informed Mr. Brewster in his last letter that the doctors had advised him that his left arm would be permanently paralysed.

Bill had a special word for Ginny. He expressed his sorrow that she had lost her brother Benjamin but was certain that she would soon have Tovell home with her. 'We've got them on the run now. There'll be no holding us. It'll be over soon – you'll see. Like Mrs. Brewster says, the war at sea is all but over and I bet they'll be no more air-raids on London or anywhere else, after what happened two nights ago.'

'Of course,' exclaimed Mary, 'you were in Yarmouth on Monday. I was forgetting.'

'The place was packed with people,' said Mrs. Westgate. 'Our landlady told us it was just like a pre-war Bank Holiday Monday. It was as though everyone had decided to forget there was a war on and enjoy the kind of Bank Holiday at the seaside they'd been used to in the old days. We had a lovely day ourselves, didn't we, Bill? We watched the Navy Day fete and the sports tournament in the Wellington Pier Gardens, and we went back to the pier again in the evening to see a charity show in the theatre.'

'That's when we first realised something was up,' added Bill, excitement creeping into his voice. 'This young chap was on stage singing. The programme said he was a pilot from the Air Station. We used to wave to them when they patrolled over this area. Half-way through his song they pulled him off stage. All the other blokes in the building wearing the same uniform – they're not Navy anymore, are they, but Royal Air Force? – rushed off too. Not long after that it was the interval and we went outside for a breath of fresh air.'

Mrs. Westgate took over the story. 'We were leaning on the railings at the end of the pier, looking down at the beach, when we realised there was a lot of activity going on further along.'

'Next thing we knew, 'planes were taking off and flying over our heads,' explained Bill. 'They still seem so tiny to me even though I'm sure they're very different from the ones we knew. Anyhow, after the show, off we went back to our boarding house with never a thought that death was so close at hand.'

'When we heard about what happened yesterday morning, I felt quite ill,' confided Mrs. Westgate. 'If just one of those Zeppelins had got through, think how many people could have been killed – us included.'

'This morning's newspaper had a full account – I was reading it on the train here – but I expect you've already seen it.' Lydia Brewster nodded but the others seemed keen to hear the rest of the story so Bill continued. 'The paper says five airships crossed the North Sea and the Yarmouth pilots found three of them cruising in formation parallel to the Norfolk coast, following the coastline just like that first damn thing did when we were stationed here. It was the young man who'd been singing at the charity show and his observer, a Canadian, who went after the leading Zeppelin and shot it down. Bill picked up the paper and found the article. 'Look, here it is. *Temporary Major Egbert Cadbury, holder of the Distinguished Service Cross for his earlier successes against the Zeppelins, and Captain Bob Leckie, having watched the Goliath sink in flames to the sea, then gave chase, damaging a second airship before a jammed machine-gun forced them to return to their Air Station on Great Yarmouth beach.* The Hun had had enough by then and the rest of 'em turned back and headed for home. I reckon they'll stay there!'

'Have the Zeppelins spoiled your holiday and put you off Yarmouth?' asked Emily.

'It'd take more than a Zeppelin to do that,' Bill replied, 'In fact, I've persuaded Gladys to pack up and move to Yarmouth permanently.'

'It was the sight of that long sea-front that did it,' explained Mrs. Westgate. 'It gave him a hankering to be a showman again. He shed twenty years just thinking about it.'

'Well, why not?' asked her husband. 'Yarmouth could do with a boxing booth like I used to have. That was the life – travelling round the countryside …. But I'm too old to travel these days. A booth on the sea-front or on one of the piers would suit me fine, and the sea air would be good for both of us.'

'But surely, it would be very unwise for you to box again, Mr. Westgate?' said Lydia anxiously.

'Oh, I wouldn't be doing the boxing, ma'am,' answered Bill. 'But there's nothing wrong with my voice. I'd still make a darned good barker. What I've got in mind is that our boy would be the boxer. He's been quite a champion in his time – better than I ever was.'

'But would he agree to move his home and family?' asked Mary.

'The way things are going he might have to move anyway – to find work,' said Bill seriously. 'Quite a few of my pals and his too, have been invalided out of the services recently but not many of them have been able to get their old jobs back. It's not that their injuries have made them incapable of doing the work, just that their bosses don't want them back. In some cases the trade isn't there anymore but in other cases the bosses have managed without help for so long they intend to go on doing so and save the wages. Now the way I see it, the war's going to end soon and millions of soldiers are going to be demobilised at the same time. They're all going to be hunting for work. I think our Sam will be glad to join us – and I know his missus and the grandchildren will be. They'll jump at the chance to live at the seaside.'

'You'll need a big house for all of you,' said Phyllis.

'And you'll need a lot of money coming in. Do boxing booths make that much?' enquired Mrs. Ellis.

It was Mrs. Westgate who answered. 'We've got it all sorted out. We'll take a boarding house and I'll run that with my daughter-in-law and the girls. The men can take care of the boxing booth. I quite fancy myself as a seaside landlady.'

'I think it's a splendid idea,' said Lydia enthusiastically. Everyone else agreed with her.

At that moment, Ted, who had been too busy eating to comment on anything which had been said previously, gave the proposal his approval. 'Cor, blast, that's right!' he exclaimed. 'We'd have somewhere to go on our trips to Yarmouth. There's nothing like a shrimp tea with a few cockles and whelks on the side, that there int!'

V

The day after the Westgates revisited Haisbro, on the eigth of August 1918, the second Battle of the Somme began at Amiens. This was a very different affair from the first Battle of the Somme; the battle which was printed indelibly on Tovell's memory. Fascine carrying tanks moved forward in great numbers followed by columns of infantry. Overhead, aircraft, copying the lesson learned from the enemy, darted back and forth in support of the troops. On their wings and bodies they carried the markings of the new independent Royal Air Force.

'Well, Tovell!' Major Webb called out, 'everywhere you look you see *Winston's Follies* – over five hundred of them this time, according to the old man. They say the Australians over at St. Quentin have the Mark V. We've got the bit between our teeth. Nothing will stop us now.'

'I hope you're right, Sir,' replied Tovell cautiously. 'I'll believe it when we see the Hindenburg Line again and break it for good this time.'

The advance continued unchecked. Now it was the turn of the Allies to push the Hun relentlessly back. By the twenty ninth of August the town of Cambrai was once more within sight. Lieutenant Colonel Bradshaw, Major Webb and Tovell stood in a dilapidated fire post looking at its shattered skyline through their field glasses.

'It's strange to think that if luck had been on our side, we would have been standing here, surveying Cambrai, nine months ago,' said the colonel.

'Indeed, Sir,' agreed Major Webb, 'but for the damn Bolsheviks.'

'They certainly cost us the victory last year,' Tovell admitted, 'but I think, Sir, that perhaps they will help us to victory this year.'

Major Webb looked at Tovell as though he'd gone mad. 'You're talking in riddles, man.'

The colonel intervened. 'Tovell is referring to the anti-war movement which has been brewing in Germany ever since the Bolsheviks took over in Russia and made peace last year. If that anti-war feeling spreads .... We already know that the morale of the German soldier has reached low ebb. That, probably more than anything else, accounts for our sweeping successes of the last three weeks.'

'It's only two months since we were in the depths of despair ourselves,' said Tovell. 'If the Americans hadn't arrived in the nick of time and boosted *our* morale, who knows .... Maybe, as the colonel says, it's morale more than anything else which wins or loses battles.'

'Time will tell, gentlemen,' the colonel concluded. 'Get back to your men and try to snatch some sleep. Tomorrow we start the onslaught on Cambrai. The town still lies a few miles ahead of us. Let's not make any assumptions. It's most unlikely that the enemy is going to lay down its arms and invite us in.'

The Hindenburg Line fell to the British at the end of September and by the fifth of October, so had Cambrai. It was the ninth of October before Tovell walked through its war ravaged streets. He found a quiet spot and sat down on a pile of rubble. The mail had caught up with him and he had a letter from Ginny which he wanted to enjoy in peace. He took the envelope from his pocket and opened it carefully. As he had suspected, there was another photograph inside. He gazed at it lovingly for a few moments before turning to the letter. At once he felt he could hear Ginny's voice speaking to him.

My dearest, I didn't want to tell you this till the danger was past, 'cause you've got more than enough to worry about, but this area has been hit by the influenza epidemic. Several little ones and old people have died. I'm sorry to say that Auntie May and Uncle William both went down with it. Dr. Lambert say that wasn't safe to be in the house with them. Lizzie and Bobby wouldn't leave me but little Alec stayed with Mary. None of us caught it, thank the Lord, but Auntie May was soon taken. Uncle William say to her, 'You've been the best pal a man could have, gal. That won't be long afore I'll be joining you.' He died himself two days later. Dr. Lambert had told the undertaker not to be too hasty so we were able to bury them both at the same time. I can't get used to this room without them but I'm glad they're together. We'll be just like them, won't we, my dearest? We'll grow old together still thinking the world of each other, just like they did. Dr. Lambert say the disease is worldwide. That could kill even more people than this horrible war. Life isn't fair, is it?

And there's something else I gotta tell you. I hope you won't mind seeing as you don't like digging, but Mrs. Brewster say we ought not to delay. She helped me with the writing to the Council. They've made the lease of this smallholding over to you, so when you come home – and I pray that'll be soon – you'll be a countryman.

Allied successes continued throughout October and in a long series of victories they drove the enemy back through Belgium to the borders of Germany. They re-captured the Belgium coastline, the British reached the river Schelde, the French advanced over the river Aisne and the Americans, going into action as an independent army on the French right, progressed down the river Meuse. On the twenty ninth of October the German fleet, anchored at Kiel, mutinied. The revolution quickly spread to all the main towns and cities throughout Germany. As in Russia the previous year, the government had to bow to the will of the people and on the sixth of November negotiations for an armistice began. Three days later the Kaiser abdicated and fled to Holland together with his family.

The eleventh of November 1918 saw Tovell and a group of his men in a shallow trench near the river Schelde. Gunfire was intermittent and distant. He took a watch from his top pocket and watched the hands move until they reached eleven o'clock. Simultaneously, the cry went up along the length of the trench, 'Cease fire! Cease fire!' Cheering broke out and men embraced one another and shook hands.

A young soldier, no more than eighteen, turned to Tovell and asked, 'Is it really over, Sergeant Major, Sir? No more fighting?'

'No more fighting,' Tovell replied. 'The armistice – the truce – has just begun, at the eleventh hour, on the eleventh day of the eleventh month. Now they'll talk peace but for us the war is over.'

Tovell's slow sombre tones had worried the lad. Anxious for reassurance, he said, 'But *we* won – didn't we, Sir?'

Tovell looked around him at the scene of devastation before him; trees stripped of foliage, mud barely covering corpses. 'Did we?' he muttered. Then he smiled at the boy and said, 'Yes, technically we won but the victory really goes to the German people for forcing their leaders to ask for this armistice.' He patted the young soldier on the shoulder. 'Just be glad it's ended, lad,' he said as he passed him and made his way along the trench. His progress was slow; there were so many hands to shake; so many cheery words of relief and congratulation to exchange, but at last he reached his commanding officer's dugout.

'Come in, Tovell, come in,' Lieutenant Colonel Bradshaw invited warmly. 'Take a drink with Major Webb and me.' Tovell felt it would be churlish to refuse in the circumstances.

He felt the same a little later when he met with his NCOs. As the senior Warrant Officer, it was his duty anyway to propose the loyal toast to His Majesty the King. There was no way either that he could not propose a second toast, to the man who had brought them through the conflict – Lieutenant Colonel Bradshaw. There, Tovell's break from abstinence ended. He passed on the colonel's good wishes, and his warning to remain vigilant in case some of their former enemies had not heard about the truce or had decided to ignore it. Then he was away to reflect in quiet solitude and to share his thoughts in a letter to his beloved.

Ginny happened to be cycling through Haisbro village when the vicar received confirmation that the armistice had begun. He had assembled his bell-ringers in anticipation of this happy event and Ginny was nearby when the peals rang out. She immediately dismounted, propped her bicycle against the wall of the churchyard and went into the church. There she wept tears of relief and joy and gave thanks that Tovell and her brothers would no longer be in danger. By the time she came to leave, others were entering the church on a similar mission. They exchanged hugs and handshakes just as their menfolk were doing on the other side of the North Sea.

November the fifteenth was officially declared V-Day – Victory Day.

There was a party for all the children and everyone had a Union Jack to wave. There was singing and dancing in St Mary's Church Room. Constable Hadden turned a blind eye to the rounds of drinks being bought at the *Admiral Lord Nelson* and to the fact that the landlord had a temporary lapse of memory and forgot all about closing time.

On the whole, however, the festivities were somewhat subdued. Rationing was still in force, but even more to the point, the little community continued to be saddened and in mourning for the loss of several of its members: husbands, sons, brothers and fathers to the battlefield and other loved ones to the recent scourge of the influenza pandemic. Not surprisingly, the special service of remembrance and thanksgiving which was held in the church was very well attended. The vicar read out the name of every man in the locality who had given his life for his country and he ended the service by quoting the words which the Prime Minister, David Lloyd George, had used a few days previously when he had announced the armistice to the members of the House of Commons. *At eleven o'clock this morning came to an end the cruellest and most terrible war that has ever scourged mankind. I hope we may say that thus, this fateful morning, came to an end all wars.'* The vicar then asked the congregation to join him in praying that this would indeed prove to be the war that had ended all wars.

The war was over by Christmas – Christmas 1918. Ginny reflected on the irony of that when she awoke on Christmas morning – still alone in the big double bed. Tovell was not home and her brothers were not home – none of the soldiers from the village or the surrounding area was home yet. This would seem a strange Christmas; almost an anti-climax after the initial joy at the cessation of hostilities. The house was so quiet; no Uncle William cursing because the fire would not pick up quickly enough to boil the kettle for his early morning tea; no Auntie May singing in the scullery as she stirred the correct amount of oats into the pot for the porridge. How she missed them. Thank heaven the Brewsters were holding their usual Christmas Day party this year. At least the children would have an enjoyable afternoon. She must pull herself together and be cheerful for them.

1919

I

By January 1919, the regiment had returned to Cambrai. They were to establish order and assist with the restoration of the town and its facilities. The buildings had been largely destroyed during the German occupation; firstly they had been subjected to onslaughts by the German artillery as they endeavoured to occupy the town and subsequently, by the British artillery as they endeavoured to end the German occupation. Lieutenant Colonel Bradshaw had set up his command post on one of the main streets in a house which had miraculously retained its frontage intact whilst those adjacent to it had been reduced to rubble. Tovell hurried there one morning after being summoned by a messenger. The colonel's batman appeared at the front door as the soldier was about to enter. He had luggage in either hand. Tovell had always liked Williams; he reminded him of his old friend Ted – even down to the Norfolk dialect.

'Come you in, Sergeant Major,' Williams greeted him, backing away to let Tovell enter. 'The colonel's waiting for you.'

'You look cheerful this morning,' said Tovell. 'Moving headquarters again?' he asked, nodding at the cases.

'Oh, I'm cheerful alright, Sir. You ent wrong there. That's because we're going home – colonel and me.'

Tovell was shocked – and alarmed. He could not imagine serving as Regimental Sergeant Major to any officer other than the colonel. His concern still showed in his face when he stood in front of his commander. 'Williams says you're going home, Sir,' he blurted out at once.

The colonel was amused and, Tovell suspected, rather pleased at his reaction. 'Only for three weeks. I'll be back. You don't begrudge me a bit of home leave, do you, Tovell? I came over with the British Expeditionary Force in 1914 and haven't been home since. My wife would have visited me in France, of course, and she suggested as much

305

several times but I wouldn't allow it – couldn't take the risk.

Well, to business. Here's a copy of the instructions I've given to Major Webb – just in case he mislays his copy,' the colonel added hastily. 'See that we hold the fort, won't you? Work has to go on – so much to do.

Walk with me to the motor car, Tovell,' he added as he put on his cap and picked up his attaché case.

The colonel was in a jovial mood – Tovell had never seen him like that. The prospect of being released from his military responsibilities and enjoying instead the company of his family, albeit only for a short while, showed in his face. He seemed a different person now that he was relaxed. He looked years younger – in fact, Tovell realised that he was probably a few years younger than he was. Williams, his face a broad grin, was standing in the road loading the luggage into the boot of the vehicle. When he returned to the house, Tovell commented on how happy the man was.

'Yes, a good man, Williams. I couldn't manage without him. He's been with me for years as batman and groom. He used to be a worker on my father-in-law's estate. He can't wait to get home.'

Tovell's interest was aroused. 'May I ask where your home is, Sir?'

'Norfolk. It's my adopted home just as it is yours, Tovell. We live near my wife's family home on the North Norfolk coast.'

At that moment there was an explosion in a nearby street. The dust cloud could be seen above what was left of the buildings opposite. A group of small children, thin, dirty and ragged were scavenging among the ruins. They scarcely paused in their search for food – or anything else remotely worth having. Explosions meant nothing to them – they had been hearing them almost since birth. The only difference now was that the shells went off unintentionally – if some person or animal ventured where they had hitherto lain hidden and unexploded.

The colonel looked at the children, the smile gone from his face. 'I'm glad you'll be staying with me for the next few months, Tovell,' he said quietly. 'These poor people have suffered so much. We must move as quickly as possible to bring them some relief from their suffering.'

Williams had returned with the last piece of luggage and was holding open the rear door. 'Well, must be off, Tovell,' said the colonel, returning to his former cheerfulness. 'Think of me in a few days, exercising the horses along the beach; galloping through the shallows with my children, the salty spray in my face.' As he started to climb into the car he paused and added ruefully, 'But it'll take a lot of salty spray to clear away the smell of the last four years.'

Tovell saluted the colonel and then leaned forward so that he could wave to Williams as the batman climbed into the front seat alongside the driver. As Tovell stood back from the road, he thought happily of how someone might be waving him off in seven months time when it was his turn to follow the same route home to Norfolk that the colonel was taking now. He smiled as he reflected that for years he had supposed that when the time came for him to leave the Army he would be full of regret – and full of fear, anticipating a meaningless future. He had imagined himself begging to be allowed to carry on – but that was before he had met Ginny.

II

It was August 1919 when Tovell stepped from the train at Stalham Station. The porter ran up to him and shook his hand. 'Welcome home!' he said warmly. 'Welcome home! Old Ted's horse and cart's tied up over the road. He must be in the *Kings Head* mardling with Kath.'

Tovell stood on the station steps and looked around him. It was mid-morning and very hot, but it was quiet; it was not market day so there were few vehicles about. Nothing much had changed, he reflected, until he caught sight of a man in a bedraggled uniform, sitting crossed-legged on the ground near the steps. The man had a placard round his neck which read, *Old Soldier – No Work.* Tovell put his hand in his pocket, stooped down and placed a pile of coins in the man's upturned cap. The man mumbled something as Tovell crossed the road to the public house.

Ted Carter was leaning on the bar, his back to the door. The landlady saw Tovell at once but she said nothing so he was able to creep up and put his hand on Ted's shoulder. The old man turned round. He was so overcome that he was unable to speak and he just embraced Tovell.

'Knew I'd find you here making eyes at Kath,' the soldier chided his friend. 'Don't you ever do any work for your poor master, you old devil?'

Ted quickly recovered. 'All I was a-doing was taking my dinner break a mite late. And be you glad that I did, bor, 'cause now I can give ye a lift home to Whimpwell Green'

The landlady leant over the bar and hugged Tovell. 'Funny – we were just talking about you – saying it must be five year.'

'Yes,' agreed Tovell. 'It's five years almost to the day that I first walked into this bar.'

'Welcome home,' she said sincerely. 'Have a drink on the house. What'll it be?'

'Have you got lemonade, or ginger beer, or something?' asked Tovell.

Ted was aghast. 'Cor, blast, bor!' he exclaimed. 'Don't tell me you've gone teetotal.'

Tovell laughed. 'Don't worry, I still like a drink – but in moderation. It's two years and eight months since I last saw my Ginny and Lizzie and Bobby – and I haven't seen little Alec at all. There's no way I'm going to hug and kiss them with booze on my breath.'

The landlady placed a mineral water in front of Tovell. 'Good health to you. And have you finished with the Army?'

'Yes, I've finished for good – retired after twenty five years. It's been hard seeing others go home but I had to stick it out and do my full time because of the pension – now I've got a family to consider.'

'Ginny's brothers got home last February,' said Ted. 'Most of the locals – them that could come home – got back afore spring.'

'Yes, Ginny wrote that they all got their old jobs back. They were lucky. London is full of beggars like the poor chap over there.'

'Old Eddie,' Ted mused. 'He dint work on the land. I forget now who he did work for but he wouldn't have him back.'

'From the despair of the trenches to the despair of the gutter,' said Tovell sadly.

'Anyway, what are you doing here?' asked Ted, changing the subject, 'Ginny int expecting you till next week. She'd got it all planned. She was going to have all the littl'uns turned out in their Sunday best and lined up on the platform to meet you.'

Tovell grinned. 'The Army had miscalculated the leave I had owing to me. I didn't send Ginny a telegram because every time she's got one of those it's been bad news. I didn't want to upset her.'

'Well, come you on, bor. Let's get you home.'

Tovell closed the gate quietly behind him. Blackie was sprawled out asleep in the sunshine. Tovell crept past him and made his way down the path between the neatly cultivated rows of vegetation. He could see Ginny, Bobby and Lizzie working at the far end of the smallholding, their backs to him. Before he had reached them, a noise made him look to his right. Alec was sitting beside a row of carrots surrounded by the ones he had half-eaten and then discarded. The child looked up and grinned at him. Tovell put down his kitbag, picked Alec up, brushed the soil away from around his mouth and continued along the path. When he was close enough to the little group of workers, he said quietly, 'Don't tell your ma this, but I'm relieved to see you're a chip off the old block, son.'

Ginny gasped and swung round. Her face lit up. She ran to Tovell and he caught her with his free arm. Lizzie and Bobby leapt upon him and Blackie rushed down the path barking madly. They clung together, laughing and crying for joy.

EPILOGUE

On the first of April 1923, responsibility for HM Coastguard passed from the Admiralty to the Board of Trade, with the provision that the service should be primarily employed for coast watching and lifesaving.